INSTRUMENT OF DEATH

Mack Bolan couldn't stem the
madness infecting the world, but
he could stop the ultrasecret
consortium's drive for power—
a juggernaut of terror sweeping
through Europe. Bolan had been
fighting evil for a long time. He was
good, the best. But then they
captured his mind. And that made
him deadly!

Accolades for America's greatest hero Mack Bolan

DON PENDLETON's
MACK BOLAN

Sudden DEATH

A GOLD EAGLE BOOK FROM
W⊕RLDWIDE

TORONTO • NEW YORK • LONDON • PARIS
AMSTERDAM • STOCKHOLM • HAMBURG
ATHENS • MILAN • TOKYO • SYDNEY

First edition February 1987

ISBN 0-373-61407-1

Special thanks and acknowledgment to
Peter Leslie for his contribution to this work.

Printed in Canada

Victory at all costs, victory in spite of all terror, victory however long and hard the road may be; for without victory there is no survival.

—Sir Winston Churchill

I don't care about a terrorist's motives—money, power, even pleasure—they are the stuff of twisted dreams. My mission is to make sure that their ugly dreams don't come true.

—Mack Bolan

To all the men and women worldwide, who unstintingly devote their time to the war against terrorism.

PROLOGUE

It was a long shot—almost five hundred yards, the sniper estimated—and the target would be moving. The midday sun was hot. So hot that the rubber shield behind the Bausch & Lomb Balvar 5 telescopic sight on his rifle, pressing into what the French call the *arcade* of the eye, was causing the skin to sweat. Moisture trickled down the lid, threatening to cloud the cornea.

From his exposed position on the flat roof of the thirty-eight-story apartment block, the sniper flicked a sideways glance at the rectangular elevator housing. For the tenth time he rehearsed his escape routine: through the housing's open doorway and onto the roof of the car that was blocked on the top floor. Lift the inspection hatch and drop to the interior. At the fifteenth floor stop the car and exit, then follow the corridor to the left. Climb through the window that opened onto the fire escape. Descend, and at the tenth-floor level all he had to do was leap across to the balcony of the adjoining building where a window of an apartment would be standing open. Stash the gun in a closet from which the backup team would remove it before he hit the street. Then down the service stairway, through the entrance lobby and out. Easy.

Just as long as the damned sun didn't make him sweat so much that it fouled his aim.

The sniper edged back from the elevated lip of the roof and rested on his haunches. The unbearable heat wafting up from the asphalt blasted his face. Tiny droplets of moisture dewed the backs of his fingers. He wished he could finalize the contract from the shade beneath a striped beach umbrella, as cool as those tourists on the ritzy waterfront four hundred and fifty feet below.

The assassin caressed the rifle. It was old, hand-crafted half a century before by the London gunsmiths Holland & Holland. There were delicate arabesques engraved on the silver plates above the semipistol grip behind the trigger guard. The butt was of satin-smooth rosewood. There was no magazine: the twin twenty-four-inch barrels had to be loaded like a shotgun. But the sniper found that the absence of rapid-fire facility was more than balanced by the deadly accuracy that derived from the length of the barrels. He had removed the original aperture sight, which folded flat against the butt, and had modified the stock to support the Balvar. He had worked on the weapon himself.

The glare shimmering off the ocean was hurting his eyes. Ideally he would have preferred to wait until the sun had moved around a little more, but he had no control over the target's movements and no idea how long it would remain accessible. The thicker parts of the asphalt roofing were softening in the heat. He decided to get it over with before conditions got worse.

A lever between the two hammers released locks holding barrel to breech. He slid it aside, tipping forward the barrel assembly so that he could load.

The brass cartridge cases slipped into place with satisfying ease. There were two more rounds in his pocket, but that was just fail-safe material. If he didn't score with the first couple of .30 caliber softnoses, he might as well go back to the airport.

The sniper took three wads of tissue from the breast pocket of his tan suit. Unfolding and using each one in turn, he dabbed perspiration from the skin around his left eye socket, carefully dried the eyeshield of the telescopic sight, and wiped the sweat from the fingers and palm of his hands.

From another pocket he removed a miniature transistor receiver tuned to a local radio station and settled the ultralightweight earphones over his head. Then he snapped the gun shut and moved forward to take up his former position by the coping.

The voice of the sports commentator came softly over the sniper's earphones. When he was quite comfortable, he lowered his eye to the sight, adjusted the cross hairs fractionally and took up first pressure on the No. 1 trigger.

"WHICH IS IT TO BE, France or Holland?" the commentator breathed into his microphone. "Excitement ripples through the ranks of spectators anxiously seated around this center court of Monte Carlo's championship tennis stadium. The charity match between the prime ministers of these two countries stands at two sets all, and five games each in this final set. How are they going to decide it?"

The multimillionaire singles star who was umpiring the game wanted to know, too. He called the players up to his raised seat by the net. They played well enough for their age—not up to Forest Hills or Wimbledon standards, of course, but well enough to elicit an occasional gasp from the jet-set crowd who had paid up to a hundred dollars to the cancer research fund for their seats.

"Gentlemen," he said, "how do you wish to settle this? Do you want to play it out?" He stole a glance at his watch: he wasn't being paid by the hour; he was on a flat fee. "Do you favor a tiebreaker? Or would you prefer sudden death?"

"Well, of course we *could* play it out," the Frenchman began dubiously, "but we've had no service breaks in this set, and it could go to thirteen-eleven or even nineteen-seventeen..."

"Oh, sudden death," said the Dutch premier, whose turn it was to serve. "We don't want the champagne in the bar to warm up!"

The star nodded. The players changed ends for the final game.

The Dutchman tossed the ball into the air. The racket flashed, the ball sped toward the far side of the net...and the server dropped to the court with a hole between the eyes, hitting the ground before the ball.

A gasp erupted from a thousand throats. A woman screamed. The star half rose from his chair, his mouth open. The Frenchman gaped too, allowing the ball to bounce past him. Then, his face a mask of consternation, he dropped his own racket and sprinted forward, leaping over the net in an attempt to aid his stricken opponent.

In midair he appeared to catch his foot and trip on the tape along the top of the net. He fell flat on his face on the red hard court.

This time it was a fifteen-year-old ballboy, running out and then seeing that the surface beneath the prime minister's body was a darker red, who screamed.

A fist-sized hole had been blasted through the Frenchman's white shirt between his shoulder blades.

The echo of the second shot was lost in the concerted cry of horror from the crowd.

A WEEK LATER, three hundred and seventy miles northeast and again at midday, Otto Jaecklin, president of the Zuricher Industrial Bank and member of a Swiss cantonal assembly, was being chauffeured through the Taunus Mountains in West Germany on his way to a European summit in Bonn.

Halfway up a steep hill, below the *schloss* in the old town of Kronberg, a young woman pushing a baby carriage stepped out from a medieval alley and started to cross the road without looking right or left.

She was directly in front of Jaecklin's car, only a few yards away. The chauffeur swore as he stomped on the brake pedal. The big Mercedes sedan shuddered to a halt with its rear end slewed across the cobbled street.

Two bikers, anonymous in black leather and vizored helmets, stopped on either side of the sedan. Glass imploded as two silenced Skorpion VZ-61 machine pistols pumped a hail of lead at Jaecklin and his driver.

Both men crumpled in their seats as blood and bone splinters sprayed the custom-built beige leather interior of the Mercedes. The woman let go of the baby carriage, which carried nothing but empty bottles hidden beneath a pink blanket. She ran to the larger of the motorcycles and leaped astride the saddle behind the rider. Both bikers then wheeled their mounts around and roared off downhill in the direction of Frankfurt.

The baby carriage rolled after them, glancing off the fender of the stalled Mercedes, and continued on with increasing speed until it crashed through the window of a hardware store.

"THAT'S A BEAUTIFUL GUN," the Unione Corso organizer said admiringly. "Originally a sporting rifle?"

"It still is," the sniper replied. "You know—big game."

"A pity there is no magazine, even if there are two barrels. It must be a nuisance, constantly having to reload."

"I've never had to use more than two shots," the sniper said stiffly.

They were crouched on a ledge halfway down a two-hundred-foot cliff of rose-pink granite, overlooking the bay of Girolata on the western coast of Corsica. The rockbound citadel of Calvi, perched above the neat rectangles of a new vacationers' marina, was sixteen miles to the north. In front of them two small sailboats cruised toward a crescent of sand on the bay. Immediately below, a powered vessel gleaming with brass and polished mahogany lay at anchor on the improbable blue of the sea.

On the foredeck was sprawled a topless brunette, her tanned breasts glistening with suntan oil. Her companion was line fishing from the cockpit—a heavyset man of fifty with a crew cut and iron-gray hair curling on his chest.

A second powerboat nosed around the headland from the direction of Calvi. It was a French-built Arcoa 900—a five-berth speedster with a fiberglass hull and twin 125-horsepower Couach diesels. A sailor in a striped jersey stood at the wheel, but his passengers—there were four or five of them—seemed to shun the heat, preferring to remain behind the double-glazed windows of the saloon.

The sniper was also in the shade this time: a granite outcrop sheltered him and his mafioso companion from the sun, and the irregular stripes of shadow thrown across the weathered cliff face effectively hid them from the people aboard the boats. The sniper was focusing a pair of Zeiss binoculars. "That the guy?" he asked, jerking his head toward the man fishing from the cockpit.

The Corsican nodded. "Commissaire Georges Codorneau himself—big-time boss of the Paris antigang squad," he said derisively. "Officially here on vacation, but in fact seconded to the local law in Ajaccio with a briefing to put the bite on the Families and squash these separatist bastards blowing up tourists' cars with plastique."

"Too bad he never got the chance to finish the job!" the sniper said. He raised the twin-barreled rifle, leaned his elbows on a shelf of rock and peered through the Balvar sight.

The crack of the shot echoed around the bay from cliff to cliff and sent seabirds screaming into the cloudless sky, where the contrails of a jetliner heading for North Africa mirrored the white brushstrokes of the Arcoa's wake.

Commissaire Codorneau folded forward over the transom and slid into the sea, clouding the water with the blood still pumping from his shattered chest. "Better take out the bitch, too," the sniper said, shifting his position as the girl pushed herself upright on the foredeck.

"Is that really necessary?" the Corsican asked.

"Of course it's necessary," the sniper said irritably. "She's not his wife, is she? The bodies will be found together. They may think the killer's a jealous lover. There'll be a scandal, and the press will make a fucking meal of it. Anything that undermines public confidence in our marvelous security services is a bonus."

He fired the second round.

He was an Iranian, but he could have passed for southern Italian. The name on his passport was Graziano, and his birthplace was given as Pescara. He was an expert lover, and the Alitalia stewardess who had spent the night with him thought she had never enjoyed the Rome stopover so much.

Before she boarded the flight for Oran the next morning, he offered her a gift—a twin-speaker Aiwa 350 FM radio and stereo cassette player. Presents already, the stewardess thought. And this one was expensive, considering all the features and the weight of it. She recalled the no-expense-spared dinner in the Via Veneto and the great night in bed, and decided that she could hardly wait until their next date.

The bomb in the stereo set exploded as the Boeing 747 began to climb to its operational height over Civitavecchia, decompressing the cabin and tipping the jet into a death dive that the pilot could do nothing to avert.

Most of the wreckage was strewn over the grounds of an infant school at Santa Marinella, where the stricken plane plunged through a glass roof.

Among the three hundred and seventeen dead was a first-class passenger named Beniamino Alonzo, a strongman who had just been appointed Minister of Home Security in Italy's new government.

Five miles offshore, a dark man with thinning hair and a military mustache limped down the companionway of an Arcoa 900 cruiser and switched on the video receiver in the saloon.

There were four expensively dressed, middle-aged foreigners seated expectantly on the leather divans. After he had showed them the videotape of the Boeing disaster, the dark man ran the tape of the Girolata killings, the Monte Carlo tennis murders and the slaughter of the Swiss official's Mercedes in Kronberg.

The man who seemed to be the leader of the quartet stood. He was American—a tall, spare sixty-year-old with shell-rimmed glasses and silver hair crimped close to his skull. He wore a cream suit and lizard skin shoes. He raised his glass of champagne toward the display screen.

"Admirable," he said. "I think we agree, gentlemen, that this will do very well for a start. Now it is up to our...shall we say our colleagues...to perfect plans for the really big ones."

1

"It's strictly a no-win situation," Hal Brognola said, sucking fiercely on his unlit cigar. "And it gets worse every day. In Europe terrorist atrocities are on the increase an average of ten percent per year. Since 1981 Paris alone has been hit by more than one hundred, most of them bombings and assassinations in the street. In the past twelve months, five long-distance railroad flyers have been derailed with bombs. They hijacked a whole train in Holland, an ocean liner in Alexandria and heaven knows how many jetliners."

"Dammit, Hal, tell me something I don't know," John Gregson, the high-ranking CIA operative seated opposite Brognola, protested. "We even know that these attacks are orchestrated. We know who writes the score and who pays the bill."

"Leaving aside the mass attacks on our own people in Lebanon," Brognola continued imperturbably, "we've seen senseless massacres at four international airports." He ticked them off on his fingers. "Munich, Lod, Rome, Vienna. Then there are the attacks on half a dozen department stores, not to mention the slaughter at railroad stations in the rush hour at Bologna, Milan and Marseille." He laid down the stogie in an ashtray and leaned forward, a bulky man with a tired city face and a rumpled suit.

"And now," the gruff voice continued, "the guys writing the score, as you put it, have changed key. Two premiers, a Eurocrat and a couple of top security chiefs in ten days. Not to mention several hundred innocent passengers and the crew of a plane."

"It's a question of degree," the CIA man began. "We don't read it as an entirely new shift in their—"

"Bull!" Brognola interrupted. "Gunning for the top brass *is* a new departure. They've always stayed away from that before—kind of an unwritten law, almost—because they've always been shit-scared we might retaliate in kind, send out hit squads against Khadaffi, Assad, Khomeini or the Palestinian bosses. Now it seems they don't give a goddamn. Plus of course you have this...." He gestured to a copy of the *Washington Post* that lay beside the ashtray.

The front page carried a five-column heading: "612 Drowned in Channel Car Ferry Disaster." And beneath this, underlined in red marker, was the subhead: "Bomb in Container Truck Shattered Hull Says British Police Chief."

The operative moved uneasily in his chair. He didn't like the way the conversation was going, but the man opposite him in the creased suit had the ear of the President—and heads could roll fast in Langley.

They were on Brognola's home ground, too. He was, in fact, White House liaison for this damned Stony Man Farm complex to which the Agency man had been summoned—the camouflaged 160-acre base in Virginia's Blue Ridge Mountains from which Uncle Sam's covert and secretly funded antiterrorist campaign operated.

Beneath the sprawling collection of farm buildings and outhouses, shielded from public view by miles of rolling forest, one of the world's most sophisticated communications systems linked an underground operations center with high-grade and high-tech intel banked in computer installations all over the Western world.

Brognola and the Company man sat on each side of a rustic wooden table, sheltered from the summer sun by an arbor outside one of the barns, but the agent had a shrewd idea that he was very soon due to be fed fresh information gleaned through the myriad antennae of that ultrasecret network. And he didn't want to hear it.

"If the guys responsible for these killings are caught," Brognola said, "what happens? Their buddies hijack another plane, and the lives of several hundred more innocents are bargained against their release...when they will at once start planning more hits."

"Sure," the CIA man said. "It's a pattern. But I don't see what—"

"I'll tell you something, Gregson," the Fed said somberly. "It wouldn't take much of an acceleration in terrorist activity to provoke a climate of fear in Europe in which the normal man and woman would think twice before taking a train, visiting an airport, going down the subway or even doing the week's shopping." He sighed. "The situation will get worse until some government over there has the guts to bring back the death penalty for terrorist acts. After all, there isn't much sense hijacking a jetliner and bargaining the lives of the passengers against the return of accomplices if they are already six feet under!"

"It's getting worse for the Europeans," Gregson said.

"Sure it is. But you guys at Langley are the last ones to start playing isolationist at this stage of the game. If the social order in Western Europe breaks down— and that's just what we're talking about—you know who's going to move in and take over."

"Okay, Hal. But what are we supposed to do? Half these crazy bastards are free because the French cling to the idea that they have to make their country an asylum for political refugees. Political refugees, my ass!" Gregson spit in the grass at his feet. "Ninety percent of the world's fanatics are free to come and go in that country. And I won't even mention the arms and explosives filtered through Mideastern embassies in Paris and Rome and Bonn—stuff that the security people can't touch because it's smuggled through in diplomatic pouches!" The man from Langley sounded personally affronted.

"I'm not arguing," Brognola said mildly. "Let me show you something." From an inside pocket he took a creased cutting torn from a glossy magazine, unfolded it and smoothed the paper on the table. "This was published in *Figaro* magazine," he said. "It's a satellite photo showing the whole of Paris, street by street. It illustrated a story headlined 'Fifty-five Million French Are Scared,' and a small red star was superimposed on the site of each of the fifty worst terrorist attacks in the past few years. What does the pattern suggest to you?" He pushed the cutting across the table.

Gregson studied the picture. "The attacks are pretty evenly distributed," he said. "They cover the whole city except the northeast corner. That quarter is completely blank."

"Exactly. That's the area where all the immigrants are concentrated. It's practically a ghetto—and you don't shit on your own doorstep."

"But that is exactly what I'm saying. That's where they go to ground, the Palestinians and the Iranian—"

"You have to remember," Brognola cut in, "that if the guys on the international terrorist circuit can pass unnoticed in that part of town, they're mingling with a couple of hundred thousand honest working people who have every right to be there—Algerians, Tunisians, Moroccans, immigrants arriving legally from ex-French colonies like Senegal, many of them with French nationality. The government can't throw them all out."

The Fed fished a fresh cigar from his breast pocket and jammed it into a corner of his mouth without lighting it.

"So what are we supposed to do?" Gregson asked.

"Right now there's nothing we can do. Not officially. Not even officially covertly. We get bad press over there anyway. If there's a strike of workers at the Renault automobile factory, it's been stirred up by the Americans. If fanatics attempt to stage a revolution on some obscure island in the Mediterranean, they've been funded by the CIA. Everything's our fault. The fact remains that we—and the Europeans with us—are at war. It's not a war we can fight openly, nor is it a war where we can even use the same weapons as the enemy. Too many innocents would get killed. But that's what they're trying to goad us into doing—fight it their way."

"So?" A frown furrowed Gregson's forehead.

"So until free world governments take a harder stand on the law-and-order question, we play this war a different way—from the inside, because there *is* a change in this latest wave of terror. Until now the attacks have been orchestrated, as you call it, by the Soviets, via the KGB. It's indirect, of course, with arms and money and free training facilities for urban guerrillas, but the latest intel feeding in to us here suggests a different scenario."

"How different?"

"The thugs carrying out the hijacks and the killings are the same—Iranian splinter groups stoked up with hate by the mad ayatollahs, Palestinian extremists, spinoffs from the IRA. But the guys pulling the strings are different. As far as we know, the KGB have a clean sheet on this one. Somebody else is writing the script."

"Okay, surprise me. Who's the guilty party—according to your superintelligent computers?"

Brognola shook his head. "No idea. Zero indications. That's why we have to put in a ferret."

"A ferret?"

"To smell out the new masterminds, to force them into the open. A ferret with a license to kill."

"You mean you're asking me to brief one of our—"

"I'm asking you nothing."

"I don't get it," Gregson said. "I figured you would want the Company—"

"I want the Company to do nothing," the Fed cut in once more. "Exactly that. Not to lift a finger."

"Meaning?"

"My ferret's on your hit list. I want him taken off it. I want you guys looking the other way when he goes into action."

"Who is it?"

Brognola removed the cigar from his mouth and leaned forward, mere inches away from Gregson's face. "Mack Bolan," he said.

"Bolan! But he..."

"Happens to be the best goddamn infiltration agent and combat specialist this country has ever produced."

"I'm familiar with Bolan's reputation," Gregson said stiffly.

"Yeah, and official intelligence organizations hate free-lancers because initiative louses up the bureaucracy." Brognola sat up very straight and stabbed the cigar toward the CIA man. "But this time you lay off. Understood?"

Gregson spread his hands in a gesture of resignation. For the first time since his arrival he looked almost happy. He wasn't being asked to sign anything, spend Company money or get involved in any kind of operation. And turning a blind eye to the activities of a professional was at least better than being fucked around by the amateurs on the National Security Planning Group.

"It says someplace in the Bible," Brognola observed, "that the meek shall inherit the earth. Obviously the guy who wrote that had never heard of Khadaffi or Khomeini. So long as there's no summary execution for terrorists caught in the act, the meek are going to go on being shit-scared. Until the silent majority in all countries stand up and shake their fists and insist on that legal reform, Mack Bolan will remain the terrorists' death penalty.''

2

A hot wind blew spirals of dust across the concrete apron in front of Tel Aviv's airport terminal. The sunlight, blazing down out of a sky the color of beaten brass, sparkled off the Plexiglas canopy above the flight deck of an El Al Boeing refueling outside Satellite Number Five.

Mack Bolan rode the third car in a string of baggage carts being tractored out to the plane from the security check beneath the departure lounges. Crouched behind the stack of valises, suitcases in expensive leather and plain vinyl luggage, he looked as anonymous as any of the other baggage handlers loading the jetliner's cargo hold. It was only when he uncoiled his six-foot-plus frame and stood upright in the shade beneath the wing that his physical power became evident. Bolan weighed in at two hundred pounds, all of it steel-cored muscle, and it was clear from the grim set of his jaw and the determination in his ice-blue eyes that he was a man who meant business.

Wrists and ankles protruding from the ill-fitting, borrowed El Al uniform, Bolan glanced warily left and right among the ground crew servicing the giant jet. Although the man was a disguise expert, there were some structural factors it was impossible to alter, and none of these men was the right shape or build to be the terrorist Bolan was looking for.

Extraspecial precautions were being taken on this flight because Isaac Goldschmidt, a big wheel in the Knesset, would be among the first-class passengers, on his way to address a plenary session of the Euro-Parliament in Geneva. All baggage, hold as well as cabin, had been passed through scanners, and travelers checking in were obliged to unpack each case entirely in front of hawk-eyed customs and security officials.

Tossing the suitcases up to a handler standing in the open hatch beneath the plane's belly, the Executioner was nevertheless unhappy—a gut reaction had set the hairs on his nape standing upright.

Bolan knew nothing yet of Hal Brognola's meeting with Gregson, but by chance he had himself been on the trail for several weeks of Graziano, the Iranian killer who traveled on fake Italian ID papers. He had no idea if the hit man had been alerted to the fact that he was being tailed, but it was undeniable that Bolan had lost the guy in Rome. And it was right after this that the jet taking off from Fiumicino was sabotaged.

And now Graziano had shown up in Tel Aviv.

Bolan knew nothing of the Alitalia stewardess either, but the airport seemed the likeliest place if a hit was to be made.

One thing he did know now—it had been news to him when he had arrived in Israel—was that Graziano, despite his nationality, didn't belong to a fanatic Jihad group sent out from Iran to spread terror in the capitals of the West. He was, in fact, a professional, a gun for hire. Except that his specialty was explosives rather than firearms.

Thus Bolan's concentration on the airport.

The intel had come via a contact of the Executioner's in Mossad, Israel's superefficient intelligence service.

A Mossad operative in Rome had been alert enough to spot Bolan in the embarkation area at Fiumicino and had radioed ahead, so that a self-effacing individual at Immigration had politely asked the Executioner to follow him.

Fortunately the official in the security interrogation room had been an old buddy. Aaron Davis was the least Jewish-looking guy it was possible to imagine—a thin, lanky, freckled redhead, with a snub nose and the pale, flat eyes of the northern European. As a Mossad agent, he found the image useful.

"Okay, Mack," he had said with a friendly smile. "I guess we can cut out the formalities. What brings you here?"

Bolan had told him.

"How did you know Graziano was here?"

Bolan had told him. An underworld tipoff from a gold smuggler whose life he had once saved.

"You must understand that we can't pretend we don't know you're here. We can't tolerate any lone wolf activity on our territory. But we're grateful for the info. Our people hadn't gotten onto Graziano yet. So if you'd care to work along with us—in a strictly noncom role—maybe between us we can locate him and take action. But any rough stuff must be left to us. Okay?"

"Understood."

"Come to my office. We'll get a printout on the guy. But you've actually been tracking him. What can you tell us about him that the computer can't?"

"Personal stuff? Mediterranean type. Passes for southern Italian. Medium height. Stays in two-star hotels, usually with a restaurant attached. Sometimes wears a mustache, sometimes a beard, sometimes neither. Hair can be cropped or curly. The only thing he can't, or won't, disguise is a limp. He walks with a limp."

The printout had told them that Graziano's real name was Sadegh Rafsanjani. That he was twenty-seven years old and had once been part of a suicide squad selected by Hussein Montazeri, the successor-designate to Khomeini in Teheran, to destroy targets in Europe. That he had broken away and hired himself out as a free-lancer after following an instruction course organized by the chief of the East German secret police, General Markus Wolff. And it was on that course that he had acquired the limp.

It was not known whether Teheran had been angered enough by his defection to put out a contract for the contract killer, or whether they had figured it would suit them to leave him on the loose dispensing death right and left. Any kind of destruction was grist to the mad mullahs' mill.

The final line on the printout had read: "Attention all operatives: this man is extremely, repeat extremely, dangerous."

Aaron Davis had agreed to let Bolan follow up his hunch and had arranged cover as a baggage handler...on the understanding that he would remain unarmed and communicate with Mossad agents posted around the airport the moment he saw anything suspicious.

The Executioner had had his own ideas on that.

Sure, he'd communicate. But for him, unarmed had been completely out of the question. And Davis, being a savvy agent, hadn't needed much convincing by Bolan that he would need firearms. So Davis had provided him with a Beretta 93-R, a carbon copy of the one Bolan usually used.

Sweating in the dry midday heat, he could feel the comforting weight of the Beretta now, pressed hard against his ribs by the too-tight uniform as he hefted the last of the suitcases to the guy in the belly of the aircraft. No chance of a fast draw here. But in any case it didn't look as though there was going to be any shooting. Neither he nor the handler above him—the nearest of the Mossad men—had observed anything remotely suspicious. They'd be calling the passengers soon; they couldn't hold up the flight any longer.

Could he have been mistaken? Had his hunch been wrong?

It was always possible. But why else would the hit man have come into the hotbed of anti-Muslim activity? No other VIP flight was planned in the immediate future.

They had covered everything, hadn't they?

The cleanup crew from the maintenance unit...the hand baggage...the stuff in the hold and the few freight containers...the passengers themselves and their effects...the crew...the bins for duty-free goods and in-flight magazines—a favorite hiding place for arms stowed ahead of takeoff by the ground crew accomplices. The Boeing itself had practically been taken apart by Mossad experts. Yeah, they'd covered everything that could be—

Suddenly Bolan's eye registered something. His muscles tensed, his pulses racing.

Not *everything*.

Not the one last-minute operation that was always delayed until the passengers trooped aboard.

The loading of the food containers. It was a mid-day flight: the cabin crew would be serving prepacked airline lunches.

The first of the aluminum containers, shelved with dozens of cellophaned trays, was being forklifted up to the forward hatch at the other end of the airplane at that very moment.

Bolan saw the feet of the white-jacketed attendant from the airport commissary between the small wheels on the far side of the second trolley.

The Executioner raised himself on tiptoe. He saw a tall, thin guy with a hooked nose.

The third was fat and balding.

The man wheeling out the fifth trolley was in the open, in the full glare of the sun, thin, stooped, a little older than the others. He looked as though the heat were too much for him. Only the man with the fourth remained completely hidden by the container.

Bolan jumped up onto the rail of the baggage cart, steadying himself with one hand on the lip of the open hatchway above. He craned to see over the top of the trolley.

A man of nondescript height. Bolan placed both hands on the hatchway rim and flexed his arms, drawing himself up a few extra inches.

He saw dark hair, a bulbous nose, a Zapata mustache. Above the nose he saw gold-rimmed glasses.

But the man's head bobbed in an unusual fashion with each step he took. It could only mean one thing. A limp!

Bolan exploded into action. His hand darted into the coverall and unleathered the 93-R as he leaped to the ground. "Search the trays!" he yelled to the Mossad man above him. And then he hurled himself toward the line of aluminum containers.

Bolan berated himself for not thinking of it before: if he could talk his way in as a baggage handler, a man with unlimited funds—and maybe associates inside—could as easily take a one-time job with the cafeteria service.

The Executioner would later learn that fifteen of the lunch tray pies carried wadded plastic explosive with wristwatch timers beneath their crust—fifteen small explosions blasting off within seconds of each other, enough to rip off the nose and flight deck and send the Boeing hurtling to its doom.

The killer saw him coming and took off. He ducked beneath the tailgate of a refueling tanker, ran around the Boeing's nosewheel and dashed across the apron toward a TriStar boarding at another satellite.

Seeing him momentarily out in the open, with no cover, Bolan stopped, sank into a combat crouch and raised the Beretta in a two-handed shooting position, ready to drop him.

But in the instant the Executioner sighted the 93-R, Graziano dipped his hand into his pocket, whirled and shot his arm out.

Bolan recognized the egg-shaped RGD-5 as it arced his way. He knew the Soviet-made antipersonnel grenade was lethal up to a radius of twenty yards. The concrete of the apron was hard, and the thing would roll.

It was no time for heroics.

He leaped sideways, dived for the cover of the nosewheel and rolled, twisting frantically away from the deadly explosive, his arms shielding his head, neck and face.

The concussion drummed his feet against the ground and the blast seared his body from heel to head. But the fragments scythed through the air above his prone frame, and apart from a deep scratch across the back of one hand, he was unscathed.

By the time he was on his feet once more, Graziano had produced a Tokarev pistol and had shot the driver of a low-slung maintenance cart designed to slide beneath the wings of executive jets. The guy lay on his back on the tarmac with a lacework of blood webbing out from beneath him.

Graziano took his place at the wheel. The electric cart accelerated toward a parking lot reserved for airport personnel, a jam-packed space between a repair hangar and the end of the terminal buildings.

The Mossad men behind Bolan were shouting; they dared not fire because he was between them and the target.

The Executioner thrust aside the bewildered driver of a tractor hauling a train of baggage cars to the TriStar, uncoupled the machine and set off in pursuit. The chase zigzagged between runway marker lights, stalled ground crew vehicles and decorative palms in concrete troughs, neither of the vehicles capable of much more than twenty miles per hour.

They were still eighty yards apart when Graziano reached the wire fence dividing the lot from the field. He scrambled onto the hood of the cart and leaped over. He was immediately whisked into a waiting white

Mercedes 190, which shot toward the gates with a screech of rubber.

Bolan vaulted the fence and raced up to a courier who was dismounting from his motorbike. "I'll need that," he snapped. "Check with Aaron Davis." He snatched the machine away from the protesting rider, flung himself across the saddle and began to chase the Mercedes.

The white sedan raced toward the center of town.

At the far end of a broad tree-lined avenue, beyond the steel and glass horizontals of modern apartment blocks, the sea lay bleached of color by the midday heat. But soon the Mercedes swerved away from the geometrical perspectives of the twentieth century toward the Arab quarter, the ancient city of Jaffa.

The bike was a high-geared Suzuki, with a fat-tired rear wheel. On the long, straight stretches it had been easy enough for Bolan to build up enough speed to keep the Mercedes in sight, but once the killer's car began twisting through the narrow, crowded streets of the quarter he found the lack of low-end punch a handicap.

With its horn blaring, the sedan forged through groups of gesticulating merchants and between kiosks and market stalls. Bolan followed as best he could, wrenching the handlebars right and left, occasionally touching the cobblestones with a steadying foot, in his effort to keep the Suzuki operable as he forced a passage through the throng.

At last the car drove beneath a Moorish arch at one side of a labyrinth of covered souks where the crowd was even more dense. Before Bolan could make it, tall gates swung shut to block off the courtyard beyond. He saw the killer and two other men leap out of the

Mercedes and run for a doorway, and then he was alone with the crowd whose murmurs had become increasingly hostile the more he penetrated the quarter.

Clearly the Mercedes men were locals—with friends.

Many of the Arabs at the entrance to the market were dressed in long robes; others, wearing jeans and sweatshirts, looked more militant; some had adopted Western dress beneath the traditional burnoose. They crowded menacingly around as Bolan was forced to brake the bike in front of the tall wooden gates. Hands plucked at the baggage handler's uniform. A foot shot out and kicked the front wheel of the Suzuki.

Bolan realized this wasn't the best place for a guy wearing the uniform of an Israeli airline to be cornered.

The murmurs were swelling to a roar. Bolan could see raised-fist salutes and threatening gestures in back of the robed characters surrounding the bike.

Backed against the gates, he dismounted, drew the Beretta and fired a shot into the air. He had no wish to kill innocent people, however mean their masters' propaganda had made them.

But he also had no wish to be torn to pieces by an enraged pack under the influence of mob fury. Furthermore, he was determined to stay with Graziano and the men who had rescued him.

The men in the forefront of the crowd shrank back momentarily as the shot echoed between the market stalls. Then the roar turned to howls of rage. A phalanx of Arabs surged toward the Executioner.

He glanced upward. Above his head, a lamp hanging from a decorative wrought-iron bracket projected from the stone archway over the gates.

Drawing a deep breath, he rammed the gun back into its holster, tensed his calf muscles and jumped up, reaching for the bracket. His fingers touched the sun-warmed metal, wrapped around the lowest bar and held. He swung back and then forward, shooting out his legs toward the attackers. His heels thudded against the chests of the two leading aggressors to send them sprawling back against the men behind.

For a second there was confusion. Then knives flashed, and the attackers reformed and rushed again, trying to claw him down. But the respite was enough to allow Bolan to swing himself up and hook one heel over the tiles crowning the arch.

An instant later, as the mob screamed their frustration, he had hauled his whole body up. With a quick glance at the empty Mercedes and the deserted courtyard, he dropped from their sight.

He landed like a jungle cat on the cobblestones. Beyond the car, a fountain bubbled beneath an orange tree. The blank white walls of the flat-roofed buildings enclosing the yard were pierced by three arched doorways. With the Beretta unleathered again, Bolan ran for the one on the right, the one through which Graziano and his companions had fled.

Flattening himself against the sidewall, the Beretta seeking targets at arm's length, he slid around into the passage beyond.

No movement. No shots. They had left no lookout to try to stop Bolan or to warn them. He ran to the far end of the passage. There, to his right, was a door. Another corridor twisted away to the left.

He hesitated for a heartbeat, then tried the latch on the door. It wasn't locked. Behind it he could hear men's voices; they were speaking in Arabic.

Bolan kicked the door open and leaped, following the Beretta into the room beyond.

He saw two elderly bearded men reclining on oriental mats, one on either side of a low table set with small porcelain cups and a copper pan from which rose the steaming fragrance of coffee. Mouths agape, the men started up in astonishment and anger.

"Sorry," Bolan said hastily.

He backed out and turned to race down the twisting passageway, ignoring the cries of outrage behind.

It lead to another courtyard, a shadowed thirty-foot rectangle slashed by a single bar of sunlight halfway up one wall. Two Arab children were bouncing a ball in the shade. They were about five years old. Two doors led out of the yard, one straight ahead, one in the sunlit wall. "Which way did my friends go?" the Executioner asked. The children stopped playing and stared at him.

"My friends," he repeated more urgently, gesticulating this time as he realized they couldn't understand English.

One of the children started to cry. Bolan realized he was still holding the gun and hurriedly holstered it. The other child, eyes still wide, pointed wordlessly to the door straight ahead.

Bolan ran to it, listened, heard nothing. He opened the door.

He saw a tiled corridor leading into what seemed to be some kind of apartment house. There were doors on either side and a stone stairway curling upward at the far end. Voices, muted and indistinguishable, could be heard all around. A woman laughed shrilly. From somewhere above the quavering tones of Arab music rose and fell.

Bolan paused halfway along the hallway. Were those footsteps he could hear above? He ran to the stairs and bounded up two at a time, keeping to the inner wall.

Empty.

Another corridor. More doors. But here one side of the building opened out onto a balustraded patio at a higher level. Red and blue flowers grew in profusion in a row of huge pottery jars, and there was another, larger fountain gushing into a stone basin. Beside a ruined wall on the far side of the patio, steps rose crazily among ancient brickwork to an alley that climbed again between the old houses.

Bolan ran toward the steps. He didn't believe the killer would have gone to ground in this warren so near to his failed hit; it was more likely that he was using it as a blind, being escorted through by local associates to pick up another car on the far side.

The hunch was confirmed more quickly than he expected.

His ears registered the crack of a pistol a millisecond after a round smashed into the brickwork only inches from his left shoulder. He flung himself flat on the stairway.

In open ground beneath the sunny stonework, he let loose an exploratory round in the general direction of the ambusher. The ricochet whined skyward, but he must have been fairly close because he heard a scrambling movement among the rubble. A stone dropped and clattered down the steps.

Then Graziano's accomplices made their mistake. They were deployed on either side of the steps, hoping that when Bolan dived out of range of the first gunner, he would automatically put himself in the sights of the second.

But the number two man forgot, when he rose from behind a crumbling wall to draw a bead on his target, that the sun was behind him.

His shadow jerked onto the stairway and then undulated down toward Bolan.

Rolling over onto his back with the Beretta in single-shot mode and held in two hands over his head, the soldier triggered the 93-R three times in lightning succession before the Arab could fire.

The first round, blasting up from below, drilled the soft flesh beneath the gunman's jawbone, pierced tongue and palate and cored the frontal lobes of the brain.

For a moment the man was pinned against the sky. The second and third 9 mm parabellums, smashing up into the rib cage and slicing through one shoulder, held him there for a timeless instant. Then he toppled forward and down onto the steps with the blood forming a crimson cascade as it frothed from beneath him.

The Tokarev he had been holding bounced and slid after him. Bolan reached for it and coiled himself for the next move.

His fighter's instinct, honed razor sharp by years of combat in the killing zone, urged him to act now, fast.

The remaining gunner, the one who had fired first, knowing precisely where Bolan was, would expect him to move now, to seek fresh cover, perhaps to slide back down around the corner at the foot of the stairway. He would be moving himself, ready to cash in on that belief.

Bolan decided to do exactly the opposite. Pushing himself upright in a single lithe movement, he leaped to the center of the flight and sprang up several steps, a gun in each hand.

It was a hell of a chance to take, but it paid off.

Flitting between a fallen column and another section of the broken wall, the hardman, on his way to enfilade the Executioner, was caught in the open.

He gasped, raising his gun arm as he hurled himself back. His finger tightened on the trigger of his automatic. But Bolan beat his reaction time. The steely muscles of Bolan's forearms were already shuddering with the recoil as the two weapons in his hands spewed death toward the column.

The gunman's chest was already split open, the flesh between his shoulder blades parting to let through a mess of blood and bone splinters and fragments of heart and lung tissue before the first slug exploded from the barrel of his weapon.

The shot went high. Bolan's rounds slammed the killer back against the gore-spattered column. He slid to the ground, twitched once and lay still.

Bolan cleared the rest of the stairway, leaped over the body and ran on. But the alleys of the Arab quarter, heavy with the stench of refuse and rotting fruit, deserted in the scorching noonday heat, curved away left and right with no hint of the direction Graziano had taken.

This time, at the cost of his companions' lives, the terrorist had gotten away.

Bolan stripped off the airline uniform in a doorway and made his way back down stepped lanes of ancient cobblestones to the market. In normal civilian clothes, he passed inconspicuously through the jabbering throng, past booths of silversmiths and leatherworkers and stalls where sweetmeats were roasted beside stacks of rugs from Ispahan, until finally he emerged into the wider streets of a residential quarter beyond which was the seafront. Eventually he found a taxi to take him back to the airport.

3

"Thanks to you we found and defused the bombs," Aaron Davis said when Bolan had made his report. "We'll get Graziano another time. Right now there's someone waiting to see you in the VIP lounge."

Davis accompanied Bolan to the lounge, and even from a distance Bolan had no trouble recognizing his longtime friend, Hal Brognola.

"Good to see you, Striker," Brognola said.

"Same here, Hal. But whatever it is that brought you all this way must be very important."

"You don't know the half of it, guy. There's this terrorist campaign, this scheme to eliminate the top men in each country. It started with Olaf Palme in Sweden in '86—they never did find out who was responsible for that, or why—and you know how far it's gone now. If it hadn't been for you and Aaron Davis, there would have been a seventh chalked up today, along with another planeload of innocents."

"And there are more planned for the future," Bolan said. "Is that what you're saying, Hal?"

Brognola nodded. "A very specific, a very special plan," he said soberly. "But we don't know yet exactly what's behind the plan. Or who's behind it. Oh, sure—" he raised a hand as Bolan was about to interrupt "—we know the idea is to create a panic situation in general. But for whose benefit?"

"You say not the Russians?"

"The Russians are happy to benefit from any panic situation. They're happy to supply arms and advice to any revolutionary organization, whatever its aims. Armenians, Basques, Corsican nationalists, Shiites, the IRA, they can all rely on a helping hand from Moscow. But the Russkies don't gun for heads of state." He shook his head. "It's not their style. The brains behind this one don't do their thinking in offices above Dzerzhinsky Square, that's for sure."

"Where do they do it?"

"I wish to hell we knew," Brognola said. "They work out of offices in Damascus and Teheran and Tripoli, as far as the tacticians—the guys who plan each individual hit—are concerned. But they no longer use their own units to make the hits. They put out contracts and pay professionals to do it. And as for the strategists who tell the guys in Damascus and Teheran and wherever what the score has to be..." He shrugged. "Your guess is as good as mine. Because neither they nor the tacticians nor the soldiers in the field can be tied in directly with a single killing. They've all got iron-clad alibis. We need your help on this one, Striker."

Bolan remained silent for a moment, a look of intense concentration on his face.

"If it's that serious," he finally said, "I could run up against operatives from the Company. They could be following up—"

"The guys from Langley, just this once, will be looking the other way. The French are too busy trying to guess which of their politicians don't take graft from the sheikhs. The only other team you might run up against would be the Circus, from London—and right now they're busy looking after Ireland."

"Okay," Bolan said. "Lay it on me, every detail."

Brognola recapped the conversation he had initiated at Stony Man Farm with Gregson of the CIA and added more intel shaped since then by the base's computer complex. "You'll understand why we can't do anything officially on this one," he said when he was through. "But personally I guarantee full cooperation, one hundred percent. You'll take it on, guy, won't you?"

The gruff voice had softened suddenly on a pleading note. Bolan favored him with a crooked smile. "If they can penetrate us, we can penetrate them, whoever they are. Sure, I'll try to sniff out a lead and go wherever it takes me."

It would, he thought, be a pleasure—and something like poetic justice if he made it. It was through a penetration agent, a mole in the White House, that the Executioner had found himself an outlaw for the second time in his life.

The guy had been a KGB plant. And it had been through him that an attack on Stony Man Farm had taken the life of Bolan's woman. Grief and fury had led Bolan to bypass the law and kill the mole with his own hands in front of the President, actually in the Oval Office. That was a lapse the administration couldn't forgive. And the security bosses, too, had been mad, because they would have preferred to keep the deep-cover sleeper in place and use him as a convenient channel of disinformation.

So the Executioner had continued his personal war out in the cold; he had quit the Stony Man operation.

"Do you have any idea where to start, Striker?" Brognola asked. "Do you figure there could be a lead if you reconnected with the bomber who escaped you today?"

"Uh-huh," Bolan said. "I know where to start all right. It's where I go afterward that could be tricky." He grinned. "But first up, I'll need your help. I want a ride on something fast from the Sixth Fleet. And then I want a navy chopper to land me secretly at night on the outskirts of Algiers."

SEAN RIORDAN, opposition leader in the Irish Dáil, had a hangover. He had flown in to New York from Dublin the day before, been feted by the local branch of the Irish police federation, wined and dined by an Irish-American Friendship society and acted as cohost with the ambassador at a late-night embassy reception.

Apart from the hangover, there was also the question of jet lag.

Now he had to stand in for a sick foreign affairs spokesman at a meeting of the UN Security Council where the participation of the Irish army in yet another Mideastern peacekeeping force was to be discussed.

Riordan was a florid, heavy man, and he found the humidity in New York trying. Perhaps, he thought, if he took a brisk walk and breathed in enough fresh air, it would clear the buzzing in his head enough for him to think clearly. There were a number of tough points he had to make to the Council, and he prided himself on referring very seldom to his notes. He left his hotel, walked to the far side of Central Park and took a cab to the UN building from there.

A small dark Hispanic-looking man who had traversed the park eighty yards behind Riordan slid a miniature transceiver from his pocket, extended a short aerial and spoke rapidly for twenty seconds. The white Cadillac Eldorado that he flagged down a few minutes later deposited him at the United Nations half a block behind the Irishman's taxi.

Riordan had met up with two of his advisers on the sidewalk. There was still five minutes before the session was due to open. Together they walked toward the pressmen, photographers, guides and onlookers gathered on the steps. Riordan was sweating; he mopped his brow and dabbed at his nape with a green handkerchief as he walked.

The Hispanic sidled up to someone in the crowd—he, too, looked Hispanic—and handed him something small in a plastic bag. The onlooker took the bag in his other hand and put it in his pocket.

Riordan and his companions began to climb the steps. Cameras clicked, electronic flashes winked in the sun, and a pressman called out a question that the politician brushed aside.

The two Hispanics were higher up now, as if seeking a clearer view of the celebrities. The man who had been handed the bag pointed out Riordan, holding his arm high and straight in front of him.

Riordan was still mopping his brow. He raised his other hand and flicked irritably at his nape, as if to chase away a fly that was bothering him.

The two Hispanics moved away from the crowd.

Sean Riordan suddenly stumbled. His mouth opened, and he uttered a loud gasp. His legs appeared to be boneless, and he crumpled to the steps, rolled over and down and finally lay on his face with out-flung arms.

The advisers knelt beside him in consternation. The cameramen moved in, and someone ran for a doctor. By the time he arrived Riordan was dead.

A heart attack, they said; a heavy man with high blood pressure, the fatigue of a long flight, a social program that had been...well, too taxing. Plus the New York climate of course and the strain of an important speech to be made.

It wasn't until the autopsy that they found the tiny feathered blowpipe dart, with its steel tip smothered in deadly curare, hidden in the curly hair on the nape of Riordan's neck.

4

One hour before dawn, Bolan was lowered from a U.S. Navy helicopter onto the flat roof of one of Brognola's safehouses in an area of Algiers projecting out into the ocean on the first of the small islands that encircled the harbor.

Unusually for that part of North Africa, it was raining. By the time the chopper pilot had finished apologizing to the Oran Area Controller for an "inadvertent" intrusion into the airspace of his sector, the Executioner's skintight blacksuit was sodden and his combat boots squelched at every step as he flitted like a ghost through the narrow cobbled streets behind the old Arab seaport.

Beyond the new yacht basin, street lamps garlanding the curving waterfront esplanade cast wavering reflections on the wet pavement. Rain bounced knee-high off the deserted streets and ran in streams down the steep lanes and stone staircases that linked the modern city with the age-old houses of the Casbah.

That was where Bolan was headed. A somber shadow in the downpour, he hurried through colonnades below the high white buildings fronting the harbor, skirted the bright lights of the Place Bugeaud and began the long uphill trek. His own silenced Beretta was holstered beneath his left arm. Big Thunder, his stainless-steel .44 AutoMag, was secreted, together with lightweight Arab robes, in a neoprene pouch clipped to his belt. Both weapons had been supplied by Hal Brognola at the Executioner's request.

Water gushed and dripped and gurgled on every side as he climbed past stepped alleys and cobblestone squares to reach the huge bazaar that flanked a battlemented mosque on the heights above the city.

The mosque, crowned by three domes and five minarets, was separated from the market by a covered passageway supported on Moorish arches. Sheltered by these, Bolan stripped off his wet clothes, rolled up the combat suit and stuffed it in the pouch, then dressed himself in the Arab robes. His face was already darkened, and a small black mustache adorned his upper lip.

The robes were special. The burnoose was bound in black and red; the white djellaba was covered back and front by an embroidered blue apron in the manner of a medieval tabard. Together they distinguished a tribe of Berber nomads whose men towered above the majority of Arabs. Dressed this way, Bolan hoped his own six-foot-plus height would escape attention among the swarms of different tribesmen who would soon be crowding the bazaar.

Just after dawn the rain stopped, the low clouds scudded away to the northwest, and the sun burned from a clear blue sky.

By six-thirty a sprawl of bivouacs, umbrellas and rattan shelters crammed the open space from wall to wall as merchants arrived and began to set out a profusion of fruit, vegetables, material, garments, brassware and preserved meats. Fifteen minutes later the place was vibrant with color, tiger-striped with dense shadow in the alleyways between the stalls as buyers and sellers mingled in a babel of a hundred different dialects, bargaining, gossiping and joking among the shouts of stallholders crying their wares.

Around the veiled women shopping for food, Bolan saw Algerians and Moroccans in modern suits, bejeaned students from the Gulf states, fellahin dressed in shift and fez, white-gowned Bedouin from the desert and Tuareg from the High Atlas with fierce, proud eyes beneath their black headdresses.

Tall Berbers too, wearing robes like his own, moved below the awnings. Once he saw these, the Executioner moved warily out from under the arches and began threading his way through the crowd. Big Thunder and the Beretta were leathered snugly beneath the djellaba, and the pouch with the blacksuit was strapped to the inside of one thigh.

The contact was on the far side of the bazaar, near a row of wooden vats that were filled with dyes used to color the newly cured hides that were made into belts, purses and slippers for the tourist trade.

The vats were there all right. He could smell the rancid odor of the skins over the syrupy aromas drifting from a kiosk displaying figs, dates and pastries decorated with honey and nuts. Two men in tarbooshes and striped shifts were stirring the dyes. At a nearby booth a haggard European in a white suit was discussing the merits of a hand-tooled twin-barrel sporting rifle with an Arab gunsmith. It was a vintage Holland & Holland, Bolan's professional eye noted as he passed. Modified to take a Balvar sight. Very nice. He approached the tanners.

Mutual identification was to be by the well-tried and often-used method of matching two halves of a torn ten-dollar bill. Bolan reached for a pocket on the inside of the robe and took out a slim billfold. He was about to remove the torn half when he was pushed violently in the small of the back.

He stumbled, tripping over a kneeling figure that had suddenly materialized at his feet, and fell headlong. He felt the practiced fingers snatch the billfold from his grasp before he hit the ground.

Bolan was on his feet again in an instant. But the thieves—two kids about twelve years old—were already twenty yards away, dodging the knots of buyers surrounding the stalls. One of them was clutching the billfold openly in his hand.

Bolan was furious at himself for being mugged as easily as any gawking tourist; worse, without the torn ten-spot his rendezvous was scratched and the whole Algiers trip screwed up. He had to get that billfold back.

He sprinted after the young delinquents.

The boys scampered along the cloister beside the mosque. Bolan raced after them, the robe hitched up, scattering merchants and buyers right and left as his powerful figure forged through the crowd.

At the far end of the arched passageway, the thieves ran out into the open air—a blazing white courtyard barred with shadow—and then dashed down a narrow lane between windowless stucco walls. The alley twisted, ran through a gatehouse pierced by a pointed arch and ended in a steep flight of steps curling upward between the mud-walled Arab dwellings. Still breathing effortlessly, the Executioner pounded up in pursuit.

Beyond the stairs there was another courtyard. There were people in this one: prostitutes with kohl-fringed eyes and red mouths sitting by an open doorway; men in striped shifts, others in robes. Bolan heard guttural murmurings and Arabic expletives as he clattered past. Once again hands plucked at his garments and an outthrust foot almost tripped him again. Then he was through and gaining on the youths along another lane.

But now he could hear the sound of running footsteps behind him as well.

The alleyway turned a corner and divided. The two boys separated, each taking one branch. Bolan followed the one with his billfold. He was less than ten yards behind, his feet striking echoes from the pavement. The kid plunged through an open gateway with the Executioner at his heels. Bolan had a confused impression of flagstones, a small fountain and sunbrowned foliage behind iron railings. Then he was in semidarkness, chasing the boy down a corridor inside a tumbledown house.

The end of the corridor was a black rectangle—an open doorway with a lightless room beyond. The young thief turned and stopped, holding up the billfold with an impudent grin.

Bolan snatched it back ... and as he did so the kid leaped nimbly aside. At the same time Bolan felt himself pushed again.

He went staggering forward through the doorway, tripped down a short flight of stone steps, barely saved himself from falling, and was finally brought up against a wall on the far side of the room.

Behind him, the door slammed shut.

Bolan opened his mouth to shout. But before he could voice his rage, there was a scraping noise in the dark and then the abrupt flare of a match. A moment later the serene light of an oil lamp widened and spread over the room.

It was a small room, hung with rugs. He saw two divans, cushions, the obligatory low table, a shuttered window.

Behind the table stood a middle-aged man with a red face and thin dark hair brushed over a balding scalp. He was dressed in a bush jacket and short khaki pants.

The Australian gold smuggler—the guy Bolan had come to Algiers to see!

"What-ho, sport! So glad you managed to make it after all."

"What the hell is this, Wally?" Bolan demanded, still angry.

"Sorry about the unconventional intro, mate." The smuggler was unabashed. He shook out the smoking match in his hand and dropped it into an ashtray on the table. "Fact is, I couldn't think of any other way to get you here."

"But it was arranged. The contact in the bazaar—"

"Yeah, I know. But my mates working the dye vats were caught by local intelligence a few days ago. The bastards there today work for the secret police. If you'd presented your half of the ten-dollar bill, they'd have had you inside for what they call interrogation. You know, a spot of putting the boot in and then the electrified balls. That's why I sent Hassan to block you before it was too late."

"Hassan?"

"Kid who led you here. Smart little nipper. That was a bright idea, pinching the wallet. Gave you an excuse to follow him without anyone suspecting it was a bloody guided tour. Hassan and his mate have done a lot for me." He clapped his hands. "They can do a bit more now and make us some coffee."

The door opened, and the boy appeared, grinning cheekily at the Executioner. Bolan flipped open the billfold and gave him a whole ten-spot. When the coffee had been served, the Australian poured the fragrant liquid from the long-handled brass pan into frail cups supported in filigree metal cradles and asked, "All right, squire, what can I do for you this time?"

"There are things I need to know," Bolan said.

Wally Boardman chuckled. Passing wafers and nuggets and sometimes whole ingots of gold from continent to continent, from country to country, under the eyes of the smartest customs investigators on earth, had left him with an unrivaled knowledge of the underworld and its ways. "Isn't there always?" he said. "Okay, shoot."

"This latest wave of killings," Bolan said. "The top-brass assassinations. These are not just the usual dime-a-dozen terrorist excesses. There's an organization behind them, a guiding hand—and this time, they tell me, the hand doesn't belong to Ivan."

Boardman frowned. "There are rumors," he said slowly. "What exactly did you . . . ?"

"I want to know whose hand the glove fits," Bolan said.

The smuggler drew in a long breath between his teeth. Most of those were gold, too. He shook his head. "That ain't a question a wise man asks," he said.

"I want to know."

"You should try someplace else then. I can't tell you. I don't know meself."

"You must have heard rumors. You just said so. All I want is a lead. It won't be traceable back to you."

"It's not that, Mack. This isn't a question of smoking out a nest of expatriate Armenians or a PLO splinter group. This is big-time stuff, sport. And I mean big."

"So it's big. So give me a big lead, Wally."

"This is dangerous material," Boardman said seriously. "Forget it. That's the best lead I can give you. Drop the whole idea, whatever it is, and leave things be."

Bolan tried another tack. "There's a professional killer who calls himself Graziano. He planted that bomb that brought down the plane at Rome, and he almost scored another at Tel Aviv a couple of days ago. We stopped that one, but afterward I lost contact. I believe the guy's part of a band of hired guns used by the organization. Do you have any idea where I might be able to pick up his trail again?"

Boardman sighed. "Don't say I didn't warn you," he replied. "But this character's very small beer, or so I've heard. There's another one, a loner they call the Marksman. They use him for individual hits, like those politicos in Monte. There are others on the payroll, too. But it seems the one called Baraka is the guy they're training for the big one, the really big one that'll shake the world."

"Baraka?"

"It's a code name, of course. An Arab word meaning... well, something like a blend of charisma, star quality and panache."

"I get the picture. And this... Baraka is being trained...?"

"I'd want a promise of your help if I was to take it any farther," Boardman said.

"Just ask."

"I've got to get out of here, see. I told you that the local fuzz nabbed my mates. They know I'm someplace here in the old town, but they don't know exactly where. So right now I can't move. I can't even send out for a bloody drink. Dead stop on the alcoholic beverages. Religion forbids the locals to touch a drop."

"It's a deal," Bolan said. "You help me, and I'll get you out of here."

The lines of anxiety tightening the flesh around the Australian's mouth slackened a little. "Good man," he said. "You were asking about this Graziano. Smalltimer, like I said. But Paris, France, is the place if you want to catch up with him again. Belleville, La Villette—he's always around one or the other, between hits. Can't tell you about the Marksman. He moves about. Very thin guy with one of those lived-in faces."

"You were telling me about the one they call Baraka," Bolan prompted.

"Yeah. Well, I only know what I heard, of course."

"You said he was being trained for a big one."

"Not so much trained, sport—they say he's some kind of an expert anyway—but groomed, rather. Briefed and rehearsed."

"What is the big one? Who or what is the target?"

"Search me. I'm only repeating hints and gossip. But big enough to make even the pros scared. Tell you who might be able to help, though." Boardman picked up the filigree cradle and sipped from the cup. "You'd have to be crafty, but if you could get around Friedekinde..."

"Friedekinde?"

"You know—the old triple-F. After all, it was from their work, their labo—"

The sentence was never completed.

A storm of glass splinters exploded into the room as the shutter over the window was kicked violently in. At the same time there was an appalling clamor of shots from outside—the deadly, deafening rattle of a machine pistol punctuated by two single, deeper reports.

The cup and its cradle disintegrated in Boardman's hand. Coffee splashed the white wall, to be blotted out instantly by a mist of blood and brain tissue as the smuggler's body jerked obscenely under the impact of a hail of slugs.

Slammed back against the wall, the carcass slid to the cushions, leaving a smear of crimson on the pale partition.

At the first sound of smashing glass, Big Thunder was out and tracking. Bolan had whipped the .44 AutoMag from beneath his robes. But as he whirled toward the window, there were shouts in the passageway outside. He heard the shrill cries of the boy, Hassan, over the stamp of feet on the flagstones.

The door burst open, and Bolan saw Hassan backing into the room and leaping down the short flight of steps with a huge six-chambered .455 Webley service revolver held in his two hands.

The big handgun roared once, twice, a third time.

In the corridor someone screamed. Ears ringing
with the concussions, Bolan had overturned the marble-topped table onto its side and dropped behind it.
"Here, kid! Quick! *Down!*" he shouted urgently.

But before the boy could turn or fire a fourth time,
an Uzi submachine gun opened fire in a single, long,
lethal burst from outside the door. Bolan could hear
the 9 mm parabellums smacking into Hassan's frail
young body as he heaved frantically at the table to
move it into a position from which he could command the passageway.

The boy was no more than a bundle of blood-
stained rags on the cushions beside his master. Choking with fury, the Executioner raised himself from behind the table long enough to let loose three rounds
from the AutoMag.

There were four men in the corridor. One was
sprawled on the ground nursing a shattered shoulder.
Two more held some kind of automatic weapon. Bolan took out the hardman with the Uzi. Big Thunder's boattails smashed into his chest, the impact
drilling him back. The automatics came up to spit
flame as Bolan dropped back behind the tabletop. The
marble shivered, cracked and split as the slugs flattened against it, but none came through.

Okay, the warrior thought, seething. Small-bore
stuff—5.62 mm perhaps—or low muzzle velocity, or
both. He'd risk a shot around the end of the table instead of over the top. But first he'd fire one blind and
hope to scare them momentarily with a ricochet.

He could see the top half of the doorway above the
edge of the marble. He raised his arm and squeezed
the trigger. Big Thunder belched fire. Plaster dust

blossomed from the vaulted ceiling of the corridor, and someone yelled.

Before the echoes of the answering volley had died away, Bolan was at the table end with a wide-angle view on one of the gunners. Once more the blast of the AutoMag rocked the room. The guy dropped his automatic and pitched forward, both hands clutching at the blood pumping from the hole in his thigh.

But now there was movement behind the Executioner. Men jumped down into the room through the shattered window. One, two, three, four—tough-looking hoods with dark features and pockmarked faces. Swiveling desperately to meet the new threat, Bolan saw that he didn't have a chance.

They were all carrying handguns. One toted a Czech Skorpion machine pistol. Two of them also swung leather-covered lead blackjacks.

Was this the way it was to end then? He knew it had to come some day... but not trapped like a rat, cornered in a stone room with no exit and gunners in front and behind.

At least he'd take some of the bastards with him, one for each of the 240-grain deathbringers that remained in Big Thunder's magazine. In the hundredth of a second it took for the thought to form, he raised the gun.

But instead of the numbing, mind-blowing shock of bullets blasting him apart, a completely different attack surprised him from behind as he pressed the trigger.

A blanket was thrown over his head, and strong arms encircled him. The shot plowed into the floor. Then he was struggling like a madman as they all rushed in.

His arms were pinioned. Steely hands grasped his ankles. He heaved and threshed with titanic strength beneath the stifling folds of the covering. The fight swayed left and right over the stone floor. But there were at least four of them, grunting and cursing as they strove to bring him down.

Then there was the sharp crack of a glass ampoule breaking and a gust of sickening fumes in the dark. Chloroform? Ether? Trilene? Bolan's mind reeled; he felt his struggles become uncoordinated. The black world beneath the blanket spun around him.

He was down. They held him among the cushions. Was he really floating or just rising up from the divan? After that it was just a stinging sensation, a sharp prick, no worse than a bee sting really, as the needle plunged into his thigh.

Very slowly, darkness fell in on him through the walls.

5

The car was a scarab-green Renault with white leather custom-built seats. It purred sedately along Route Nationale 83 from Cernay to Guebwiller, past the huge Bollenberg vineyard at Rouffach, and on to the outskirts of Colmar, where the medieval frame houses, steep-roofed above their oak-and-beechwood half-timbering, blazed with scarlet geraniums beneath every window.

There were five men in the Renault. The driver was German, a stocky, bullet-headed character of about fifty, wearing a tan chauffeur's uniform completed by a cap with a shiny peak. The man beside him, tall, heavy and muscular, was completely bald. He looked as though he could have been an enforcer for a collection agency or a punch-drunk ex-pug.

The two passengers in the back seat nearest the doors had the air of professional men—lawyers or doctors or academics, perhaps. The older one peered out at the Alsatian countryside through thick-lensed pince-nez with gold rims. His companion's eyes were hidden behind dark wraparound sunglasses.

The man between them was tall, too. His face showed little interest as they passed through Kientzheim, Riquewihr and Hunawihr. Staring right and left at the vineyards flowing like a green sea to wash against the tree-clad slopes of the Vosges, his eyes remained vacant.

"Don't you remember this journey?" the man wearing pince-nez asked. "Can't you recall any of these towns, these villages?"

The man in the middle shook his head.

"Sometimes it helps to revisit the places you knew well. It triggers some kind of release mechanism that brings back the whole picture," the younger man said. Careful shaving hadn't eliminated the blue shadow tinting his cheeks and chin.

"I don't remember it at all," the man in the middle said.

"Total memory loss is always distressing," the older man said. "All we can hope to do... Well, let's put it this way. There's this black curtain surrounding you. If we can somehow provoke a tiny rip in the material, then maybe you will see enough through that rip to let you tear the whole curtain apart and see what lies beyond. Or, more properly, behind." He favored the man who had lost his memory with a wintry smile.

"The rehabilitation of the amnesiac," the man with the blue chin said pompously, "is almost always partial in the initial stages. Like a jigsaw puzzle—first one piece falls into place, then another, until finally the whole scenario is complete. You know who you are, where you are, and why you are. That's important. You must have a reason for existence."

"We'll do everything in our power to help you," the man with the gold-rimmed pince-nez promised.

Still driving north, they passed through Ribeauvillé. Between white slatted shutters, the window boxes here too were bright with flowers. Storks had built huge spiky nests on metal frames above the chimneys. "I don't remember anything at all," the amnesiac complained.

"You will," the German chauffeur said over his shoulder. Five miles before Sélestat, he turned left off the highway and took a white dirt road that twisted up toward the hills.

Far above the plain, the Renault skirted the horizontal strata of a sandstone bluff crowned by the ancient château of Haut-Koenigsbourg. The turreted castle, built of honey-colored brick with a square-towered keep topped by a pyramid of green tiles, looked out from its wooded height across receding parallels of vines toward the thin gray ribbon of the Rhine.

Up here the village houses were no longer frame but stone-built, with overhanging eaves to protect the inhabitants from winter snows.

Higher still, curious gray outcrops appeared among the tall grasses of the upland meadows. Some were domed, some barrow-shaped, with rounded or rectangular apertures situated among weeds and tangles of briar. Occasionally, half hidden by saplings or thickets, smaller cylindrical shapes were visible with horizontal slits facing east. For the first time, the man who had lost his memory showed some interest.

"What are these?" he asked when the road had circled a particularly large barrow that seemed to be sunk below a grassy bank and surrounded by a narrow trench choked with nettles.

The man with pince-nez laughed. "One of the most expensive mistakes in history," he said. "They called it the Maginot Line. You're looking at the remains of one of the linked forts. They were supposed to beat off the attack in World War II if the Germans crossed the Rhine.''

The amnesiac's eyes brightened. He repeated the words. ''Maginot . . . Line.''

The men on either side of him exchanged glances.

''It was built between 1930 and 1936,'' the younger man said. ''It cost three hundred million francs, and it covered the French frontier all the way from Luxembourg to Switzerland. The French had learned the lessons of 1914, and they weren't going to be invaded by the Germans again. Too bad it never occurred to them that the Germans would be ungentlemanly enough to walk around one end of it, through Belgium and Holland, and attack from the rear!''

The chauffeur laughed.

''The casemates you see aren't stone but pre-stressed reinforced concrete—twelve feet thick with a twelve-inch steel lining. They used to have case-hardened steel covers over the lookout posts and observation towers, but of course they're gone now.''

''Maginot!'' the man who had lost his memory said once again. The word seemed to fascinate him.

''He was the minister who signed the order for it to be built. It was he who gave the go-ahead,'' the chauffeur said.

Fifteen minutes later, on the western side of the crest, the car turned through a crumbling gateway and stopped in the yard of an abandoned farm.

Bleached rafters showed through the roofs of the outbuildings where the tiles had become dislodged. There was no glass in the farmhouse windows, and the wall above one had been blackened long ago by a fire. When the five men got out of the Renault, thistles and weeds growing in the yard reached their knees.

The chauffeur led the way to a brick wall that surrounded two sides of the derelict property. It was about fifteen feet high with a grassy bank on top of it—and the bank, too, was overgrown with briars and other vegetation.

In one corner of the yard, a fig tree grew out of the wall. Below it were the rusted remains of what had once been a three-ton army truck. A sycamore sapling had split apart the floorboards of the tireless wreck and was growing out through one of the cab windows. Hidden behind its three-pointed leaves there was a low, arched opening in the brickwork.

The chauffeur brushed aside a curtain of creeper and disappeared from view. The others followed.

They were in a dark vaulted passageway smelling of mildew and damp. Somewhere ahead of them, water dripped.

As light from the entrance faded, the tunnel turned a corner. Ten yards farther on, the chauffeur halted. His knuckles rapped metal five times.

Light flooded the passageway as a steel door opened. On the far side stood a swarthy man with close-cropped hair who could have been the twin brother of the chauffeur. "You're late, Klaus," he said.

"Who's complainin'?" the chauffeur said. "We're here, aren't we? Nobody asked me to clock in yet."

"Some people have other commitments. Some of us have to keep a believable cover going," the swarthy man said.

"Willi!" the man with pince-nez said sharply. "Klaus! We can do without this kind of nonsense. There's a job to be done here. In any case, Willi, we won't keep you long."

"Okay, okay. No offense, Doc," Willi said.

They were standing in a cellarlike, brick-floored room, not much bigger than a cell. The light came from an old-fashioned oil lamp. A broken chair, an empty wooden crate and a table covered in rat droppings were the only furnishings. There was no window, no skylight, no other door.

Willi shifted the table, kicked aside some dead leaves and revealed a trapdoor. He seized an iron ring and pulled it open. Carrying the lamp, he climbed down the iron rungs of a ladder to a much dryer, airier corridor below. When the others had followed and Klaus, who brought up the rear, had lowered the trapdoor, he blew out the flame in the lamp and clicked a switch. At once the passageway was illuminated by a row of low-power electric bulbs set in the arched roof.

They walked perhaps a hundred yards along a straight flagstoned tunnel. Willi unlocked another steel door. Beyond it was a room that looked like the entrance hall in a hospital—white walls, shining tiles on the floor, fluorescent lighting above a gray steel desk with a telephone switchboard installation.

At the far end there was an open-cage elevator.

They crammed in. The grille slid shut with a hydraulic hiss. Slowly the car descended past a metal catwalk that overlooked a cavernous chamber fitted out with monitors and a vast computer terminal winking with red, blue and green lights. A distant generator hummed, and there was the smell of ozone in the air.

The elevator bounced to a halt on a lower level in what seemed to be a gymnasium. The amnesiac saw wall bars, a punching bag, a rowing machine. "You have been here before," the doctor with pince-nez said. It wasn't a question.

The amnesiac smiled. "Maginot," he said.

"You know who you are now. You know your name."

"Maginot."

"No, no. *Your* name, not the name of the place." The voice was gentle. "Your name is Baraka, is it not." Again this was a statement, not a query.

"I don't remember."

"You must remember. Your name is Baraka. Ba-ra-ka. Under no circumstances must you forget. If you forget, we cannot help you. What is your name?"

"Baraka?"

"That's right. Good. You *must* remember that."

The man with wraparound sunglasses had said nothing for a long time. He spoke now. "Isn't it time we ran a check? Identification is fine, but we want to know, don't we, if the expertise can still be tapped? If the previous acquired skills remain?"

"Quite right, Paul," the doctor said. He turned to the bald ex-pug. "Mazarin. Get the dog."

The huge thug grinned, revealing yellowed tombstone teeth. He turned and went out through a door at the far end of the gymnasium. Baraka walked to a row of filing cabinets, opened the door of a steel cupboard at one end of the bank and took a bottle of mineral water from the miniature refrigerator inside. He drank.

"You see, Paul!" the doctor said excitedly. "He *can* remember—he does. When there's no pressure, no strain, the old instincts, the conditioned reflexes take over!"

Mazarin returned, leading a snarling Doberman pinscher on a leash. "All right," the doctor said. "Let him go."

Mazarin unclipped the leash. The dog growled, its teeth bared. Saliva dripped from its slavering jaws. The doctor feigned a kick in its direction. Howling, the big dog leaped for him.

The doctor drew a small automatic from his pocket and fired once. The Doberman yelped, staggering in the middle of its spring, and dropped to the floor, threshing from side to side. Blood flowed from its chest.

The doctor fired a second shot, loud under the low ceiling. The dog twitched and lay still.

"The animal was about to attack me," the doctor said calmly, turning toward Baraka. "It was an enemy. You know what an enemy is—someone or something that threatens you. What do you do if you are threatened by an enemy? To protect yourself, you kill him. If he is dead, he cannot harm you."

"This is a lesson you must learn," Paul added. "We believe you have the skills to eliminate enemies, buried someplace in your past. Soon we shall find out. For the moment, it is enough that you show us you have . . . digested . . . the doctor's lesson."

"What do you do if someone shows you an enemy?" the doctor asked softly.

Baraka's face hardened to a chilly mask. "Kill," he said. "Kill, kill, kill."

6

The "impregnable" forts of the Maginot Line were designed to cover overlapping fields of fire with a high-explosive barrage from 75 mm and 88 mm artillery, supported by 135 mm howitzers, mortars, grenades, various calibers of antitank cannon and machine guns fired from armored "pepperpots" strung out on the heights between each strongpoint. Observers in a steel command post sunk in the highest part of each bunker coordinated the defensive strategy.

Each concrete shell, shored up by a twelve-foot-thick rampart of earth and rocks, its casemates bristling with gun barrels, was something like an ungainly warship sunk up to the turrets in the green slopes of the Vosges.

The firing points were linked by a honeycomb of galleries, passageways and staircases, with elevators to three or even four lower levels that could penetrate as far as three hundred feet below the surface.

The blockhouses were provided with dormitories, an infirmary, a telephone exchange, mess halls, recreation rooms, electricity generators, air-conditioning, poison gas filters and armories housing several thousand shells. Steel bulkheads sealed off each sector of the redoubt, there was an ammunition hoist with an eighteen-ton counterweight, and aerial monorails transported charges of up to two and a half tons at a time to each firing point.

The larger forts were staffed by a crew of up to twelve hundred men; some were used as barracks for infantry who were supposed to stream out and mop up the vanquished remnants of the attackers once the artillery had done its deadly work. There were separate entrances for men, munitions and stores as well as the tractors that worked inside the bunkers. Some of the entry tunnels surfaced as far as a mile behind the line.

In fact Hitler's generals ignored the Maginot Line until they had overrun practically the whole of the rest of France. When they did attack at last, the pepperpots proved extremely vulnerable to the Wehrmacht's 88s—and the "impregnable" casemates, undamaged by the shells of the German artillery or the bombs of Stukas, fell easily to the determined assaults of grenades, flamethrowers, smoke bombs and, once the French machine gunners had been silenced, parcels of explosives inserted on long poles.

The survivors, their weapons destroyed, were forced to seek shelter on the lower levels. And there, because the ventilation system was unable to extricate either smoke or the heavier-than-air carbon dioxide, most of them asphyxiated.

Forty-seven years later, their machinery and equipment long gone, the entrances sealed or mined, the interconnecting network of tunnels closed off, the blockhouses had become part of the landscape, of no more interest than the natural rocks or trees.

The stronghold in which the man called Baraka was to be programmed was an exception.

The doctor had bought the derelict farm many years ago as a speculation, intending one day perhaps to transform the property into some kind of mountain clinic. It was only later that he found the sole entrance to the bunker that the demolition squads had missed. Once he and his associates realized the complexity of the galleries to which it gave access, they saw immediately the multiple uses to which such a vast secret enclave could be put. And they began secretly refurbishing the interior with the latest mechanical and electronic apparatus.

It took a long time. They would never have gotten away with it if it wasn't for the fact that this entrance was on the doctor's private property, that the nearest village was almost ten miles away... and that immense care was taken to maintain the farmyard in its derelict state.

Adventuring children, gypsies or hoboes who did stumble on the creeper-covered arch could in any case penetrate no farther than the first steel door, when they would naturally assume that the rest was sealed off in the usual way.

Among the doctor's more sophisticated innovations was a small biochemical laboratory, high-tech video equipment with a specialized viewing room and underground advanced technology workshops where microelectronic detection and bugging devices could be perfected. On the lowest level, a soundproofed 150-yard firing range had been installed.

Before Baraka was taken there, Paul and the doctor wished to test the effect of the Doberman "lesson" on his damaged mind. The younger man signaled to Mazarin and pointed to a wrestling mat occupying a fifteen-foot square in the center of the gymnasium. "All right," he said. "Take him."

The tombstone teeth gleamed briefly. Without warning, the bruiser leaped at Baraka, kicked his feet from under him, caught him as he fell and threw him bodily onto the mat. He launched himself through the air and landed heavily on the fallen amnesiac, groping for nerve centers he could use to immobilize him.

Baraka's reaction was immediate, instinctive—and impressive.

He threw off the big bald man with a double heel-of-the-hand attack that thudded against his temples, extricating himself and springing upright while Mazarin still lay on the floor.

As Mazarin in turn surged to his feet, surprisingly lightly for a man of his bulk, Baraka squared off into a karate stance, one arm close in to his side, the other held out.

Mazarin grinned wolfishly. He liked it when they fancied themselves experts at the so-called martial arts! Rising onto his toes, he ran in and blasted off a flying jump kick at Baraka's jaw. Swaying unexpectedly back, Baraka rode it, shook his head and swiveled, scything in a cross-body *shuto* stroke as the big man coasted back onto the mat.

Then, as the target shuddered away, he dropped a high side kick to the sphenoid and feinted another *shuto* aimed at the throat. Mazarin ducked beneath that and unleashed a punishing *seiken* blow, a ram's head punch carrying all his weight that slammed against Baraka's diaphragm and sent him down.

He rolled away from a heel that thumped his ribs, shoving himself upright as his opponent dashed in with a tae kwon do head kick. Baraka dropped back

onto the mat and seized the outthrust foot as it rocketed toward him, twisting with all his strength to speed
Mazarin on, fueled by his own impetus, until he
crashed against the wall bars and slid to the floor.

"Amazing!" Paul murmured. "The ego suppressed, but the id—the original reflexes *and the
thinking behind them*—functioning normally!"

"Not *thinking*," the doctor corrected. "The reflexes are subconscious. The id, as you say, taking
charge. As we hoped."

The combatants were locked in close body conflict
now. Although the ex-pug was at least thirty pounds
heavier, Baraka's sinewy form seemed his equal in
force and resilience. There was a brief period of wrestling throws, holds and locks, then Mazarin broke
from a conventional scissors grip and dexterously im-
mobilized Baraka in the deadly position known as the
Boston Crab—an excruciating arch-back hold in
which too much struggling on the part of the victim,
or too much force exerted by the victor, could result in
a snapped spine.

In professional bouts, the Boston Crab inevitably
elicits a submission. Baraka wasn't a professional . . . but he wasn't beaten either. Grunting with effort, he freed an arm and slashed a devastating *shuto*
with the plank-hard edge of his hand at Mazarin's
crotch. The blow landed with a hollow thwack, hard
enough to echo around the gymnasium after it hit the
genital protector that the ex-pug wore beneath his
pants.

Mazarin laughed. He relaxed his hold, and the two
men stood up.

The doctor noticed that Baraka wasn't even out of
breath. "Excellent," he said approvingly. "For a while

there Mazarin was your enemy. You did the right thing. You attacked to protect yourself. Now we shall see about another kind of attack."

Beyond the gymnasium, an escalator brought them down to the low-level shooting gallery. Klaus, Willi and Mazarin stayed behind, but there was already someone on the range. Standing by the racks of rifles and handguns was a thin character with a hollow-cheeked, cadaverous face deeply etched with lines. He was cradling a twin-barreled sporting rifle.

"Marksman," the doctor exclaimed, "I didn't know you were back!"

"I don't like nobody to know where I'm at," the man replied. "As it happens, it's sooner than I thought. There was a job I had to organize in Algiers—"

"Algiers!"

"Yeah. It seems someone was getting too close. Knew more than was good for him, know what I mean?"

"But why Algiers?"

The Marksman shrugged. "It was convenient. Guy was passing through. Then I heard he got himself blocked and holed up there. It's not a bad place—they don't ask too many questions."

"And so you came by here...?"

"I figured I'd put in a little practice while I was waiting out the deadline to collect from the boss."

"Swell. Maybe you'd care to set an example for our friend here." Paul nodded at Baraka.

The Marksman shrugged again. "Whatever you say."

There were paper targets painted with concentric circles thumbtacked to the soundproofing material covering the wall at the far end of the gallery. He fired twice in quick succession then broke the gun, inserted two more rounds and fired again.

The four bullets had made a single clover-shaped hole in the center of the bull's-eye. A three-quarter-inch group.

The doctor smiled. "Remarkable. You can fire a gun, can't you?" he said to Baraka. "Why not have a go yourself?"

Baraka nodded. His face expressionless, he walked to the racks, picked five cartridges from an ammunition box and selected a Springfield M-1903 sniper's rifle.

Paul nudged the older man. "You see? Automatic reflex," he whispered. "That's the one he picked before!"

Baraka loaded his shells into the five-round magazine. Standing in a casual attitude, he raised the rifle to his shoulder and fired five times, manipulating the strong bolt firmly and confidently each time.

The first shot pierced the bull's-eye dead center. The four others blasted, one after the other, the heads from the thumbtacks pinning the target in place. The paper detached itself from the wall and drifted to the floor.

The doctor repressed a smile. "Satisfied about those retained skills?" he asked Paul.

The Marksman's eyebrows were raised, although whether this was due to surprise, admiration or jealousy wasn't clear.

Ten minutes later, Paul and the doctor took Baraka to the highest point of the old bunker, up beneath the concrete dome.

The doctor unlocked a heavy door, climbed a short flight of steps to the turret and walked across to a steel shutter blanking off the casemate. On the outside, the shutter was stained with more than forty years of rust and weather. Inside it was oiled and shining, moving soundlessly in metal grooves let into the concrete, once he had withdrawn bolts, dialed a combination on the locking mechanism and twirled the handle that raised it.

Across the broad sill of the old firing slit, they looked out over the weed-grown dike, across a slope of meadow, and then down a steep-sided wooded valley with a stream coursing beneath the trees.

At the bottom of the valley, framed by the cleft in the foliage, a short stretch of highway traversing a bridge that spanned the stream was visible.

Two automobiles crossed the bridge, and then a bus and a truck loaded with farm produce going in the opposite direction.

The doctor gestured at the distant strip of road and the toy-sized vehicles crawling along it. "The range is two thousand yards," he told Baraka. "Suppose an open car was stopped on that sector of road you can see—stalled there for a couple of minutes, say. If you had the right kind of rifle with the right kind of telescopic sight, do you think you could pick off an enemy if he was a passenger in the rear seat?"

For the first time, Baraka's smile was spontaneous and warm. "No problem," he said.

7

Mack Bolan awoke and stared at a ceiling ten feet above his head. The ceiling was white, yellowing slightly at the corners as if it hadn't been repainted for some time. From the center of the ceiling a worn electric lead supported a fluted 1920s-style lampshade in pink frosted glass.

The lamp wasn't illuminated; light filtered into the room through net curtains drawn across a double-casement window.

Bolan turned his head. He was naked, lying on his back in a bed, the covers drawn up to his chin. Instantly he was wide awake, his fighter's instincts honed by years of continuous danger. He remembered every detail of the massacre in Wally Boardman's room. Everything up to the sting of the needle.

So they hadn't killed him. Where were they keeping him prisoner? And why?

He flexed his limbs experimentally, testing out the restraints they would have put on him.

There were none. His arms and legs moved freely.

Puzzled, he sat up and threw aside the crisp sheets. He glanced around his prison. About fifteen feet square, it looked like a cheap hotel room. A table, a single chair, an old-fashioned pearwood closet, a wall light above the bed. There were two doors. One, half open, showed the tiled interior of a bathroom.

Bolan swung his feet to the floor and stood up. He felt fine. No post-Mickey Finn hangover. No headache.

He went to the window. It looked out onto a white-tiled airshaft, stained with years of city grime. A fire escape passed the window, zigzagging six or seven floors down to a small square yard lined with trash cans. Bolan tried the catch. It opened easily. He leaned out and breathed in warm air. Above the shaft white clouds moved across a blue sky.

A row of windows like his own, one above the other, studded the far wall of the shaft. On a lower story he could see a young woman with dark hair fastening the clasp of a brassiere behind her back. He withdrew into the room, his brows knitted into a frown.

He went to the closed door and tried the handle. The door wasn't locked. He opened it a crack.

A carpeted corridor with more doors, all of them numbered, stretched before him. His own was room 72. Outside one of the others, a tray laden with used dishes, a coffeepot and part of a bread roll rested on the floor. In the distance he could hear the humming whine of a vacuum cleaner.

Thoroughly bewildered, the Executioner closed the door and sat down on the bed. If this was some kind of elaborate setup to fool him, similar to the one in the movie where the spy believed he was in a Nazi prison camp but was actually in a faked-up suburban garden in London, then they were sure spending a lot of dough to make it convincing.

He padded into the shower room. A stranger looked back at him out of the glass. He still had the stained skin and the mustache.

He felt his jaw. No more than the usual one-day stubble. There was an electric razor, toothbrush and soap on the shelf above the hand basin. He had never seen any of them before.

Before he shaved he went back into the bedroom and opened the closet. Underclothes—his own—were on a shelf, as were a black turtleneck sweater, jeans, sneakers and a lightweight raincoat. On the floor of the closet was a zippered canvas holdall that was unfamiliar. He opened it.

Inside he found a neatly rolled combat blacksuit; two holsters with straps; one Beretta 93-R, one .44 AutoMag and ammunition clips packed into a waterproof neoprene pouch; a waistbelt with holster clips; and a billfold.

He opened that. There was money inside, including the torn ten-spot.

By this time, Bolan was genuinely perplexed.

If this was really a hotel, why was he here? Why had they left him his weapons? If they were going to do that, why take him in the first place?

The only thing missing from his gear was the lightweight Berber outfit he had assumed as a disguise when he had gone to the market to make contact with Boardman. For most of the rest they must have turned over his hotel room in Algiers.

Algiers? But where was he now? The atmosphere, the sounds of life around him, the very odor of the air he breathed was wrong for North Africa.

Where then? He went to the window and listened. He heard the distant sounds of traffic, a horn blaring, the seesaw bray of an ambulance or a police car. A jetliner droned somewhere in the sky. At the foot of the shaft there was a clatter of plates and a dispute in a language he couldn't recognize.

Bolan dressed. If it was a setup, he'd play along. If it wasn't, if the hotel was genuine... well, he'd learn nothing staying here. There was a key on the outside of the door. He locked the door and walked down the passageway.

Around a corner at the far end there was a hallway with stairs and an elevator shaft. A girl who looked Vietnamese was vacuuming the floor. "Good morning," Bolan said experimentally. The girl looked up, smiled and said nothing.

The buttons on the elevator control board inside the car ran from eight through one to RC. He hit the lowest one.

The car sank. RC? *Rez-de-chaussée?* Street level? Well, Algeria had been a French colony until the early sixties.

The elevator deposited him in a small lobby, which contained a desk, a phone switchboard and a register. A girl with spectacles and very short hair was behind the desk.

"Bonjour, Monsieur Bolan," she said, smiling.

The Executioner repressed a start. His name was known.

Behind the girl he saw posters advertising budget vacations in Tunisia, Morocco, the island of Réunion. "Do you feel better today?" she asked.

"I feel fine," Bolan said. "Er... what time did I check in yesterday? I, uh, might not have been... myself."

The receptionist spun the register around to face her and opened it. "Ten-thirty in the evening," she said. Not looking up at him, she continued, "Your friends made the reservation by phone. A celebration, they said. You were deceived by the strength of our local *pastis*."

He stared at her. Maybe it was a real hotel. "But you were no trouble," she reassured him hastily. "They helped you upstairs and then left at once. Absolutely no problem."

"Yeah," Bolan said. "My friends."

He walked out through revolving glass doors into sunshine.

His eyes took in a wide flagged square with a statue on a plinth in the center. Cars were parked on the roadway surrounding the paved area. There were old houses with mansard roofs and, towering skyward, an enormous baroque church that took up one whole side of the square.

Bolan stared up at the vast neoclassical facade. He knew the church. St. Sulpice, in the Latin Quarter of Paris.

Paris!

Frowning, the Executioner swore under his breath.

He walked half a block to a café in the rue de Rennes and ordered a strong black coffee. For minutes he sat gazing at nothing, trying to make some sense out of that day and the day before, trying to find the connection between them.

There was no connection. Nothing made sense.

Following Brognola's briefing, he had hoped to regain contact with the underworld know-all, Wally Boardman. He had believed Boardman could put him back on the trail of the killer, Graziano. And Gra-

ziano, he thought, would lead him to the world terrorist organization Brognola wished him to unmask.

Well, he had found Boardman. And the Australian
had been murdered to stop him from talking.

The killing—and that of the boy, Hassan—had
nothing to do with the Algerian police or the fact that
they were onto the Australian's gold smuggling racket.

So why had Bolan been spared?

If the aim of the operation was to abort any investigation into the terrorist organization, why hadn't the
goons mowed down the Executioner when he was a
sitting duck?

Why had he simply been knocked out with an in-
jection and taken away?

Normally that would have been because they wanted
to find out how much he knew. But if he'd known
anything at all, he wouldn't have been there asking
favors of the Australian!

In any case, he had no evidence of interrogation,
torture or the use of truth drugs. He'd examined his
body carefully for hypo marks, and there was only the
one in his thigh that he'd gotten in Boardman's place.
He'd no recollection whatever of any kind of... well,
any kind of anything. He'd woken up after a good
night's sleep. Between the attack in Algiers and his return to consciousness in the hotel room his mind was
a complete—and peaceful—blank.

Plus he felt fine.

Which left the second burning question: why Paris?

What conceivable reason could there be for wasting his informant, drugging the Executioner himself
in North Africa and then dumping him here...
complete with his weapons, his ammunition and his
money?

Bolan couldn't find a thread of logic to connect all that. He ordered another coffee.

Just what had he learned from Wally Boardman before they had gunned him down?

Not much. The Australian had advised Bolan to let the investigation drop because it was too damn dangerous to ask questions, and he'd proved the truth of that with his own life.

He'd said, to use his own words, that it was very big-time stuff, and that apart from Graziano, he knew of at least two other pro hit-men on the organization payroll—one called the Marksman, the other, Baraka. This Baraka, Boardman had told him, was being... groomed for some ultimate horror hit, and Bolan's best bet would be someone with the name of Friedekinde, but it would need very careful handling. There was also the obscure reference to "the old triple-F."

The only other thing Bolan had learned was that Graziano was a small-timer...and that customarily he holed up between hits in the Belleville or La Villette districts of Paris.

Well, Bolan himself was in Paris, wasn't he? He shook his head. That last thought suggested a link that was so crazy it wasn't worth thinking about. Except that he had to think about it, because he had no other point of departure.

It depended on whether the killers had overheard his conversation with Boardman before they'd opened fire. And how much of it.

If they had...no, it was insane, but if they'd patched in to the whole scenario, one reason he had been brought back to Paris with his weapons could be that they *wanted* him to get on Graziano's tail.

Because Graziano himself knew too much and it was a convenient way of eliminating him? Or because the man was no more than a coincidence and there were two separate groups working against each other? In which case, following Graziano would be a false trail as far as Brognola was concerned.

Bolan gave up. None of it made sense.

But what the hell. He was here anyway. Forget the lunacy, he told himself. He might as well follow up the little he had and see what came out of it.

Baraka and the Marksman could wait. He'd never heard of either of them, and he had no in. He'd prospect Belleville and La Villette later. Right now he'd run a soft probe on Friedekinde, whoever or whatever it was.

That was, of course, if the guy had anything to do with Paris. He could just as easily be in Damascus, Amsterdam or Vienna.

Boardman's words came back to Bolan: *You know—the old triple-F. After all, it was their work, their labo—*

What did they mean? What work? What labor? How had it helped the organization? Was the triple-F an acronym... and if so what did it stand for? A society, a guerrilla group, a company? Or were there simply three names beginning with that letter? If so, it was a fair guess that Friedekinde was one of them.

That prompted another thought: it was just as Boardman was about to explain the three Fs that the guns had opened up. If they had listened in on the conversation, or even the last part of it, that could imply that Friedekinde was the most important lead, the key to the whole thing.

Bolan paid for the coffee and walked to the nearest phone booth.

On the shelf beneath the directories someone had left a copy of *Le Monde*. Idly Bolan glanced at the headlines. None of the stories seemed familiar, nor were they follow-ups to anything familiar. Then he saw the date. The fourteenth.

Boardman had been killed on the eleventh.

Bolan was stunned. It had taken them not twenty-four but seventy-two hours to get him here! In between he had lost two whole days....

There had to be some explanation, Bolan thought. Smuggling an unconscious man, plus weapons, across international frontiers could be tricky. A small boat across the Mediterranean perhaps, and then a car or truck or ambulance up past Lyon to Paris?

The Executioner didn't think so. A group this organized would have executive jets or a chopper available.

So what then?

So that was just one more mystery to add to the long list. And what difference did an extra one make among so many?

Bolan swiveled the name directory down on its pivot and opened the hard covers. There was nobody in Paris listed under the name Friedekinde. He flipped back a couple of pages. Nothing with the acronym FFF.

He had no better luck with the street directory, and there was no point consulting the yellow pages, because subscribers were entered under professions and he had no idea what business Friedekinde was in.

The guy was either unlisted or based in one of the other three hundred and eight major cities in the world.

Bolan sighed. He closed the books and walked out into the street. He saw no sign of a tail, though he knew there would be one. They—whoever "they" were—had brought him to Paris for a purpose, even if he didn't know what that purpose was yet. So it stood to reason that he would be under continuous surveillance.

So far he hadn't been able to spot anyone. But it could be the Vietnamese girl with the vacuum cleaner, the café waiter, the guy sweeping garbage along the sidewalk gutter near the phone booth, the telephone lineman with his feet dangling among the coaxial cables beneath the open manhole on the far side of the street.

The streets were crowded, too. If it was a question of professionals—maybe two people on foot, a couple on bicycles and a pair of automobiles, switching every half hour—he knew he wouldn't have a hope in hell of flushing them out.

Let them work for their dough. He'd take the subway up to the Place Blanche in Montmartre, a cab to La Villette, and then walk on down through Belleville toward Place de la Bastille. Graziano, he knew, was something of a playboy. He liked to hang around high-class women. He didn't mind spending money. So it wouldn't be too difficult to locate the kind of bars in those areas that such a man would frequent.

If he could get his hands on the terrorist, maybe he could choke some intel about Friedekinde out of him.

8

It was the middle of the afternoon. Bolan had found
the La Villette neighborhood counterproductive; until the second half of the nineteenth century, it had
been part of what was called the Zone, a no-man's-
land between the inner and outer ring of the old city
defenses frequented by ragpickers, hoboes and the
dispossessed. It wasn't much better now; it remained
a bleak wasteland of railroad marshaling yards,
abandoned factories, and dock basins linked by canals crossing vacant lots overgrown with weeds.

The swarming, colorful ghetto of Belleville looked
more promising. Bolan had no fixed plan of action.
Graziano would doubtless be known to the precinct
police, but he was unwilling to make his search that
official—especially as he himself could still be on some
Parisian wanted list for all he knew.

In a network of narrow streets choked with market
traders and children playing among battered automobiles parked along the curbs, he drifted from café
to bar to club, sometimes asking a casual question,
sometimes just keeping an open eye.

It wasn't until the fifth or sixth that he struck pay
dirt at an afternoon strip club. Dimly lit by pink-
shaded lamps, there was a space at the far end of the
bar where a succession of big-breasted blondes took

off their clothes as they writhed and swayed to the
hard rock screaming from speakers in the four corners of the room.

Bolan sat near the bar. Only half a dozen tables were
occupied, mainly by North Africans whose own customs or religion forbade them to watch such exhibi-
tions at home. He ordered a beer and allowed a
brunette with an enameled face and a red dress that
looked as if it had been sprayed over her curves to join
him.

She ordered champagne, and he paid the usual clip
joint price—from which, he knew, she would receive
a small commission—for a glass of syrup and water.
With the mustache and the stained face, it was conceivable that he could pass as a Libyan or Tunisian,
quite possibly from the neighborhood. So he felt safe
enough making conversation, asking questions, without being thought a police spy or the wrong kind of
journalist.

He called the barman over and ordered a second
round.

Bolan knew how these places worked. As a rule, the
management reckoned each customer was good for
three rounds. After that came the pitch . . . and then it
was too late for questions.

The pitch came in three sizes. The woman held out
the promise of sexual delights in a love nest "just
around the corner." She would take the cash in advance, agree to meet the john outside after she had
changed out of her working clothes and then wouldn't
show. Or she might be a genuine fast-throw hooker. In
that case the ante would be upped and there would be
cubicles upstairs. Or more likely, there would be a

curtained alcove at the other end of the room where the girl and her customer could get together.

In each case a quick turnover was vital. The guys who ran those places weren't paying the strippers so that a handful of rubberneck jerks could stay all afternoon over a single glass of beer.

The flip side of Paris's latest hit single was halfway through and the third blonde was revealing her breasts when the bartender brought the third round to the table and the pitch was launched.

The brunette's mascaraed stick-on lashes were as stiff as iron railings. Bolan was surprised she had the strength to bat them as she cooed, "I always did like tall, macho types with blue eyes. I like a guy with muscle. And you got some powerful shoulders there. The thought of your hands makes shivers run down my spine." There was a pause before she continued. "Tell you what, darling, why don't we—?"

Bolan was familiar enough with French to understand what she was saying. Besides, he thought wryly, the language she was speaking then was international in its intent.

"As powerful as Graziano's?" Bolan asked, diving into the deep end.

The girl's eyes opened unnaturally wide as if counterweights in back of her doll face had swung down.

"Emilio?" she exclaimed. "Graziano? You're a friend of Emilio's! Baby, you shoulda told me. But you just missed him. He left with Clara half a minute before you blew in."

"You know where he was headed?"

"The Bluebird, I guess. Or maybe Las Vegas Nights. Clara has a thing about the hatcheck girl there." The brunette sniffed. "Look, seeing you're a buddy of Emilio's, I got a better idea. I know a joint just off the rue Morand, and my place is—"

"Another time, maybe." Bolan pushed back his chair. He left a couple of bills on the table. "I've got business with Emilio. But thanks for your time."

"Quickest way to the Vegas is out the back, past the bathroom and across the lot," she said. "It's the way Emilio always goes."

Bolan nodded. "Sure," he said. "Thanks again."

He threaded his way past the tables. The third blonde's buttocks were shaking and wobbling. Through the red draperies below the illuminated Toilettes sign, a short passage led to an open doorway, a yard with two evil-smelling toilets and a vacant lot.

As soon as the curtain dropped behind Bolan, the brunette hurried back to the bar. "Toni," she said to the man behind the bar, "get me Max on the house phone. This is urgent."

THE LOT WAS BIG. It was, in fact, a demolition site, where a whole block had been flattened in a slum clearance scheme. But the reconstruction hadn't started yet.

Wrecked car bodies stripped of everything movable, piles of used tires, bottles and cans in stacks of rotting household garbage, iron bedsteads and broken pots littered the rubble-strewn ground between brick-lined pits where wildflowers grew among the smashed drainage pipes.

Old two-story houses backed onto two sides of the lot, and there was a high fence with wire gates ahead. Beyond this, Bolan could see soot-blackened warehouses and a couple of high-rise apartment blocks where the new concrete was already cracked and stained.

It was presumably in that direction that Graziano and his companion had gone. Perhaps there was a pass door in the fence, or a portion of the wire gates that opened. Bolan hurried across, his shadow long in the rank grasses.

In the center of the lot a section of paved roadway—the remains of a lane that had once been a cul-de-sac—ran alongside a pit filled with yellow water. Discarded trash cans lay on the far side of the pool.

The first shot hit one of the containers with a noise like a ten-pound hammer battering a steel door. Bolan was flat on the pavement, rolling, with his arms above his head and the Beretta in both hands before the echo of the report registered in his ears.

His tails—if they were still there—couldn't be gunning for him: they could have done that more easily in Algiers.

So who was the attacker? If it wasn't one of the hardmen who had drugged and then dumped him, could it be a buddy of Graziano's alerted by his questions in the neighborhood? Graziano himself?

If so, did it mean that his wild idea—that Graziano and the new terrorist organization weren't connected—might be true?

Or was it no more than a coincidence? Some independent villain out for a tougher-than-usual mugging? A kid stoned out of his mind who'd do anything, kill anyone, to get the cash for a fix?

Vital question: was the shooter after Bolan *as* Bolan, as an unwelcome, unidentified snooper who must be silenced; or just as a convenient mark? If it wasn't the last it had to be one of the other two, because nobody else could possibly know he was in Paris. He hadn't known himself until he'd woken up in the hotel that morning!

The thoughts flashed through his head as he kept rolling, waiting for a second shot that would give him a clue, a direction, a hint where to aim.

It came quickly enough, a heavy-caliber slug that gouged a furrow in the tarmac beside his head and scuffed dirt into his face. This was no hophead kid firing blind, but a pro who knew what he was doing.

But the near miss enabled the Executioner to locate the ambusher's firing point—the skeleton of a miniature three-wheel delivery truck that had once been powered by a motorcycle engine. The tricar was lying on its side, and the gunman was crouched by the rusted floorboard.

He whipped around to the far side as Bolan squeezed off a three-round burst that shook the steel plating and sent one ricochet screeching off the differential housing.

Bolan came to his knees, firing a single shot to make the hidden marksman keep his head down, and then dashed toward the trash cans. Over the stamp of his own pounding feet he heard the distant thumping jangle of rock music from the strip club.

The third shot—and a fourth immediately afterward—didn't come until he was almost level with the galvanized bins. He dived full length behind them, and then there was another pause.

A gun with no more than a two-shot capacity, Bolan guessed. He figured it for some kind of express rifle, judging by the whipcrack report—something far crisper and less hollow-sounding than the reverberations of modern handguns. The pauses were bonuses, allowing him peril-free movement each time the guy reloaded.

Bolan decided to offer himself as a decoy, tempting the gunner to let loose two more, which would give the Executioner the chance, now that he knew the score, to seek proper cover in the lull that would come immediately after.

Bolan shuffled down to one end of the row, raised an arm above the level of the trash cans and fired a shot at the tricar.

For an instant he showed himself beyond the end of the row, as if in readiness to run for a pile of broken bricks topped with motor tires, a piece of cover ten yards nearer the wire gates and safety. And immediately the rifle cracked out once, twice. A slug pierced a lid above one of the empty, deformed bins with a noise like a shot from a Bofors antiaircraft cannon. It was no more than an inch from the Executioner's momentarily visible shoulder.

Its companion was a hunch shot prompted by Bolan's own misleading maneuver. It was aimed at the space he was expected to fill when he made his run, to nail him as he left the cover of the bins and dashed for the tires.

The high-velocity round glanced off the corrugated side of the container at waist height and caromed skyward with a high-pitched whine.

Bolan was on his feet and moving, all right... but he was springing away in the opposite direction, hurling himself toward a burned-out panel truck that was much farther away toward the middle of the lot, but which would give him much better all-round protection in case the sniper also moved.

He made it. The gamble on the killer's need to reload after two shots paid off, but only just.

A hole appeared in the roof panel above his head,
and another round took away the heel of his shoe and
sent him sprawling as he threw himself through the
gap where the rear doors of the truck had been.

Panting, Bolan dragged himself toward the front
end of the wreck. The farther away he was from the
rear, the wider his angle of view on the tricar...and
the more chance he had of enfilading the guy behind
it.

The bulkhead separating the cab from the engine
compartment was missing, along with the motor itself and the gearbox and pedal controls, so it was
possible to crawl through beneath the scuttle to the
scorched and oily space that had once housed the cylinder block.

Better still, the hood that covered the engine had
also been removed.

Bolan had a choice of vantage points. Crouched, he
could peer over the axle and brake drum out through
the wheel arch, or he could rise suddenly up over the
louvered edge of the hood long enough to risk a shot.
The rifleman would be expecting him now to do just
that—but through the glassless cab window or around
the pillar of the empty windshield.

The extra few feet would once again give Bolan the
advantage of surprise. He would have time to choke
out another three-round burst and drop back out of
sight in the moment it took his adversary to adjust the
target site he had in mind and switch his aim.

From beneath the wheel arch he could see part of
the gunman, but only two shoes and trouser legs as far
as the knees. The guy was lying behind the floor-

board. It was difficult: there was no percentage wasting lead in an attempt to score on a pair of limbs when the best he could do was wing the bastard. Let the sniper take the initiative one more time, Bolan thought, and then waste him once he showed.

The gunman took the initiative all right, but he also took his time.

Bolan mastered his impatience. Years of guerrilla combat experience had taught him that a savvy warrior doesn't move before he's ready, mentally as well as physically.

Clouds passed across the sun now. A wind rustled the wild grasses patterning the vacant lot. In the distance the pulse of hard rock music was momentarily drowned by an angry chorus of horns as drivers less patient than the Executioner expressed their frustration at some holdup caused by a delivery truck in a narrow street.

At last the feet behind the tricar moved.

The guy was about to kneel. Bolan saw the barrel—no, two barrels!—of a rifle appear through a hole in the floorboard where the shock absorber for the single front wheel had once been fixed.

He backed off a few inches from the wheel arch.

It was too difficult a shot angled upward around the brake drum. He would have to fire over the top of the hood. And in any case it was at the Beretta's maximum range.

One of the rifle barrels jetted flame. The single round tempted a reply, but Bolan knew the killing slug would come soon after. The panel truck's bodywork quaked under the impact.

Bolan waited in his turn. What kind of a greenhorn did the man take him for? The rifle would be trained on the cab window, first pressure probably applied already, anticipating his appearance.

Bolan knew he had to do it before the guy's concentration on that window lapsed, before he started to ask questions, to ponder other possibilities.

Suddenly Bolan sprang up into view, as near the charred radiator grille as he could get, and blasted a three-in-one at the tricar. Then he dropped as quickly as he had risen.

He could have taken his time. With no chance of hitting the sniper himself, he had aimed at the twin barrels, hoping to damage the weapon, to scare some unexpected reaction from the man behind them.

He scored.

The barrels jerked upward under the stunning shock of the 9 mm parabellums. Involuntarily a finger tightened on the trigger. The gun fired; the second shot went into orbit.

Bolan heard a cry of pain as the damaged gun was wrenched savagely from its owner's grasp.

Mack Bolan remained immobile. There were no more shots. Were they going to keep up this act until nightfall, or until a third person walked across the lot and one or the other could make it to safer terrain?

The sun reemerged, flooding the lot with golden light. A thin bright shaft flashed suddenly above the floorboard of the capsized three-wheeler.

The gun barrels canted upward? Bolan screwed up his eyes against the glare. No, it was something slimmer, something that moved. He saw a hand.

The telescopic antenna of a radio! A walkie-talkie transceiver. And still no more shots.

The killer was calling base. That disposed of the idea that this was a casual villain on the lookout for an easy mark. Bolan was the victim of a planned ambush. Planned since he had gone into the strip club, for he hadn't known he'd be crossing the lot until just before he'd left there.

Either the guy's rifle was so damaged by the Beretta slugs that it was no longer usable, or he'd run out of ammunition. With that kind of target rifle, Bolan knew, snipers carried only a handful of spare rounds, since there was no clip and customarily they would be confident enough, sure enough of their skill, to rely mainly on a first-shot capability. Bolan wondered if this was the killer they called the Marksman.

If so, was he calling for reinforcements or for fresh supplies of ammo?

The answer wasn't long in coming. A section of fencing at one side of the wire gates was swung aside, and a powerful motorcycle roared into the lot. The rider, crouched low over his tank as the machine bounced across the rough ground, was clad in black leather, with a shiny black crash helmet and visor covering his head.

Zigzagging between the pits and puddles and refuse piles, the bike zoomed up to the far side of the tricar, halted for a second with the exhaust snarling as the rider revved the engine, and then, gears whining, howled back toward the exit.

Only this time the rifleman and his weapon were on the back.

The gunner was leaning forward, one arm around the rider's waist, the rifle clasped to his own chest with the other. It was difficult to make out individual features at that distance, but Bolan thought he'd know him again if he saw him—a lean man with a lined, cadaverous face.

The bike and its two riders leaned over and roared out through the gap in the fencing.

Strategic withdrawal, or just a tactical retreat?

Bolan rose to his feet and stepped out of the open engine compartment of the wrecked truck. He hesitated. Was he being watched from a window of one of the old houses surrounding the lot? Through a telescope from an upper story on one of the tower blocks? Spied on through a hole in the fence?

He recharged the Beretta's magazine and unleathered Big Thunder from beneath his sweater. With a quick glance around him, he began striding toward the gates. Whether the killer was returning with a fresh supply of ammunition, with a new weapon, or with reinforcements, it made good sense to get out. Or as far out as he could.

He had about two hundred yards to go. He was a little over halfway when he again heard the roar of motorcycle engines, more than one this time, approaching beyond the fence.

Fifteen yards away he saw the remains of a ramshackle cabin—probably constructed by kids—built out of a collection of oil drums, corrugated iron sheeting, lengths of rattan and rotted gunnysacks. Most of the roof had gone, but it was better than open ground. He ran toward it and dropped behind the waist-high walls.

Three bikes, smaller and noisier than the first, swung into the lot. Between two drums Bolan could see that the helmeted riders each held a mini-Uzi on the saddle before him.

He was familiar with the weapon. The scaled-down version of the full-size Israeli submachine gun could be fired on full-auto from the hip—a perfect weapon for a biker steering with one hand—and its 9 mm deathstream, spewed out at a rate of twelve hundred rpm, could make mincemeat of a victim at anything up to a hundred and fifty yards.

Bolan dropped to his hands and knees. The shack was built on a slight rise on the undulating surface of the lot, and there was a depression in the center of the hillock—not deep enough to be used as a foxhole, but again better than nothing.

The riders had spotted him. The bikes accelerated and began to circle the cabin at a distance of about fifty yards.

That was fine by the Executioner. At least the attackers weren't at the limit of his range this time. But he had to act fast . . . and first.

The moment those blowback-operated miniature SMGs began pumping their deadly hail at the shack from three different directions, he was finished. Right now they were on their third lap, revving the bikes one after the other so that the rattle of the detonations beneath those wraparound bolts would be masked once they started shooting.

Bolan had to act before that. They knew he was there, but they didn't know his exact location. He would take out one for starters at least.

Prone now in the depression, he sighted Big Thunder between two of the drums and waited for one of the machines to wheel into view. The rider had just raised a walkie-talkie to his mouth. Bolan shot it out of his hand.

There would be no reporting back to base on this action. If Bolan made it to the base, he wanted it to be a surprise.

The second flesh-shredder from the stainless-steel AutoMag catapulted the rider from the saddle with blood jetting from his chest and neck. He crashed to the ground as the bike fell on its side, rear wheel still spinning and motor screaming.

His two companions opened fire as Bolan hurled himself to the far side of the shack. Slugs ripped through the iron sheeting, tore the rattan to shreds and pierced the drums in a murderous tattoo.

They were aiming downward at the depression where they figured he would be. But Bolan was on his feet now, bent low to stay below the wall, on the far side of the shelter. Sweeping it from side to side, it could only be seconds before one or the other of the remaining killers caught him below the knee.

So it had to be surprise yet again. Plus the fact that they would be forced, facing an armed adversary, to be careful with their own ammunition.

It doesn't take long for a thirty-two-round magazine on full-auto, firing at twelve hundred rpm, to exhaust itself. So they had to shoot in very short bursts, because once they were forced to reload—unless they rode out of range and allowed the Executioner to take the initiative—they would be sitting ducks.

He relied on this . . . and on the unexpected; something that would faze them while they were still directing their fire through the flimsy walls at the ground.

They continued circling, the rasp of the two exhausts rising and falling as they wrenched at the handgrips.

Immediately after a brief volley from each that scored the entire floor of the shack, Bolan played his wild card.

He slammed one of the oil drums onto its side and kicked it to start it rolling toward the lead biker. Since they were within one bike length of each other, the first rider had to stop firing and try to regain control of his machine with the other hand. The second rider ran into the same problem.

But the surprise move had the desired effect, and in the instant that their attention was distracted, Bolan leaped up onto another drum, Big Thunder making target acquisition. He unleashed a quick double punch at both bikers, before they had a chance to correct their mounts.

The first rider fell forward over his handlebars with his torso smashed open. He toppled to the ground with the machine, its motor stalled, on top of him.

The second arched backward in the saddle with a gurgling shriek, gloved hands flying up to the scarlet jet spraying from the flayed shreds of his throat. The mini-Uzi dropped to the ground.

The bike careened on, veering from right to left as the imperfections in the ground altered the angle of the front wheel.

Finally, as the machine gradually lost way, the wheel dropped into a pothole, twisted at right angles, and the rear of the bike canted upward.

The dead rider was flung clear, his mount tipped over onto its side. Gasoline from a hole in the tank, which had been punctured by one of the Executioner's 240-grain slugs, gushed over the hot cylinders.

There was a sudden burst of flame, the smothered whump of an explosion as the vapor from the volatile liquid ignited, and then the whole tank went up in a blazing fireball, a column of black oily smoke boiling skyward.

Bolan ran from the shack to escape the scorching heat. If the command post for the assault had been at the Bluebird or Las Vegas Nights, he wanted to be there before news of his own success filtered through the grapevine.

He releathered his two guns, selected the bike in the best condition, kick-started the engine and rode out of the lot.

9

The Bluebird was a café-bar. It was across the street from one of the stained concrete tower blocks, a corner site loud with jukeboxes and pinball machines, bright with chrome and gaudy plastic tables.

Bolan knew instinctively—as instinctively as he had ridden straight there on his acquired bike—that it wasn't the right place to find Graziano or whoever it was who had organized the ambush in the vacant lot.

It was too sleazy. A villain might have a stake in the place businesswise, but he would never use it himself.

In the many countries and cities that his everlasting war had taken him, Bolan had noticed that the predators on the wrong side of the law—whether they were terrorists, pro killers or ordinary hoods—invariably hung out in the same kind of place.

However much money was spent, however high the denizens had risen in the hierarchy of crime, there was always an atmosphere, a social context, a certain sleaziness that characterized these places. They were manicured fingers stained yellow with tobacco, tuxedos worn with a stubbled chin.

From the days of Al Capone, through the Genovese wars, right up to the Executioner's own conflict with the Mafia, mobsters as well as international con men, smugglers and fanatics from one or the other of the lunatic revolutionary organizations had this one thing in common: the spending of money in haunts that were usually flashy, expensive . . . but inelegant.

Places in fact where they felt at home. Among friends.

Spaggieri and Jacques Mesrine, the two most wanted men in France during the seventies and eighties, weren't to be seen dining at Maxim's; the Baader-Meinhof killers didn't rent suites at the Four Seasons in Hamburg; Albert Anastasia wasn't a habitué of Sardi's; and neither Biggs nor Roy James among the Great Train Robbers ever checked into the Connaught Hotel when they were in London.

Las Vegas Nights in the Belleville quarter of Paris would have suited any or all of them—and doubtless had, at one time or another, numbered Mesrine and Spaggieri among its clients.

It was on the first two floors of a gray stone block between a Moroccan couscous restaurant and a mini-supermarket boasting a sidewalk display of oriental spices and tropical fruits.

There would, Bolan knew without looking, be a fire escape and a rear entrance with a yard off a lane that led to a street in another block.

High-backed booths separated dining tables ranged on each side of a narrow entrance hallway, and behind this there was a wider space with a long bar, a cold food counter and marble-topped tables where drinks were served by shirt-sleeved waiters wearing long white aprons. A brass foot rail shone below the bar, and an illuminated sign reading Billard stood over the entrance to a poolroom in back.

Although it wasn't five o'clock yet, huge seafood platters were being served to several couples in the entrance hall. Inside, groups of dubious-looking men played card games around the bar.

But the real gambling, Bolan knew, would be in rooms on the floor above whose approaches would be monitored by video cameras.

A wide staircase at one side of the poolroom led there.

Two girls, their breasts barely covered by low-cut sequin tops, displayed their legs as they sat on bar stools. A third, with a close-cut cap of black hair, was talking to a curly-headed blonde with fishnet stockings and a Cupid's-bow mouth who stood behind the hatcheck counter at the foot of the stairs.

Bolan wondered if the dark one could be Clara. He walked through and approached her. "Emilio around?" he asked curtly.

She jerked a thumb at the stairs. "In the blackjack room."

He nodded and climbed up into an atmosphere combining equal parts of air freshener, sweat and the odor of stale cigar smoke. A hundred-piece string orchestra replayed easy-listening music through speakers positioned alongside the cameras above each door along the hallway.

No guards with double-breasted jackets not quite concealing the bulge of a shoulder holster stood near these doors. The cameras were better informed. The rooms, labeled Baccarat, Roulette, Blackjack, Poker, would be supervised by mild-mannered little men with lapel mikes who would politely enquire, "Who?" each time anyone wanted in.

Bolan didn't give the mild-mannered little man on the far side of the blackjack door time to ask his question. He twisted the handle, shouldered the door and made his entrance with a gun in each hand.

"Nobody moves, nobody gets hurt. Just answer the questions," he growled.

There were six men around the baize-covered table, plus the guy on the door and two enforcers who stood behind the dealer with their backs to an exit.

"Hands on the table," Bolan advised the six. "And you—" he turned to the doorman "—go stand with your buddies in back. And don't try anything stupid." He thrust the Beretta and the AutoMag out a little farther to emphasize his point.

His cold blue glance swept the table. Graziano was sitting on the dealer's right. "Okay," Bolan said. "Who ordered the ambush . . . and why?"

The dealer was a dark, muscled man with a mustache, a pockmarked skin and the eyes of a Mideasterner accustomed to giving orders. He and the other four players—they could have been Algerian diplomats, Turkish white slavers or football managers from Morocco, all with the same hard stare—turned their faces toward Graziano.

Graziano made no attempt to bluff his way out of it. "So you got away?" he said. The big nose, the gold-rimmed glasses and the mustache were gone. His hair was different, too, but no doubt he still limped.

"You should have sent back the first guy," Bolan said.

"His fancy rifle was fucked," the dealer said sarcastically. "So we had to send in what we had."

"Punks," Graziano said. There was contempt in his voice. "How the hell would they know what to do?"

"At least they follow orders," the dealer said. "They don't double-cross the people who trained them to free-lance."

"They won't be following any more orders," Bolan corrected.

Graziano, who had flushed angrily at the dealer's rebuke, turned to him now. "What do you say now, Max? Still believe in your goddamn amateurs?"

"We'll see about the difference between amateurs and pros in just—" very slowly Max turned his left hand so that he could look at his watch "—in just two and a half minutes."

Bolan frowned. He didn't know what to make of the guy, with his air of authority. What was he getting at? Bolan backed away slowly so that he was within reach of the entrance door. "Nobody's answered my question yet," he said, gesturing with the two guns. "I'm waiting."

"Look, mister, this is a private game you walked in on," Max said. "Six guys playing cards. Not one of us armed, and—"

"Oh, sure."

The dealer spoke over his shoulder to the three men standing behind him. "Rafael, Ahmed, Kemal—show the gentleman."

"Slow and easy," Bolan warned. The gun barrels shifted slightly their way.

The three men unbuttoned their jackets and held them wide. No shoulder holsters. The three faces were expressionless.

"Turn around," Bolan ordered. "Lift the jackets."

No weapons on the hip or clipped to the belt. That didn't mean there wasn't a .22 on the inside of the thigh or a knife strapped to the ankle, but it would do for now. As long as they stood straight.

"And you," Bolan said to the card players. "What do you have to show me?"

One by one the men rose and executed the same maneuvers. The first four were clean. Graziano and the dealer, Max, were the last. Bolan's fingers curled around the triggers of his guns as the terrorist began to rise.

Suddenly the window glass shivered, and a porcelain vase on a shelf at the far side of the room tinkled against its twin as a distant explosion shook the building.

"Well, Sadegh Rafsanjani, there's one thing you did right," Max said to Graziano. "Too bad it was just for money rather than the Cause."

Graziano appeared annoyed by the use of his real name. "The effect's the same," he said sullenly. "A few dozen more out of the way. The department store in the rue de Rivoli—the Toy Fair on the top floor, just before closing time. It was hidden up among the sprinklers. Six kilos." He smiled then. "With luck, although the blast was directed downward, part of the roof could come down."

"The way the Alitalia plane came down in Rome?" Bolan queried through gritted teeth. Out of one of the windows he could see a mushroom of black smoke rising above the rooftops down near the river, obscuring the twin towers of Notre-Dame.

"A beautiful job that was," Graziano said. He shook his head. "And clever, too, the way I used that stewardess." He glared at the Executioner, and the admiration in his voice faded as he added, "If it hadn't been for your damned interference, Tel Aviv would have been even better.''

Mack Bolan's icy reserve had left him only a couple of times in his adult life. Coolness, objectivity, the correct weighing of pros and cons, of cause and effect, refusal to let the heart rule the head—these were all attributes on which his existence often depended.

It was the cold-blooded smugness, the insufferable self-approval of the man that made Bolan lose his own cool. He had calmly admitted the murder of three hundred and seventeen people and now congratulated himself on the fact that, seconds before, God knows how many more had been ripped to shreds, blasted to bloody eternity or were lying maimed and screaming somewhere below those roofs.

The smoke rose darkly into the sky. In the distance the shrill warble of police cars and the bray of ambulances increased.

Seething with fury, Bolan was scarcely aware of the signals from mind to muscle that ordered his fingers to squeeze the triggers.

He fired both guns at once.

At a range of fifteen feet, two separate shots from the .44 Magnum and a triple burst from the Beretta slammed into the killer's chest, pulped his face into an unrecognizable hash of raw meat splintered with bone, sprayed brain tissue from the back of his head and catapulted him and the chair in which he was sitting several feet away from the table to crash over backward onto the floor.

There was smoke in the room now, and the acrid odor of gunfire. When the stunning effect of the multiple concussions subsided, Max rose to his feet. He seemed quite unafraid now that Bolan's gust of fury was spent.

He walked across to a window that overlooked the street. "Perhaps, Mr. Bolan, your questions are answered now?" he said calmly. "Like who ordered the ambush from which you escaped."

"And why?"

"I cannot help you there. This man—" he glanced with distaste at the gory body on the floor "—was what you Americans term a gun for hire, a professional murderer. We supplied certain...facilities ...because we were asked—"

"Such as three killer kids on bikes? And a guy with a double-barreled rifle? A guy known maybe as the Marksman?"

"And because it might have suited us to assist those for whom Sadegh Rafsanjani was working. But he wasn't one of us. To find out his reasons, you would have to ask his employers."

"Not one of us? Who is 'us'?"

Max slid a gold cigarette case from an inside pocket, selected one, lit it with a jeweled Cartier lighter and blew smoke. He made no reply.

"And your reasons? For helping out?" Bolan insisted.

Max smiled frostily. "I am afraid that is a professional secret. In any case—" he looked down once more into the street, his voice suddenly hardening "—such questions have now become irrelevant."

The warble of police sirens was very loud. Bolan heard gunned motors, the screech of brakes outside, the sound of running footsteps.

"The police are raiding this establishment. As arranged. They will find nothing amiss, no rules broken, nothing out of order below. But up here there is a dead man," Max said.

He paused. Bolan heard a commotion downstairs. There were shouts, scuffles and the shrill of whistles. The word "Police" was repeated several times. A girl screamed. In the blackjack room nobody moved.

"Apart from myself," Max continued, "there are seven witnesses here who saw you shoot down this man in cold blood—a man seated in a chair who had made no attempt to threaten or attack you. An *unarmed* man. The same witnesses can testify that you forced your way in here with guns already in your hands."

Bolan's lips twisted into a wry smile. "Neat. And the confessions that prompted me to...shoot? I suppose nobody heard those?"

"I think you will find that nobody heard anything. In fact, you burst straight in and fired without a word. Isn't that right, gentlemen?" He looked around the room.

The doorman and the silent hoods nodded. One of the card players said, "Busted in and blasted the poor bastard. Just like that." The other three said nothing.

Bolan didn't hesitate. There were footsteps on the stairs. Faced with a setup...and cops, possibly cops on Max's payroll, tipped off in advance, there was only one thing to do.

Get out. Fast.

Covering his face with his arms, he took three quick steps and launched himself through the rear window in an explosion of glass and splintered wood.

10

Mack Bolan landed on the iron grille separating two flights of the fire escape, the impetus slamming him against the rail.

There were cuts on his hands, his sweater was ripped and one razor-sharp glass fragment had gashed a shin. But the damage was minor—the barrels of the pistols, smashing first into the pane, had knocked away most of the window before his body had followed.

Angular shards were still separating themselves from the shattered frame and clattering to the ironwork as Bolan took to the stairway.

Not the section leading down but up.

His fighter's eye, taking in the scene at a glance, had picked out the blue uniforms lurking in the yard at the foot of the fire escape, the disguised prowl cars blocking the lane outside and the suspiciously idle loungers in windbreakers, hardmen who had cop written all over them, standing nearby.

He had no wish to become involved with the French police—especially with a rigged murder charge and a genuinely dead man to explain away. Justice, as meted out by the Executioner, wasn't looked upon with favor by the functionaries of the law.

There was a second advantage to an upward climb: if he could get away in an unexpected direction, there was a chance he could shake off the invisible mystery men tailing him, whether or not those guys were connected with the ambush and the police trap.

There were three more floors above him, and then the dormers projecting from the mansard roof. The fire escape went all the way. Bolan took those stairs three at a time. But he didn't go all the way.

It was too obvious. The cops would have radios. Already there was shouting below, although no gun had fired yet. By the time he made the top, he would be under surveillance for the rest of the trip.

One story below the dormers, the fire escape platform was beneath a small double window that looked as if it could belong to a kitchen or shower room. On either side of it, cracked and peeling shutters were pegged back against the brickwork of the wall. The wood of the window frames was dried out and in need of paint, too.

The windows of French houses open inward. With the butt of the AutoMag, Bolan thumped once, hard, at the two frames level with the catch.

The old wood splintered, the catch tore away from the hasp and the windows burst open. He vaulted over the sill.

He was in a kitchen that was absolutely bare except for two used wineglasses and a cup half full of cold coffee in the sink. An antique gas-operated icebox hummed noisily by the door. He heard cries of alarm from an inner room. He ran through.

The apartment was a seedy one-room walkup. On a bed Bolan saw two naked figures. They lay on their backs and were propped on their elbows, looking at him in disbelief.

Stunned at the sight of the blood-streaked apparition brandishing two guns, the two people on the bed were unable to shout a second time. Bolan ran to the front door. "Please, don't mind me, carry on," he panted, nodding to the dark-skinned man on the bed.

Bolan slid back the bolt on the door and erupted onto a narrow landing that revealed a flight of uncarpeted stairs leading upward.

The door to the top-floor apartment was flimsy. He holstered his guns and charged it with his shoulder. The door crashed open. The apartment was the same as the last. Only this time it was empty.

He opened the dormer window above the street. Below, the roadway was jammed with police vehicles, but most of the cops seemed to be inside the building. The few left to guard the cars weren't looking up. Bolan climbed out onto the rotted wood of the sill, hauled himself up onto the tiles roofing the dormer and began a perilous traverse of the mansard's upper slope.

From the far side of the street, helmeted construction workers stared out at him from the empty egg-carton cells of an uncompleted concrete apartment block.

Crouched below the level of the ridgepole, Bolan made his way between tall stacks of chimneys to the building next door. Easing himself up to the crest, he peered down the far slope.

He was looking at the backyard of the supermarket. The yard was busy. A semitrailer with the name of a mass-producer of canned soups emblazoned on its side was backing up through the gateway. Youths in white coveralls helped direct a forklift to unload cartons from a container on a flatbed. In between, girls stacked empty packing cases and cardboard boxes by a row of small delivery vans.

Bolan ducked back out of sight and continued his crawl until he reached the building beyond. The roof here was ten feet lower. But once again there was a fire escape.

He made up his mind. There was no way he could make it to the yard down the supermarket's own fire escape. They'd watch him all the way...and the cops would be waiting with open arms when he landed. But if he could make it on this third stairway down as far as the wall dividing the two properties, maybe he could drop over into the yard unseen.

He was betting that all the inhabitants of this third block would be hanging out their front windows to see what the hell the law was doing inside Las Vegas Nights.

The hunch paid off again. Bolan lowered himself over the gable end until he was suspended at the full stretch of his arms. That left him only a couple of feet to drop to the roof below.

Even so, it wasn't easy. The tiled slant was steep. He turned one ankle under as he landed, fell backward into a sitting position and began to slide. Only a desperate grab at the lead jacket crowning the ridge saved him from plummeting to the street four floors below.

Thanking his lucky stars that the mansard wasn't slippery with rain, he regained the crest, slid down the far side until he was astride a dormer and jumped from there to the fire escape.

Nobody challenged him as he cat-footed down the zigzag flights of the iron stairway.

Finally there was just one more flight to go. Luckily the owners had invested in a counterbalanced extension, the kind that couldn't be reached from the ground but swung down to earth when someone stepped onto it.

Bolan leaped from it to the top of the wall as it began to tilt. He dropped into the supermarket yard behind the packing cases.

His escape plan relied on the small Renault panel vans with sliding doors being ready to go. There were three of them, all parked facing the gateway and with their loading doors open. He could see through into the cab of the two nearest, which held no supplies at the moment.

No keys hung from the ignition of either van.

Bolan bit his lip. The girls stacking the crates were indoors right now, but they would be back in the yard again with a fresh consignment at any time. He looked over at the third vehicle.

Filled paper bags and cartons laden with groceries covered the loading space...and the engine was idling. A thin plume of exhaust smoke curled from the tail pipe.

No driver was visible. But to reach the van, Bolan would have to pass the guys who had been directing the forklift. They had now moved across to the semi and, with the aid of the forklift, were shifting a huge pyramid of soup cans down from the tailgate.

He glanced swiftly around. There was an open door behind him. He could hear the girls' voices approaching along the passageway beyond. The men moving the soup cans had their backs turned. Then the light suddenly faded as clouds obscured the sinking sun and a few drops of rain fell.

It was now or never.

Bolan rose to his feet and ran.

Grimy with soot from the roofs, one pant leg blood-soaked, his face also stained red where his gashed hands had brushed it when he'd hung from the gable end, Bolan presented a frightening sight. One of the girls screamed. The men near the semi swung around, open-mouthed. Two cops he hadn't noticed darted out from behind the dairy produce flatbed. A third appeared in the open doorway that led to the supermarket storeroom.

"Hey! Where are you going?" a voice shouted.

"Stop! Police!" another yelled. A whistle blew.

"He's making for the gates!"

"Cut him off!"

"Stop that man!"

The driver of the flatbed leaped down from his cab and joined the two cops, sprinting across the yard in an attempt to make the gateway before the Executioner. The men in white coveralls near the semi stood and stared. The semitrailer driver was nearest the Renault. He stood squarely in the Executioner's path, a burly colossus in denims and a fatigue cap, his wrestler's arms held wide.

Bolan had no time to trade punches. A karate offense was the answer. Without pausing in his stride, he launched a flying jump kick at the driver's head. The blow knocked the big man off-balance long enough for Bolan to dodge around him, but the others were close behind.

The forklift operator had lowered the wooden pallet stacked with soup cans almost to ground level. Bolan whirled, his arms windmilling. The carefully stacked pyramid erupted, toppled and burst apart. Cans clattered, bounced and rolled all over the yard. The flatbed driver went down, bringing one of the cops with him. The semi's driver hopped on one foot, howling as he nursed a cracked shin. The second cop was brought to a standstill and the one dashing from the storeroom stepped on a rolling can and landed on his back.

Bolan leaped in through the open door of the delivery van, dropped into the driver's seat, slammed the lever into first gear and gunned the engine.

As he pointed the Renault in the direction of the gateway, Bolan had a confused impression of plainclothes police converging from both sides of the lane, of onlookers scattering as he slammed two wheels onto the sidewalk to squeeze between a prowl car and the wall. Then the cops in windbreakers were behind, and he was sliding the van around a right-angle turn into a broad highway with stores on either side. A single shot had smashed a side window and gouged a fresh cut where the first wounds had already congealed across his knuckles.

The rain was falling more heavily now, spotting the windshield and making the roadway slick. Bolan switched on the wipers and kept his foot down.

He was heading south and east, away from the center and police headquarters on Ile de la Cité, toward the huge traffic circle at Place de la Nation. From there he could easily make the woods surrounding the lake in the quarter of Vincennes by the confluence of the Seine and the Marne.

But it was almost five-thirty; at any moment office workers would debouch onto the streets. Traffic, already heavy, would become snarled in the rush hour jam.

He had to make Place de la Nation before the half hour.

In the Vincennes woods he could ditch the van and make a clean getaway. After that? He shrugged. He wasn't going back to the hotel, that was certain. He'd play it by ear.

Just as long as he could somehow pick up the scent again and follow Brognola's directive.

He hurtled across Boulevard de Belleville, took a curving one-way that led to the vast Père-Lachaise cemetery and forked left into Avenue Philippe Auguste. Just over a mile now to the Place de la Nation circle.

But the rain was falling heavily. The umbrellas were up. Already the traffic flow was slowing.

The Renault's steeply raked windshield, immediately above the radiator grille and well ahead of the front wheels, gave the driver a great view, but Bolan wasn't sure how the little van would take a corner on a wet road.

He found out soon enough.

Two hundred yards past the Lachaise intersection, two prowl cars, cutting through the traffic with sirens shrieking, passed him in the other direction. He heard the screech of brakes and a squeal of rubber on the roadway. In the rearview mirror he saw the prowl cars skidding around in a tight U-turn to follow him.

He leaned more heavily on the gas. The van was easily identifiable: it was bright daffodil yellow with Day-Glo green script on either side. Clearly the cops had an APB out for him.

The engine hummed and throbbed beneath his feet as he kept the pedal to the floorboard. The tall van swayed crazily as he wrestled it past a forty-ton trailer in the face of an oncoming stream, its tires hissing on the wet roadway.

He swung left into Alexandre Dumas, nearly tipping the Renault over. This was another one-way, heading east. If he could lose the cops, he could circle around and approach Place de la Nation from another direction. The speedometer needle quivered. He had topped sixty. At least there was nothing coming the other way now.

The images of the prowl cars began to recede in the mirror.

Then suddenly the cars and trucks ahead began slowing. He was approaching a busy neighborhood shopping center.

The sidewalks were crowded, and there were fruit and vegetable stalls laid out beneath glistening umbrellas by the curb. Pickups and delivery trucks clogged the street between four shiny strips of asphalt where streetcar tracks had once been laid. Bolan cursed and braked, spun the wheel and accelerated and then braked again. Behind him the clamor of sirens grew louder.

He cut in between two buses, swerved past a truck loaded with a stack of cases containing mineral water and narrowly missed a head-on collision with a cab. He hadn't realized that the street had become two-way again when he had passed the intersection.

Suddenly there was a clear stretch. He hit the gas once more. The needle was approaching the limit on the speedometer dial when he took in the lights at a main crosstown intersection ahead.

He was less than a hundred yards away when the green turned to amber and then almost instantly to red.

Bolan braked momentarily, felt the wheels begin to go, released the pedal and then—realizing he could never stop in time—declutched and shifted down, deciding to go through with it.

He hit the intersection just as the traffic held back by the lights on the cross street was released. Brakes squealed over the furious honking of horns as the van plunged in among the flood of vehicles converging from either side. Bolan leaned on the horn, stamped on the brakes again and wrenched at the wheel. The arc of clear glass swept by the windshield wipers was suddenly filled with the shapes of cars shooting past in every direction.

Even then he might have made it if one of the Renault's rear wheels hadn't run into a groove worn in the asphalt covering the old streetcar tracks. The wet surface was slick with grease. The little van lurched, slewed sideways and then spun around out of control when the rear end broke away. One of the tires rolled off the wheel rim. Bolan sat helpless in the cab while the intersection whirled dizzily past.

The Renault sideswiped a bus crammed with standing passengers, skidded between two cabs and then shot across the slippery roadway. Homeward bound crowds screamed and scattered as it mounted the sidewalk, slammed against iron railings protecting a crowded stairway leading down to the subway and then bounced back into the road to cannon off a pedestrian refuge and turn over on its side.

Bolan found himself clinging to the buckled wheel with broken glass showering all around him. He was shaken but unhurt. Pushing open the driver's door that was now above his head, he dragged himself out.

The police cars were zigzagging toward him through traffic stalled all over the intersection, the shriek of their sirens drowning the cries of the crowd and the hiss of steam from the Renault's burst radiator. One of the front wheels was still turning as the Executioner dropped to the ground.

Men and women were rushing toward him, some offering to help, others shouting and shaking their fists.

A Honda 250 motor scooter rocked to a halt beside the wrecked Renault.

"Quick! Jump on behind!" the helmeted, leather-clad rider yelled from beneath the rain visor.

Bolan leaped for the little bike without thinking. He wrapped both arms around the rider's waist as he sat astride the saddle and the Honda jerked forward.

The scooter arrowed between the two police cars as the lights changed again to green, roaring across the intersection and heading east before the rest of the traffic had started to move.

By the time the prowl cars had swung around to follow, the scooter was three hundred yards ahead . . . and long before they hit anything like a respectable speed, the rider had circled between two iron posts blocking the entry to a narrow lane and had shot away between tall, old houses where the cars were unable to pursue them.

It was only then, feeling the pliancy of the waist and seeing the glossy stream of black hair cascading below the back of the helmet, that Bolan realized his rescuer was a girl.

11

Her name, she told Bolan, was Fawzi Harari. She lived on the eighth floor of an enormous nondescript apartment block, one of a group on the northern outskirts of the city.

Without the crash helmet, he could see that she was beautiful. Blue jeans and a lightweight sweater did nothing to hide the tight curves of a voluptuous body. Large liquid brown eyes and a slightly broad nose and mouth combined with honey-dark skin to hint at a North African or Arab origin.

The Honda scooter was chained to a rail among rows of shiny Renaults, Peugeots and Citroëns bought on credit by the new poor who lived in the state-subsidized blocks. The bare concrete passageways stank of urine. Graffiti sprayed over the metal walls of the elevator mingled racist slogans with plugs for the local football team and crude sex images. Some of them were delicately executed in Arabic characters.

"Why?" Bolan asked after they had sunk gratefully into imitation leather armchairs. The apartment was clean, sparsely furnished, featureless.

"I had to find someplace fast," she said. "People from my country are not always welcome in France."

"I don't mean why you chose this apartment. Why did you rescue me? How come you were there to do it?'' Bolan was still breathless after a whirlwind ride that had taken them in and out of the rush hour traffic halfway around the freeway circling the city.

Fawzi Harari walked to the window. She twitched aside one of the handmade draperies and looked down at a huge asphalt yard pockmarked with futuristic children's play structures. Several hundred kids milled and shrieked between the blocks, but very few were using the chutes and frames and cement tunnels the architects had designed for them. "I had special reasons," she said without turning around, "for wanting you . . . free."

"Such as?"

"Such as my brother, Hassan."

"Hassan?"

"The boy they killed before they took you away. In Algiers."

"You mean Boardman's kid? The one who led me back to his place? That was your brother?"

Still with her back to him, she nodded, the glossy black hair bouncing between her shoulder blades.

"I'm . . . sorry," Bolan said awkwardly. "He was a brave kid, and he put up a great fight. It was unforgivable."

"It will not be forgiven," she said in a choked voice.

After a pause, the Executioner rose and stood behind her. He put a hand on her shoulder. Her body was shaking. Below, the kids in the playground tumbled and yelled. "What is the connection?" he asked gently. "I mean, why keep me at liberty?"

"I should have thought it was obvious. You were there. You were shooting at the people who killed Hassan. His murderers were your enemies. You seemed to me the only person...big, strong enough...the only possible person to strike back."

"You want me to avenge your brother?"

"I believe," she said carefully, "as long as you are free from those people and free from the police, that whatever it is you are doing *will* avenge him."

She turned to face him. The tears on her cheeks were drying. Bolan's smile was crooked. "Fawzi, what do you know of me?"

"That you are a man of courage and initiative. That you made a rendezvous with Monsieur Boardman because he had some information concerning—" she paused "—concerning certain activities the world considers illegal."

"Anything else?" And before she could answer, Bolan played another hunch. It was the use of the word *considers* that tipped him off. "Activities you are concerned in yourself?" he prompted. "Illegal activities concerning what people call...terrorism?"

She blushed and looked away. "Not anymore."

"Tell me."

"It was when we were students. I had two cousins, boys a little older than me, who were very much involved. The AMER was strong in Oran, where I was at college. You know how it is."

Bolan nodded. AMER—Arab Militants Against European Repression—was yet another splinter group from the main body of the holy war extremists orchestrated by Khomeini and his cronies from Iran. They were mainly young, fanatic, their immature passions inflamed and manipulated with ruthless cynicism by the men who used the envy of the dispossessed to satisfy their own lust for power. The letters of the acronym also happened to spell the French word for bitter, *amer*.

"You figured it was brave and romantic," Bolan said. "Getting your own back on countries who for centuries had exploited your people, spreading the Word of the Prophet, cleaning up the decadent West. A catharsis by fire and the sword. At first you distributed leaflets, went to meetings and listened to inspiring speeches, joined in with the rent-a-mob guys and gals who manifest and riot any time there's a television camera within range. It was all very exciting. And then . . . ?"

"Then I found I was in deeper than I liked. There were organized groups staging small holdups to get money. Somebody was killed. Half a dozen of us were sent over to Italy, and I found after we got there that we had been ordered to place a bomb inside a synagogue. I . . . I drove the getaway car. Fortunately the police found the thing and defused it before it exploded."

She sighed and shook her dark head. "I was not totally convinced of the religious angle anyway. I couldn't believe you were damned unless you belonged to our faith. I realized how stupid and pointless and wrong the jihad creed was. We were killing and maiming people just like ourselves—the people you see in this block, people you see in the subway. For what? What good did it do us? They were not responsible for our troubles."

"You quit?"

"I sort of disappeared. I had an excuse. Our parents were killed in a car crash. I had to look after Hassan. I went back to Algiers."

"But you still saw your friends in AMER?"

"Just my cousins. But they had been sent to Beirut. They only visited occasionally on their way through."

"And then Hassan joined the other side?"

"Not really. He was..." Fawzi bit her lip. "He was a smart boy. But he was not interested in politics. Not at his age. Yes, he did little jobs for Monsieur Boardman. But even if they were not always strictly legal, they had nothing to do with the people the Australian knew. Hassan could use the money...and he was there."

"How do you mean—he was there?"

"We live—lived—in the same house as Boardman. On the floor above."

"So that's how you knew about *my* business with Wally? That's how you knew so much about the gunfight and...what happened after?"

"I was outside the window," she confessed. "I saw those men burst in, and I ran down and hid in the courtyard."

"And you saw them take me away? But how did you find me in this town?"

"My brother was dead," she said fiercely, "so there was nothing I could do for him. Not personally. But if I stuck with someone who had tried once already to save him..."

"How did they get me away?" Bolan asked.

"They had a panel truck, and they stowed you in it. They left the...the dead, even their own. They rolled you up in one of Monsieur Boardman's rugs, a Persian prayer mat they took from the wall."

"And you followed the truck on that little scooter all the way to Paris? How could you—?"

"It is not so difficult, with a small maneuverable machine and people who do not suspect they are being followed. Why should they have suspected? They knew you were alone."

"Over a short distance, yes. But to Paris . . . ?"

"There was a boat in the harbor about to leave for Marseille. They must have had an . . . arrangement . . . with the port police, and the customs people on the other side. They drove straight on in Algiers and straight off again when we arrived in France. I had money with me. I managed to buy a ticket and scramble aboard at the last minute."

"And in France?"

"I knew they were taking you to Paris. I overheard them talking on the boat. So I put the bike on a train, and I was waiting at the exit from the highway when they arrived after an all-night drive."

"And then you followed me when I left the hotel?"

"Yes, but that was not so easy," she admitted, "because this time they were following you also. They wanted to see what you would do, I guess."

"You keep saying 'they.' Just who are 'they'?"

"I do not know, I swear. Dangerous people."

"Nothing to do with AMER?" Bolan asked.

"Certainly not. But they have levers. They can put pressure on AMER. On other clandestine organizations, too."

"How do you know?"

"As I said, I do not attend meetings anymore, but my cousins trust me. They talk freely in front of me when they visit."

"And?"

"Something very big is going on. It seems that AMER, the PLO, the FPCQ, Abu Nidal's FRAL, even the IRA, the Corsicans and the Basques, have all been warned to lie low. Their activists must all arrange to have alibis on certain dates. The new people do not wish anyone else claiming credit—or being blamed—for their operations."

"But you don't know anything about them at all?"

"I know the reasons why they want the Islamic revolutionaries and the others to keep quiet—because they are using professionals. My cousins disapprove. They think it cowardly to pay outsiders for work that should be done by volunteers, for a cause."

"They're dead right," Bolan said. "Except that what they call work should be stamped out altogether. This sacred cause, naturally, is ... ?"

"The revolt against the Satans of the West who have contaminated the 'purity of Islam.' A holy war against the vices and corruption and injustices of the non-Muslim world. They want to establish a worldwide Islamic republic, to impose this on a world they have systematically destroyed." She laughed scornfully. "They are already claiming the return of Andalusia and a good third of this country!"

"Luckily they fight so much among themselves over what is and what is not the true Islam that their impact is diminished," Bolan said soberly. "The threat is there just the same. But you're telling me this has nothing to do with these new terrorists? So what *is* the cause for them? Antisemitism? Communism? Some other form of pan-Arab conspiracy? A worldwide slave state?"

She shook her head. "I have no idea. I only know what I hear my cousins say, and they do not know, either."

"Beats me," the Executioner said. "Too many things here don't stack up at all. It's a very big deal, just the same, with real money behind it. Pro hit men don't come cheap. Nor does the kind of organization directing them. Nor does the kind of operation they pulled on me. Do you have any idea how many tails they laid on me here in Paris?"

"At least four. Perhaps more. I cannot say definitely. It was too difficult making certain they did not discover that I was on the same trail myself."

"You were taking some risk, getting that close to me," Bolan said. "You didn't see who was giving the orders?"

"A man called Max Nasruddin seemed to be the boss. I saw him once before with my cousins in Algiers. A dark, chunky man with a mustache. He limps."

"I didn't notice the limp," Bolan said, "but he was the guy directing the setup back in that Las Vegas Nights club."

"I think he is a very dangerous man," Fawzi said.

"They're all dangerous men. Fanatics who refuse to let the rest of the world do its own thing are always a danger. You can check that in any history book. Such people must be stopped."

Bolan walked away from the window. It was dusk, and the children were being called in to eat. Outside the apartment he could hear footsteps, shouts and the whine of elevators. "I've dedicated my life to the destruction of these people," he said. "Whoever they are."

"I know," she said. "That is why I know, too, that Hassan will be avenged."

"How much of my conversation with Boardman did you overhear?" Bolan asked.

"Not much. Hassan heard the beginning and came up to tell me. I heard enough to guess a little about your motives."

"If you were still upstairs when the killers broke in, you wouldn't have heard my final questions and the answers Wally began to give. Does the name Baraka mean anything to you?"

"The *name*, Baraka? No. It is a common enough word in my country, but not as a name. It means—"

"I know what it means," the Executioner cut in. "It's probably a code name, anyway. Did you ever hear Boardman or your cousins speak of someone called Friedekinde?"

The girl's nose wrinkled as she frowned in concentration. "I think I may have heard it," she said slowly, "but right now I cannot say where."

"No sweat." Bolan glanced at his watch. It was eight o'clock. "Is there a radio in this apartment?" he asked.

"Yes, a small transistor in the bedroom," she said.

He went through and tuned in to the France-Inter national network. A broadcaster was already a few seconds into the evening news.

"...the device, which bomb disposal experts estimate as at least five kilos of plastique, was apparently lodged in the roof above the department store's top-floor Toy Fair. It exploded at the busiest hour, shortly before closing time. First estimates place the casualties at eighteen dead and fifty-two injured, some of them seriously, but salvage men working with cranes

and cutting equipment fear there may be more victims beneath debris at one end of the department,
where a section of roof collapsed under the force of
the blast. It is feared that there may be many children
among the casualties.''

Bolan bit back a curse, suppressing the anger he
could feel rising within him.

It was exactly this kind of horror that the Executioner had pledged to stamp out. The kind of slime-
bucket creeps who could plan and carry out a thing
like that deserved to be annihilated the way he had
wasted Graziano that afternoon. There were no re-
grets on that score. The newscaster continued: ''So
far, no organization has claimed responsibility for the
outrage. The mayor of Paris and the minister for home
security were at the scene of the disaster, directing
rescue operations, within fifteen minutes....''

He switched off the radio and walked back into the
living room. ''Nice people, your cousins' friends,'' he
said.

Fawzi didn't reply. She was staring out the window
again. Something about her attitude warned Bolan
that things had gone wrong. He joined her and moved
the draperies aside.

She pointed wordlessly at the yard below.

Beside a plastic play chute, a black Mercedes sedan
had drawn up and was waiting with the engine idling.
A thin plume of smoke issued from the tail pipe and
assumed a reddish hue in the illumination from the
rear lights. Four men had climbed out of the big car.
The driver was still at the wheel.

Three of the men, bulky silhouettes in the sodium
lights above the yard, lounged against the sedan. The
fourth stood by the front fender and lit a cigarette.

Even from the eighth floor, Bolan could see in the sudden flare of the match that it was Max Nasruddin.

"But they couldn't have followed us here!" Bolan exploded. "Not through that jam on the freeway!"

"They did not," Fawzi said. "They must have known already. In other words, the team following you must have discovered that somebody else was following the same trail. They must have put a tail on me also."

"Smart," Bolan admitted. "I think we better get out of here. Is there an emergency exit?"

"Yes. If you can stand the smell."

"Could we get to your scooter from the exit without them seeing us?"

"Certainly, if they stay where they are, but not if they have men watching the whole block."

"They may not be certain which block, which apartment—or at any rate which window—relates to you," Bolan said. "They may not know for sure we've gotten back yet. Watch them and tell me if anyone moves. And don't let them see you, okay?"

"They will know," she said. "But we can always try."

Bolan whipped into the bathroom, cleaned up his hands and the gash on his leg, washed the stain from his face and peeled away the false mustache.

"They are separating and heading toward the main entrance," Fawzi called out. "Max is still with the car."

The Executioner was in the doorway, towel in his hand. "Okay," he said. "We split."

The girl was right about the stairway. It smelled like dead fish. They switched on the light timer and ran down.

Heavy iron locking bars had to be pushed up to open the emergency doors, and it was impossible to do this without making a hell of a noise. The steps continued down into a basement. "Is there a garage?" Bolan asked.

"No," she whispered. "Just the furnace room, storage area, a laundry and some cellars. But there is a loading hatch for the delivery of things. If we could lift up the trap..."

They could. Bolan stood on a packing case and cautiously raised half of the iron trap a few inches.

The bike was on the nearer side of the parking lot, beyond a stretch of trampled grass and a line of dirty bushes. There was no sign of the pursuers.

Bolan hitched up his sweater and eased off the safety of both guns. They waited, peering out at the deserted yard in the harsh yellow light. "There was one thing I forgot to ask you," he murmured. "The triple-F. Three Fs. Or just the acronym FFF. Do any of *those* ring a bell with you?"

"Of course," she said, smiling. "It is a logo. A trademark, if you like. What the French call the *sigle*, of a clinic."

"What?" Bolan began. But she laid a finger across his lips. Footsteps approached over the hard earth beneath the grass. One of the thugs from the Mercedes had turned the corner of the building.

Bolan lowered the iron trap until it was only open a crack. The man walked calmly past the bushes, scanned the automobiles in the lot and disappeared around the far corner of the block.

"Okay—" it was Bolan's turn to whisper "—let me have the keys to the padlock and the bike. I'll start it up, ride over and pick you up. That way, we'll attract less attention than two going at once—and when we're up, we'll also have the advantage of speed and maneuverability.''

"Right," she murmured. "Except I will go myself. There is a knack to starting it. If you do not make it the first time, we will have the whole bunch around here.''

"Whatever you say," he agreed reluctantly. It made sense, but he didn't like it.

He raised the trap and hoisted her out. The pliant, supple feel of her young body, the warm weight of her breasts on his hands, stirred a sudden pang of tenderness in him. He was struck by Fawzi's tawny beauty. At once his mind conjured up the image of the delicate satin friction of skins, the luxury of a bed....
He put the thought out of his mind. There might be time for such indulgences later.

If there was any later.

If ever his private war let up for a week, a day, an hour.

Maybe.

Fawzi raced across the grass, crouched below the bushes, made the rail and silently unlocked the chain. The scooter started at the first kick, unexpectedly loud in the silence. She leaped into the saddle and careered toward the loading bay. Bolan was already outside the hatch, waiting.

The rasp of the little scooter's exhaust was suddenly obliterated by an appalling clamor. Two machine pistols on full-auto, shockingly violent in the suburban evening, spat death from the direction in which the lone hardman had appeared. Muzzle-flashes flickered mauve and electric blue against the yellow sodium glare.

The shooting was followed at once by three single shots fired from around the corner of the block by the first man.

Fawzi Harari was literally lifted from the saddle by the impact of the death hail aimed at her. Sickeningly Bolan could hear the thwack of the heavy slugs as they ripped through her tender flesh.

Blood spurted purple in the pitiless overhead light. Projected several feet by the stream of lead, the girl crashed onto her back on the asphalt with outflung arms and lay still.

Mack Bolan was on his feet and running, a red mist of fury behind his eyes.

The killers with the SMGs were half hidden by one of the play structures, but he could sight them through a cement tunnel that lay between the grass and that obstacle.

The tunnel was about two feet in diameter and maybe ten feet long. The center of each man's body was momentarily visible as they emerged and began moving forward to check the result of their murderous work.

Bolan fired the AutoMag four times.

The big stainless-steel handgun bucked savagely in his two-handed grip. The skull-shattering 240-grain boattails streaked through the cement tube to zero in on the Executioner's targets, two for each man.

Terrible in their destruction, the slugs ripped through flesh and bone and cartilage, dropping the terrorists like slaughtered beasts. They were dead before they hit the ground.

For the second time that day Bolan lost his cool. He had fired from behind the bushes. Now he hurled himself out into the open, his face twisted into a mask of rage, until he stood over the fallen Honda like an avenging angel, eyes searching for the first man, the guy who had fired the single shots.

For the gunman standing thirty feet away at the corner of the block Bolan was an angel of death.

Completely unnerved at the sight of his quarry standing out in the open, totally without cover, he froze for one fatal instant with astonishment.

That fiftieth of a second cost him his life.

The shot, when it came, went wide, for Bolan had already fired. Smashed full in the face by the huge .44 caliber bullet, the killer was flung back against the wall of the building with his head almost torn from his shoulders. The body slumped to the ground, leaving a giant splash of blood fanned out over the concrete.

Bolan ran to the girl. Lights went on all over the block, windows opened and voices sounded their irritation in the night air.

There was nothing he could do for her.

Fawzi's slender body was completely riddled. A spiderweb of blood, glistening horribly as it congealed in the sodium light, rayed out from beneath her in all directions.

Only her face, impassive in death, the large eyes staring sightlessly upward, was untouched.

Gently Bolan pressed the lids shut.

With murder in his own heart, he ran to the other corner of the block.

The black Mercedes was already moving away. Max was sitting beside the driver. In the reflected light from the instruments, Bolan could see that he was lighting another cigarette.

He emptied the AutoMag's magazine at the sedan, but the big car was too far away for him to score.

Sickened at the useless waste of a young life, the Executioner went back to the scooter, picked it up, restarted the engine and rode out of there.

12

Four men sat watching a scene being played out on a television set. On the screen a tall, powerfully built man stood firing two guns at once. One of them, a silver-colored weapon, looked awesome. The other appeared to be some kind of submachine gun. The slugs slammed into the chest of an olive-skinned man seated at a table. The impact lifted him out of the chair and drove him against the wall.

A third man, who wore a mustache and whose face appeared pitted, stood from the table and walked to the window. "Perhaps, Mr. Bolan, your questions are answered now?" he said. "Like who ordered the ambush from which you escaped." There was a reply from the man with the guns, then the guy with the pockmarked face spoke again. "This man was what you Americans term a gun for hire, a professional murderer." And then later: "But wasn't one of us. To find out his reasons, you would have to ask his employers."

Max Nasruddin, the man with the pockmarked face on the TV set, switched it off and slid the videocassette out of its slot. "I think that should be enough to convince you gentlemen," he said. "The remainder of the meeting, which ended as planned with Bolan's escape, is not relevant."

The four men who had been watching the clip nodded their approval. It was the tall, spare American with shell-rimmed glasses and silver hair crimped close to his skull who acted as spokesman for the others.

"Admirable," he said. "I think we must all agree that Mr. Nasruddin has organized this particular part of the scheme in a way that should please everybody."

"Sure, it's what we wanted," the youngest of the four said. He wore a lightweight charcoal suit from Savile Row with a single rosebud in the buttonhole, but his English was heavily accented. "The traitor, Sadegh Rafsanjani, has paid for his betrayal of the jihad with his life, and that is as it should be. The fact that the supreme punishment was at the hands of an infidel will please Hussein Montazeri in Teheran."

The third man was a petrodollar millionaire many times over. He came from one of the Gulf states, but he was to be seen more often in New York or Paris or Tokyo than he was in his tiny home country. "What about the girl?" he asked. "Did that too work out as planned?"

"The problem has been . . . taken care of," Nasruddin said. "Unfortunately, for technical reasons, there is no videotape of this operation. I can assure you, however, that the solution was—" he smiled bleakly "—final."

"No problems?" the American queried.

"We lost three men," Nasruddin said. "But they were expendable. They have already been replaced."

The fourth man had a sullen face with bushy eyebrows. His name was Shell Pettifer, and he was director-general of a multinational consortium that marketed electronic hardware and software ranging from the simplest of home computers to the directional equipment in the nose cones of space rockets.

He spoke now for the first time, a gravel-voiced monotone that was nevertheless vibrating with suppressed power. "Let's get this straight," he said. "Graziano, Rafsanjani, whatever you want to call him, had to be eliminated because he knew too much and because once he himself was known, through Bolan, to the Israeli authorities, he could have compromised our master plan. The fact that his death can be presented to the Iranian revolutionaries as some kind of retribution for betrayal of their cause may be of help to our friend Farid Gamal Mokhaddem—" he nodded toward the man with the rose in his buttonhole "—but the real aim of this operation, successful I agree, was to load Bolan with a murder charge."

He looked around the room—they were sitting in a tiny viewing theater off the computer complex in the old Maginot fortress—and then continued, "So far, so good. The assassinations have been well organized, and the fact that no organization claims credit for them helps to maintain a generalized climate of fear. The blast in the rue de Rivoli entrusted to Graziano was an excellent impromptu idea. It triggered Bolan's rage, and it added one more element to the destabilization of society that we're aiming for. But what of the long-range plans? These elite assassins, how are they shaping up? In particular, how is the Baraka operation progressing?"

"As scheduled," Nasruddin replied. "I'll call in the doctors, and you can question them yourself. They can give you a more comprehensive analysis than I can."

"Is Baraka here now?"

Nasruddin nodded. "The indoctrination will be a success," he said. "But perhaps you should ask the medics themselves to report. They can explain just how far it has gone, and give you visual proof, if you want."

"I think that would be a sound idea," Pettifer said, "in view of the time and money involved."

The doctors were brisk and businesslike in their starched white jackets.

The older one removed his pince-nez and polished the lenses with a silk handkerchief. "It is a little difficult to explain the technicalities," he said, "but the programming is, as you might say, 'taking.' Slowly but very surely."

"Can't you speed it up?" the petrodollar millionaire asked. "Time is money."

The younger doctor, still inscrutable behind his wraparound shades, replied. "It is the first time the drugs—or this combination of them—have been used in this way. The calculation of the doses, often quite extraordinarily small, and their exact relation to one another, require great care. And at each stage the effect of their administration, short-term and long-term, must be minutely noted. And the program, if necessary, equally minutely adjusted. Hasty action could be fatal."

"You must remember, too," the older man said, "that however clever and ingenious Monsieur Nasruddin's manipulations and maneuvers are, the subject is only sporadically available to us. And even when he is here, the visits are necessarily short."

The younger doctor spoke again. "If ever there was a breakthrough—a connection in the subject's mind— between the old imprintation and the new, the entire project would be ruined. And it could be very dangerous for all of us. Considering the strength involved.''

"We can at least demonstrate to these gentlemen that there has been no weakening whatever in acquired skill during the transfer,'' the doctor with pince-nez suggested. He turned to a stocky character at the back of the room. "Willi, fetch the tapes and run us the recordings of the Doberman scene, Baraka's fight with Mazarin and the shooting gallery test.''

"Impressive," the American commented when the tapes were through. "Now what about the others? What news on the three German kids, the Hispanic and his buddy, the Corsican, the two Irishmen and the Marksman?''

"Just a difference in degree," the young doctor said. "There's no question there of reimprinting. They're all disillusioned fanatics who decided to settle for money. But there's a certain amount of conditioning to be done, a necessity to remove or suppress various prejudices, so-called moral stands and preconceived ideas that might affect or even hinder their work on our behalf. This is not necessary in the case of the Marksman. He's an artisan, schooled in the most efficient methods of destruction, and proud as hell of his expertise."

"See how mad he was when Baraka did better than he did in the shooting gallery!" the doctor with pince-nez said, chuckling.

His companion nodded. "With the others," he said, "the conditioning is to render them into the state of semiautomata, what the popular press would call zombies. They carry out their orders without question. The Marksman doesn't ask questions, not even of himself. He does the job and pockets the money. Period. Reasons don't exist for him."

"Understood," Pettifer said. "Maybe we could see the system at work now? I have to be at a meeting with the Eurocrats in Strasbourg before dark."

"Of course," Max Nasruddin agreed. "Doctor, if you wouldn't mind leading the way to the conditioning section?"

They trooped through the computer complex— staffed now by a girl and three young men in white coveralls, all intent on taking notes from the flickering green rows of text unscrolling, pausing and vanishing from the racked VDT screens in front of them. An elevator took them one stage higher in the interior warren of the fortress, and from there a moving walkway carried them several hundred feet laterally to a glass-paneled viewing room that looked over a space resembling an army briefing unit or a university lecture theater.

Exploded diagrams showing the working parts of handguns, rifles, SMGs and even artillery pieces had been pulled down from wall hangers on one side of the big room. The bullet-headed German, Klaus, who acted as chauffeur to the two doctors, was standing by a table on a raised platform opposite the viewing window. A projector on the table was throwing the image of a town plan onto a screen that stood on a tripod nearby. The network of streets and squares and avenues was itself crisscrossed by a web of waterways. Klaus was talking, tapping sections of the plan from time to time with a wooden pointer.

"They are organizing a contingency operation for the elimination of Jaap van Leeuward, the Dutch information minister, in Amsterdam," Nasruddin explained. "The class will terminate in a few minutes, and then you can watch Mazarin schooling the younger ones in unarmed combat—all of them except Baraka, in fact."

"Why not Baraka?" Mokhaddem asked, glancing at the small group of men and the single girl at their desks.

Nasruddin smiled. "Baraka could teach Mazarin," he said.

"And he has absolutely no recollection?" The American was staring curiously at the star killer-to-be, towering over the others as he concentrated on the screen.

"None whatever," the older doctor said firmly. "You will see later in the gallery, if you have time. We offer a series of pop-up targets for him to shoot at, all of them portraits of eminent people—actors, sportsmen, diplomats, industrialists. He is to fire only at his enemies. You will be surprised at those he chooses."

"I see there is a certain amount of... shall we say... subliminal persuasion on hand anyway," the petrodollar tycoon commented, indicating a series of posters and placards displayed on walls all around the lecture hall.

It was an odd collection. All of them were World War II propaganda publications, some French, some German, and even a British one warning that Careless Talk Costs Lives. But they had one thing in common.

They included such slogans as The Enemy Is Listening, The Warmonger Who Threatens Your Future, This Soldier Is Your Foe, Join the Fight against Tyranny and—from the odious and infamous "anti-

Jew'' exhibition in occupied Paris—These Are the Bloodsuckers Responsible.

But whether the figure on the poster was a Nazi soldier, a fifth columnist, Stalin, a French general or Winston Churchill, each one had been doctored, with the original face replaced by that of a prominent present-day diplomat or statesman.

The largest poster, and the most prominently displayed, had depicted a ranting and raving Hitler tearing the map of Europe to pieces and feeding the shreds into his mouth—with the slogan beneath: Whatever the Cost, This Man Must Be Stopped!

Faked and reprinted, the features above the swastika armbands were now those of the President of the United States.

Nasruddin was smiling again. ''We don't actually go the whole way,'' he said, ''making them believe they actually *are* operating as secret agents in World War II. But they are all people who have been conditioned to serve a cause. And here, in this militaristic atmosphere—no matter that the 'enemy' uniforms are from both sides—we give them one. They serve and obey.''

Farid Gamal Mokhaddem turned up the lapel of his immaculate suit and sniffed appreciatively at the rosebud. ''If only they knew!'' he said.

13

Clinic was the key word. Even so, Bolan had to spend a whole morning in the reference section of the Bibliothèque Nationale—France's equivalent of the Library of Congress—before he finally located the source of Wally Boardman's phrase, "the old triple-F."

"Of course," Fawzi Harari had said when he'd remembered to ask. "It's a logo. A trademark if you like. What the French call the *sigle*, of a clinic...."

There had been an everybody-knows-that quality in her smiling reply that had to mean this clinic, whatever it was and wherever it was, had some close connection with the girl or with her ex-associates. Which meant in turn that it could be vital to the Executioner. But before he could ask where the clinic could be found, death had sealed the girl's lips forever.

Death in the form of Nasruddin's assassins.

They had paid already for that brutal and despicable act; the account with the guy who had ordered the killing would be settled later.

In full.

Right now, identification of the clinic took priority.

The medical directory that at last surrendered the secret told Bolan that it was in the Val de Ruz, near Neuchâtel, in the western sector of Switzerland.

The clinic was called the Friedrich Friedekinde Foundation.

The description in the directory was succinct.

The place had been founded in 1936 by Friedrich Friedekinde, an Austrian pupil of Freud and Jung, as a study center for research into the behavior patterns of psychotics and patients who suffered from schizophrenia and personality disorders. Inheritor of a fortune from his rich industrialist family in Vienna, Friedekinde had endowed the clinic before his death in the 1950s with enough funds to continue research independently of the huge fees contributed by the small number of rich patients sent there.

The present director was Wilhelm Friedekinde, the founder's son. He was a graduate of USC, MIT and Harvard Medical School. Under his leadership, the work of the foundation was now directed more toward a scientific search for the underlying causes of delusions, persecution mania and hysteric amnesia.

Clinical experiments were monitored under the supervision of Professor Otto Schloesser; laboratory work was headed by Dr. Paul Hansen.

Bolan took notes, committed them to memory, tore up the paper he had used and fed the pieces into a waste disposal bin.

He had looked up the meaning of the French word *sigle*.

The dictionary gave the meaning "abbreviation."

Okay. Three Fs were an abbreviation of the clinic's full title—although, not making a pronounceable word such as UNO or NATO or SALT, they could hardly qualify as an acronym. But there was certainly a logo or trademark, as Fawzi had said. The medical directory reproduced it.

The symbol was in fact a monogram—three overlapping capital Fs arranged clockwise, one after the other, in a circle.

The whole device bore a curious resemblance to a swastika with six arms instead of four.

Bolan stared at the printed page.

You'd have to be crafty, but if you could get around Friedekinde...

Those words, Wally Boardman's suggestion for an approach to identify the men behind the new terrorism, had been almost his last.

What had he said after that?

The quote about "the old triple-F."

After all, it was from their work, their labo—

And the sentence had died in his throat as the gunmen had opened fire.

Was the word going to be...laboratory, not labor?

He returned the reference books and decided to go to the Val de Ruz, near Neuchâtel, in Switzerland.

14

The route passed via the information room of the American embassy and Hal Brognola. Bolan chained Fawzi Harari's Honda scooter to the railings surrounding the courtyard, joined the trickle of tourists filing in from the Place de la Concorde, the Rue Royale and the tree-shaded length of the Champs Elysées and told the uniformed U.S. marine at the top of the steps that he had an appointment with Colonel Pforzheimer.

This coded request, used by field agents from all the U.S. intelligence services, got him past the security checks at the entrance and the reception desk in the embassy lobby and up the gracious curving stairway to a plainclothes Fed installed behind a smaller desk on the mezzanine. The man was trying hard to look like a minor diplomatic official.

The fictitious colonel's rank changed each month: when he had made major general, he was demoted to lieutenant and started over. Just like in real life, Bolan reflected wryly as he asked the Fed the second, failsafe question, in a different code, that would oblige the embassy cypher section to put out an all-countries emergency call for Brognola to call in.

Luckily the presidential liaison was in Rome, attending an antiterrorist seminar called by Interpol chiefs in the wake of the latest wave of assassinations. He could be in Paris within three hours.

Bolan waited impatiently in a small anteroom that looked out over the Avenue Gabriel. Half a mile away, beyond the summer crowds strolling under the chestnut and plane trees in the Tuileries gardens, beyond the neoclassical facades of the Louvre, wreckers and salvage crews were still sweating to extricate the bodies of victims from the bombed department stores. The death roll had now risen to thirty-one.

HAL BROGNOLA LOOKED HARASSED. His white seersucker suit was more creased than usual, his hair mussed, the cigar jutting from his grim features unlit. In one hand he held a strip of paper torn from a teletype machine. When Bolan had reported on the mission so far, he handed it over without a word. Bolan read:

FLASH
COPENHAGEN, THURSDAY (AP)—TERRORIST BOMB EXPLODED EARLY TODAY IN UNDERGROUND GARAGE ERIKSSON DEPT STORE NEAR TIVOLI GARDENS COLLAPSING STREET-LEVEL SALES FLOOR INTO FIRE STARTED AMONG PARKED AUTOS CASUALTIES FEARED HEAVY MORE LATER.

''More later!'' Brognola quoted, tapping the wire service's sign-off slug with a furious forefinger. ''How many more, for crying out loud. How much later? Striker, this has to stop.''

"It will," the Executioner promised grimly. "But it will take time. You know that."

"Sure, I know it. But how much time do we have until the panic spreads? Last night, a couple of hours after the bomb down the road was detonated, a perfectly innocent Algerian laborer was beaten to death in the Place de la Bastille—just because he had Arab features. How much time do we have before the whole damned continent goes up in flames?"

Bolan spread his arms and sighed. He made no reply.

Brognola continued, "Word is that this latest terror wave is the work of dissident extremist splinter groups—the same unrelated groups bugging us for the past five years. The story comes with the rumor that, this time, they're getting no help from Ivan. According to the latest intel from Stony Man, the first part just isn't true."

Bolan nodded. "I know it," he said.

"The Company penetrated the so-called Red Army Faction in West Germany," Brognola said. "Their man was blown. His body was found in a suburban gutter in Munich last night. A hit-and-run accident, they said." He snorted his disbelief. "But he got through a final message before they wasted him. He said neither the RAF nor the French Action Directe fanatics they're in cahoots with had anything to do with the latest hits. He said they had specifically been warned to lay off. He said Abyll Abu Hamad's Palestine Liberation Front had been given similar orders. And we know ourselves that the Lebanese Armed Revolutionary Faction has been inoperative since the head man, George Abdallah, was jailed by the French.

There's no evidence that the IRA, the Armenians, the Basques or the Corsicans are involved."

"I know all that," Bolan said. "You told me. They're using pros, working to a definite plan. And whoever the guys giving the orders are, they're big."

"Tell me something *I* don't know," the Fed grunted. "But they've got to be identified, tracked down. Terminated, as the boys say, with extreme prejudice before any more damage is done."

He crumpled the teletype message into a ball and tossed it into a wastebasket. "And no crap about public trials with smart-ass lawyers to get them off. No prison sentences that will trigger another set of skyjacks with their buddies bargaining innocent lives as hostages against their release. Politico-diplomatic expedience, cynical self-interest and plain rule-book inefficiency has stopped the governments of our world from cleaning up this garbage," Brognola shouted. "Now it's up to you to do it for them. You got me?"

"Uh-huh," Bolan said gently.

"I'm sorry, Striker." Calming down, the big Fed became contrite. "This thing is getting me down. Now...I guess you're in need of help. So tell me why I just left a good lunch and flew eleven hundred kilometers in an uncomfortable army jet, okay?"

"Intel," the Executioner said. "Friedekinde, Wilhelm, an Austrian national living near Neuchâtel, Switzerland. Anything known. Ditto the Friedekinde Foundation clinic. Nasruddin, Max, nationality unknown. Cool and ruthless, rotten through and through. Seems to be some kind of organizer. A pro contract man known as the Marksman. Schloesser, Otto, and Hansen, Paul, both doctors in Switzerland. Anything and everything on all of them."

"You'll have it," Brognola said. "We'll go down to the cypher room now and borrow a satellite."

In the long basement corridor, they passed a stiff-backed man of about fifty with gray hair and a clipped mustache. He was wearing a chalk-striped worsted suit with a Brooks Brothers necktie and a button-down shirt.

The hand he raised in answer to Brognola's greeting was barely high enough to be polite, and the glance he shot at Bolan was positively resentful. Neither his eyes nor his mouth smiled.

"Assistant military attaché," Brognola explained. He grinned. "They hate us here. Free-lancers and wildcat individualists decidedly unwelcome. For them, anything that isn't Company business, fed through the Paris resident, is practically a violation of the Constitution."

"Tough," Bolan said. "Well...if I fall down on the job, I can always plead the Fifth Amendment!"

"Don't even think it, guy!" Brognola said.

The Stony Man computer complex wasn't able to offer much. The check run on Friedekinde and·his clinic via the linked CIA-FBI-NSC-Interpol data banks came up with nothing. The two Swiss doctors were clean also.

Max Nasruddin was Lebanese. Twice jailed for falsification of documents and attempts to defraud the government. He had been commandant of the terrorist training camp at Barandak, near Teheran; technical advisor at the guerrilla camp of Fakilabad, near Meched, where two captured Boeings, a 707 and a 727, were used to "educate" future hijackers in the niceties of piracy in the air; and chief lecturer at Mandharia, where Islamic children were indoctrinated, from the age of eight years, in the use of modern arms and explosives against the infidel.

Supplementary intel concerned conflicting underworld rumors about the killers of Sean Riordan, Alonzo and the Swiss diplomat. A final addition to the coded signal read:

> These are considered small-timers compared with the hit man code-named Baraka, who is supposed to be under wraps until some spectacular (but unspecified) outrage planned for later this month. Will advise if supplementary material feeds in. Warning meanwhile: this man is reputed to be deadly, repeat deadly dangerous.

Bolan sighed. "So, Baraka again," he said. "I have to flush out this character, that's for sure. I have a hunch that if I find him, the whole deal will disintegrate."

"Let's hope you're right," Brognola said. "Where do you aim to start, now that the Graziano thing has burned out?"

"This clinic. I know it's zero-rated by the Stony Man analysts, but it's the only lead I have. Boardman seemed to figure it as the key. The girl knew about it. And if she knew from her cousins, then it has to be connected in some way."

"Okay, Striker. You're in the driving seat. Is there anything I can do?"

"Yeah," Bolan said. "Could be the local law has a warrant out for me in connection with Graziano. This creep Nasruddin certainly implied that the whole setup was faked with that in mind. So I want to get out of town—and into Switzerland—unseen."

"I don't think I have the power to ask the police—"

"I don't mean that. I want you to get me some clothes, a shirt, the nearest thing you can find to my combat blacksuit—a one-piecer in black, covering me from wrist to shoulder and neck to ankle in light-weight cling material. And black sneakers. And a biker's crash helmet—in black also."

"The rest was window dressing, wasn't it?" Brognola growled. "You knew damned well there'd be no additional hard news on those bums. You had me come all the way here from Rome just to do your shopping, right?"

He punched Brognola on the shoulder. "Don't be sore, Hal. It may sound like a chicken-feed operation to you, but these few things could get me out of trouble, and you're the only guy I can trust to do it in secret, and remain silent afterward. Like I need your help, see. Isn't that what 'liaison' means?"

"I still don't see what good they'll do you," the Fed complained one hour later when he returned with the stuff the Executioner ordered.

Bolan held up his black sweater. "I'll use this to hide the hardware," he said. "As for the rest—what could be more anonymous, more difficult to identify during the summer vacation, than a guy riding two hundred and fifty miles on a scooter with his face hidden by a regulation crash helmet and visor?"

15

Each time there was a revolution or a change in the system of government during the nineteenth and early twentieth centuries, many French aristocrats and rich bourgeois families would flee across the border into Switzerland, together with their gold and jewels. It wasn't surprising, then, that Neuchâtel was said to be more French than any town in France.

Certainly, Mack Bolan thought, as he navigated the crowded city center on the Honda scooter after his long and exhausting ride, the atmosphere of the place was more Gallic than Swiss.

There were no Alps near Neuchâtel. It lay at the northern tip of a narrow twenty-mile-long lake, with rolling pastureland on one side and the wooded crests of the Jura Mountains on the other.

Lanes twisting between the tall medieval houses around the twelfth-century château were redolent of the smells Bolan always associated with France—rich, gamy odors, the savory aromas of cooking done in wine, the sugary warmth issuing from pastry shops, the hint of coffee and the acrid tang of black tobacco.

There was a waterfront with a wooden-decked jetty from which the lake steamers took aboard passengers for Colombier, Concise and Yverdon. Was it here, in this quiet country town, that the destruction of Europe's social order was being planned?

The Friedekinde clinic, Bolan discovered, sipping a beer beneath a striped umbrella at the pierhead café, was well-known. It was two or three miles out of town, the waiter told him, on the road that led north to the village of Valangin.

It was a restful location for the mentally disturbed, the Executioner thought, riding past the place a half hour later—wildflowers by the roadside, cattle browsing knee-deep in meadows, the summer sun gleaming on a distant triangle of lake water glimpsed through a gap in the trees.

Old man Friedekinde must have been loaded, too, he thought. The ten-foot brick wall topped with broken glass enclosed between twenty-five and thirty acres of woodland and park.

There was a stone gatehouse flanked by tall, gold-tipped iron gates with the triple-F motif worked into the scrollwork. Beyond them, the entrance driveway curled off between dense cypress hedges, hiding the house.

The waiter, happy to linger gossiping on the sunny quayside, had told Bolan that it was modeled on a Moorish-Venetian palazzo built on Cap Ferrat for Beatrice de Rothschild in 1905. He had never seen it himself, but deliverymen said it was a real crazy pad.

They were dead right. From the fork of a lime tree on the far side of the country road, Bolan was able to focus his binoculars on the clinic and the formal gardens surrounding it. He saw a symmetrical two-story facade in terracotta stucco, with white sandstone facings and two wings enclosing a center section pierced by Moorish arches on slender pillars. The shallow, shingled roof was surmounted by a white balustrade.

At right angles to the wide terrace in back, a hundred-foot rectangular ornamental pond led between rows of tropical shrubs to a domed pavilion. Fountains played at ten-foot intervals down the center of the waterway, which was dotted with islands of lotus in bloom, lending the place the air of a Mediterranean Taj Mahal.

There was a stable block in back, and beyond its clock tower, Bolan could see the slanted glass roofs of workshops and laboratories.

Very interesting.

A sanctuary for the insane rich or a front for terrorists?

The problem was to decide on an approach, a way of getting in there to find out. Bolan wondered whether he should use a direct tack, posing as a newspaperman hoping to do a photo story on the place. Or perhaps a ruse, pretending to be a fellow medic in search of technical information on their discoveries.

The other route, of course, would be illegal entry, with the hope that he could stay undetected long enough to unearth some intel that would give him a lead, one that would help, in Boardman's words, "to get around Friedekinde."

The big question was: did Friedekinde himself know of the terrorist conspiracy or was he in some way an unwitting accomplice? Assuming that the conspiracy and the clinic *were* related.

There was no way he could answer the question, Bolan decided, before he had a chance to find out more about the clinic and the way it worked, and before he had a chance to check on the Foundation's director and make up his own mind about the kind of man he was.

Because there was always a possibility—faint but not to be ignored—that he was the victim of a chain of coincidences, that Boardman had been mistaken, that Fawzi Harari had known of the place in a different context, that the clinic, in fact, was no more and no less than what it pretended to be.

A soft probe, then.

So it was frontal approach, negative. If the personnel really were innocent, how could he be sure the front wasn't just a cover-up to hide guilt? Equally, if they were guilty... well, they would feign innocence, and they would be forewarned that Bolan was on their track.

He decided on a covert entry.

He scanned the house, the gardens, the surrounding park, as closely as he could. No sign of dogs.

Focusing the high-powered field glasses minutely, he examined the ground, concentrating on the spaces between stonework and shrubs, between a yew hedge and a line of statues at one side of the pond. He couldn't see any signs of trip wires, video scanners or the short posts on which sensors were customarily installed. That didn't mean there weren't any, but it was an indication.

He climbed back to the ground, remounted the scooter and rode around the property. The lane bounded two sides of the area; the remainder of the circuit was rough ground, through the woods that stretched back along the Val de Ruz to the Jura foothills and the fourteen-hundred-foot peak of the Tête de Ran.

Scaling the wall, with its razor-sharp shards of glass embedded along the top, was no sweat for a man of the Executioner's experience and agility, especially if there were no snarling Dobermans or German shepherds on the far side.

He made it just after dusk, in the most likely—and therefore unexpected—place, fifty yards from the entrance gates, figuring that the sections of wall that ran through the wood were more likely to be closely watched, especially since there was no rear entrance to the stable block.

There were canvas saddlebags on each side of the Honda's rear wheel. Bolan stripped off his sweater and stuffed it into one. From the other he took two objects encased in dull black plastic, one about the size of a cigar box, the other the size of a pack of cigarettes.

He had run the scooter in close to the wall and had steadied it on the kickstand. His Beretta nestled snugly in the shoulder rig, the AutoMag holstered on his right hip. Now he clipped the two plastic boxes to his belt and hoisted himself warily up until he was standing on the little machine's saddle.

Balanced precariously there, he flung a length of burlap he had found at an old campsite in the woods over the glass fragments cemented into the wall. Standing that far above the ground, with his height, he could just reach up and grip the coping with his fingertips.

He drew himself up until his shoulders were level with the top of the wall. He paused and listened, fingers, wrists and biceps aching. There was no sound from the other side of the wall. In the distance he could hear music from a fairground on the outskirts of Neuchâtel. A lake steamer gave a short blast on its siren.

He continued to pull himself up until he could wedge one foot on the coping. In the next moment he dropped noiselessly to the grass on the far side of the wall.

He unclipped the larger of the two plastic boxes and flipped a switch. This was one of the goodies supplied by Hal Brognola. Similar to a radar detector used by motorists, the box would bleep softly and a red light would glow any time it came within range of any kind of electronic sensor or magic-eye beam.

Holding it in front of him, the Executioner glided silently between bushes, through a plantation of young trees and past a sunken garden to the pavilion that looked over the waterway.

The detector remained mute. No dogs barked. No voice challenged him from the dark.

From the rococo pavilion he could look straight down the length of the ornamental pond to the palazzo. Lights showed in two of the downstairs windows and between the slatted shutters covering several more on the upper floor. A slight breeze moved the lotus leaves and stirred the somber surface of the water.

Bolan stole past the tropical shrubs and crouched below the terrace. There seemed to be no guards patrolling the outside of the building. After a while, he rose until his head was above the top of the terrace balustrade.

Through one of the long, uncurtained windows he could see a book-lined study and a green-shaded, counterbalanced lamp pulled low over a desk littered with papers. An elderly man with gold-rimmed pince-nez sat writing at the desk.

Bolan moved to the second window. He saw what was clearly some kind of reception room—the honey glow of ancient wood, vases and figurines in glass-fronted cabinets, a group of leather armchairs. Two men stood by an eighteenth-century inlaid French buffet loaded with bottles and glasses. The older was florid, white-haired, about sixty years of age; the younger blue-chinned, his eyes hidden behind wrap-around dark glasses.

Hell, Bolan thought, they sure didn't put much value on security!

One of the windows was slightly open. He could hear snatches of conversation as the white-haired man poured drinks.

"It was Ruth Benedict who first noted the effect of psilocybin on the Pueblo Indians as long ago as 1934...."

"But haven't we found here, Paul, that drug-associated behavior change in the patients...?"

"...a case of controlling the extradrug varia-bles..."

"...an effect indistinguishable, as Abramson observed, from that obtained with microgamma doses of LSD. And talking of ethyl alcohols, do you prefer soda or just ice with your Scotch?"

Shoptalk. Doctors having an exchange of views on the uses of chemotherapy in the treatment of nut cases. Normal enough—even though lysergic acid diethylamide and psilocybin were psychedelic drugs. Bolan had heard that they could be used on schizo patients in the more extreme cases. He was preparing to move away when a sentence from the younger man—Dr. Paul Hansen, he assumed—froze him in his tracks.

"But in this case it's the thought block that counts. Baraka shows no evidence whatsoever of ability transformation."

Baraka!

Bolan concentrated all his senses, blanking off everything but hearing in an effort to hear the older man's reply. But the words were mumbled, and immediately afterward he moved toward the window, causing the Executioner to duck below the balustrade. "There's a breeze blowing up," he said. "At my age, you want to keep out of drafts."

The window closed.

Bolan cursed. He couldn't hear anything else. But at least it proved he wasn't on a wild-goose chase: there *was* a connection between the foundation and the terrorists.

If the clinic's director was the guy writing in the study, that still left one question unanswered. If, on the other hand, the florid white-haired character pouring drinks was Friedekinde, the answer was affirmative: he too was heavily into the plot.

Bolan decided to pay a visit to the laboratories.

There should be records there, some kind of bookwork, filing cards even, on the patients—a case history, perhaps, on Baraka, if they were experimenting on the mysterious master killer.

If so, there was a possibility that he could find a lead to the man's movements.

And through him, maybe, to the shadowy elements behind the conspiracy. For Bolan was already convinced that the clinic was no more than an intermediate stage in the plot. The total lack of security precautions argued that.

It was a good time, anyway, for a clandestine check on the labs. It was a fair guess that they would be devoid of people after working hours, whereas there would be an unknown number of nursing staff, servants and possibly patients in the house. He could hear someone whistling and the scrape of a bucket around the corner of the building now.

He cat-footed around the opposite wing and crossed the stable yard. A black Mercedes sedan, a Citroën ambulance and a couple of lightweight pickups were parked on the cobblestones.

At the far end of the yard there was a high wall with a wooden door inset. The door wasn't locked. He went through and found himself in a vegetable garden, the scents of herbs aromatic on the night wind.

The garden was bounded on one side by the rear of the laboratory block. There was a door there, too. This one was locked.

Bolan unclipped the second, smaller plastic box from his belt. This small, sophisticated device was magnetized. It clamped firmly to anything that had metal buried within two inches of the surface. A lock for instance. On the outside there was a dial calibrated with figures.

Once the box was fixed firmly over the keyhole, the Executioner manipulated the dial this way and that until he heard the tumblers fall. He opened the door and walked into the lab.

A pencil flashlight showed him a row of windows above a tiled workbench complete with sinks, fume cupboards, Bunsen burners and microscales in glass cases furnished with deionization equipment. He pulled venetian blinds down over each window and risked sweeping the beam around the room.

He saw shelves of chemicals in jars and the usual laboratory equipment. Insulated wires and lengths of rubber tubing linked the copper condensation coils and glass components of some complex experiment set up in front of a locked poison cupboard at the far end of the lab. At one side of the cupboard, a glass door led to an office.

There were filing cabinets in there, along with ledgers on shelves and printed forms filled in by hand and clipped to sheaves of computer printouts. Bolan sat down at the table and started to read.

He set aside copy invoices from pharmaceutical companies, medical equipment suppliers' order forms, a daybook recording the clinic's financial income and expenses and salary slips for doctors, nurses and household employees. Thick notebooks logging the results of experiments carried out by researchers were of little use to him since they were almost entirely expressed in chemical formulae, which he couldn't understand.

He saw from the foundation's letterhead that the board of directors included Sir George Caversham; Admiral Hervé Dutrand-Cheville; Farid Gamal Mokhaddem; Senator Shell Pettifer; Sayed Mahdi al-Jaafari; and Montessori Giotto.

Caversham, he knew, was a big wheel in the London stock market, a useful figurehead for companies wishing to float shares. The admiral was a retired defense adviser to the French navy, Giotto the industrial relations chief to Italy's largest manufacturer of automobiles. Mahdi al-Jaafari was gossip column material, a playboy educated at Oxford who kept a close watch nevertheless on his immense holdings in oil. The others didn't ring any bells for Bolan.

No hint of anything shady there, he thought. He found a box file in a drawer of the desk in which case histories were summarized. But the patients were identified only by code letters. The treatment, expressed in medical shorthand, could have been instructions for the manufacture of a fission bomb, for all Bolan knew.

Patients were subdivided under the headings NEU and MAG. Did the first of these imply Neuchâtel, that is, inpatients at the clinic? If so, there were only five of them—three men and two women, all suffering from paranoid delusions of one kind or another, if he read the abbreviations correctly.

But what could MAG stand for?

The larger number of patients under this heading were clearly nonresident, for the dated treatments— the coded entries varied a lot—took place at odd intervals, and the length of each was unrelated to the others.

Without a key to the identities masked by the code letters, it was pointless to continue. Bolan searched everywhere, but he could find no key, no deciphering notebook, no master card in the box file.

Pondering his next move, he flipped idly through the pharmaceutical invoices. Among the expected analgesics, local anesthetics, disinfectants and tranquilizers, there was what seemed to him an abnormally large number of orders for very different substances: bufotenin, lysergic acid diethylamide, sodium amytal, TMA, adrenolutin—all of them, Bolan knew, in the category classed generally as hallucinogens.

He shrugged. It was a research clinic, after all. Hadn't he read someplace that such psychedelic drugs had successfully been used stateside in the treatment of alcoholics, as well as psychotics and schizos?

One thing was for sure: none of this stuff bore the slightest relation to arms, explosives or terrorism in general. It would be a waste of time delving any farther here. If proof existed of Friedekinde's connection with the plot, it would have to be sought elsewhere.

The palazzo?

Bolan glanced at his watch. It wasn't far off midnight; he had spent more time than he realized in the laboratory. The flashlight beam was beginning to fade.

But even if the principals were still working or talking, surely the domestic servants, the patients and the medical staff would be asleep by now?

In a house that size there would be room for maneuvering.

He raised the venetian blinds, slipped out of the lab and relocked the door. Back in the stable yard, he checked out the palazzo's rear facade. There were no lights showing from the kitchen quarters, and none through the shuttered upstairs windows.

A quick circuit of the building showed him that all three of the doctors he had seen were now drinking in the reception room. The conversation was animated; it looked as if it might be a long session.

Bolan stole back to the side of the house that was opposite the stable yard. The upper floor offered no problems to a penetration specialist trained in the expertise of secret entry. There were trash cans behind a fence, there was an outhouse roof, a stack pipe, a broad windowsill. It took him ten minutes to make the sill, open the shutters, lift away the circle of glass he had cut with a small diamond tool and reach in to ease back the catch. He pushed open the casement and climbed inside.

After a moment of silence, he swept the pencil flashlight beam around the room. For some obscure reason it looked vaguely familiar. A narrow bed, a desk, a door to a bathroom.

There was a half-full bottle of Scotch on the desk, an overflowing ashtray and a folded newspaper on a night table. To his surprise, instead of the sterile clinical odors he expected, the place smelled of stale cigar smoke and sweat.

Something was wrong.

It wasn't just that he had made a miscalculation: he had hoped the window would have been at one end of an upper hallway, not in the wall of what seemed like some servant's room.

No, the alarm buzzer in back of his mind was vibrating; it was something much more positive than that. His subconscious fighter's sense had noted something out of place and was signaling him to watch out.

He stood very still, listening.

Then he swept the weakening flashlight beam slowly back over the bed, the newspaper, the ashtray, the bottle, the desk . . .

The bottle!

The surface of the amber liquor was swaying inperceptibly from side to side.

Somebody had put that bottle down, plunked it hastily down, only seconds before, when they had heard him at the window.

He continued the even sweep of the pale pencil of light around the room, as though he had noticed nothing. But now he was noticing everything, especially the heavy draperies covering an alcove that was presumably used as a closet for hanging clothes.

And the tips of oversize brown shoes just visible beneath them.

So the penetration specialist trained in the expertise of secret entry hadn't been so smart after all!

Bolan flicked his flashlight off, unleathered the AutoMag and launched himself into the dark where the draperies had been. He aimed a kick just below a slight bulge he remembered in the invisible material.

His foot thudded into something yielding. He heard a gasp of pain, and something heavy dropped to the floor.

Continuing his advance, the Executioner ripped aside the curtains and swept his free hand over an electric light switch he had seen by the door. The room blazed into dazzling brightness.

He was tall, bald, and massively built, and he needed a shave. He would always need a shave. He stood in jeans and a vest with his mouth open and his hands clasped to the lower part of his belly, fighting for breath.

''You again!'' he choked as air wheezed back into his lungs.

As far as Bolan knew, he had never set eyes on the guy before. But this was no time for asking questions. He booted a fallen revolver under the bed, reversed the AutoMag in his hand and danced back out of range as the giant lumbered out of the alcove after him. Once he let those gorilla arms wrap around him he would be finished.

He ducked underneath a roundhouse left, launched his own hard fist in a second attack on the big man's belly and then took a right cross on the shoulder that sent him spinning across the room to sprawl back over the bed.

Winded or not, the giant was quick on his feet. Still grunting with pain, he hurled himself at the Executioner with clawing hands. Bolan lay on the bed, drew back his knees and straightened his legs as the huge body hit his feet.

The guy staggered away far enough for Bolan to spring upright. A colossal fist slammed against his cheekbone with a force that seemed to split his skull apart. And now the hamlike hand straightened out, the plank-hard edge forward in a karate stance.

But by this time the butt of the heavy stainless-steel AutoMag was swinging in a short arc toward the bald head. It clipped the man behind the ear before he could attack again. He dropped facedown on the floor with a thump that shook the room.

Bolan leaped astride his back and slugged him again. Harder this time. The giant had been struggling to rise. Now he dropped and lay still.

Bolan sprang catlike to his feet. Any kind of struggle in a house makes a disproportionate amount of noise, especially on an upper floor, especially a no-holds-barred fight between two big men. The fabric of the building acts as an acoustic amplifier, the floorboards as a resonator. And a deadfall by a hulk as heavy as the Executioner's opponent must have woken everyone in the entire house—and tipped off the doctors downstairs that this was no simple case of an inmate blowing his or her crazy top and being forcibly restrained by muscular nurses.

Jerking open the door, he ran out into a long passageway dimly lit by low-power light bulbs enclosed in wire cages in the ceiling.

He had had more than his share of hunches already on this mission, but there was another to be followed now.

With that curious and mysterious déjà vu feeling that everybody has at one time or another, he *knew* as he dashed down the corridor that he must turn right at the T-junction, that the main stairway lay to the left. There would be an unmarked door at the end of the passage that led to a service staircase that must connect with the kitchens.

Angry voices sounded from the foot of the main stairway. A door opened somewhere behind him. He flashed past doors with glass inspection panels behind which he glimpsed patients in white hospital beds. An image was imprinted on his mind of one woman sitting up open-mouthed and screaming.

He opened the unmarked door. True enough, concrete stairs led downward.

At the foot of the stairs he ran across an empty kitchen bright with stainless-steel sinks, white enameled deep-freeze units and copper pans hooked along one wall. The door to the stable yard was locked, but the key was on the inside. He twisted it, reholstered the AutoMag, opened the door and hurried out into the night.

The yard seemed twice as wide as it had before.

Bolan took in the alternatives with a single searing glance.

The car? The pickups? The ambulance?

No ignition keys. No materials—and no time—to hot-wire them. The iron entrance gates barred the only way out, and they were probably electrically controlled. In any case a phone call could alert the gatekeeper and have him waiting, maybe with a gun.

Down past the ornamental pond and the pavilion, with a desperate leap for the wall and the Honda on the other side?

No way. He had seen floodlights installed in the tropical shrubs on either side of the water when he'd come in. One flick of a switch, that way, and he'd be center stage, with all illumination systems go.

Behind the stables, then, and hightail it for the wall where it ran through the woods?

Right.

He sprinted past the vehicles and turned the corner of the block. Another wall, an archway that led to an orchard.

Bolan ran through.

As he passed beneath the arch, a floodlight set in the brickwork above his head blazed into life. He halted, pinned against the dark and as vulnerable as a specimen on a microscope slide. Blinded by the brilliance, he squeezed his eyes almost shut.

"Mr. Bolan!" a deep voice intoned. "How nice of you to pay us another visit. But why go to all that trouble? Why not just knock on the door and ask your questions directly?"

Bolan said nothing. The voice stirred no memory in him. On the fringe of the pool of light cast by the flood, he could just make out the figure of the florid man with white hair.

"In case you should be contemplating anything foolhardy," the voice continued, "I must warn you that two of my colleagues are standing in the darkness, one on either side of me. Each one is armed...and although we may not be experts like yourself, at this range, in this light, you would be a target hard to miss.''

The Executioner's muscles tensed; his fingers itched for the feel of Big Thunder's butt, so near on his right hip. There were bushes no more than ten feet away on his right. How far away were the other two? Could he beat their reaction times? Did he dare risk a sudden dive—and a punishing burst from the AutoMag to cover his retreat?

''All right, Mazarin—'' the white-haired man was staring at a point behind Bolan's shoulder ''—don't hit him too hard.''

The oldest trick in the world. Bolan of all people, seasoned fighter as he was, didn't intend to fall for it.

Except that this time it wasn't a trick.

He heard the whistle of the blackjack as it zeroed in on his skull.

Then, for the second time that week, the sky fell in on him.

16

It was raining in Amsterdam. Too bad, Information
Minister Jaap van Leeuward thought as he waited to
greet his guests beneath the scarlet canopy outside the
Central Station; the city should have been at its best in
this summer season, with the tall, narrow houses reflected in sunlit canals, a blue sky visible between
leaves not yet fallen from the waterside trees. Oh, well,
there was always the hope that the color inside would
compensate for the lack of it in the streets.

Van Leeuward was to accompany his opposite
numbers from Norway, Sweden, Denmark and West
Germany to the official opening of an exhibition at the
world-famous Rijksmuseum. The show, intended to
reunite modern masters from all over the world, would
make a fascinating contrast to the traditional Ver-
meers, Van Dycks and Rembrandts that were normally the museum's main attractions. It was expected
to draw big crowds during the two months it would
remain open.

The ministerial cavalcade crossed the bridge that
spanned the network of waterways surrounding the
station and rolled slowly down the Damrak toward the
Koninklijk Palace. The route had been closed to ordinary traffic, and there were black-leather-suited
mobile police every few yards, but the bad weather

had kept the expected crowds away. At the last moment a Mercedes 600 and three Cadillac limousines had been substituted for the open cars originally planned.

The rain blew in gusts across the huge square in front of the palace and silvered the Gothic spires of the Nieuwekerk just behind it. The square was deserted, though small groups of Amsterdammers waved from beneath the trees lining Rokin and around the Mint Tower.

Police outriders leading the procession turned right between two canals and then swung left to cross the bridge over the Singelgracht. The huge bulk of the museum, set in formal gardens, was on the far side of the wide canal.

As the driver of the Mercedes twirled the wheel to follow them, a man sitting behind an upper window in a house beside the canal pressed a remote control button on a directional radio device, detonating a hundred pounds of plastic explosive packed into a motorboat moored close to the bridge.

There was a livid blast of flame and a shattering roar as the boat disintegrated and the bridge parapet with half the roadway was sheared off and sent hurtling skyward.

Three of the six motorcycle outriders, together with their machines, were blown to pieces—a shower of metal fragments, entrails and bloodied morsels of flesh and bone fell back onto the remains of the bridge along with chunks of masonry pulverized by the explosion.

A fourth policeman was wrapped around a lamp standard with a broken back. The two survivors sat dazedly on the sidewalk, staring at the gaping hole in the roadway through which their machines had fallen into the water.

The front of the Mercedes 600 was crumpled by the shock wave, and both front wheels were blown off as the huge limo slewed across the bridge. The chauffeur and a bodyguard beside him were cut by glass fragments. But Van Leeuward and his guests, sitting behind armored windows in the rear of the car, were unharmed.

The six cops bringing up the rear of the cavalcade screamed to a halt. Five of them raced toward the column of smoke and dust hanging in the air above the damaged bridge, leaving one to shout an urgent report into his radio.

Doors jerked open as shocked officials poured out of the three Cadillacs; men and women ran from the canalside houses. Van Leeuward and his companions emerged from the leading car, wondering helplessly what they could do.

This was where the bomber and his associates had been smart. It was assumed that the very carefully calculated and minutely prepared explosion was a near miss, a failed attempt to assassinate the five politicians.

In fact, Van Leeuward alone was the target, and the blast had achieved precisely the effect desired: to halt the motorcade and get him out of his car.

The bodyguard, mopping the blood streaming into one eye from a gash on his forehead, must have had in that split second a premonition, for he swung around and tried to push the information minister back into the Mercedes.

He was too late.

Two distant rifle shots cracked out above the hub-bub of voices and whistles and sirens.

The bodyguard was flung backward over the hood of the limo with blood frothing from a fist-sized hole between his lungs.

Van Leeuward was hit between the shoulder blades, the high-velocity bullet tearing away half his heart as it burst out through his rib cage. He took a single step forward on rubber legs and fell, dead before he reached the chasm at the side of the bridge and dropped into the canal.

Eight towers with pyramid roofs crowned the Rijksmuseum. By an attic window beneath the rain-wet tiles of one of the two tallest, the Marksman focused field glasses on the commotion around the blown bridge. Satisfied, he broke the twin-barreled Holland & Holland rifle, ejected the cartridges and stowed them in his pocket. The gun, still hinged in a wide-angle V, he stuffed into a gunnysack along with the binoculars, a waterproof coat, the remains of a packet of sandwiches and a roll of wallpaper.

He was wearing stained white coveralls. Slinging the sack over one shoulder, he picked up a can half full of white paint with a wide brush suspended from the handle. Making no attempt to move quietly, he plod-ded down the hundred and eighty stairs that spiraled from the roof to the foot of the tower. A uniformed commissionaire waved from the main entrance as he walked out into the rain.

The Marksman waved back, rolled his eyes heaven-enward in disgust at the weather and called out, "Fucking rain! Wouldn't you know when there's out-side work to do!"

The commissionaire nodded sympathetically. The Marksman trudged around the corner and loaded his stuff into a small unmarked panel truck. He got in, started the engine and drove away.

Half an hour later, when most of the available police in the city were cordoning off the area around the museum, a young woman pushed a baby carriage onto the Arrivals concourse of the Central Station and joined the crowd waiting to meet passengers from the Antwerp-Rotterdam express.

The streamlined flyer drew into the terminus. The crowd surged toward the barrier. Nobody noticed the young woman walk quickly away from the baby carriage.

The explosion killed seventeen people, maimed more than fifty and slightly injured one hundred more.

Two leather-clad youths on motorbikes were waiting outside the station. The girl leaped astride the pillion of one, and they rode away.

Approaching the first intersection, they saw a prowl car approaching at high speed, the blue light on its roof flashing.

Momentarily the solo rider panicked, believing the cops were already on their tail.

The rider signaled wildly to the other two, leaned his bike steeply over and headed for a narrow side street. But the pavement was slick with rain, the tires lost their grip, the machine slid away from under him and he rolled onto the road.

The police driver could do nothing. He was traveling at fifty miles an hour, and the boy was dead ahead. The body was thrown twenty feet, and the biker's skull cracked open on the sidewalk.

The dead man carried no papers. His clothes were unmarked. The motorcycle had been stolen three weeks before in Belgium. The mini-Uzi beneath his windbreaker was part of a consignment hijacked by the Red Army Faction from a West German army base two years previously. The body was never identified.

The other biker and his passenger rode on unchallenged and made their way through Belgium to Luxembourg and then France.

IT WAS RAINING in Neuchâtel, too—a thin drizzle blowing off the lake that woke Mack Bolan to the fact that he was lying on wet grass and his head ached like hell.

On wet grass? He opened his eyes and saw clouds. At the edge of his vision there was a wall. Beside the wall a Honda 250 scooter was balanced on its kickstand

What the...? With the return of consciousness, the instant combat-trained awareness of the world, his place in it and the events leading up to the crack on the head that had knocked him out, came a flood of questions.

Why had they released him? Why here, back with the scooter? Once they realized he was onto the terrorist-clinic connection, as they must have done, why hadn't he been killed?

What was this "You again!" from the giant who had slugged him, and the reference by the old guy to *another* visit?

Was he injured? Had he been drugged, tortured, interrogated?

Bolan sat up. He was wearing the sweater he had taken off and stowed in the Honda's saddlebag before he'd made his clandestine entry into the clinic the night before. They must have dragged it on over the blacksuit when they'd dumped him.

He couldn't have been here long, because the garments weren't sodden, only damp on the outside, and clearly the drizzle had been falling for some time.

He felt each limb experimentally. No broken bones, no cuts, no scars. Even the lump on the back of his aching head was barely noticeable. He pulled up sleeves, unfastened zippers. No needle marks.

Even the Beretta and the AutoMag were still in place, snug beneath the sweater in their holsters. He unleathered both and examined them. The magazines were there, both loaded. Spare clips still rested in the pouches attached to his belt.

Only the electronic sensor detector and the magnetic auto picklock were missing.

Why?

Drugs—and they sure had plenty in there—didn't have to be administered with a hypo syringe of course. But if he had been fed pentathol or some other truth drug while he was out, then questioned, there wasn't much he could have told them.

That his mission was to track down the terrorists? They would have known already through Boardman and the fact that he had killed Graziano in Paris.

That he had found out nothing else and still had no lead—except the clinic's connection to the plot? The fact that he had been caught breaking in there would already have proved he was wise to that.

In any case, in his experience people exposed to truth drugs usually retained some hazy recollection of the session. He remembered nothing.

What was crystal clear—it was unarguable—was that the plotters, or at least those connected with the clinic, *wanted* him free, were prepared to release him armed, wished for some reason to leave him on the loose.

When he would presumably continue the chase. And they didn't give a goddamn? Bolan didn't get it. It was baffling beyond words. They had treated him like a fish too small to count among the catch and thus thrown back into the sea.

Did that mean the racket was so big they didn't have to fear anyone, even the Executioner? Or could it imply that the doctors at the clinic were more squeamish than the terrorists about killing in cold blood...that there was a conceivable difference of opinion that could be exploited?

Obviously priority number one was to find out every single thing he could about the damned clinic and the people working there. His pierhead waiter friend, and others like him, were the most likely source of useful gossip.

Before that, a couple of strong black coffees would help clear his head; after that, maybe he could straighten out his thinking.

Bolan started the scooter and rode back into town. If anyone was checking his departure from the gatehouse, they didn't show themselves.

He stopped at a workers' café on the outskirts and ordered his coffee. Somebody had left an English language newspaper on the next table. Idly he leaned across and scanned the front-page headlines.

"Dutch Government Resigns over Security Issue," he read across five columns in the number one spot.

And then below: "Opposition Chief Accuses Police of Laxity in Van Leeuward Killing."

A separate panel boxed farther down the page carried the query: "Was Dead Gunman the Station Bomber?"

Bolan pulled the newspaper over and read the stories through. There had been antigovernment riots in The Hague, the lead story said, after the Amsterdam atrocities. Railroad workers were threatening strike action unless more stringent precautions were taken against terrorists.

It seemed the disasters had shocked Holland two days earlier. He was surprised he hadn't heard of them before.

He sighed. The death campaign was heating up. How much worse would it have to get, how many more innocents must die, before he was in a position to throw a monkey wrench in the works of the scum planning these horrors?

He drained a second cup of coffee, glanced at his watch—and froze.

It was ten to eight, but he wasn't looking at the time. His eyes stared unbelievingly at the date.

Yesterday was Tuesday. Today should be Wednesday.

The window in the watch face told him it was Friday.

He grabbed the newspaper and scanned the front-page masthead beneath the Gothic-lettered title. Friday.

Bolan bit his lip. It was a replay of the Paris hotel scene. Once again he had lost two whole days. Only this time there was no thousand-mile journey in a Mercedes to account for it.

If they'd held him at Friedekinde's place since Tuesday evening, how come he didn't remember any of it? Not even the fuzziest, spaced-out recollection?

It worried the hell out of him, not because of this particular mission, but for a more personal reason.

Was his body, his head, finally beginning to succumb to the ravages of his everlasting war? Was nature, aided by events like the double blackjacking he'd suffered recently, conspiring to bring him down?

It was a sobering thought—a thought he wanted to push away but one that had to be taken into account.

But before he could worry any further, life supplied a more immediate problem.

Across the street from the café there was a gas station. A black Mercedes sedan had just stopped by the pumps for a refill.

There were, of course, plenty of black Mercedes sedans in Neuchâtel. But this one happened to be the antique model he had seen in the stable yard at the Friedekinde clinic. As part of his routine combat pattern, he had played his flashlight beam on the license plate and memorized the number—that was one thing he did remember. Now the limo was within fifty yards of him.

The chauffeur, a swarthy, stocky, bullet-headed man, was alone in the car. While the attendant was filling the tank, he climbed out and crossed the road to a cigar store next to the café.

Bolan threw coins on the table and left. He crossed the road.

The tank filled, the attendant had returned to the gas station office.

The rear of the big car was hidden behind the pay kiosk.

Bolan acted on impulse. Good or bad, the risk he was going to take would provoke a reaction—and here was an opportunity too good to pass up.

Was the trunk unlocked?

He pressed the button above the license plate. It was.

The lid swung slowly open. Bolan checked that the locking mechanism could be operated from inside. It was simply a matter of manipulating a hook-shaped catch against a strong spring.

With a hasty glance around—empty sidewalks, the attendant still in the office, the chauffeur at the cigar store—he folded himself over the sill of the trunk and pulled the lid down on top of him.

Soon afterward Bolan heard voices. Then a door slammed, the engine started and the car moved away.

In total darkness the Executioner weighed the chances of his impulse paying off. If the Mercedes returned to the clinic, he'd be inside again, unobserved, and there was surely intel to be gathered there someplace. If, on the other hand, the Mercedes was tanked up because a journey was planned, he wanted to know the destination.

Provided no baggage was stowed in the trunk.

If it was . . . well, he would have to rely on the Beretta, already unleathered and in his right hand, the surprise element and his own talent for survival to get him out of it.

From the shortness of the trip and a gravelly scrape that could have been iron gates opening, he guessed they had returned to the clinic.

Almost at once four, perhaps five, passengers got into the car. The body sank slightly on its springs.

Doors slammed again. The Mercedes turned around and started off again.

The huge trunk wasn't hermetically sealed, but fresh air was scarce, and the aromatic stink of gasoline from the newly filled tank helped to make breathing even more of a chore. In the close, hot darkness of his self-imposed prison, Mack Bolan soon found that his lungs were laboring. His clothes dried quickly on the outside . . . but inside they were damp with sweat.

It was a long journey, at first uphill and then down again—crossing the misted crests of the Jura?—followed by an interminable flat stretch, and then more uphill twisting.

If there was conversation among the passengers, Bolan couldn't hear it. The even beat of the engine and the discreet boom of the exhaust pipe beneath the trunk were having a soporific effect. If it wasn't for the fact that his headache grew worse with every undulation in the road surface, he might have slept.

Two hours and fifteen minutes passed before the car bumped along a rough track and finally halted. The engine was cut. Doors opened. The body rocked as people got out. Bolan heard voices fading away to his right.

He waited ten minutes before he was convinced that the chauffeur had also left and he dared spring back the catch of the trunk lid. Apart from a slight sighing of wind, the silence was total. He was certain the Mercedes was parked in some isolated place and was prepared to take a chance that it was a place where nobody would have an overview of the car.

The mechanism of the catch was simple all right, but the spring was strong; he was unable to exert enough strength with his fingers and finally had to snap back the greased metal with the barrel of the Beretta. The lock flipped open, and the lid began to rise.

Rain drifted into the trunk. Screwing up his eyes against the unfamiliar light, he saw a widening rectangle of gray sky fringed by the leaves of a chestnut tree.

Bolan inhaled grateful lungfuls of fresh, damp air and climbed out.

He was in an abandoned farmyard knee-high with weeds. He saw a fire-scorched building with rafters showing through a hole in the sagging roof, a wall topped by a grassy bank, the rusted wreck of a truck.

Warily he circled the building. There was nobody in sight. The surrounding countryside was masked by trees.

It was ten minutes before he found the opening beneath the fig tree.

Before he could decide whether to explore the dark passage revealed beyond, he heard the distant mutter of a motorcycle engine. The sound grew louder, the beat more rapid and the exhaust note more laboring as the rider shifted down. He had already concluded that the farm was on high ground. This proved it; the bike was climbing a steep hill.

When it became clear that the machine was approaching the farm along the grass-grown track, he ducked beneath the wreck and flattened himself under the differential casing, the Beretta ready to fire.

He saw the bike's wheels slowing through the weeds. The motor wheezed into silence. The machine was leaned against the wall ten yards away. He heard two voices, a man and a girl.

"Am I glad that's bloody over!" the girl said. "I feel like I was kicked from head to heels by a horse."

"I told you it would be a long ride. Better than risking a police check on public transport, though," the man replied.

"I still wonder what happened to Dirk after he fell."

"He fucking bought it. You know that. You read the paper."

"Yeah, but it could be some kind of cop trick. To make us, you know, think that—"

"Bullshit. The stupid bastard lost control and got himself wasted by that cop wagon."

Drops of moisture pattered on the rusty cab as the branches of the fig tree were thrust aside. Bolan heard the couple's footsteps recede down the passageway. He heard the code knock: two long, two short, a final long.

Slow, slow, quick-quick, slow.

The sound of a door opening, closing. Silence returned to the deserted yard, broken only by the tick of cooling metal and the hiss of raindrops spitting on the hot cylinders of the bike.

Bolan crawled out into the open. He parted wet leaves and cat-footed down the dank passage.

Counting the footsteps, he knew the couple hadn't gone far. With the faint illumination from the exhausted batteries of the pencil flashlight, he located the ancient steel door.

He waited, listening.

On the far side of the door, silence. In the corridor, the stealthy drip of moisture, a distant moan of wind.

Bolan lifted his left hand, hesitated and then repeated the code knock.

17

Dash . . . dash . . . dot-dot . . . dash. The rhythm of the code knock was somehow as familiar as the morse signal for the letter *V*—and the opening phrase of the Beethoven symphony the Allies had used as a *V*-for-Victory signature to announce their clandestine radio transmissions during World War II.

Mack Bolan repeated it.

And a third time, with a little more force.

The door remained closed.

Could he have been mistaken? Had the knocking he heard originated someplace else? No, a door had opened, must have opened, or the two bikers would still be there.

Was there a second door?

Bolan explored the farther depths of the curving tunnel, playing the weak beam of his flashlight over roof, walls, floor.

The roof was arched brickwork, and the walls were brick, too. Moss, lichens and subterranean plant growths with pallid stems like the fingers of drowned men patched the crumbling surface. Here and there along the flagstoned floor puddles reflected the light where moisture had seeped through the vaulting above.

No more doors.

After forty feet the passageway turned again, and Bolan was faced with a mass of rubble that blocked it completely.

The slant of bricks, earth and fragments of masonry had collapsed a long time ago: it was covered with spiderwebs. The dead gray veils heaved slightly in the disturbed air as he advanced. He saw bat droppings on the edge of a pool of stagnant water filmed with green slime. The air was dank, earthy, tainted with the staleness of vegetable decay. Clearly nobody had come this way in a long time.

Bolan returned to the door.

Rust, grime and rivulets of dried mud that had trickled down from a fissure in the roof caked the surface. But the faint illumination from the flashlight showed telltale brightness at the extreme edges, where the steel sheet fitted against the door frame. The door was in constant use all right.

He paused, thinking. Four or five men had driven for more than two hours to get to the deserted farm. He hadn't actually heard them knock, but their voices had faded in this direction . . . sure, and where the hell else could they be?

A little later, the bikers had shown up and been admitted.

According to the girl, they, too, had come a long way.

No prizes, then, for figuring out that some kind of meet, and an important one at that, was going down.

So there could be others on the way.

The terrorists? Max Nasruddin, the Marksman, members of the team he hadn't heard of yet? Could be.

The most vital point: were the two bikers last to arrive or were there others on the way?

Bolan hadn't seen any other cars, nor any other bikes. He took a chance on the hunch that the men in the Mercedes had been early arrivals, that more were expected to complete the picture.

Maybe his own knock had remained unanswered because whoever was on the door had to escort people past some second security check inside.

He switched off the light, eased the Beretta out into the open and gave the code knock for the fourth time.

Dash, dash, dot-dot, dash. *Slow, slow, quick-quick, slow.* Something flashed in his brain. It reminded him— He lost it.

The door opened immediately, revealing, thanks to the light from an oil lamp, a stone-walled cellar and a stocky man built like the chauffeur. He wore a jersey and jeans and held a Browning-style automatic in his hand.

Bolan was standing back, but the illumination was strong enough to reveal his build and height.

The bullet-headed doorman's mouth dropped open. "You! But who the—?"

Bolan struck.

The barrel of the Beretta streaked downward, cracking against the wrist of the hardman's gun arm.

He yelled, dropping the automatic.

Bolan hurled himself into the cellar, adjusting stride and balance as he moved, pivoting just right so that his left fist, with the wrist locked steady, slammed with all his weight behind it against the tight-fitting jersey between the two descending curves of the guy's rib cage.

Breath whooshed from the big man's lungs.

On the backswing from that punishing blow to the solar plexus, Bolan's own gun arm swept up with the Beretta's barrel to split open the doorman's left cheek.

Half stunned by the attack, winded and blind with pain, the hardman crashed back onto a rickety table that disintegrated with his weight.

He was groggy, but he was tough. As Bolan leaned in to hook steely fingers under the belt around the doorman's waist, he thrashed his legs sideways and kicked the Executioner's feet from under him.

Bolan sprawled back against the wall. The doorman struggled free of the splintered table and leaped . . . not for Bolan, but for the fallen automatic. Bolan stamped on the guy's damaged wrist one-tenth of a second before his outstretched fingers reached the butt.

The guy swore, yellow teeth bared, the teak face creased into an expression mingling agony, frustration and rage. Bolan kicked the pistol away as the guy sprang back, facing him in a half crouch.

With a grunt of effort, the hardman launched himself again, his unhurt fist cocked and ready for a murderous blow.

In the moment that the man's arm drew back, Bolan dropped to a squatting position, fingertips brushing the damp floor.

With no target for the unleashed haymaker, the guy overbalanced, pitched forward and spilled over the Executioner's bowed shoulders.

Bolan rocketed up as he hit, and the doorman made a half turn in the air to land flat on his back.

He stayed there: he had rapped his skull against an iron wheel that operated bolts on the inner side of the half-open door and knocked himself cold.

Bolan rolled him onto his face, whipped the belt from the waistband of his pants and lashed his hands behind his back. There was nothing else he could use in the cellar. He saw only splintered wood, dead leaves, an ancient chair. He ripped away the man's jersey, tore it into strips, bound his ankles and wadded another length into a makeshift gag, which he jammed into his open mouth and tied in place.

It wouldn't keep the guy hog-tied for ever, but he wasn't going to open his eyes for a while anyway.

Bolan located the trapdoor. He closed the outer door, spun the wheel, then brushed leaves aside to expose the iron ring. He pulled the trapdoor open and climbed warily down the ladder into the lit passageway, lowering the hatch after him.

Now came the tough part. The entrance door, for example, could well be wired to relay the code knocks to a control room below, to flash a warning light, to ring a bell. Because it was evident from the condition of the cellar that nobody stood guard there all the time.

If Bolan's hunch was right and there were more people expected, the fact that their knocks remained unanswered would tip off whoever was inside that the doorman was out of action.

By that time, Bolan would have to be out of sight.

But that wouldn't be possible until he made the second steel door, one hundred yards along the passage. It stood ajar. Evidently the doorman had expected to return with someone right away.

So there *were* more arrivals scheduled.

Bolan peered around the door into the white-tiled entrance lobby, dazzled temporarily by the fluorescent lights.

Blinking, he saw the back of a blond girl in a white jacket seated near a telephone switchboard behind the desk. As he watched, a red light winked on the board, and she plugged in a headset. He couldn't hear what she said, but a moment later she hooked up the set, rose to her feet and walked to an open-cage elevator at the far end of the lobby. The cage whined down out of sight.

There were two doorways, one on either side of the shaft. Bolan padded across the tiles and opened each in turn.

The first led to a storeroom stacked with crated electronic equipment; the other opened onto another passageway. He slid through and closed it after him.

Back to brickwork and an odor of mildew and molds.

In the roof, low-power lamps glowed again every few yards, but it was obvious that this part of the complex was much older than the shining, aseptic lobby—in line, he guessed, with the farmyard entrance, the first door and the cellar.

He passed an alcove arched into the wall that held an oak desk grainy with age, a wheel-back chair with a split seat and a wooden filing cabinet.

The desk was bare, its drawers empty. He tried the cabinet. The top drawer jammed; he had a hell of a job prying the dried wood open a couple of inches. There was nothing inside. From the easy way the cabinet rocked when he leaned against it, he figured the others could also be empty.

Behind the desk, a chart yellowed with age was tacked to the alcove wall.

He moved in. The nearest tunnel light was some distance away, and the recess was in shadow. He had to use the last of the flashlight power to make out the faded lettering at the top of the chart.

It was headed: "Saales No.4—GHQ 52nd Bn. VIII Div. Art."

Beneath this he saw what looked like an exploded diagram of a mining site, webbed with galleries, shafts, ladders and stylized representations of machinery.

At random, Bolan traced out some of the lines that linked parts of the diagram to captions set around the perimeter of the chart.

He read: "Overhead monorail to shell armory. Eighteen-ton counterweight for ammunition lift. Stairway to MG turret 16. Generator housing. Decontamination chamber for officers. Block H: access to 88 mm observation tower."

He drew a deep breath. You didn't have to be an Einstein to relate the aged chart to the underground complex he was in.

With his fighter's knowledge of modern warfare and its history, he had suspected it from the moment he'd seen the opening in the grassy bank above the farmyard. If he was right, it could have been the German or French side of the Rhine. Now the old chart clinched it—the wording was in French.

He had penetrated a surviving underground fortress that had once formed part of the Maginot Line!

It figured, of course; it made good sense.

What better place for a terrorists' rendezvous, for a guerrilla training camp, perhaps? Geographically it was practical, too. A little over two hours' drive from Neuchâtel, it was probably—he recalled World War II campaign maps—in the Vosges, somewhat south of Strasbourg, overlooking the Alsace plain. Easily accessible from Paris, from the western part of Germany, from Luxembourg and the Low Countries. Perfect.

Bolan had never heard of Saales, but it was clear from the chart that this had been a key artillery observation post in the French defense system. What he needed now was a contemporary chart detailing the changes and modernization. It would be a hell of a help for instance, he thought wryly, if he could happen on a piece of paper that would tell him where he was in relation to the rest of the restored fort.

Because even if the old wall chart had been small enough to take with him, it wouldn't have been that much help. It showed the original workings of the place in cross section all right, but there was no floor plan of each separate level, and that was what he needed. Whatever alterations they had made, the general layout had to remain the same; the heavy construction equipment necessary for any modification of that would have drawn too much attention to the site.

It seemed that there were four levels. The topmost, accessible only from the farther reaches of the fortress, had housed the artillery and automatic weapons designed to cover through concrete casemates the terrain that fell away toward the Rhine.

Below that was the level he was on.

Lower still, two more sets of galleries ran off on either side of a central shaft. Fashioned at first to accommodate the ammunition lift that had linked magazine and firing points, this was now, Bolan reckoned, the site of the open-cage elevator he had seen.

The wall chart showed stairs and companionways running between the various levels, but whether these were still in existence he would have to find out.

Memorizing as much of the general layout as he could, he moved on along the corridor. Turning sharply right, the tunnel passed three openings in the outer wall and then stopped abruptly. The entire width had been bricked up.

Bolan surveyed the openings. Shaped like an arched window, each ran from waist height to the tunnel roof.

The arches were carved from solid rock, piercing a wall more than two feet thick. But these "windows" carried no glass. A faint light filtered through from the far side, accompanied by a hint of ozone and a distant, barely heard thrumming that could have been a generator.

Heaving himself across the sill of the first arch, he peered cautiously through . . . and down.

He was in an opening—one of six; three more were visible on the far side—up near the roof of a lofty cavern. The chamber, which rose clear through two, if not three levels, must once have been the magazine. But the shelves and stacks and ledges crammed in 1940 with shells, grenades, rockets and antitank ammunition now held a bewildering array of high-tech electronics.

Fronting the racked data banks and computer terminals, three men, white-jacketed, sat in front of VDT screens manipulating keyboards in the greenish light flickering from the unscrolling, constantly changing texts.

Beyond, red and blue pilot lights winked underneath a row of video monitors, each displaying a different image. Bolan hazarded a guess that these were relayed from scanners placed at strategic positions all over the redoubt. At this distance, he was unable to make out details or recognize characters, but one of the screens showed a number of people grouped around a desk in what looked like a lecture theater.

Bolan wished he was among them.

For if he was to check out the fortress in a meaningful way, find out how it was used and why, he must somehow first get to one of the lower levels. The passage he was in was a dead end, and apart from the storeroom and the entrance lobby there was nothing else on this one.

Except the elevator.

Sure, the elevator. But it would be better if there was some other way of getting down, since he had no idea how many people staffed the fort, where the elevator ended up, or whether it was within range of a scanner.

Shoving his head and shoulders farther into the opening, he glanced once more at the technicians below. Two were intent on their screens and keys; the third was speaking to the blonde from the reception lobby.

He could hear the voices, but echoes under the cavern roof blurred the words into an unintelligible mumble. No chance of guessing from the conversation how long she was likely to linger before she returned to that damned elevator.

He poked his head far enough out to recon the wall between and beneath the arches. Smooth rock. No footholds, no pipes, no shelves within leaping distance, no fire stairs.

No way.

No, if he had to lie low in this blocked passage until everyone was gone, it would have to be the elevator. He moved quietly back toward the door leading into the lobby.

He opened the door a crack.

One of the lights on the switchboard was flashing. There was nobody behind the desk.

Bolan opened the door and moved softly into the lobby.

There was a metallic clunk behind him. He whirled to see the empty elevator cage sinking from sight.

The blonde had taken it down. She hadn't returned yet—most likely she was calling it right now, to bring her back.

So if she had to call it, if it had been at this level, someone else must have brought it up after she had gone down. Someone leaving the fortress.

Someone who, if they hadn't made the discovery already, would at any moment stumble on the trussed-up body of the unconscious doorman.

Unless of course the elevator was one of those that returned automatically to the point of departure each time the grille clanged shut after use.

Bolan wasn't prepared to take the chance.

If they started a search for the doorman's attacker, he would have to hide. But where? There wasn't too much choice. The dead-end passage was too obvious; there were no possibilities in the alcove halfway along. The bright, bare lobby offered no suggestions. It was too late to use the elevator.

It had to be the storeroom on the far side of the shaft.

He opened the door and went in there.

He switched on a light. That chance had to be taken if he was to find a hiding spot before the hounds were unleashed. He would switch off as soon as he heard the baying.

If there was a hole to be found.

The stacked crates of electronic merchandise filled most of the available space. Maneuvering his tall frame along the narrow lanes between each stack, the Executioner found that most of them were too heavy for him to shift unaided. The only place that looked halfway possible was in back, opposite the door. There, a couple of dozen wooden cases of computer hardware were ranged as high as his head along the wall.

But there was a stone ledge eighteen inches high running along the foot of the wall. Between the wall and the upper part of the stack there was therefore a gap.

Wide enough for an agile guy to squirm in there?

Affirmative.

Not that this was a sure-fire hole where a fugitive could rest easy and escape the most rigorous search: the swiftest glance, the mere flick of a flashlight beam would mean discovery. And the search would be rigorous: apart from the dead-end passage, the storeroom was the only place on this level an intruder could be.

Bolan bit his lip. Would they know for sure that he hadn't taken the elevator and pressed the Down button? Was there an Up? If the answer in both cases was negative, they'd tear the place apart. So?

Maybe it would be better if he simply stood behind the door and came out with guns blazing when they passed by.

Backing awkwardly out of the narrow space, he realized with a start of surprise that he had moved one of the cases.

It was big, tall enough to take a four-drawer steel filing cabinet and a little wider. And it was empty, the opened side toward the back wall. Above it, a two-by-four carton was heavy, packed full of insulated coaxial cable, according to the stenciled lettering along one side.

Bolan tried the empty crate and found that he could wedge himself in there. And the interior...yeah, inside the box were ranged the wooden slats that had originally been nailed over the opening.

He returned to the door, cut the light and felt his way back to the ledge. Inside the empty crate, he crouched and propped up half a dozen of the slats to block the opening, holding them in place with his two forearms. A searcher leaning his head against the wall to squint along the space above the ledge would now see no more than the backs of a row of cases, all of them apparently nailed up with the lids in place.

With luck.

Less than a minute later he heard the voices.

Angry, querulous, sometimes shrill, all talking at once, they created a blast of sound that conveyed no meaning to a man hidden behind so many baffles of wood and plastic and wire.

The door of the storeroom burst open.

Now he could hear words.

"Bastard has to be someplace around here. I don't see where else—"

"Shut your mouth and look! Didn't Willi give you an idea who he was, what he looked like?"

"Willi's still out. He walked into a heavy one."

"Let's take a look at the storeroom. He's got to be..."

"...lousing up an important meet this way. The more time we waste up here..."

Light streamed between the slats of wood. Bolan held his breath. He heard footsteps, panting, the scrape of wood. "Would one of you mothers help me shift this damned crate?"

The light brightened, faded again. A flashlight beam explored the space above the shelf. "Not a sign. I can't think what—"

"Hey!" Someone shouted from the lobby. "Willi came round, and he says it was Bolan who jumped him!"

"What the hell . . . ?"

"How could he have found—?"

"Would you guys just cool it?" The deep voice, unruffled as ever, was surely Max Nasruddin's. "Listen, I'm telling you it doesn't matter. Surely you're not so dumb you can't see that? It's not important. Leave him be. If he's in, he won't get out."

"Yeah, but—"

"Forget it. We have more important things to talk about right now. Willi has to go back to his job. When we leave, Gerhard and Rizzo can remain here in the lobby. If he wants out, he has to come this way, and they can block him. If not...what the hell. So he stays and the medics fix him later. Don't you see, it don't matter a goddamn whichever way."

A click and the darkness was back. The door closed. Bolan heard the voices fade, the jarring of the elevator gates, the descending whine of the car.

So they were leaving a pair of hardmen when the others completed their business and split. Okay, it seemed he had zero chances of finding out what this business was while they were still inside the fortress. But two guys he knew for sure would be outside the door in the lobby, two guys who already believed the storeroom was clean—hell, the odds weren't too long there. He would wait until Max and the others left, and then he would try his luck.

It was a long wait.

The luminous dial on his watch told him it was eight minutes past five when the elevator cage finally groaned upward with its cargo of...what? Terrorists? Murderers? Screwball lab researchers?

They were jabbering away in the lobby. Among the voices he could identify those of the guy who had brought the news of Willi, the biker girl, a guttural German accent he took to be Klaus, the chauffeur, and Nasruddin's cool, insolent drawl.

The elevator whined down and returned with a second shipment. The volume of talk on the far side of the door increased. Bolan could pick no more than an occasional word from the babel.

Somebody wanted to know how long they had to wait until "the Spanish thing" took off. A deep voice announced that the RNA molecules in the brain manufactured special proteins that were related to the function of memory. The girl asked if someone could give her a ride into Strasbourg. Nasruddin was quoting dates.

Finally they did leave...in twos and threes, allowing a couple of minutes between each group. They didn't want to make too much of a road show as they left the abandoned farm and picked up their transport wherever they had hidden it, the Executioner imagined.

At last it was quiet.

Bolan tried to imagine the two hardmen he knew were on the other side of the door. They didn't talk. He heard a scrape of shoe leather, the flare of a match.

From time to time one of them whistled some out-of-key tune. He tried to guess their positions in the bright-tiled, well-lit lobby, to visualize the guns they would hold.

He squirmed out of the crate and stood upright. His knees cracked like pistol shots in the silence, and Bolan froze. He smiled wryly to himself when he realized that no one else had heard. He drew a deep breath, easing open the latch on the door.

With a gun in each hand, he flung the door wide and erupted into the lobby.

A warrior fighting the forces of evil, Mack Bolan could feel no pity. In a war you didn't ask questions first and then shoot if the answers didn't please you. Whether or not these were the hands that planted the explosives, fingers that set the timer or squeezed the trigger, the two men were examples of collective guilt, morally responsible for hundreds, maybe thousands of innocent deaths.

He was squeezing two triggers himself as he hurled himself across the lobby toward the entrance door.

There was a man in a windbreaker behind the desk. He was sitting with a mini-Uzi laid across his knees. The other guy was older, thickset, standing by the door to the dead-end passage—a pockmarked, rock-hard face above a cradled H&K MP-5 submachine gun.

Total surprise, violent movement from an unexpected direction—the soldier relied on these for the tenth of a second advantage that he needed. His faith wasn't misplaced.

With Big Thunder in his right hand, the Beretta in his left, he roared out firing blind for the second time on this mission, a tornado of flaming death.

One arc of hellspray found a target right away: Big Thunder's 240-grain boattail flesh-shredders homed in on the guy at the desk before he could grab his Uzi. The Beretta's lethal hail fell on stonier ground: the shots went wide of the gorilla flattened against the passageway door. He lifted the gun while splinters of tile gouged from the wall by the 9 mm slugs were still in the air and triggered a couple of shots at the Executioner.

But Bolan was already diving into a shoulder roll: the H&K deathstream streaked over his head while he was on the floor. He came up out of it by the entrance door before the thunderous echoes of that first volley had died away in the low-ceilinged room. The hardman thumbed the SMG onto full-auto and swung the barrel, but his reaction time was too slow.

From his half crouch by the door, Bolan unleashed a three-round burst from the Beretta that cored the gorilla's chest in the instant that he fired. It was followed by a single pulverizer from the AutoMag that found no target. For the 93-R's 9 mm rounds had punched the guy hard enough to burst open the passage door and send him sliding on his back on the floor several feet beyond.

Three small jets of dark crimson fountained momentarily from his chest and then subsided as his heart stopped beating.

Bolan swung around to the deskman.

He was still breathing, but only just. One of the AutoMag's slugs had torn away the top of his left arm, another had creased him above the ear and a third had clearly punctured a lung. He was slumped in the chair that had tipped back against a wall cracked and starred by the near misses. Most of his blood was in his lap or puddled on the floor beneath, but an obscene pink froth swelled and deflated over the hole in his chest.

Glassy eyes swung upward as Bolan stood over the desk. He saw through the gory stains marking one side of the gunman's face that it was the biker kid who had ridden in with the girl. If he'd been left as end-stop, that explained why the girl was looking for a ride.

There was a gargling sound from the bloodied face. The guy was trying to speak. Bolan bent toward him.

The voice was a whispered croak, with pauses to allow blood bubbling in the windpipe to subside. But the words when they came were clear enough at first. "You didn't have to . . . you shouldn't . . . we only had or . . . orders to hold you. We weren't to . . . take you out. Shit, all we had . . . do . . . only to keep . . . keep . . ." The voice died away into a mumble.

"Keep what?" Bolan said. "Orders to keep what?"

"Keep . . . you . . . for next—" the words were now as toneless as the wind rustling over dead leaves "—for the next . . . session . . ."

"What session?" Bolan said urgently.

The wounded man's mouth was gaping. A thread of red spittle swayed from his lower lip. He gave a deep groan, struggling to push his head away from the wall. Dry lips twisted into a contorted grimace, and a curious spasmodic choking noise shuddered the top half of his body. He was laughing.

The eyes swiveled to fix on the Executioner. Briefly a puzzled expression flitted across the guy's face.

"As if . . . you . . . didn't . . . know!" he gasped.

"Know what?" Bolan cried. "What do you mean?"

But the man choked again on the next word, gagging as blood gurgled from his mouth. He stiffened suddenly, and then went totally limp, his head lolling sideways as he slid slackly from the chair to the floor.

Bolan sighed, then straightened. He thumbed shut the eyes of both dead men and went to the elevator. He pressed the lowest button. The grille slammed shut; the cage sank down into darkness.

18

Before he attempted any detailed investigation, the Executioner decided to make a swift recon of the entire underground complex. That way, in an emergency, during any future visit, he would have the layout of each level, together with its potential of attack and retreat, fixed firmly in his mind.

Because he knew he would be coming back. And when he did there was going to be trouble—most of it, he hoped, for others.

The elevator deposited him in the gymnasium.

He noted the variety of the equipment, walked through to an anteroom and saw that an escalator led down from there to a level that was still lower—an excavation, he realized, that must recently have been quarried from the rock because there was no indication of anything that far down on the old chart he had seen.

This lowest level was the firing range. Bolan whistled when he saw the scope of the armament stacked there. Racked at the back of the stand were Winchester repeaters, Mannlicher Express hunting rifles, specialized snipers' guns and every modern infantry weapon from an M-16 to a Parker-Hale M-82, from a Heckler & Koch caseless assault rifle to a Czech-made Makarov.

Uzi and Ingram SMGs jostled for pride of place on a long counter with Walther MPKs and Bergmann, Schmeisser and Skorpion machine pistols.

But it was the handgun collection that really took Bolan's breath away. There was everything from an old .38 Police Special to the latest VZ-82 fabricated by Omnipol in Prague. He saw Pythons and PPKs, Berettas and Brownings, Combat Magnums and Cobras. There was more than one version of the Parabellum automatic, incorrectly known as a Luger, a Webley service revolver and even an old, angular, long-barreled Mauser Military from World War I.

Labeled trays of ammunition gleamed behind flaps of Plexiglas; three or four dozen manuals and instruction booklets were ranged along a shelf above the SMG counter.

At one end of the stand, a glass door led to a small armorer's workshop where a Russian-made Kalashnikov had been dismantled and laid out for cleaning. On the same bench, Bolan recognized a number of one-off, one-shot weapons that didn't look like guns at all. They were in the form of fountain pens, flashlights, cigarette lighters, women's vanity cases and other domestic gadgets.

What was screwy, too—it was clear from notices and warnings pinned up here and there—was that this was no secret arms dump, no cache destined to equip elitist future terror groups. The weapons here were supernumerary—for teaching, familiarization and practice only!

The guys running the show, Bolan reflected as he walked to the butts, sure as hell were in the money.

He whistled again when he saw the stack of photo faces waiting to be fixed to the pop-up target figures on the snap-shot mechanism. There were more than thirty of them, and the names read like a directory of Europe's most eminent, most powerful and most talked-about headliners. They were certainly training a mean assassination squad here.

He took the moving stairway back to the gymnasium and explored the galleries on the other side of the elevator shaft. First, the lofty computer cavern, then a projection studio equipped for film and video viewing. In back of this small room, a spiral stairway rose to a comfortably furnished office suite.

Beyond the wide desk, the liquor cabinet and the filing bank, doors opened onto the iron catwalk that ran along one wall above the computer complex. The left-hand end of the railed gallery abutted on the rock wall of the cave; on the right there was an arch.

Bolan went through and found himself in a passageway that took him past the elevator shaft to a biochemical laboratory he judged to be above the gymnasium. Washrooms, kitchens and a refectory separated this from an electronics workshop. Research here seemed to be concerned with the perfecting of middle-range microbugs. An enlarged diagram of a two-headed Continental 0011 hung on one wall, several types of FM handset receivers lay on the bench, and he saw at least a dozen miniaturized transmitters in transparent plastic boxes.

At the far end of the workshop an arch led to a cement-walled hallway. This was roughly circular in shape. Through a second archway immediately opposite, Bolan saw the humped shapes of a generator and turbine casings. Six doorways opened off the remainder of the hallway.

One of these gave access to the lecture theater, another revealed a stairway leading down to the gymnasium anteroom, a third—blocked by a locked steel grille—wound upward into the dark. He imagined this must lead to the old casemates and the site where the armored observation tower had once been, the highest level inside the fort.

The three remaining doorways were bricked up. Bolan figured they closed off passages running out to minor firing points designed for snipers and machine gunners.

Okay, so there were two ways, apart from the elevator, of switching from one to the other of the two main levels—the stairway linking hallway and gymnasium; the spiral between the office suite and the viewing room. Had he missed out on any others? He decided to make a second lap and headed for the stairs.

Crossing the gymnasium, he was aware that pangs of hunger were gnawing at his belly. He'd eaten and drunk nothing since his morning coffee in Neuchâtel. Thirst was more acute than hunger: the air-conditioned atmosphere of the redoubt had made his throat dry. Absently he walked across to a row of filing cabinets, opened the door of a steel cupboard at one end of the bank and took a bottle of mineral water from the miniature refrigerator inside. He drank.

It wasn't until he was going through a pile of ledgers, medical treatment charts and notebooks covered with cryptic annotations that he found in the office desk that he paused to wonder how it was that he had known where to go for his drink. He shrugged. Another hunch—he was used to them paying off now.

The charts listed treatment given to a score of "patients," many of them expressed in chemical formulae, some quoting the kind of drugs ordered by the researchers in the Neuchâtel lab. Amounts were expressed in micrograms and milliliters, together with dates and handwritten comments in the Results column on the right of each sheet. The comments were in a psychiatrist's shorthand that Bolan found hard to understand: "Resp var c moon... Percep chg antag + Sod Succ i v... Regress x 3... Synesth sens modal fus."

The patients this time were identified by first names—Rizzo, Gerhard, Julie, Jean-Paul—and certain cross-references Bolan was able to make from memory showed that these were in fact the same people listed under the MAG heading in the Friedekinde clinic. MAG for Maginot.

Patient was a euphemism: Bolan was reading a documented account of drug medication deliberately fed to known killers. The inclusion of Gerhard and Rizzo, the two guys he had wasted in the lobby, proved that.

Baraka's chart was the longest of all, running to three sheets with dates stretching back more than six months. Bolan jotted down some of the formulae, drug names and abbreviations, since the treatment for the star assassin seemed more variable, more delicate and a hell of a lot more complicated than the others. Brognola would know someone who could deduce the kind of behavior such chemical indoctrination might produce. Maybe they could even get a lead on the big deal planned for this number one killer.

For the moment, however, Bolan couldn't turn up any indications other than the medical records.

He did find listed cross-references for several of the named terrorists, and also for the Marksman and an individual referred to simply as "the Corsican," neither of whom appeared to have received any medication, for their names weren't on the charts. Most of these references were followed either by "Morgue" or "VCR," sometimes by both.

Hazarding a guess that the former implied newspaper clippings rather than the end product of the killers' work, Bolan searched the cabinets and found one drawer filled with files relating to every terrorist outrage, hijack, holdup and bombing during the past three years. The clippings had come from most European dailies and weeklies and the most influential papers stateside.

Where the new organization had been involved, as in the English Channel car ferry disaster, the sabotage at Rome airport and the bombed rue de Rivoli store, neat names were printed on the outside of the folder: Cobbold, Graziano, Marksman, Gerhard.

Some of the folders were also tagged "VCR."

Bolan went down to the viewing room.

In the projectionist's booth behind the six rows of padded club seats, he found a library of videocassettes and half a dozen cans of film. The cassettes were all noncommercial products, each marked on the spine with a name.

The Executioner felt the hair on his nape rise, and a chill raced through him as he read those names.

Alonzo, Codorneau, Jaecklin, Riordan, Van Leeuward . . .

All prominent men.

All recently murdered.

Did this mean that the savages organizing the assassinations currently shaking Europe were callous enough to record the evidence on tape?

It did.

Bolan switched on the giant television screen and slotted in a cassette.

The screen flickered, chased lines up, down, relapsed into color and then steadied on a tennis court surrounded by crowded tiers of seats fronting a palm-fringed backdrop of tower blocks and condos. Behind the modernistic steel and glass buildings, limestone cliffs stood against a hard blue sky.

Monte Carlo?

Check. With mounting horror, the Executioner watched the assassination of two prime ministers at the end of their match.

He changed the cassette.

The tapes were expertly edited. Some of them incorporated shots from two different cameras. One— the murder of the French antiterrorist chief, Codorneau—had been shot from a boat.

The backs of Bolan's hands were tingling. Trying to control his fury as the catalog of crimes ran on through tape after bloody tape, he found he was drumming nervously with his fingers on the arm of the seat.

On the screen two bikers emptied their SMGs through the windows of a stalled Mercedes on a German street.

Bolan clenched and unclenched his hands, forcing himself to concentrate on Nasruddin and the elusive, mysterious Baraka, who was being groomed in this very bunker for God knows what atrocity. Baraka, whose secret he was resolved at all costs to unveil, whose satanic plans he had sworn to thwart.

Every hint, every rumor, every indication that could suggest a lead to the monster was a step in the right direction. And there were cassettes here, he had seen, labeled "B—Training."

If *B* did stand for Baraka, he might at least—at last—see what the bastard looked like. He returned to the projection room, selected a cassette at random and slotted it in.

The lighting wasn't brilliant, but he could see that the camera had been mounted high in a corner of the fortress's gymnasium. Perhaps they recorded from the video scanners he had noticed in every part of the redoubt.

The two doctors Bolan had seen at the Friedekinde clinic were in semicloseup. "Let's see the result of the Doberman lesson," the older man said.

A huge, bald gorilla with tombstone teeth walked into shot. The younger doctor, the one with wraparound shades—Dr. Paul Hansen, Bolan remembered—nodded and turned toward the thug. "All right, Mazarin," he said. "Take him."

The camera panned as the giant leaped suddenly at a tall muscular man who had appeared in the frame, kicking his feet from under him and catching him as he fell to hurl him bodily down on the wrestling mat.

The Executioner sat forward on the edge of his seat, craning to see the man whose back was still to the camera.

Mazarin had jumped the terrorist-in-training, groping for nerve centers he could use to immobilize him.

Baraka threw him off with a double heel-of-the-hand attack that slammed against Mazarin's temples, extricating himself and springing upright while the giant still sprawled. For the first time he faced the camera.

Bolan suppressed a shout.

He sat rooted to the seat, frozen with horror.

The other tapes had made his flesh creep, but this was totally bizarre.

Something had made him vaguely uneasy, something about the terrorist's carriage, his stance, the moment the camera picked him up. Now the unease crystallized into a spine-chilling certainty, for there could be no mistaking those ice-blue eyes, the face with its resolute mouth and determined chin. He saw it in the mirror each time he shaved.

The image of the terrorist on the screen was the image of himself.

He was Baraka.

19

Mack Bolan was thunderstruck. He found himself unable to accept what his eyes told him must be true.

His first reaction was total disbelief.

The man on the screen was a look-alike, a ringer, someone already schooled and trained—but trained to impersonate and discredit the Executioner. It was a plot to blacken his name and destroy his reputation as a fighter for justice.

It had happened before. The KGB had meticulously groomed and trained a Bolan look-alike who had publicly murdered a popular European labor leader while the Executioner himself was in the country. That was one of the reasons he was still on the hit list of so many of the world's intelligence services.

Except that this time there was no ringer involved.

The blank-eyed unarmed combat expert throwing Mazarin around on the screen *was* the real Mack Bolan. A dozen personal quirks and movements and reflexes underlined the truth. And as he dazedly ran the rest of the tapes, Bolan was forced to admit to himself that by some evil alchemy he was, *unknown to himself*, being programmed to act as a terrorist.

The thought made his blood run cold.

It was the most recent cassette that was the clincher. The tall sharpshooter gunning down images of the world's most prominent statesmen and diplomats in the shooting gallery wore on his right hand the cuts Bolan had suffered from flying glass during his flight from Nasruddin and the police in Paris.

He looked at his own hand. The scabbed cuts were still there, and they checked.

The dates made perfect sense, too. The first cassette, recording the fight with Mazarin and the shooting duel with the Marksman, was dated the twelfth and thirteenth of the month. These were the two "lost" days between Bolan's visit to Boardman in Algiers and his awakening in the Paris hotel.

On the last tape, where he was firing at the pop-up targets with famous faces, a newspaper was visible on the counter of the gallery, and the front page bannered the Van Leeuward killing. The date of this "treatment" coincided with the two missing days following his capture at the clinic. Hell, he must have been here in this same damned fortress, *yesterday*!

No wonder he'd known subconsciously where to go when he'd needed a drink; no wonder Willi the doorman, Mazarin at the clinic and Friedekinde himself had in effect said "*You* again!" each time he showed. No wonder Nasruddin had drawled, "Ah, leave him be. The medics can fix him."

The way it seemed they had somehow fixed him before. And fixed him good.

But how? His discovery answered a few puzzling queries but raised a host of issues that were far more serious.

Such as, what kind of devilish drug treatment could turn a man's mind around so that he became temporarily the opposite of his natural self, could turn a freedom fighter overnight into a terrorist assassin?

And leave him, two days later, back in his normal guise, with no recollection at all of the terror phase?

Such as, how the hell had they managed to lay their hands on him, again without his knowledge, in order to force that treatment on him?

Okay, the last two sessions had been after he'd been blackjacked—but there were other one- or two-day gaps of which he had no memory at all. How had they gotten to him?

What kind of chemical could erase from a man's memory the fact that he had been doped?

If they could do those things and get away with it time after time, it didn't matter too much whether Bolan was wise to the plan or not: they could still use the same methods to take him next time.

He'd figured they must be damned sure of themselves to leave him loose in the fortress, even if there were gunners to prevent him splitting, with all the evidence of their devilry lying around. Now he saw what Nasruddin meant—if they could take him any time they wanted, and if Bolan was unable in any way to relate mentally to Baraka, it didn't matter whether he knew or not. There was nothing he could do about it: the two would remain separate entities, with Bolan ignorant of Baraka's deadly aims.

The Executioner was never a man given to fear.

He was frightened now.

He went back to the office and took out the Baraka medical charts again. If Hal Brognola's shrink was to have any chance of combating the treatment—and if Bolan was to act successfully against its results—the guy must have *all* the details, right down to the last microgram, not just a few liftouts at random to give the flavor of it.

There was no photocopier in the place. Bolan found some blank paper and laboriously transcribed the whole works—formulae, drug names, dates, amounts, length of each session and marginal comments. It took him over an hour.

While he was working with his hands and eyes, his mind was free to roam, racing over a recap on the past few days, evaluating the action he did remember.

If his discovery posed agonizing problems, at least one question was answered by it.

The thinking behind his Paris saga.

They didn't kill him in Boardman's place for a very good reason: they wanted him, *needed* him alive.

He had been brought to the French capital, he supposed, because the political asylum situation in France allowed them to staff the city with hired help that would have been arrested and probably deported elsewhere—hired help that Nasruddin used as a team with orders to keep tabs on him. They wanted to know where he was at any time, so that they could move in when they thought it necessary and take him for future treatments.

Another reason for bringing him to Paris was so that he could be provoked into taking out Graziano, who had become expendable once he'd been unmasked at Tel Aviv. This, they knew, would hang a murder rap on Bolan and keep his head down so that they could more easily locate him. And the execution of Graziano the traitor could be used to keep the jihad activists in Teheran sweet.

But completion of that particular puzzle raised two more minor questions to which he could find no answer right now.

First, the attack in the vacant lot.

How did that stack up against the fact that they needed him alive? Had it been, as he'd first thought, Graziano acting on his own to protect himself against Bolan, whom he knew was on his tail?

Uh-uh. The second wave of attackers, the biker kids, had been supplied by Nasruddin. And he, like the Marksman himself, was part of the main conspiracy.

Were the attacks *intended* to fail? Were they a ruse to sting him into action, to steer him toward Las Vegas Nights, where he was set up to eliminate Graziano before witnesses, with a planned police raid due?

Was the whole routine a trick to get him on the run?

No way of knowing.

Then there were some other events that didn't make sense. Fawzi Harari had told him the two missing days between Algiers and the Paris hotel had been taken up with a sea voyage to Marseille followed by an overnight truck ride to the capital. She claimed she had tailed them all the way.

But they must have transported him in a private plane, because the tapes proved that those two days had been spent right here in the redoubt—the last but one training session.

Why had the girl lied?

He had no time for evaluating honesty, though. For the moment Bolan was more worried about the immediate future. Because although he had uncovered the truth of Baraka's identity, he was no nearer the identity of the big wheels behind the plot, the guys who pulled the strings for Nasruddin and the others.

He shook his head. It remained one hell of a problem.

"Can I help you?" a female voice said suddenly behind him.

The woman standing in the doorway was blond and slender. Her features were chiseled, and her eyes were as blue as the Executioner's own. But apart from the attractiveness, Bolan thought there was an unhealthy pallor to her skin. She had a generous, curvaceous figure, but looked sick and wasted. Her shoulder-length hair was lusterless. Beneath the makeup, the skin of her face had lost its elasticity, and there were lines of tiredness around her mouth as well as dark circles under her eyes.

She was wearing a white lab jacket over black stretch pants and a blue shirt. Bolan recognized her as the girl who had been working the switchboard in the lobby when he'd come in.

"Help me?" he repeated. "You probably could. How did you get here?"

"Tell me," she said, ignoring the question.

Bolan studied her. A little neurotic maybe? You'd have to be to work in a dump like this, even if you didn't know what went on. But harmless? She was leaning against the doorpost, thumbs outside, fingers inside the pockets of the jacket. There was no sign of a weapon.

Could he trust her enough to ask the vital question?

He decided yes. And he would play it straight.

"You know who I am," he said. "But I just found out who *else* I am. There's something the first me wants very much to find out about the second. Maybe you could help me?"

"What's the question?"

The question was crucial. Ever since he'd seen that first tape and had survived the shock it had produced, he had been shoving it to the back of his mind, unwilling to face the implications—and the consequences—of the wrong answer.

He drew a deep breath and asked the question.

"Has my second self...has Baraka...been sent on any missions yet? Has he been...used...to eliminate anyone, plant a bomb, sabotage a train or plane?"

"You mean has he been personally responsible for any deaths?" she asked with a wry twist of the mouth. "The answer is no, not yet."

"You're certain?"

"Certain as can be. I do the filing here. I prepare the dossiers and organize the videocassettes. No operation has been activated in Baraka's name. He's still in the training sector."

Bolan heaved a sigh of relief. The specter haunting him ever since his discovery, the fear that he might already—even if unknowingly—have been guilty of killing the innocent, had been dispelled.

"The big wheels," he said. "Do you know who they are?"

"The big wheels?"

"The guys in the boardroom, the bastards who give the orders."

"I don't think—"

"I know Nasruddin seems to be the man in charge of operations. And the two doctors take care of the experiments. But somebody has to give them their orders. There must be men above them. Men who dreamed up this whole sick operation, who had the money to modify this old Maginot fort. Do you know who they are?''

She shook her head. ''No one speaks of them. Max brought four guys down a few days ago, very cagey characters, didn't want to be recognized.''

''But you did recognize some of them?''

''No. I don't know who they were. One looked like an Arab. Another had a rose in his lapel. They all looked classy.''

''I'll bet,'' Bolan said. ''How come you're still here anyway? Why did you ask if you could help?''

The girl looked uncomfortable. ''I was supposed to stay behind and take care of closing up the place after everyone had left—everyone except the two waiting in the lobby for you, that is. But . . .''

''Well?''

''I was kind of tired. I figured I'd lie up a few minutes in the rest room. While I was...while I was there, I heard shooting. I came out and I saw you moving around. I followed you. That's all.''

Bolan studied her face, noted the tiny muscular twitch, the shadowed eyes. ''You're hooked on something, aren't you?'' he accused. ''You were shooting up, weren't you? That's what you were doing in the rest room—shooting up.''

She blushed, nodding miserably.

''And you came to offer help because you knew who I was and you thought maybe *I* could help *you*?'' Bolan played the long shot.

It paid off. She nodded again. ''I want out,'' she said.

''So get out. Walk away.''

"I can't kick the habit. I've no money of my own. Max keeps me supplied. It's a condition of the... It's the only way I can make out."

"How did you get in? How come a kid like you can stomach working with people whose business is *killing*?"

She was crying now, the tears channeling through the makeup on her cheeks and diluting the mascara to blacken the dark circles under her eyes. She shook her head helplessly.

Slowly at first and then in a flood, it all came out. Her name was Julie Marco.

And, yes, Bolan had heard the story hundreds of times. In fact, it had touched him personally, where he lived, had become the reason for his everlasting war.

"Julie," Bolan said when the girl had finished, "I can help you."

Tears glistened on her cheeks again. "If only you would," she whispered.

"I will," he promised. "You *want* out. That's half the battle won already. But I'm going to ask you to do something for me first. I want you to stay here a little longer, to keep me in touch with what goes on, with what *I'm* programmed to do. Because I'm going to break these guys into little pieces—and Baraka along with them! But I must have inside intel. Will you help me?"

"Yes," she said, dabbing at her eyes with the back of one hand.

"Okay," Bolan said. "Now, do you know anything that *is* planned for Baraka, any possible hit in the future?"

She shook her head. "I've heard them say it's going to be the big one, but I don't know what it is. There's nothing in the files about it."

"Right. I arrive here and get some kind of drug pumped into me that transforms me into Baraka. I have a list of the drugs they use. But how do they get me here? It seems they can knock me out somehow and transport me here without my knowledge of it. Do you know what method they use? There's nothing about it in the medical files."

Again the blond head moved from side to side. "No idea. My work starts when I clock you in."

"Lastly then, do you know anything of any other hits planned, any future hits that don't involve Baraka, but may have been assigned to other killers?"

This time Julie nodded. "I have no details," she said, "but I heard Max talking to the Corsican about the...the elimination of a Spanish official."

"That's right," Bolan mused. "I heard someone ask about 'the Spanish thing' while I was in the storeroom."

"I think it's the minister for tourism, Alfonso Velasquez. It's supposed to be when he's on a goodwill visit to London. You know, to check out some compromise on Gibraltar or something that the Spaniards have been agitating for for years. There's a bomb planned outside the Iberia airline office at the same time. It's supposed to scuttle the talks and lead to bad feeling."

"Do you have the date?" Bolan asked.

"No. It depends on the minister's schedule, and that hasn't been finalized. I think they said it was to be when he's addressing a meeting of the Anglo-Hispanic Friendship Society."

"Julie, you've got to keep in touch," Bolan said urgently. "As soon as you learn that date, you've got to let me know."

For a moment she looked scared. "As long as it's something you could have found out for yourself from the files, on some future visit," she said dubiously. "I could tip you off when to come again, when there will be written evidence. Because if a leak could be traced back to me that would be it. I'd be found OD'd in my room with enough circumstantial proof strewn around to convince a coroner it was suicide ten times over."

"Just trust me," Bolan said. "I wouldn't drop you in it, kid."

Julie smiled tremulously. "I have to lock up now. You could have run out immediately after the shooting. I never saw you, right? But I'll have to report . . . well, whatever I see on my way out."

Bolan visualized the lobby and then asked, "Tell me, is there any way into this place besides the tunnel by the fig tree?"

"Yes, of course," she said. "The storeroom hatch."

Bolan slapped his open palm against his forehead, mentally cursing himself for not having thought of it. Of course they had to have some way of getting all that heavy electronic equipment in, and the other stuff installed below. None of it could possibly have been maneuvered down through the trapdoor in the cellar and along that narrow tunnel. "In the ceiling of the storeroom?" he suggested.

"That's right. Two steel plates that open upward hydraulically, with an electric crane above."

"I never thought to look *up*." Once more he conjured up the layout above and below ground, mentally estimating distances. "I suppose the hatch is hidden above in one of the farm buildings?"

"Behind the skeleton of a tractor in the old barn," she confirmed.

When she was through and they had made their way out past the gruesome evidence in the lobby, she showed him the button, concealed on the top surface of an ancient oak beam, that operated the hatch.

They emerged into a night brilliant with stars. A warm wind blowing off the Rhine stirred the tops of the trees surrounding the farm.

"Where do you live, Julie?" Bolan asked.

"Strasbourg," she replied.

"But that's quite a way, isn't it? How do you get there?"

"Thirty-four miles. I walk to Saales and catch a bus. That's only three miles. Max says it's good for my health. He won't let me hitch a ride with the others. He says the exercise counteracts the bad effects of my habit."

"Well, you're getting a ride tonight. There's a bike here, and I don't think the owner's going to need it anymore."

20

Hal Brognola's expert had been brought to Paris all the way from Washington. "Nutty as a fruitcake, the whole diplomatic community," he told Bolan. "I never stop working."

A psychoanalyst by profession, he was also an expert on drugs and was often called in for consultation by the Federal Narcotics Bureau.

His name was Greg Toledo. He was short and wore oversize glasses, and his bald scalp was covered in freckles. Bolan guessed he was around forty years old.

They met in the embassy interview room overlooking the Avenue Gabriel.

"Interesting," Toledo said in a high-pitched voice when he had been briefed on the Bolan–Baraka substitution. He smoothed the fringe of hair that remained on his head and fingered a wispy mustache. For the third time he scanned the charts the Executioner had brought from the old Maginot fort. "All these drugs, you see," he said to Brognola, "are psychotomimetics."

"Say again?" Bolan said.

"Psy-choto-mi-met-ics. They are agents that mimic certain abnormal mental conditions. Their combination, as outlined here in this case history, is fascinating. Now what do we find?" He ticked off each entry on a finger. "Psilocybin—that's the famous Mexican mushroom—telepathine, soma, TMA, microgamma doses of LSD-25, all administered in minutely varying quantities at carefully calculated intervals. Amazing."

"Those are all hallucinogens, aren't they?" Bolan inquired.

"Each of them," the analyst said, nodding, "is capable under certain conditions, in certain amounts with certain subjects, of producing paravisual phenomena. Of making them hallucinate, if you prefer.

"What makes this case particularly absorbing is the planned interaction of the agents, each imperceptibly modifying, stimulating or acting as a catalyst on the action of the other. There are, you will know, great differences in degree. The synthetic LSD, for example, is ten times stronger than psilocybin and a hundred times more potent than mescaline, the original psychedelic. The one thing they have in common, all of them, is not so much these so-called visionary effects as the fact that they ruthlessly strip away the fences we surround ourselves with. They penetrate the masks we hide behind when we face the world. And we suddenly see ourselves as we really are. Psychologically it can be frightening, even terrifying. It is this that gives people what they call a bad trip. Because they can't retreat from that reality until the effect of the drug wears off."

"Okay," Bolan said. "So how can they turn me into a terrorist?"

"This—it's only my guess, mind—would have something to do with the phenomenon known as imprinting."

"Which is?"

"The system we build up from birth, like all living creatures, to relate ourselves to the world around us. We learn that the first large moving object we see—our mother—means comfort and security. We learn how to distinguish that moving object from others. We learn that a flame means heat means pain. We learn that water makes you wet and reflecting surfaces shoot you back an image of yourself. Later we learn that the image is false, the opposite of ourselves. And later still we begin to build our sense of values, the moral code by which we live."

Toledo shuffled the medical charts and patted the edges straight with his fingertips. "The psychedelic drugs," he said, "are believed to suspend these imprinted patterns, to erase them temporarily. It has also been suggested that during the period of suspension a subject may be *re*imprinted with a different pattern. A different set of values. I believe this is what is happening in your case."

"You mean it alters the sense of right and wrong?" Bolan asked.

Toledo sighed. "Those terms are relative to the persons using them. They're subjective, arbitrary, nonscientific values decided upon by each individual or group of individuals themselves. I may label as right an action you choose to label wrong. But, in effect, yes, you could say that."

"He gets around to it eventually," Bolan remarked.

Brognola winked. "You said that on one of the tapes the doctors mention the fact that digital expertise—acquired skills if you like—was unimpaired?" he asked the Executioner.

"That's right," Bolan said.

"Well, that accounts for it, Striker!" The Fed sounded pleased with himself. "You're the perfect choice for the job, a natural for programming as an undercover killer of the innocent."

"What do you mean?"

"Your previous history has shown you to be precisely the opposite," Brognola said. "That's your imprinting. But your muscular and autonomous nervous systems are clued in to the type of work required of a terrorist just the same. You're an excellent penetration agent. All your skills have conditioned you for the kind of existence a terrorist leads. You're just on the other side of the fence, that's all."

"Too right." Unexpectedly the shrink lapsed into the vernacular. "All the enemy has to do is, in effect, alter the target in your sights."

"And this can go on happening each time they pump the stuff into me in the right amounts?"

"Basically, yes. It's a little like posthypnotic suggestion."

"Okay. I'll buy that. But I guess I had to be available for your hypnotist to make the original suggestion, right? I mean like the first time they got to me."

Toledo nodded.

Bolan was about to say something more, but suddenly he paused, thinking. Then he turned to Brognola. "Remember when I took that blow on the skull in northern Italy, Hal? I was taken to a hospital somewhere nearby, wasn't I?"

"Sure. They lifted you across the border into Switzerland. It was the nearest place with the right kind of care. But it wasn't a hospital, it was a clinic."

"You remember the name?"

"Sure I do. It was called the Friedekinde Foundation."

Bolan was incredulous. He realized now why parts of the clinic had seemed so familiar to him, why Friedekinde had talked of his coming *back*: he *had* been there before. He turned to the analyst. "Granted that I was an amnesiac the first time they got to me," he said, "and that I'd been knocked out immediately before the last two sessions, can you think of any way they could have gotten to me, any way they could have taken me without my knowing, the times I was programmed in between?"

"I can think of dozens," Toledo said cheerfully. "The tiny pellet in the back of the calf, fired from an umbrella gun the way the KGB did in London with that Bulgarian defector who broadcast anticommunist stuff over the radio. Toxic material in your food or drink. A miniature thorn in your shoe. What the press call a sleep dart. You'd have forgotten the tiny mosquito sting before you hit the ground"

"And I'm open to that kind of attack?"

"Unless you stay closeted in one room with a guard outside. And even then they could get to you through your food. There are so many choices." The analyst shook his head. "You can get alkaloids so poisonous that a small amount smeared on the inside of a sleeve will put you out as soon as it touches the hairs on the back of your hand."

"That's nice to know," Bolan said. "But how come I've no recollection of the knockouts or the treatment after? I'm not an amnesiac anymore."

"That's another question altogether. I'd be guessing again here, but I can only think of one way it might be done."

"It *was* done," Bolan said.

"Very well. But first I have to give you a crash course on the functions of the human brain."

Bolan sighed. "Shoot."

"You have ten billion neurons or brain cells in your head, Mr. Bolan. Any one of them, at any time, can be interacting with some twenty-five thousand others. This means that the number of possible associations mentally is staggering. Each of those neurons transmits a tiny electric current and contains, among other things, twenty million molecules of ribonucleic acid, RNA for short."

"Yeah." Bolan nodded. "I heard a guy at the fort talk about RNA chains."

"The RNA manufactures protein molecules, and these are related to the function we call memory. Are you with me?"

"At a distance."

"Good. This electrochemical network, inconceivable in its complexity, is the anatomical structure of consciousness. Now, it has been found that certain chemicals stimulate the production of RNA. Secondly, it has been proved with laboratory animals that increased RNA—and thus increased protein in the brain—enables animals to remember better, learn faster. They get smarter. Then the back room boys decided to try the reverse process. They injected rats and mice with a chemical that *interferes* with the production of RNA."

"And they got dumb animals?"

"Exactly."

"What was the chemical?"

"I think they call it puromycil."

"Could it be used on humans?"

"If it was, I'd think the effect would be just what you describe—total memory loss of recent events, with long-term recall unaffected."

"And when the drug wore off—" this was Brognola "—the subject would be back to normal, but the memory loss would remain?"

"Correct."

"Yeah, but just a minute. You say the animals get dumb. So what about this digital skill routine? You said—and the videotapes proved it—that Striker's military expertise would be unaltered."

"You don't understand," Toledo said patiently. "Certainly they remained unaltered—*when he was under the influence of the other drugs*. But presumably the puromycil would only be injected when the, uh, training was through and the skills weren't required anymore."

"But they'd be back in there again next time around when they laid hands on me for another session?" Bolan said.

"Yes."

"And this...this reimprinting would remain kind of dormant until the next psychedelic treatment?"

"I guess so."

"Okay," Bolan said. "All that makes sense, in a screwy kind of way. I find it spooky, but at least I'm not going crazy."

"Not with the tiny controlled doses they're giving you at the moment."

"Now one more thing," the Executioner said. "Suppose I find out, as me, that Baraka is being programmed to pull off something real bad. And suppose I know beforehand when he's going to be knocked out and then given the treatment and briefed to do it. And suppose, finally, that I want to pretend to go through with it but in fact louse up the deal..."

Toledo looked interested. "I'm supposing," he said.

"Right. Is there anything I could take before they got to me, you know, some kind of antidote? Are you familiar with anything, any drug or chemical that would stop these hallucinogens having their usual effect on me?"

The analyst smoothed out the mustache with a forefinger. "Again, this is not really my area," he said slowly. "But I believe there are certain other drugs—some of them quite common—that can block, inhibit or even cancel out for a short time the psychotomimetics. But I'd have to check with a couple of colleagues in that line."

"Do that," Brognola said.

"As soon as I get back. I'll contact you when I have the necessary information."

"Make it fast," the Executioner said.

21

The phone rang in the bedroom of a back-street hotel in Strasbourg. Mack Bolan swung his legs off the bed and reached for the receiver. It was Julie Marco.

"The Spanish thing has been finalized," she told him. "The Connaught Rooms between Kingsway and Drury Lane in London. The Corsican and the Marksman have been briefed to make the hit, each from a different location. The Iberia bomb will be placed by Olga Kurtz, the woman who did the Amsterdam station and acted as a decoy in the Jaecklin killing in Kronberg. Her MO doesn't change. She uses a baby carriage, with the stuff concealed beneath a blanket."

"You wouldn't happen to know the snipers' MO on this particular occasion?" Bolan asked. "Like the firing points they'll use?"

"No. Only the date. The twenty-ninth, around eight in the evening. It's left to them how they work it out. But there'll be a camera there someplace recording it."

"I know what the Marksman looks like from the Baraka tapes, but I don't have a face for the Corsican. Do you have a photo in your files?"

"No way. Max runs a dead stop on visuals. No evidence. There's not a photo of anyone in the whole place."

"What does he look like?"

"He looks like . . . well, like a Corsican. Bulky, tanned, big black mustache, short curly hair. Very dark shades all the time."

"Got it. No special distinguishing marks?"

"No, not that anyone could see when he's dressed. Oh, by the way, you will drop by the fort and leave traces, won't you?"

"As I promised."

"Good. There's nobody there tonight or tomorrow. It's all in the dossier I activated. Top left-hand drawer of the desk in the office. It's not locked."

"Relax," Bolan said. "Even if they find out I know, you'll be in the clear."

"Great. Everything I told you is in there."

"Thanks, Julie," Bolan said. He heard a click, then replaced the receiver.

As soon as it was dark, Bolan left the hotel. When he was ready, he'd allow himself to be found again, offer himself as a guinea pig—as long as Greg Toledo had found some chemical to counteract the drugs they would use on him.

Meanwhile there was this Spanish hit. Bolan knew the surveillance team or teams had lost him, and he wanted it to stay that way, which meant he had to lie very low indeed.

He took the bike. He left the old town, riding through the network of narrow, twisting streets past steep-roofed old houses with overhanging carved wood gables dwarfed by the soaring red sandstone tower of the Gothic cathedral.

It took him some time to find the abandoned farm again. From Sélestat onward, through the vineyards and up along the forested ridges of the Vosges, one steep unmarked lane looked much like another. Also, when he had left with Julie, he had thought only of getting back to the city and hadn't paid much attention to the route.

But finally he found the rutted track that led to the ruin, bumping along it and out into the yard. He cut the engine and leaned the bike against the wall. There were no stars tonight, and the wind was stronger. Bolan guessed there would be rain before dawn. He wished he had brought some kind of jacket to cover his blacksuit.

The two sagging doors of the barn were chained together, with a rusty padlock joining the links. But he had no difficulty pushing them far enough apart to squeeze through.

This time he had brought a larger flashlight. He switched it on as soon as he was inside. Dust motes danced in the brilliant beam, and a bat flew squeaking through the tunnel of brightness as he directed the flashlight upward to locate the roof beam with the electric button behind it.

The hatch's panels were thick—half-inch steel plates covered with twenty inches of compounded earth covered in straw. He saw with astonishment as they whined apart that the whole storeroom ceiling had been hinged to open in two sections.

He stood at the edge and played the beam downward. The top of the tallest crate was ten feet below him. He leaped lightly down, scrambled to the floor and went through into the lobby.

Only then, when the storeroom door had closed, did he switch on the lighting master control. He didn't want any illumination escaping through the hatch and out the barn doors to alert any curious passerby that there was an occupant within the farm.

The lights blazed on, dimmed, then brightened again as the generator automatically cut in. Bolan took the elevator down one level and went through to the walkway and the office.

The dossier was in the drawer as Julie had told him. He leafed through the three pages of typescript. The briefing was as she had outlined it. The only additional factor was the mention of a British contact called Cobbold, who was to help the snipers with locations and arrange a getaway car for the woman.

Bolan closed the file. Leaving it open on the desk was a little too obvious he decided. He would make it look as if an attempt had been made to cover up.

He placed the folder awkwardly among the other papers, so that it stuck out of the rest, then pushed the drawer not quite shut and knocked over a tall vase full of dried grasses so that it smashed on the floor. He went back to the elevator, rode up to the lobby, cut the master switch and reentered the storeroom in the dark.

Groping his way through the blackness, he found the big packing case and clambered to the top. It was going to be quite a leap to make the top edge. He stood upright.

His head cracked against something solid.

Bolan swore. He unclipped the flashlight from his combat belt and shone it upward. Eighteen inches away, the light dazzled back at him from a polished steel surface.

The two loading panels that made up the room's ceiling had been closed.

For a heartbeat the Executioner stood totally immobile. The darkness was total; he couldn't hear any sound except his own steady breathing.

Okay, either Julie Marco was a plant and had double-crossed him so they could grab him once more, or, unknown to her, Nasruddin had followed up the Executioner's elimination of his watchdogs by posting an all-night sentry outside the redoubt, someone to stay there even when the place itself, as she had correctly reported, was empty.

He rejected the first idea. If that was the case, why would they have waited while he went into the fort and did his number with the dossier? Surely they would have jumped him the moment he hit the farm. In any case, Julie knew where to find him in Strasbourg.

No, he must have arrived when the watchman was temporarily absent, maybe taking a leak someplace up among the trees, smoking a forbidden cigarette or returning to wherever he had hidden his transport to fetch a sandwich.

Seeing the hatch open when he returned, the guy would have closed them in order to force the intruder to exit via the trapdoor, the cellar and the tunnel behind the fig tree. That way he could be one hundred percent sure of covering him when he showed.

This absence told Bolan two things: one, that there was no second sentry; two, that the watchman wouldn't know for a fact that it was Bolan inside the fort.

This brought with it a disadvantage. If the guard didn't know that the target was Mack Bolan, a man his bosses desperately needed to keep alive, he would probably shoot to kill.

Very quietly the warrior lowered himself to the floor. He left the storeroom, walked through the lobby to the long tunnel and made his way up the ladder to the trapdoor. He pushed the trap open and climbed up into the cellar. For a moment he switched off the flashlight.

Somewhere on the far side of the steel door, the killer would be waiting for him.

Bolan concentrated all his thoughts on the layout of the entrance. He tried—as he always did in combat situations—to put himself in the position of the enemy, and then formulate his own plans.

The guy wouldn't be waiting immediately outside the door. The door opened inward, and there was too much chance that Bolan would erupt with guns blazing, the way he had in the lobby on his last visit.

It was unlikely that the watchman would choose to station himself farther along the blocked tunnel outside. Once Bolan left the cellar they would be even— and the gunman would be trapped while the Executioner could simply turn and run.

No, the guy would be posted someplace out in the yard—under the wrecked truck, on the bank above, up in the branches of the fig tree, perhaps around the nearest corner of the farmhouse with a spotlight ready to pin Bolan like some lab specimen once he heard the steel door open.

In any case he would be trigger-happy, because he would know by now that the intruder knew he was wise to the break-in. Closing the loading hatch would have proved that.

Also, he couldn't be certain that there was only one intruder—any more than Bolan himself could be certain there was only one guard.

A team would have left a sentry outside to guard the exit and the escape route. If it was a duo . . . well, both of them might have gone in. He had to take that into account.

Finally, he wouldn't know for sure that the intruder or intruders had been here before. The interior layout of the redoubt was complex. First-timers might be checking it out quite a while; the fact that Bolan was emerging after so short a time might give him a slight edge.

Once again the element of surprise.

Yeah, but emerging how?

Flat on his face, crawling on elbows and knees with a gun in each hand—to be annihilated from above with a stream of slugs in the back?

To be crucified against the blackness of the tunnel mouth while the gunner shot down the beam of light that was illuminating him?

To make a dash for it and rush out into the center of the yard with two deathbringers at the ready, only to find that he was a perfect target for a marksman concealed behind any one of a hundred bushes around the yard?

No way.

And then it struck him.

He had been thinking all along of the *blocked* tunnel: the yard exit at one end, the rockfall at the other.

But why was it blocked? How come the rockfall?

If his memory wasn't at fault it was because the roof had caved in. There was shattered brickwork in the debris blocking the passageway.

With a collapsed roof, there was a possibility that a determined man might be able to claw his way through to the open air.

It was worth a try.

The Executioner slowly turned the wheel that withdrew the bolts securing the door. They were well greased but made metallic noise as they slid through the iron guides. The door screeched quietly, grinding a speck of gravel into the cement floor as he swung it open.

He stole out of the tunnel and turned away from the exit. Before he started walking he checked that each of his guns was primed for action. The snick of the AutoMag's slide sounded disconcertingly loud in the silence.

Once around the corner in the passageway he counted his paces. At twelve he halted, listening. The drip of moisture that he remembered was near. Masking most of the lens with his fingers, he switched on the flashlight. In the dim illumination he could see that the rubble slant was ten feet ahead of him.

He splashed through the stagnant pool, almost gagging as the odors of decomposition and decay rose to his nostrils. His feet sank into the damp earth between the fragments of rock and brickwork forming the slope.

When his head was at the height of the tunnel roof, he removed his hand from the lens, chancing that the two curves in the underground passage and the curtain of leaves covering the entrance would kill any telltale glow that could give his position away.

He shone the beam upward. Judging from the depth of the grassy bank above the farmyard wall, the tunnel couldn't be far—perhaps eight or ten feet—below the surface.

He saw an irregular, funnel-shaped opening, its narrow end upward, with here and there a stone projecting through the earth, and gnarled tree roots snaking outward.

Bolan braced himself on the slope. He reached up and began digging into the earth with the fingers of his left hand.

The earth crumbled away easily enough. It was the opposite side of the funnel that was damp. Bolan continued clawing a passage up past the tree roots.

He came across a large stone, about the size of a man's head, that was blocking the hole he was excavating. He clipped the flashlight back onto his combat belt and felt around the stone with both hands, gouging away the earth, probing up into the dark, trying to loosen the obstruction.

A stream of earth and pebbles fell around his feet. Abruptly the big stone dislodged itself and dropped, narrowly missing Bolan's shoulder. It bounced down the slope, scattered spray and slime from the pool and rumbled a few yards along the brick floor of the tunnel. It was followed by a sudden rush of earth and sand that thumped down with numbing force and buried the Executioner almost up to his waist.

Cursing silently, he struggled to free himself. The damp breeze cool on his face was a relief after he had sweated so much in the fetid atmosphere of the tunnel.

Damp air? Fresh air?

He freed the flashlight and shone the beam upward once more.

Earth, wet this time, and still crumbling away. More tree roots. Stones that glistened with moisture. A patch of blackness, of dark nothing, a gap in the center of which all at once he saw the glitter of a single star.

He was through to the open air!

With a gasp of relief, Bolan dragged himself free of the earthfall. Slipping this way, slithering back as his feet slid on the precarious mound of rubble, he managed at last to reach up, grasp stronger roots and haul himself up and out through the hole in the ground.

He was in the middle of a stand of young trees about fifty feet away from the wall and the farmyard.

The gap in the clouds closed over, and the star vanished. A sudden freshening of the breeze heaved the branches of trees; there was a sudden loud pattering among the leaves. It had begun to rain.

Boots scuffing aside the undergrowth, Bolan took advantage of the sudden, unexpected rustling all around and made his way to a rise topped with tangled brier just before the farmyard wall.

He lay beneath the overhanging branches of a flowering bush, eyes straining to pierce the pool of near darkness that lay between him and the black bulk of the old farm buildings. Someplace down there a guy with a gun—probably an SMG—was waiting, tense as Bolan himself, for a figure to emerge from the tunnel mouth.

Ten minutes passed.

Bolan saw no sign of movement; no denser blur shifted against the dark. His ears caught no stealthy slither of feet, no scrape of a shoe, no rasp of cloth against stone or metal. The rain fell more heavily, drumming on the cobblestones of the yard, spattering the leaves, beating a tattoo on the Executioner's back. Somewhere down below an overflow of water gurgled away.

Bolan decided there was one way to bring the enemy into the open. He felt around in the wet grass until his fingers encountered a stone half buried in the earth. He pried it loose. It was about the size of a man's fist. Kneeling, he drew back his arm and threw the stone as far as he could in the direction of the rutted track that led to the road.

It crashed among bushes with a satisfyingly loud noise, thumped onto something hard and rolled.

"What the hell was that?"

The voice was so close—about ten feet away, below the wall, on his left—that Bolan started. His forefinger curled around the trigger of the AutoMag.

"How the hell do I know? You ain't here to ask goddamn questions. Wait in silence and then shoot, Max said."

The second voice spoke through the broken, flame-scorched window on the lower floor of the farmhouse. Bolan caught his breath. So there *were* two of the bastards!

He remained in a kneeling position, mentally evaluating the possible moves in this life or death chess game in which there were only three pieces on the board.

There was a possibility that he could take out the guy in the empty window—he remembered approximately its position, and he thought he could distinguish it as a more intense rectangle of darkness against the wall of the building.

But it would need a burst rather than a single round, and that would be self-defeating because the muzzle-flash would dazzle him enough to negate his aim: he would be firing blind at an imagined target rather than correcting the aim after a first ranging shot.

And that same muzzle-flash would pinpoint Bolan himself accurately enough for the man by the wall to drop him.

If on the other hand he went for the second man, he would have to stand and lean out over the wall to get anywhere near him, and even then he wasn't exactly sure of the guy's precise position, which would make the warrior himself an even easier target for the killer framed in the window.

No, it was his own position that would have to be changed. He would have to shoot from a more protected location, someplace where the flashes and the man behind them were at least partially screened by leaves, branches or a swell in the ground.

He rose to his feet and trod quietly along the top of the rise toward the section that was above the wrecked truck and the tunnel mouth.

By the time he reached that, he reckoned, he would have passed above the guy by the wall, so that he would have both the killers in the same field of fire, rather than one on each side of him.

The rain was pelting down through the leaves hard enough now to drown out any slight noise he made, but there was a risk that the grass and the ground beneath it would become so waterlogged that his footsteps would squeak and signal his presence.

He had to take into account also that the men below had been smart enough not to be fooled by the stone he had thrown; they hadn't automatically fired in the direction of an unexpected, unexplained noise and given their location away.

The situation called for stealth—and speed.

A few yards past the upper branches of the fig tree that grew by the wrecked truck, a second fig grew on top of the rise. Its trunk was thick, and the branches were strong and widely splayed. Bolan remembered seeing it when he'd first visited the farm in day-light....

Holstering both guns, he reached up carefully into the dark until his fingers touched a limb thick enough to bear his weight. Moving a quarter-inch at a time so that his shoulders didn't displace the leaves and send a telltale extra shower of raindrops below, he drew himself up among the branches.

The limb projected over the yard. Through the topmost leaves of the lower tree he could still make out the dark blotch he believed to be the scorched window frame. The guy by the wall would be immediately below, about ten yards beyond the truck.

Bolan moved farther out along the branch. He unleathered the Beretta, shifting his position slightly to get a wider angle on the place he believed the man to be.

The ridged rubber sole of his combat boot, which had gripped well enough on the wide trunk of the fig tree, slipped on the smooth bark of the narrower limb.

Hampered by the gun in his right hand, Bolan almost fell, clinging on with both arms wrapped around the branch as one leg swung down into space.

The branch creaked protestingly. Moisture cascaded down onto the stones below. An involuntary gasp of breath was forced from his lungs.

This time the noises were too near and too obvious to be ignored.

The gunman by the wall fired.

An SMG as the Executioner had guessed. From the astonishingly rapid rate of fire he figured it was an Ingram. Heavy slugs ripped through the leaves, thunked into the branch behind him and stung his face with fragments of bark. The branch thrummed under the multiple impacts.

Miraculously Bolan was untouched. He triggered a three-round burst just above the muzzle-flashes the instant the SMG spat fire.

He scored. There was a high-pitched scream of agony. The gun rattled to the cobblestones; he heard the clattering stumble of a human knocked off balance and slumping to the ground.

Bolan launched himself out and down.

The drop to the yard was more than fifteen feet, but the gunman in the window was already slamming a deathstream up into the fig tree.

The warrior landed with a thump that jarred the whole length of his spine, but he was upright, leaping for the shelter of the old truck before the killer switched his aim.

The guy by the wall was still hollering. Bolan finished it for him with a well-placed trio and then whipped out the AutoMag to thunder a couple of skullbusters toward the window. It was too dark for the remaining gunman to pick him out against the irregular outline of the truck: if the guy believed two different guns meant two men shooting, so much the better.

Bolan's shots were clearly wide or high because the hardman was quick—almost too quick—to reply.

Flame flickered beneath the eaves of the farmhouse; the ear-busting detonations of a machine pistol split the night. A stream of slugs ripped through the rusted bodywork of the truck.

The Executioner was already running. He felt the wind of the killstream pass over his head as he dived for a slight depression he remembered in the center of the yard, rolled, came up again and dashed for the wall of the building.

The hardman swung the deadly spray his way. Bolan leaped and dived a second time.

This time he was aiming up—for another vandalized window at the end of the farmhouse wall. He remembered there were a few shards of glass left in the frame and that half the space was covered by a loose wooden shutter weathered to matchwood by forty years of neglect.

Face shielded by his upraised forearms, he hit the window like a battering ram and burst through into the interior in an explosion of glass and splintered wood.

He had no idea of the building's floor plan, but there had to be some cover in there, and he would be no worse off in the dark than the killer.

Also he judged from the second man's slower rate of fire that his SMG was an Uzi—six hundred rounds per minute against an Ingram's eleven hundred plus— and that meant a thirty-two-round magazine, much of which must have been expended by now.

If he could tempt the bastard, provoke him into an exchange of shots, there would soon be an empty clip and Bolan could move in and clean up.

He crouched on dust-covered boards amid the wreckage of the window. The only sounds he could hear were his own breathing, water from his sodden blacksuit dripping onto the floor and the persistent drumming of rain on the roof's remaining tiles.

He waited.

Very slowly, as his eyes adjusted, the stygian blackness arranged itself into separate elements of lighter and denser dark. A low rectangle could have been a fireplace. On the inner wall a particularly somber patch must be an open doorway leading to the rear of the house. There was another in the corner by the outer wall, a few feet from the window Bolan had crashed. He reckoned this led to a passage that would connect via intervening rooms to the one at the far end of the building where the gunman was holed up.

It was the obvious approach.

He wouldn't take it.

Using all his urban guerrilla expertise, he rose half upright and moved stealthily toward the inner door. If the rooms interconnected, maybe he could enfilade the man or even come up on him from behind.

Before each step he tested the ground ahead, probing with the toe of a combat boot for loose objects on the floor, his outstretched fingers searching for obstacles, the ball of his foot checking for creaks or crunches before he allowed his weight to fall on it.

He reached the doorway. He paused, searching for the open door. Which way did it open? Was there room for him to squeeze through? Would it squeak?

There was no door.

Bolan moved silently through and waited again.

He allowed his senses to map out the dark space in front and to either side.

He was standing on flagstones instead of wood. Maybe the room ahead was the old kitchen?

When he turned to the right, a deadness in the sound of his breathing, the minutest playback of warm air onto his cheek, told him that he was near a wall.

Somewhat ahead a paler square indicated a window. Above this, in a corner of the ceiling, a darker one suggested a trapdoor, maybe with a ladder below. On the left there was space.

A barely discernible current of cooler air told him that the corridor running along the back of the house that he hoped to find was actually there.

Perhaps that was too obvious a move once again.

If he could get out that window unseen and unheard, he could steal around the end of the building on the outside and surprise the hell out of a guy who was straining every nerve to locate him indoors.

Crouched low to avoid making a silhouette, he moved over toward the paler rectangle. Two feet away from the wall he was brought up short, his hips hard against some obstacle. He explored with his hands.

There was a wide, shallow stone sink beneath the window. And the window was closed; there was still glass in the frame.

He realized it would be suicide to try to maneuver open a window that had probably been closed for years.

It would have to be the corridor after all.

Bolan moved back toward the doorway. He turned toward the passage that ran along the back of the house, probing warily ahead with his toe. His boot touched an obstacle, a second, a third.

He crouched, feeling around with one hand.

He found a hard, irregular shape the size of a walnut, which crumbled in his hand, then another, smaller one, a flat fragment with jagged edges. It too crumbled when he tightened his grasp. The floor of the corridor was strewn with rubble—plaster that had fallen from a collapsed ceiling.

It was impossible to move along it without making a noise.

Bolan bit his lip. In the instant that he hesitated, he became aware of movement—nothing so much as an identifiable sound, but certainly movement—in the room he had left.

He froze.

Yeah, as faint as the whisper of a slight breeze over cut grass ... something.

Abruptly the rain stopped.

Water dripped, ran, splashed, but the drumming on the roof had ceased.

The silence was almost tangible.

Except that there was someone breathing in the next room.

While he had been trying to work out ways of creeping around behind the gunman so that he could be taken in the rear, the guy had been playing the same number on him!

With more success.

As far as movement was concerned, Bolan was trapped. If the gunner was already in the room that Bolan had dived into, he was in a no-escape situation. He'd be shot down before he could break out of the window above the sink. The plaster-strewn corridor was probably too long for him to make the far end before he'd be in the killer's sights.

The Executioner decided that he had no choice then but to trade shots with the gunman and hope he himself had faster reaction times.

And if it was to be the last exchange of all ... well, he would have gone down the way he wanted to. Just as quickly, he dismissed the defeatist train of thought. He had to win, this time like all the other times. The Baraka deal must be seen through to the bitter end. He owed that to Brognola, to Julie Marco, to all those who would suffer if he failed. He owed it to himself.

The Beretta was reholstered. With Big Thunder in his right hand, Bolan backed up cautiously toward the sink, feeling behind him with his left. As he had hoped, the sink was flanked by a counter—a solid wood surface built against the wall with cupboards and drawers beneath.

He climbed onto the counter and stood with his head just below the ceiling.

The killer would expect his target to be standing, crouched or flat on the floor; he wouldn't be ready for an opponent up near the ceiling.

A board creaked.

By now the guy would know he had left the front room.

Bolan had been holding his breath; now he allowed his breathing to be heard.

There was a darker shape in the doorway, blurred against the rectangle of the wrecked window. The gunman was moving in for the kill.

The SMG spit flame as the gunner opened fire, knowing the target must be in that kitchen, stitching a superfast figure eight from wall to wall, from waist height to the floor.

With each flash from the muzzle of the SMG, a giant shadow leaped onto the wall behind him, jerking in and out of vision as quick as the image on a hand-cranked silent movie.

Bolan fired at the substance, not the shadow.

Big Thunder roared once, the explosion deafening in the confined space beneath the roof. Glass tinkled from the window. Plaster fell.

The edge of the counter below the Executioner's feet was shredded, but that was as near as the killer got. The gunman hurtled back with a 240-grain boattail tunneling through his shoulder, brought up the barrel of his SMG—and heard only a click above the empty magazine.

His snarled curse died in his throat as the second two-handed shot from the AutoMag smashed through his breastbone with frightful power and cored a fist-sized hole between his lungs.

Bolan jumped down from the counter and unclipped the flashlight.

The hood lay on his back in the doorway—an unshaven Nordic blonde with pale eyes that stared sightless into the beam. The rivers of bright blood that had run out from beneath him were already filming over with dust from the floor. Bolan thumbed shut his eyes and left him there.

He climbed through the window and went in search of the bike.

Seventy minutes later he was back in his hotel room in Strasbourg, dialing the local airport at Entzheim to make a reservation on the midday flight to Paris, with an onward booking to London, England.

22

The Connaught Rooms on London's Great Queen Street was a white Portland stone building of neoclassical pretensions with a pillared front. Although the place was actually a Masonic headquarters, it looked more like something Mussolini might have commissioned to celebrate the conquest of Abyssinia. There were reception suites and lecture theaters inside, and these were much in demand for sales conventions, international conferences and office parties.

It was in one of the largest of the reception halls that Alfonso Velasquez, minister for tourism in the Spanish government, was to attend a gala reception on the evening of the twenty-ninth. The reception was to be preceded by an address to the members of the Anglo-Hispanic Society, delivered by the minister himself.

On the afternoon of the twenty-seventh, Mack Bolan strolled the length of Great Queen Street for the third time. On the fringe of London's theaterland, it was a short street, not more than three hundred yards long, and unusually wide for the old Covent Garden market neighborhood that also included the Opera House, Bow Street police headquarters and courtroom, and a couple of newspaper offices.

Eight o'clock in the evening was both a good time and a bad time for a hit.

The broad flight of steps leading from the sidewalk to the pillared entrance left a target without cover for the maximum time, especially for a sniper on the rooftops opposite. And it would still be light at that time on a summer evening.

On the other hand, it was also theater time: the complex network of streets from Drury Lane to Shaftesbury Avenue, from Long Acre to the Aldwych, would be choked with cabs and drivers desperately trying to locate a parking space.

In Great Queen Street itself, however, a getaway car could easily double-park for the necessary length of time and then make it out into Kingsway—a broad commercial thoroughfare deserted after the offices closed. From there it was less than a quarter of a mile to Waterloo Bridge and an escape to the wilderness south of the river.

Bolan glanced up at the rooftops on the far side of the street—a mixed bag of buildings, eighteenth, nineteenth and twentieth century, most of them narrow, between five and six stories high, some with dormer windows set in the steep, slated roofs. He saw parapets, multiple chimney stacks, air-conditioning vents, elevator housings and the gable ends and television antennae of taller buildings in the next street.

It was perfect for a sniper with murder in his mind. And the Marksman at least—Bolan knew from the videotapes in the old Maginot fortress—favored rooftop shooting.

Someone mounting the steps in front of the conference center would be a sitting duck for a man equipped with a sniperscope above any one of the houses along the entire length of Great Queen Street.

And there would be two killers aiming at the same target.

Plus a bomb-crazy woman wheeling a baby carriage loaded with explosives in front of the Spanish airline offices.

Clearly Bolan couldn't handle it all on his own.

He didn't like to call on the police or the army—in any country. Too much red tape, too many questions, not enough urgency... and, sadly, not always enough efficiency either.

He couldn't see British cops acting with enough ferocity and determination to protect Velasquez from murderers as cold and professional as the Marksman and the Corsican. If they believed in the threat at all, they would detail a couple of men—maybe even specialists with Home Office permits to carry arms— to accompany the minister in the role of bodyguards.

Which would achieve precisely nothing if, as Bolan guessed, the killers were someplace up among the chimneys across the street.

What was required was a guard manning the access to every single rooftop over there.

The alternative would be someone who could finger the two terrorists, tail them to their chosen firing points and take them out before they could take out their target.

The Executioner realized that since he couldn't rely on the police, he'd have to handle it in his own way.

Alone.

But first he had to get a line on one or both of the killers—preferably the Marksman; at least he knew him by sight.

And the only way he could do that in a city of eleven million inhabitants was to stay put and hope that they

would show. Because they would have to recon the location, find suitable positions, then liaise with the
contact named Cobbold, who was to drive the getaway car. And for all of these things they would have
to visit Great Queen Street.

Bolan had been tipped off by Julie Marco that they
couldn't have done this already: they weren't due to
arrive in London until some hours after the warrior
himself.

So he would hang in there until they did show. And
after that . . . well, he would play it by ear.

Meanwhile there was the problem of the Iberia
bomb.

No two ways about this one: he would have to alert
the local authorities and rely on them to do their duty.

He went into a public phone booth in Holborn
subway station and dialed 999, the British alarm call
combination.

Someone with a maddeningly calm voice on the
other end grilled Bolan with the most inane questions
about the bomb threat. Bolan tried his best to retain
his composure, but shook his head and hung up.

The guy probably thought he was humoring a crank
caller.

The Executioner figured they would likely put a
trace on all calls connected with this kind of threat,
and he had no wish to spend the evening answering
any more questions from the police.

He had only just made the sidewalk when a prowl
car screeched to a halt outside the station and two
plainclothes cops jumped out and made for the row of
phone booths at one side of the newspaper kiosk.

Bolan got out of there fast.

He had no way of knowing whether the metropolitan police would take his call seriously or not. No matter, he'd done his job.

EARLY THE FOLLOWING MORNING, the twenty-eighth, Bolan went to a car rental company and hired a small panel truck. Before rush-hour traffic, he eased the truck into a parking space and fed the meter.

From the cab it was possible to squeeze past a sliding door into the rear. Bolan went through and used the blade on his knife to scrape away a couple of small holes in the coating of black-tinted rear windows. From there he could keep watch, through one hole or another, on the whole length of the street.

It wasn't until late afternoon that he struck pay dirt.

Not long before the offices closed, a man strolled along the sidewalk from the direction of Holborn subway station, glancing casually at the buildings on either side of the street. Before he reached the Connaught Rooms he crossed over to the other side—a bulky, florid man with dark, curly hair and a bushy mustache.

The Corsican? Bolan figured he had to be.

The Executioner got out of the panel truck and followed at a discreet distance.

The guy entered a doorway of one of the narrow, older houses about eighty yards past the conference center. It was a town house transformed into office suites. Bolan read the names of lawyers, an accounting firm and a book publisher on the brass plates at one side of the entrance.

At street level there was an antiquarian store selling prints, engravings and ancient maps. He could see through the display window that the Corsican wasn't in there. He climbed to the next floor. A blonde in high heels was locking the mahogany outer door of the accounting office. She flashed the Executioner a smile as she dropped the keys in her purse and hurried downstairs.

The lawyer's premises on the floor above were closed. That left the book publisher. Bolan went on up. Glass-paneled doors blocked the stairway: evidently the publisher occupied both of the top two floors and the attics—if there were any.

Bolan pushed through the doors and found himself in a reception area furnished with a desk, leather armchairs and a stack of magazines on a low table. Judging from the samples on display in glass cases around the room, the publisher specialized in political commentaries and polemics on the European situation, all of them with a markedly right-wing tendency.

A birdlike, tweedy woman with spectacles emerged from an inner door and laid a buff folder on the desk. She sat down. "Can I help you?" she warbled, looking at the Executioner.

He made some generalized inquiry about the availability of the books for the American market and added, "I was recommended to you by a friend from Corsica. In fact, I thought I saw him coming into this building a few minutes ago. Giacomo Lucchese."

She shook her head. "Oh, no. You must be thinking of Monsieur Lozano. You just missed him. He was only here a moment."

Bolan thanked her and was about to leave when the inner door opened and a tall, heavily built man with sandy hair and a ginger mustache came into the office. He was wearing a gray chalk-striped suit with a white shirt and a dark blue silk necktie. The woman turned to him. "Oh, Mr. Cobbold," she said as Bolan opened the exit door, "did you want these letters to be mailed tonight or will tomorrow morning be all right?"

Bolan didn't wait to hear the reply. He left and hurried back to the street.

Cobbold!

That clinched it. He was the liaison and getaway man. The Corsican, Lozano, hadn't really left. He would have passed Bolan on the stairs if he had. Nor, Bolan had seen with a quick glance through the open door, was he in the inner office. He had gone on upstairs to check out his firing position on the roof.

Or even, since the top of the building belonged to an accomplice, from one of the upper windows.

So where would the Marksman operate?

If he chose a position an equal distance from the Connaught Rooms but on the far side of the building, Bolan would have to find another way of eliminating both killers. But first he was determined to locate the Marksman.

It was quite by chance that Bolan saw him in the rush-hour crowds flooding into the subway station soon after five-thirty. The tall, lean figure and that lined, cadaverous face were unmistakable, even though the man wore a London Telecommunications uniform and carried a metal telephone linesman's box.

Disguised this way, he had probably been up on the rooftops all afternoon, making doubly sure he had the best of all possible vantage points. His gun could already be stashed someplace up among the chimney stacks.

Angry that he had failed to spot the guy, Bolan tried his best to keep him in sight. Maybe it would be wise—if he could tail him to a quiet enough location—to take him out right now, this evening. That way he would have only one killer to deal with tomorrow.

But keeping him in sight was beyond even the Executioner's powers that evening. The Marksman was swept down the moving stairway in a sudden crush of commuters, and although Bolan did his best to force a passage through the phalanx of men and women jamming the escalator, the tall spare figure had vanished by the time he hit the arched corridor below.

The only reward for his pains was a tirade of abuse from the people he had pushed aside in his frantic efforts to keep the Marksman in sight. He didn't even know which of the two subway lines serving the station the guy had taken.

Bolan walked the three blocks to his hotel with the problem of how to tackle the assassination plot still unsolved.

THE MORNING OF THE TWENTY-NINTH was sunny and warm, with high white clouds moving slowly across an azure sky. Between the clouds, jetliners descending to land at London's Heathrow Airport flashed silver in the clear, washed atmosphere.

Soon after dawn Mack Bolan parked the panel truck on the far side of the conference center from the book publisher's office. He reckoned it was in that sector that he had the best chance of picking up the Marksman again.

He remained in the truck all morning and all afternoon, but he saw no sign of Lozano or the Marksman.

The killer from Corsica was probably still in Cobbold's duplex; there would have been no reason for him to leave once he had selected the best place to execute his plan.

The nonappearance of the Marksman was more worrying. It was ironic that Bolan had fingered the quarry he didn't know and scored an absolute zero on the one he did. By five o'clock in the afternoon when the assassin was still conspicuous by his absence, Bolan concluded that he had to have a route onto the rooftops from one of the buildings in the next street.

Bolan couldn't stake out two separate streets at the same time. Reluctantly he was forced to adopt a wild contingency plan he had dreamed up during the hours of darkness.

At five-thirty Cobbold left his office and walked away in the direction of Drury Lane. He returned ten minutes later driving a small Opel sedan, which he parked across the street from Bolan's panel truck, facing Kingsway.

The sedan was outside a small, modern glass-fronted office block. The facade was topped by a parapet, behind which there seemed to be a flat roof bare of chimney stacks. There was, however, a two-foot serpentine conduit leading to the air-conditioning plant and—just visible from the street—the upper part of a square concrete structure above the elevator shaft. Was it from there that the killer would strike?

It was impossible to be certain.

Bolan started the truck, drove to the end of the street, made a U-turn around a traffic island and returned to park in the same place but now, like the Opel, facing Kingsway.

He eased open the lock of the panel truck's rear door and left it resting on the latch. After that it was a matter of waiting.

At seven-thirty half a dozen unarmed uniformed policemen were decanted from a dark blue minibus and took up position on either side of the entrance steps to the Connaught Rooms. This, Bolan knew, would be the normal detail to keep the roadway clear and move away onlookers when a minister of state was due.

Soon afterward a procession of cars and taxis deposited men and women who were probably members of the Anglo-Hispanic Society's organizing committee. They were followed by a number of obviously Hispanic men, presumably stewards, bodyguards, possibly even bouncers from the embassy. And after that—at first in twos and threes, later in tens and twenties—the audience began to arrive by car, by taxi and on foot.

Bolan saw cocktail dresses, white tuxedos, dark suits, a sprinkling of jeans, all of them presenting invitations at the top of the steps. For the hundredth time his eyes raked the rooftops opposite. No figure showed above the parapet; none was visible in any of Cobbold's windows.

Five minutes before eight o'clock, a white-helmeted cop astride a BMW 1100 arrived, parked the bike on its kickstand and began talking into his radio. A crowd of spectators, sensing celebrities, had assembled on the sidewalk.

Right on the hour, a Daimler limo with diplomatic plates, flying the Spanish flag, turned into Great Queen Street from Kingsway. It was preceded by two more cops on BMWs and followed by three black Jaguar sedans.

The bikes wheeled aside, the limo drew up at the foot of the steps and the Jags stopped immediately behind.

Embassy officials, wives and a couple of newspaper columnists piled out and moved toward the entrance. A man with a rosette in the buttonhole of his tailcoat ran down the steps to open the rear door of the Daimler.

Bolan had started the panel truck's engine. He scanned the street in every direction.

The Englishman, Cobbold, hurried around the corner from Kingsway, climbed into the Opel and sat behind the wheel.

A louvered shutter opened on the top floor of the book publisher's building. Someone appeared in the window. Bolan was certain it would be Lozano. He was holding a long-barreled rifle with a sniperscope. Standing back a little inside the room, the Corsican raised the rifle to his shoulder and squinted through the sight.

Bolan glanced upward toward the Kingsway end of the street. He saw a figure lurking behind the parapet of the office block. The gunman would fire through a space between two of the short stone columns forming the balustrade.

The Executioner's plan relied on speed, surprise, sureness of touch and silence alternating with sound. Above all on speed.

The man with the rosette was holding the limo door open, offering his hand to the Spanish minister.

Bolan was holding the Beretta 93-R. He had lowered the front handgrip. The gun, equipped with specially machined springs to take subsonic cartridges, now had a folding carbine stock clipped to the butt and a suppressor screwed to the barrel. Bolan's two favorite handguns were supplied by Hal Brognola via the CIA's London resident at the Grosvenor Square embassy. And it was through that same channel the weapons would leave the U.K. again.

The warrior raised the modified and silenced weapon to his shoulder, the fingers of his left hand curled around the handgrip, his thumb hooked through the extrawide trigger guard.

His right forefinger caressed the trigger.

Since the Corsican was standing back from his window and the Marksman was behind a balustrade, Lozano would be invisible to his accomplice. Bolan's plan was to take him out silently and then preempt the Marksman's action with a maneuver of his own—before the killer knew his teammate had been wasted.

The minister, together with two aides and the guy with the rosette, began to climb the steps. They were talking animatedly.

Lozano's gun was raised. Bolan squeezed off two three-round bursts, the Beretta punching his shoulder lightly as the deadly 9 mm parabellums leaped noiselessly toward their target.

There was a flash of light as the rifle spun from the Corsican's hands and pinwheeled down into the street. Bolan didn't wait to see the killer, his chest smashed open by the six-shot killstream, collapse over the windowsill and hang head downward with outflung arms. The Executioner had already dropped the Beretta and snatched up his AutoMag.

Velasquez, a small, neat man with a pointed beard, was one-third of the way up the flight of steps. Bolan's plan was simple. Now that there was only one murderer to reckon with, he would *fake* an assassination attempt . . . and hope to hell it would provoke enough confusion to stop the Marksman from isolating his target.

Crouched in the open rear of the panel truck, the Executioner blasted off six separate deafening rounds, aiming three of them just above the heads of the Spaniards on the steps, two more at the pillars flanking the entrance and one into the air.

The effect was as electrifying as he could have wished.

There were shouts and the panicked commotion of bodies moving in all directions as chips flew from the pillars and a ricochet screamed skyward. The uniformed cops whirled toward the panel truck, the bikers leaped for their machines, and guests flung themselves flat. Some began to run while others shot back inside the building.

Bolan had to hand it to the embassy aides. They manhandled Alfonso Velasquez back down the steps, pushed him to the ground between the limo and the curb and covered him with their own bodies before the echo of Bolan's last shot died away.

If the Marksman had fired during the confusion, he hadn't scored. That was Bolan's main concern. He was already in the driving seat, Big Thunder beside him, the Beretta on the floor in back. He pulled out of the parking space, floored the pedal and headed for Kingsway.

Across the street, the Opel was already moving, slewing out into the center of the roadway.

The door of the office building burst open, and the Marksman, carrying his twin-barrel rifle, pelted across the sidewalk and ran between a couple of parked cars to get to the Opel. He jerked open the passenger door and scrambled inside as Cobbold cut in front of the Executioner and sent the car, with gears screaming, hurtling toward the corner.

Bolan saw a startled flash of recognition on the face of the Marksman as he registered the identity of the man driving the panel truck. Then both cars were on Kingsway, roaring south toward the bridge and the river.

Behind them, the three white-helmeted police riders started their BMWs, slammed them off the stands and raced in pursuit.

23

Mack Bolan had been in many pursuits, sometimes as hunter, sometimes as the hunted, but this was the first time he had played both roles at once.

Cobbold was a good driver, better than average, but not as good as the Executioner. The fact that he had the faster, more maneuverable vehicle just about made them even.

At the lower end of Kingsway, he broadsided the Opel into the one-way circle around the Aldwych, corrected the slide just in time to avoid a bus, carved up three taxis returning home after the early theater trade and ran a red light to turn onto Waterloo Bridge.

Bolan maintained his distance about fifty yards behind through experience and expertise, using the gears skillfully, twitching the wheel when he felt the rear end begin to drift. He had a two-hundred-yard lead on the police BMWs, but the bikes were gaining fast. Their ability to thread through a jam on busy roads would enable them to catch up within a few blocks...and on an open road they would be almost twice as fast as the Opel. As for the panel truck, the small European-built Ford was lively, but it was no speedster.

So the cops would draw level almost at once.

Bolan was certain they would have radioed headquarters to put out an APB: prowl cars would be heading in to cut them off from all over London.

Once over the bridge, the Opel swung right and took the road past the Royal Festival Hall and along the South Bank. Still in convoy, they raced past London County Hall, the fire department center and the blackened stone towers of Lambeth Palace—with Big Ben and the Houses of Parliament blurred in the dusk on the other side of the river.

Here, beneath street lighting just switched on, the road was almost clear, and Cobbold pushed the Opel up to seventy-five miles per hour. Bolan's own vehicle began to whine in order to keep up.

The Opel tore around the complex carousel beneath the railroad tracks at Nine Elms and continued heading west. It was on the long warehouse-bordered section between there and Battersea that the cops drew level and decided to make their play alone.

Two rode up, one on either side of Bolan, and waved him curtly to stop. The third man accelerated and maneuvered his machine, exhaust howling, alongside the Opel.

He gestured fiercely, stabbing a gloved finger toward the sidewalk.

Casually the Marksman poked the barrels of his gun out the open window and fired at the bike's front wheel.

Bolan saw the two puffs of smoke whipped away by the speeding car's slipstream. Hammered by the two deadly projectiles, the wheel whipped to one side, wrenching the handlebars from the rider's grasp.

With the front wheel turned under, the BMW somersaulted, catapulting the cop across the roadway. He landed on his back, slid along the pavement and hit his head on a curb.

Horror-struck at the fate of their teammate, the cops on either side of Bolan signaled him more angrily still to stop. Bolan kept on after the Opel, now traveling dangerously fast. He reached for the AutoMag, lifted it from the passenger seat and pointed it first at one rider and then the other. He had no intention of firing, but the cops didn't know that.

They hesitated until he made a more imperious gesture with the big gun. They reduced speed, dropping behind the panel truck and remaining there, about fifty yards away. In the rearview mirror, Bolan could see the one who had looked the more scared steering with one hand while he talked into the mike of his radio.

The bikers had evidently been ordered to stay put and tail them until there were patrol cars near enough to cut across and block the route in front and behind.

The Executioner himself was following much the same plan—except that he had no prowl cars to help him. He hadn't yet decided what action to take if he did manage not only to keep on Cobbold's tail but draw level with the runaway Opel.

The Marksman had recognized him for sure, so there were only two things he could do. First, eliminate the guy along with Cobbold, which they both deserved as murderers in theory and now, with the callous attack on the policeman, in fact.

Or pretend that he was there in his Baraka role. The Marksman was jealous of Baraka's own firearms prowess; the Maginot tapes proved that. Maybe he could be fed the idea that Bolan had been sent by Max Nasruddin to see how the Marksman handled the Velasquez assassination. As a loner, proud of his lethal skills—and the reputation that went with them—the Marksman would violently resent such interference. He would interpret it as questioning his competence.

But the situation was developing too fast for Bolan to make a choice.

He could hear the warble of a police siren, then a second, some way behind. Soon the cars, two low-slung Rover 800s with blue lamps flashing on their roofs, appeared in the rearview mirror, overtaking him rapidly.

A moment later a third appeared from beneath a railroad bridge on the left and cut in between Bolan and the Opel.

It was now virtually dark.

With the solitary police car closing up to nudge his rear fender, Cobbold screeched the Opel around the traffic circle south of Battersea Park, cut back across the river and roared along the Chelsea embankment. Gnatlike, his headlamps now blazing, he zigzagged perilously in and out of a stream of trucks, buses and private cars heading west and north for the express-way that circled the city.

The Rover followed, sometimes pulling right across the roadway in front of oncoming traffic as brakes smoked and drivers swore. Bolan and his pursuers began to drop behind.

It was on the long stretch between Hammersmith and Chiswick—where there were two three-lane sectors of road separated by a central grass strip—that they decided to put the Executioner out of the race.

There was a sudden lull in the westward flow. The bikes swung wide to let the Rovers through. They raced up on each side of the panel truck, intending to overtake and then squeeze together in a pincer movement, forcing him to stop. The BMWs stayed behind, ready to pounce and disarm him as soon as he halted.

Bolan was familiar with the maneuver. He knew, too, that the police drivers, as they had been taught, would be watching the driver's silhouette, the front wheels, the brake lights for signs of an abrupt alteration in speed or direction.

Just before the Rovers drew level, he hauled up savagely on the hand brake lever. The lever, working the rear-wheel brakes only, didn't activate the brake lights.

The panel truck shuddered, slewed and slowed as it fell behind. The police cars, already homing in from either side on a collision course with a now non-existent target, clashed front fenders. With bumpers locked together, they skated across the hardtop and came to rest against a split-fence shield surrounding a sapling planted by the roadside.

Bolan swerved outside them, released the lever and hit the pedal once more. One of the bikers, braking too hard, slid straight into the enmeshed cars; the other, taken completely by surprise when the panel truck lost speed so unexpectedly, ran up onto the central strip and fell off sideways as his machine stalled.

Bolan continued as fast as he dared, keeping an eye open for Cobbold and the other police car.

A few hundred yards before the overpass that carried the road out of the city and toward Heathrow Airport, he saw brake lights blaze all along the procession of vehicles ahead of him. Gradually the snarled traffic ground to a halt.

This was a situation Bolan had feared. If he stayed with the panel truck, the only outcome could be a police interrogation, because it wouldn't take long for the bikers to resume the chase. And they could cut through this kind of bottleneck almost as fast as they could ride.

A short private road led off the expressway at right angles here. Bolan coaxed the Ford across a grass strip and up to a turning circle at the end of the cul-de-sac. He reholstered Big Thunder, detached stock and silencer from the Beretta and shoved that back into its shoulder rig. Then, leaving the panel truck with the keys in the ignition, he walked past a row of neat red-brick houses, past clipped lawns bright with flower-beds, back to the expressway.

Lamplight gleamed on the roofs of the stalled vehicles choking the roadway, but beyond there was a brighter radiance, glowing then fading beneath a canopy of smoke. As Bolan hurried closer he saw the police Rover pulled up on the grass shoulder separating the road from a footpath.

Fifty yards farther on, the Opel lay on its side against the posts of a sign warning of an intersection, with flames billowing out from beneath the hood and through the windows of the interior.

A small crowd of motorists had left their vehicles and gathered in a wary half circle by the curb. Cobbold and the Marksman stood some way off with their backs to a tall fence.

Bolan could see in the flickering light that the Marksman's face was bloodied from a gash in his forehead. Cobbold, incongruous in his gray chalk stripe, looked ruffled but unharmed. He was holding a heavy-caliber revolver in front of him. The Marksman had raised the Holland & Holland rifle to his shoulder, the twin barrels pointed at three uniformed cops halted a little way in front of the Rover.

One of the cops moved slowly forward.

"Stand back!" the Marksman snarled.

The policeman continued to advance. The Marksman fired twice, the shots curiously flat over the crackle of flames from the burning car.

The cop pitched forward, dead.

A movement of recoil accompanied by shouts of outrage swayed the crowd. A woman screamed. Seeing that the killer was now temporarily unarmed, the two remaining police moved purposefully forward. Cobbold raised his revolver.

From fifty yards away Bolan shot him with a single round from the Beretta. The 9 mm flesh-shredder pulverized his face at the level of his ginger mustache, blasting his teeth out through the back of his head. He thumped into the fence and slid to the ground.

Bolan swung the gun toward the Marksman, but he had already disappeared over the fence and into the trees on the other side.

After hastily filling in the police about the evening's events, Bolan decided it would be wise to return to France. He took the unexpected course and walked the remaining seven miles to Heathrow. After a snack at the new Terminal 4, he made the last Air France flight to Paris.

Early editions of the next day's papers were already available on the plane. "London Police Foil Terror-Bomb Attack on Airline Office," he read with satisfaction on the front page. " 'Baby Carriage Killer' Arrested." And then, lower, "Spanish Minister Escapes Assassination Attempt—Basque Separatists Suspected."

The following morning he put in an early routine call to Julie Marco in Strasbourg.

"I've been told to start two more dossiers," she told him. "There's a fifty kilo bomb due to demolish the International Culture Center in Liège, Belgium, at midday tomorrow. And Baraka's going operational—they're aiming to bring you in pretty damn quick to set you up for the big one...."

24

In theory it was a mission after the Executioner's own heart—almost an urban version of one of his lightning jungle raids in Vietnam.

The formula was the same: efficient recon, a study of the intel, then quickly in, do the job and quickly out again.

All the recon he would need had already been processed by Julie Marco. She had told him the aim of the enemy operation, the place, the time, the MO, even the outward appearance of the terrorists involved.

So far as the evaluation and eventual use of this intel was concerned, Bolan required only to refresh his memory on the layout of the town plan of Liège, and then buy a first-class round trip railroad ticket to the Belgian city.

Bolan took the reservation-only Paris–Cologne flyer, which left the Paris Nord station at seven-thirty on the morning of the thirty-first.

On the train, German waiters served him an ample breakfast. The French and Belgian immigration and customs officials glanced only casually into the first-class compartments as the train crossed the frontier, and didn't even ask to see passports.

Very convenient, Bolan mused, feeling the comforting weight of Big Thunder on his right hip and the bulge of the Beretta beneath his left arm. If you happened to be a terrorist loaded with firearms and explosives and you wanted out of one country and into another, all you had to do was travel first class. The second-class passengers were asked if they had anything to declare, had their ID checked and in some cases were asked to open luggage or remove jackets. Money, as usual, bought immunity!

The train stopped at Charleroi and Namur, depositing him in Liège at two minutes past eleven o'clock.

Fifty-eight minutes in which to foil the terrorists' attempt to bomb the Culture Center.

Just under an hour to put one more spoke in Max Nasruddin's evil wheel.

Bolan took a cab around the boulevard that circled the old town and paid the driver off at the opera house. He aimed to walk down to the Culture Center, which overlooked the Meuse River, by way of the cathedral square and the coal-black Gothic church building that presided over it—because that was the route he had been told the terrorists would take.

They would be pushing a four-wheel trolley loaded with packing cases supposedly full of archaeological specimens, similar to clerks pushing dress racks through the streets of New York's garment district. Some of the cases would be packed with specimens. One wouldn't be.

Bolan hurried down the rue Lulay, once the hub of the red-light district, now a showplace for chic boutiques, cut through to the university and made it to the river by the junction on the near side of the Kennedy Bridge.

On the way he passed through a shopping arcade where a long-haired youth strummed a guitar, accompanied on the flute by a willowy brunette.

As the Executioner turned out of sight at the far end of the arcade, the music was cut short as the boy disconnected his guitar from the amplifier. He plugged in a hand mike, turned a knob and spoke quietly for fifteen seconds.

The girl packed away her flute, and they walked toward the river.

The Culture Center was behind a thirty-story tower block that faced the aquarium and zoological institute across the sluggish yellow flow of the Meuse. The entrance was in the rue Méry. And the whole length of the street was taken up by the long horizontal length of the charcoal-gray building that housed the Center. The clifflike facade was pierced laterally by street-long slits behind which windows were hidden.

Bolan circled the block. There was a loading bay for the Center near the exit from a multistory parking garage.

A workman in blue coveralls was winding down a steel grille to block off the storage area in back of the platform at the far end of the bay. Behind it crates and cartons were stacked with cans of film and tall thin packages leaning against a wall that could have been the flats for a stage set or the elements of an exhibition display stand.

Crates?

Hairs prickled on Bolan's nape. Was he too late? Should he try to raise the alarm?

There was no sign of an unloaded trolley. He had seen nothing on his walk down from the opera house.

A three-ton Mercedes flatbed backed up into the bay had nothing between the cab and the tailgate.

He looked at his watch. It was 11:37.

The man winding down the grille had completed the job and gone back inside the building. Secretaries and clerks emerged from the staff entrance in twos and threes. The red-and-white-striped barrier pole at the exit from the parking garage rose and fell as executives drove away.

Bolan glanced up and down the rue Méry. There must be a lot of packing cases in Liège. If he attempted to alert the authorities, was it likely that he could persuade someone official, with no hard evidence to support him, to get a bomb disposal expert to the Center within twenty minutes? At the beginning of the lunch hour?

No way.

And even if he did, there was a chance that all of the crates visible behind the grille could be entirely harmless.

In the distance he heard a rumbling clatter. At the far end of the street, on the corner of the rue de l'Université, two men in white coveralls pushed a four-wheel trolley loaded with packing crates toward the river.

Bolan ran.

As he neared the street corner, he could see that the two men answered the descriptions he had been given by Julie Marco—a grizzled guy of about fifty with close-cropped hair and a beer belly, and a stocky, muscular type with Germanic features and a bullet head, obviously Willi, the guard he had knocked out in the cellar entrance to the Maginot redoubt.

They rounded the next corner onto the embankment and pushed the trolley more slowly up a rise toward the bridge and the thirty-story tower block, which was called the Residence Kennedy.

Had Julie been mistaken about the target? Many officials from the European Iron and Steel Federation owned apartments in the block. So did the leader of the Belgian steelworkers' union and a couple of Eurocrats from the OEEC headquarters in Brussels. Wouldn't that be a more impressive hit than the Culture Center behind the tower?

Hearing running footsteps, Willi glanced over his shoulder and saw the Executioner. He snapped some comment to his companion out of the side of his mouth, and they began to hurry, half running themselves as they labored up the slope with the heavy trolley. The crates, Bolan saw as he drew near, were stenciled Fragile—Objets d'Art.

It was 11:44.

Bolan palmed the Beretta.

The two terrorists continued pushing. Bolan couldn't shoot. Three people walking in the opposite direction—an elderly couple, a woman with a poodle on a leash—had just passed the trolley. He had to wait until they had passed him too and were safely on the pedestrian crossing leading to the sidewalk that overlooked the river. And by that time the trolley load was no more than thirty yards from the glassed-in entrance to the Kennedy tower.

Bolan called out and fired a single shot over the heads of the two men.

They stopped, swinging the trolley broadside on to the slope and dodging behind the stack of crates. "Go ahead," Willi jeered. This confirmed Bolan's suspicions that the crates were loaded with high explosives.

He thought quickly. Unless the contents of the crates were liquid nitroglycerin, it was hardly likely to be detonated by the relatively slight shock of a slug thwacking into a neighboring crate. And even if he scored on the crate itself, the odds on a direct hit on a detonator were long. In any case he didn't see Willi and his companion as carbon copies of the Beirut Palestinian kamikazes, who were prepared to be blown to pieces along with their booby-trapped cars. The crate with the explosives was probably on the far side of the trolley, away from the Executioner's gun, and the delayed-action timer would already have been set, almost certainly with the usual wristwatch device.

He decided to call the bluff. He pumped three shots from the Beretta just above the upper of the two rows of crates.

The two men swore and ducked behind their load, Willi managing to get off a quick round from a small automatic before he vanished. Bolan whipped behind a cast-iron mailbox set in the sidewalk and fired again.

It was 11:53.

The next few minutes were hectic, but Mack Bolan was never able to recall the action as anything other than a series of freeze-frames.

The man with the beer belly leaning around the edge of the crated trolley to aim a heavy caliber revolver at Bolan's legs, partly exposed on either side of the steel shaft supporting the bulk of the mailbox.

The small puff of smoke beside the crates.

The vibration tingling through his body as the bullet splatted against the shaft and set the whole box trembling.

His own lightning three-round reaction that winged the gunman before he had time to get back under cover; a silver fountain cascading over the sidewalk as one of the slugs shattered a glass door in the tower block entrance and the midday sun glittered on the falling glass.

Beer Belly tumbling, spilling into the roadway in front of a speeding red sedan accelerating fiercely as the driver jumped a red light at the end of the bridge.

The blood and guts steaming on the blacktop.

The trolley, which Willi shoved violently in his direction before he fled, careering down the slope, jumping the curb and rocketing across the roadway to burst through a railing above the road emerging from the junction underpass.

The explosion.

The first millionth-of-a-second flash that dimmed the brightness of the sun would always remain printed on Bolan's memory, but he would never have any recollection of the thunderous concussion or the searing blast that hurled him fifty yards back down the slope to end up half stunned against the front wheel of a parked taxi.

As he struggled dazedly to his feet, the vast mushroom of brown smoke roiling skyward from the crater blown in the lower road was still showering concrete fragments, asphalt and pieces of masonry into the river and glass was still falling from the upper windows of the Residence Kennedy.

A man with blood trickling from a cut in his forehead got out of a car that had run up onto the sidewalk and smashed its windshield. He helped Bolan to his feet. "Goddamn gas mains," he fumed in French.

"Last month one exploded in an apartment block out at Maloune. Killed four people."

Bolan thanked him, refused a ride to a hospital and limped back up toward the bridge. The red sedan was lying on its side in the center of the road, near the remains of Beer Belly.

There seemed to be no other casualties. Bolan figured there would soon be a crowd. He shouldered his way through the stream of people erupting from the tower block, running across the bridge, materializing the way they always did when there was some kind of disaster. His Beretta was lying on the sidewalk at the foot of a flight of steps. It seemed undamaged. He picked it up and shoved it back into the shoulder rig. People were too taken by the disaster to notice.

It would be useless to try to pick up Willi's trail now. He crossed the street and took the footpath at the side of the bridge.

Below, traffic was already jammed on each side of the huge smoking hole by the exit from the underpass.

Halfway across the bridge, a long-haired youth with a guitar case was packing away his amplifier. Beside him a tall, slender girl held a flute.

As Bolan approached, the boy straightened. He was holding the guitar case horizontally, the strap over one shoulder. Too late the Executioner saw that the top of the neck had been cut away, saw the circular gleam of a gun muzzle inside the case.

The young man swung toward him. "There's a gun in here, mister," he said. "If I was you, I'd turn left toward the parapet and admire the view across the river."

Bolan halted in midstride, hesitated.

"Fast," the boy said. "The gun's silenced."

Bolan turned. He approached the parapet.

The girl moved behind him. She raised her flute to her lips, but instead of blowing across it she put her mouth to one end and puffed. Instinctively Bolan raised a hand to brush away the tiny sting at the nape of his neck. But before his fingers touched flesh, the minute feathered dart had done its work and the day blacked out on him.

The couple moved quickly. The youth leaned the guitar case against the parapet. The girl glanced right and left across the bridge. "Okay," she said. "They're all watching the hole."

Together they hefted the Executioner's inert body onto the coping. A barge was chugging very slowly beneath the bridge. Over the hatches on its foredeck an awning had been rigged on four tall posts—an unusual awning, for instead of the usual canvas or sunshade material it was made of fine-mesh netting.

As the prow of the barge passed beneath the bridge arch, the net was immediately below the parapet. The boy and the girl gave a quick heave and pushed Bolan over.

He dropped down and fell into the center of the net.

The guitar player and his accompanist picked up their gear and walked unhurriedly across to the far side of the river. As they turned along the road following the east bank, the clock in the tower above the zoological institute began chiming twelve times.

25

"You don't understand," Max Nasruddin said angrily. "It doesn't matter that they missed the Kennedy tower block. There was a bomb explosion. All the papers carried scare stories. Now everyone is wondering how much worse the terror will get, why the authorities aren't doing something. What more do you want?"

"It would have been perhaps more ... impressive," Farid Gamal Mokhaddem said, "if there had been casualties."

"Certainly, but I repeat, there *was* an explosion. It got into the news all over Europe. It will add to the general air of demoralization."

"That's three hits flunked in as many days," Senator Shell Pettifer observed. "Velasquez. The Iberia office. And now this."

"So what? Flunked is a relative term." Nasruddin paced up and down between the desk and the filing cabinets in the office at the Maginot fortress. "Listen. Velasquez *personally* means nothing to us. His removal wouldn't benefit us one way or the other. Codorneau and the Italian were another matter, but this guy was no more than a gesture—one more prominent man out of the way, one step higher up the panic scale. Look at it objectively, in the light of the plan as a whole, and you'll see that it's not really important that he escaped."

"It was a failure just the same," Pettifer said stubbornly.

"Okay, okay. Bolan screwed up the hit. Don't ask me how. But the fact that it was made got us as much publicity as if it had succeeded. Don't you see? It's the same thing with the girl and the Iberia bomb. The mysterious tip-off...our fearless police force...disaster narrowly averted. All that shit. It's a natural for the media."

"But you lost the Corsican. And Olga Kurtz is in jail," Mahdi al-Jaafari objected.

Nasruddin waved a hand. "They were expendable. So was the man in Liège. They're all expendable. That's why we use pros. There's always another in need of ready cash."

He sat down behind the desk. "You've seen the Liège video. It was shot from a parked cab just down the hill from the Kennedy. Pretty spectacular, don't you think? Even if it wasn't the tower block?"

"I thought it was supposed to be the Culture Center," Mahdi al-Jaafari remarked, fingering the yellow rose in his buttonhole.

"The target was switched at the last minute. For a reason. It told us something we wanted to know... because Bolan went to the Culture Center first. It's all on the tape."

"I think Max is right," the tall American with crimped hair put in. "We're forgetting something here. The entire Liège operation was planned with a single aim in mind—to get Bolan there. Whether or not he fouled up the bomb arrangements was of secondary importance. We'd lost him after the fiasco here with the night guards. We wanted him where we could tail him again.''

He paused, looking at the three other men. ''Well, we got him, didn't we?'' he said. ''In my view anything extra in the way of explosions or newspaper stories about them are a bonus.''

''I guess you're right, Al,'' Pettifer said. ''Anything to keep the man in the street screaming blue murder...and his wife saying she's too scared to fly or even go to the supermarket anymore.''

''She'll be even more scared after today,'' Nasruddin said.

THE SUPERMARKET WAS three miles out of town on the road to Limoges—a vast, single-story, hangarlike structure with forty-six checkout desks and open-air parking for thirty-five hundred cars. Most of them seemed to be there on the afternoon of the thirty-first. Certainly the section of the vast hall devoted to sports and camping gear was unusually crowded.

At first the people examining kayak skirts and Windsurfing equipment took the two men in camouflage fatigues and face masks to be part of some demonstration or sales promotion.

The men were sitting side by side on a porch swing with a striped awning overhead. Even when they unzipped their fatigue tunics to produce mini-Uzi submachine guns, nobody paid them any mind.

Then, quite calmly, the taller man fired a short burst into a group of customers checking out the assembly of a camp stove.

A man in knee-length shorts died instantly. A child of seven threw herself screaming across a fallen mother who was pumping blood from her mouth. A bearded youth stared unbelievingly at his shattered arm. The noise of the volley was deafening.

At the same time the second man leaped onto a stack of crated scuba suits and fired at the long wall of bottles in the liquor department.

Uproar.

After the instant of total silence that follows any catastrophe, before the echoes of the SMGs died away in the girdered ceiling, panic flooded the vast hall. Shouts, sobs and a stampede of feet as men and women fought to make the exits mixed with the sound of several hundred people dropping to the floor and the lone screech of a hysterical woman.

In the liquor department glass erupted, liquid splashed and showered and wood splintered as the hail of lead swept along the rows of shelved bottles.

The two gunmen were acting crazy. The sound of shots ripped through the pandemonium engulfing the supermarket. A container bottle of camping gas exploded, and the flames set fire to the material covering poolside chairs and sun umbrellas. Within seconds that corner of the building was a holocaust of flame.

The killers sprinted from alley to alley, hosing death and destruction as they ran. They fired at anything that moved, anything that caught their eye, anything that stirred their drug-crazed minds to hatred.

The tall terrorist continued shooting when his companion had exhausted his thirty-two-round box magazine, then slammed in a fresh clip himself when the other had reloaded and opened fire again.

More terror-stricken customers fell. A huge pyramid of canned dog food disintegrated, and the cans rolled and clattered for dozens of yards in every direction.

Then at last the slaughter was over. The junkie murderers backed out and ran from the screams and the flames and the blood. They were giggling as they piled into a Land Rover and careered out of the parking lot.

The toll was forty-two dead and more than seventy injured.

SWISSAIR'S FLIGHT SR759 took off as scheduled from Nice airport at 7:40 p.m., destination Geneva. The jetliner, a DC-9, flew out over the Mediterranean, turned when it was halfway to Corsica and returned on the international airlane that passed over Bordighera and the Italian Alps when it reached its operational height of thirty-three thousand feet. It was due to land at Geneva fifty minutes later.

The plane never arrived.

Seventeen minutes after takeoff, when the dusk was gathering in steep-sided valleys between the still-snowcapped peaks far below, a slender man with a crew cut and pale, flat, expressionless eyes stood up to reach for a case in the overhead locker compartment above his seat.

The plastic-bodied Heckler & Koch caseless assault rifle that he produced had been smuggled in by an accomplice working with the baggage handlers in Nice. The woman sitting next to him, a retired schoolteacher from Milan, didn't initially recognize the weapon for what it was: the H&K G-11, with its smooth, longitudinally grooved polystyrene exterior and sniperscope carrying handle, could be a modernistic musical instrument case or some kind of precision optical device.

The man walked clumsily to the rear of the cabin. Despite the fact that the summer evening was warm, he was wearing a raincoat that flapped around his legs. Standing by the curtain that divided the toilets from the seating accommodation, he raised the gun to his shoulder.

The first indication the majority of passengers had that something was wrong was the sound of gunfire—three separate shots cracked loudly over the drone of the Pratt & Whitney jet engines. A hoarse shout from a bearded fat man and a scream from the schoolteacher were swamped in the tinkling clatter of breaking glass.

Three flight attendants—one man and two women—serving drinks from a trolley at the far end of the cabin slumped lifeless to the aisle between the rows of seats.

The outcry that swelled down the length of the cabin was drowned by a fourth shot as the terrorist gunned down the first officer, who had appeared in the doorway of the first-class cabin up front.

Then he reached into the pocket of his raincoat and drew out an egg-shaped plastic hand grenade. He extracted the pin. "Here, catch!" he called to a young man sitting by a window at the far end of the cabin.

He drew back his arm and pitched the grenade accurately over the heads of the other passengers. Involuntarily the young man raised his hands, though whether this was in automatic obedience to the direct command or simply to ward off danger, nobody knew.

The grenade—a 70 mm, 150-gram nonfragmentation HE killer developed by Omnipol in Prague—exploded as it reached him, reducing the upper half of his body to a gory pulp and smashing a seven-foot hole in the stressed skin of the DC-9's fuselage.

Air from the pressurized cabin of the jetliner blasted out into the rarefied atmosphere high above the mountains, sucking with it several dozen of the tourist-class passengers, hand baggage, bottles, the drinks trolley and the four dead aircrew.

At the same time the hurricane disturbance created an implosion between the cabin floor and the non-pressurized cargo hold beneath, buckling the airframe and shearing hydraulic feeders and control conduits that led from the flight deck to the tail group.

The captain, who had only just had time to radio a skyjack alert, was halfway through the international Mayday sign when the bomb blew a hole in the DC-9's fuselage and sent it plummeting toward the earth.

The terrorist had been ready for the whirlwind that sucked half the contents of the cabin out into the void. He had dropped down and clung to the bulkhead, which he knew was attached to one of the main fuselage formers, as soon as the grenade had left his hand.

Now he rose unsteadily to his feet and fought his way out of the shrieking horror in the cabin, past the galley and the toilets to the rear entrance and exit hatch. Pushing up the steel safety bars on the door, he forced it open against the pressure of the wind and allowed it to be whipped away by the howling slipstream.

He ripped off the raincoat—and suddenly the reason for its cumbersome size was revealed: beneath it he was strapped into the harness of a parachute rig. He forced himself to the open doorway and stepped out into space, allowing himself to fall several thousand feet before he pulled the rip cord.

It seemed a long while later that he saw the dull flash some miles to the east when the stricken DC-9 plunged into a rocky escarpment on the slopes of Mont Blanc.

26

Mack Bolan regained consciousness underneath a bush. The bush was one of a clump growing below a line of trees. The trees crowned an eighty-foot bluff, partially covered by wild grasses and scrub, that bordered a wide river. Beyond a curve in the river, he could see the roofs, spires and factory chimneys of a large town.

Bolan sat up. Apart from that fraction of a second immediately following the bomb blast, everything that had happened in Liège and in the days preceding his arrival there returned to him totally and in a single flash of awareness.

He felt fine. No headache, no apparent injuries, the guns still holstered, each in its special rig. He took them out. Still loaded—exactly as they had been when he had come to outside the Friedekinde clinic near Neuchâtel.

He touched his cheek and chin. They had even shaved him! He wondered how long he had been held this time, how much, and precisely what, had been programmed into him without his knowledge.

He wondered where he was.

Undulating pastureland stretched as far as the eye could see on the other side of the river. Long shadows beneath the trees faded as the sun sank below a cloud bank low in the western sky.

He got to his feet and walked away from the river and through the belt of trees.

Soon he came to a country road. He turned left and strode in the direction of the town. Approaching scattered houses on the outskirts a mile farther on, he was passed by a pickup loaded with crates of live chickens. Glancing at the rear license plate, he saw three numerals followed by three letters, red on a white background. And the white plate itself was rimmed with red.

Bolan frowned. Red on white?

And then, rounding a corner and seeing ahead of him a roadside sign announcing the name of the town, he halted in midstride.

The license plate was Belgian. The name of the town was Namur.

Bolan started walking again, more slowly this time. That meant the river must be the Meuse. They had dumped him only thirty miles away from the city where he had been dumb enough to let them surprise him.

How come?

Liège to Neuchâtel was two hundred and thirty miles in a straight line, more like two hundred and fifty by road; Liège to the Maginot fortress perhaps seventy or eighty less.

Something wasn't quite right. Bolan went into the first café he came to and ordered a beer. In halting French he asked the girl standing behind the zinc coffee urn if there was a newspaper he could look at.

She smiled and told him she spoke English, then reached beneath the shelves and handed him a copy of the Brussels daily, *Le Soir*. He glanced at the front page and handed it back. The lead story was about the attempted assassination of Alfonso Velasquez. "No," he said. "Sorry. I meant *today's* paper."

"That is today's," the girl said.

He stared at her, down at the date below the title and then up again. "But it says here the thirty-first."

She frowned. "Today is the thirty-first."

Bolan raised his left wrist and looked at the date slot on the face of his watch. She was right of course. The thirty-first.

But this was crazy.

He knew nothing of the net into which he had been dropped or the barge that had carried him upriver. What was certain, nevertheless, since the date hadn't changed, was the fact that he had been in the hands of Nasruddin's hoods not days but simply a matter of hours.

They'd taken him around midday. It was only just after six o'clock now.

What the hell would be the point?

No way could they have transported him to the Maginot fort, transformed him into Baraka, doctored his mind and returned him to Belgium in such a short time, even if they had flown him there in a private plane. No, there would be too much time wasted driving to and from airfields, and a chopper would be too slow, plus the fact that Bolan thought he had read someplace that it often took several hours for psychedelic drugs to take effect.

And why bring him back to Belgium?

None of it made any sense at all, not in terms of a visit to the Maginot complex or the clinic.

Okay, so they hadn't taken him out of the country.

Whatever happened in those lost six hours must have happened right here in Belgium. That was the only answer that did make sense.

But—his mind circled back to the same problem—what could they do to a guy, what possible use could they make of an unconscious man during a thirty-mile journey that took six hours?

Bolan gave up. Like so many other turning points on this damned mission, this one had him well and truly baffled.

Every time he figured he was getting someplace, a new twist came up and he found himself more puzzled than ever. He had even made the most important objective: he had located and identified Baraka. But despite the fact that he knew now that this programmed killer-to-be was himself, he was no nearer to the why, when and where of "the big one" for which Baraka was supposedly being trained.

The Executioner felt that he needed help to work on the problem. Maybe Brognola or that shrink of his would have some bright suggestions; maybe, looking at it from a fresh angle, they could dream up a valid reason for a guy to be slugged, retained for six hours and then left unharmed down by the riverside thirty miles away.

Whatever the answer, Bolan figured there was no point hanging around Namur.

It would be better to return to Paris and connect with Brognola, so that they could hammer out the possibles and probables together.

Finishing his beer, Bolan was struck by a sudden thought. He still had his round-trip railroad ticket in his pocket. And he remembered that the express, on its return journey from Cologne, called at Namur at exactly 7:00 p.m.

He had around fifty minutes to make it. And if he did, he would be in Paris at 9:50—ten minutes short of ten o'clock. He could be in the embassy cypher room before eleven, dictating distress calls to the big Fed.

Bolan put down the glass and laid some coins on the counter. "How far is it from here to the central railroad station?" he asked the girl.

She pursed her lips. "Maybe a mile."

"Would there be a cab in this neighborhood?"

She shook her head.

Bolan thanked her and left the café.

He began to run.

27

"I can only think of one reason," Hal Brognola said. "You said it was a *maximum* of six hours, right?"

"Right," Bolan said. Outside the window of the interview room, rain splashed on the roofs of traffic stalled along the Avenue Gabriel behind a truck unloading crates of beer between two lines of parked cars.

"And you're certain they weren't still on your tail when you left Paris for Liège?"

"They couldn't have been," Bolan said. "Look at the schedule, Hal. I flew to London on the twenty-seventh, as soon as I was briefed on the Velasquez hit. I don't think I was tailed, but I might have been—if they'd known where I was holed up in Strasbourg. In any case, I was recognized two days later by the Marksman after the hit had aborted. But he may have thought I was Baraka, sent to oversee his actions, rather than Bolan determined to foul them up, in which case he might not have reported it. He's a self-important character and he hates interference. Either way we can forget it. Because he vanished after the cop was killed at the end of the car chase. There was nobody left to keep track of me."

"And you lost him?"

"Yeah. Then I *walked* to London airport. I caught the last plane to Paris, but I didn't have a reservation. There was no way they could have known I was even there, let alone on my way back to Paris."

"Unless they had the Arrivals sections staked out on the other side as a matter of routine."

"At all the terminals in three different airports?"

"Maybe not," Brognola conceded. "So you're clean in Paris. You find out from your contact that there's another hit planned in Belgium the next day. You leave on the early train. Any chance they could have picked you up in between?"

"Uh-uh. I checked in at the big airport hotel, and I never left my room once I'd made that phone call. I had my meals sent up and I left for the railroad station at six o'clock the following morning—by subway."

"Okay. So let's say you're still clean when you make Liège. But they're waiting for you at the site of the hit—even though the target had been switched. What does that suggest?"

Bolan grinned crookedly. "They knew I was coming. But it still doesn't make sense. I mean, how could they have?"

"Leave aside the how, Striker. Concentrate on the why. What clse docs it suggest to you?"

"You tell me," Bolan said.

"It was a setup," the Fed replied grimly. "If they were expecting you—and they were—then you must have been led to Liège deliberately, maneuvered there. There's no other explanation."

"Led there for what?"

"Because they needed you for those six hours. It's my opinion the entire Liège operation was mounted with that one aim—to get you where they could lay their hands on you once more.''

"Why, though?" The Executioner was frowning.

"They *needed* to be in contact again. They had to be if they were to proceed with the Baraka thing. They had to know where you were so they could knock you out anytime they felt like it, as quick as they wanted, for the next stage of the training."

"But I told you, in six hours they couldn't—"

"You worked that out yourself," Brognola interrupted. "There wasn't time to take you anywhere, to work any drug routine. So this time it wasn't for any training stage."

"What was it for?"

"Like I say, I can only think of one reason. To make one hundred percent certain that they *stayed* in touch."

"You mean . . . ?"

"I think they used the time they held you to plant some kind of bug on you. Something they could home in on as long as they knew roughly where you were, something that didn't require a twelve-man team on constant alert."

"That could be," Bolan said slowly. "Let's check, huh?"

"Don't worry," the Fed told him. "I already have electronics experts waiting downstairs."

The experts were efficient and anonymous. Bolan unbuckled his shoulder rig and holster and stripped to the skin. First, they monitored his muscular frame with a radar-type scanner to check if the bug had been concealed in a body cavity or hidden in a hollowed-out-tooth.

Negative.

They used a radio-wave detector in case it was an all-plastic device; they had him talk, stop, talk again in case it was voice-operated. Nothing.

After that they turned their high-tech attentions to his clothes—seams, buttons, clasps, zippers. They tried the metal tags at the end of his laces. But it was a tiny thread of dried glue that had escaped under pressure that led them to the heel of one combat boot.

The device was between the inner sole and the nonskid heel. "Not very original," one of the experts said. And then, after he had examined the bug, he added, "It emits an ultrahigh-frequency signal that can be picked up over a radius of around three miles."

"Okay," Brognola said when it was all over. "Mystery solved, and thank you, guys. Now we go see Greg Toledo and his tame pharmacist."

The pharmacist was a full-hipped, breasty redhead with a diminutive waist and shoulder-length hair. She was wearing a white laboratory coat and glasses with huge circular frames, but neither of these accessories hid the fact that underneath she was all woman.

Like Greg Toledo, she had freckles on her forehead and across each cheekbone. Apart from that there was little resemblance.

"This is Beth McMann," the psychoanalyst announced in his high voice. "She's the best Langley has to offer. She's studied all the data you brought," he said to Bolan, "and she has news for you."

"According to the formulae you supplied," Beth said, "the normal conceptual standards by which you live would be temporarily destroyed each time they drug you. Replacing them with different criteria would be no problem for experienced psychospecialists. I've checked the international lists, and Schloesser and

Hansen, the doctors that you mention, are accepted experts with a long history of research in that direction.''

"And this reimprintation would stick? I mean they wouldn't have to start over each time they used the drugs?''

"No. It would be cumulative.''

"Until?''

"Until such time as the reimprintation was neutralized—under precisely the same medication—and the original standards replaced by a competent practitioner.''

"Meanwhile I go on knowing strictly nothing about this second self? But his implanted...immoral standards...don't affect my ordinary life? Unless I'm under the influence of the drugs, I go on thinking black is black and white is white?''

"That is so. This is because of the memory block that occurs when they give you the drug we believe to be puromycil. Without that the reimprinted standards *would* spill over into your normal day-to-day existence.''

"Is there anything I could take that would remove the block so that I could be aware of both my selves at the same time?''

Beth McMann shook her coppery head. "Not that I know of. And even if I did, you'd have to know how much had been used. And we don't. Plus the antidote would have to be taken at the same time or just before—and we don't know when that is because it's done when you're stoned out of your mind with these other drugs.''

"Right," Bolan said. "So what about these others? The psychoto—whatever they are? Have you come up with some way to combat them?"

"We're on firmer ground there," the woman said, reciting a litany of complex-sounding pharmaceutical names that she told Bolan would be able to help him.

"So if I stuffed myself with these before they got to me, the psychedelics wouldn't work anymore?"

"It's not quite as simple as that. But if you did it at the right time, with very carefully calculated doses, it could reduce the bad effects. I can't swear they would be canceled out altogether."

"Also," Toledo put in, "you'd have to know pretty accurately when you were going to be got to, as you put it, since the preventive action, as Beth says, is limited in time."

"But I'd still know who I was and what I was doing?"

"We think so. We hope so. But we couldn't promise."

"What odds will you give that it'll work?"

The analyst smiled. "My business is empiric. We observe, we deduce, we make decisions and we act on them. Beth is a scientist. For her, nothing is accepted until it's proven. But in neither case do we gamble, Mr. Bolan."

Bolan looked at Brognola. "What do you think, Hal?"

Brognola sighed. He looked out the window. The street was blocked again. A scatter of raindrops drummed against the glass. "It's for you to decide, Striker," he said. "It's your life at risk."

"And hundreds, thousands of others more innocent than mine," Bolan said soberly. "The way I see it, there's only one way to do this. I have to play along, hide the fact that I uncovered part of the plot, allow myself to be programmed yet again—but shoot myself these precautionary drugs and hope to hell I stay sane enough to get wise to the terrorists' plan as a whole." He looked at the redhead and grinned. "Miss McMann, you better make me up a package of goodies that I can carry with me at all times—along with a little instruction book that tells me how much and when."

The girl raised questioning eyebrows at Brognola and Toledo. "You heard what the man said," Brognola told her.

Later he said to Bolan, "You're going out on a limb, you know, right to the end. Because there's one thing we haven't taken into account yet. If you're going to make it you're going to need inside intel. You're going to have to know in advance when you're scheduled for another treatment."

"I know."

"And, you must know this as well as I do, the Liège setup, the fact that they wanted you there and got you there, must mean one of two things—either that girl, your contact, is a plant, or else she's blown and they've been deliberately feeding her. It's got to be one or the other."

"Yeah," Bolan said wearily. "I know that, too."

"So?"

"So I play along, the way I said. If she comes across with any more intel, I take it in—but with the knowledge that they're wise to it and will be there ahead of me."

"Wouldn't it be wiser to stay clear, to break contact?"

"I promised to help the kid, Hal," Bolan said. "She needs help. I don't see her as a double, a plant. And if, as I believe, she's leveling with me, like you say, that means she's deliberately being fed disinformation...that they know is passed on to me. In which case, once they have no further use for her, she's in real trouble, and I have to do what I can."

"Okay," Brognola said. "But we agreed that you need inside intel if you're going to make it. More than that, you need *accurate* inside intel. And whether this girl's on the level or not, that's one thing you certainly won't get through her. If they're onto her, it'll be what they want you to know and no more."

"Sure. So I take what she has to offer," Bolan said, "but with it I take the proverbial pinch of salt. Whether I *act* on it is something else. That will depend on my evaluation of the truth when it comes my way."

"And it will come your way exactly how?"

"There's a certain shrink, one Friedekinde, that I have to see," the Executioner said, and there was steel in his voice.

28

The strength of the clinic owned by the Friedekinde
Foundation was also its weakness.

It was normal to have high gates and a wall topped
by broken glass, as much to keep psychotic patients in
as marauders out. But by renouncing trip wires, guard
dogs, electronic sensors and any of the more sophisticated anti-intruder devices, Hansen, Schloesser and
the son of the founder were in effect proclaiming that
they had nothing to hide.

They could afford to do this because the activities
that they *did* have to hide took place safely out of sight
in the Maginot biochemical laboratory.

The disadvantage of course was that, although their
work remained under wraps, the crooked medics were
personally vulnerable when they were at Neuchâtel.

Their headquarters was easy enough to penetrate,
and they themselves were in turn ''accessible'' to a
determined intruder such as Mack Bolan.

Especially if he was a loner and the clandestine entry was made at an unexpected time of day.

Bolan chose to make his surprise return engage-
ment in the middle of the morning.

It was a wet morning, with the rain drifting down
from the wooded, cloud-capped crests of the Jura and
blowing across the lake in horizontal squalls. The

sound of raindrops pattering among the branches and dripping from the leaves of trees surrounding the property was loud enough to drown the noise of footsteps treading cautiously over the sodden underbrush.

Bolan selected a sector of wall that ran behind the stable block on the side away from the road. A stout branch projecting from the trunk of a Spanish chestnut fifteen feet above the ground offered him a secure enough perch to monitor the yard—and a launchpad from which he could leap over the wall.

But first he was simply going to keep his eyes open and watch.

From time to time, nurses in white uniforms passed the window at the end of the second-floor hallway. On the far side of the stable yard he saw Schloesser, followed by Hansen, emerge from the lab block. Hansen locked the door, and the two men hurried into the main building.

When he had been there twenty minutes, Bolan saw the chauffeur, Klaus, his collar turned up against the rain, run from the rear door to the stables. Soon afterward the black Mercedes purred out into the open, wipers threshing busily.

Klaus drove out through the arch and stopped the big sedan outside the villa's front porch. He gave a single discreet tap on the horn.

Bolan shifted his position slightly so that he could squint through the arch and keep the steps in view. He saw the hulking gorilla, Mazarin, holding a striped golf umbrella above his head, appear on the steps. One by one, the hairless giant convoyed Schloesser, Hansen and two other men to the Mercedes, sheltered by the umbrella. Klaus was already holding the rear door open.

The last man down was Max Nasruddin. He was preceded by a sulky-looking individual with bushy eyebrows whom Bolan recognized as the electronics tycoon Shell Pettifer, a U.S. senator who was also, Bolan recalled, one of the foundation's directors. Nasruddin and Hansen took the jump seats, and the older men sank back against the cushions. Klaus closed the door, climbed behind the wheel and drove the Mercedes away.

The Executioner would have given a lot to know whether they were on their way to the Maginot complex. If they were, it meant that Pettifer was mixed up with the terrorist conspiracy. That would certainly be a lead worth following up. Did it mean that he was at last on the track of Nasruddin's superiors?

Maybe. There was nothing he could do about it now. In any case, it was more important first to approach Friedekinde while the clinic's top man was on his own.

Mazarin had folded the umbrella, shaken it free of raindrops and gone back indoors. If the information gleaned on Bolan's previous recon still held good, it was possible that he was the only hardman left between the warrior and his target.

Bolan broke twigs from his branch and stripped off leaves. Slowly he began rocking the bared limb up and down until the wood creaked with his efforts and the rain stung his face.

When he figured he had worked up enough amplitude, he loosened his hold at the zenith of an upswing and allowed himself to be catapulted over the top of the wall.

He landed like a cat near some bushes.

It seemed to the Executioner that he had made a hell of a lot of noise. As well, he'd twisted his ankle slightly, bruised one arm and found that the sleeve of his blacksuit was ripped. But no inquiring faces were pressed against the clinic windows; no servant appeared around the corner of the building to ask what was going on.

He picked himself up, ran lightly across the wet cobblestones of the yard and flattened himself against the wall of the house below the hallway window. Carefully he edged toward the arch.

And through it.

On the terrace above the pond, he crouched and moved along below the line of casements, risking a rapid glance over the sill at the corner of each.

Friedekinde was seated at the desk in the study.

He was writing in some kind of a ledger, glancing from time to time at a sheaf of papers attached to a clipboard between the two phones on the desk. As Bolan watched, he lifted the red handset, tapped a single button on the keyboard and spoke.

Making up the clinic's "official" books, the Executioner guessed, and now he was querying something with a staffer, probably one of the nurses upstairs. The single numeral proved that it wasn't an outside call.

Crouched again below the window with the rain drumming on his back, Bolan thought about the three possible means of entry—the rear entrance through the kitchens; the outhouse roof and the stack pipe that led to the window of Mazarin's room; the main doors beneath the porch.

He rejected the first. Workers in the kitchen area would probably be innocent locals, preparing food for the staff and the few genuine patients, and he was reluctant to cause them harm.

He also tossed out his second option. Although his twisted ankle hadn't swollen, it had begun to hurt him slightly now, and the thought of putting his weight on it each time he swarmed farther up a slippery pipe wasn't appealing.

So it had to be the front door, like a respectable guest.

He crossed the rest of the terrace until he made the porch. He pressed the bell set in the brickwork beside the outer doors.

Footsteps. The door opened.

"Yeah? What is it?" Mazarin asked in a rasping, surly voice.

Using the fingers of his right hand, Bolan jabbed with savage force into the big gorilla's solar plexus before the hardman's eyes had stopped widening at the unexpected sight of the Executioner.

Mazarin uttered a choked gurgle as the muscles of his diaphragm, paralyzed by the force of the blow, ejected the air from his lungs and refused to draw in more.

He folded forward—to meet Bolan's pistoning knee beneath his chin. Bolan's left uppercut, carrying all his weight, snapped the hood's head back before he fell. The edge of a flattened hand, seasoned as teak, chopped the top of his spine to help him on his way.

Bolan tried to catch him before he hit the ground, but Mazarin was already as slack as a side of beef, and the two of them cannoned into a plaster column supporting a potted palm.

Bolan grabbed for the pot, stumbled and ended up seated with the heavy pot clasped to his chest. The column fell sideways and shattered on the black-and-white marble floor.

Originally Bolan had meant to drag the hood's unconscious body into the inner hallway, perhaps tie him up and stow him in a cupboard while he surprised Friedekinde in his den. But he figured he would have no time for that now. Mazarin had fallen heavily, Bolan himself had made some noise saving the pot, and the pillar had broken into pieces, it seemed to him, as loudly as a train wreck. Could be someone would come out to check.

He thumbed back one of the fallen giant's eyelids. Mazarin was going to be out for some time. He decided to gamble on the hope that no other visitors would ring the doorbell, so he left the guy closed in between the two sets of doors. With luck, he wouldn't be missed—and he wouldn't wake up—in the time Bolan needed.

If he was found among the broken fragments of the pillar, the finder might believe he had fallen, knocking himself out with the pot full of earth as he went down.

Until Mazarin was able to tell them differently.

So okay... it had to be fast.

Bolan maneuvered the pot onto its side, spilled some earth and moved it nearer the gorilla's head. He closed the outer doors, then slipped through the inner and shut them, too. The big warrior found himself at the foot of a curving staircase beside a table strewn with letters that he knew was outside the door to Friedekinde's study.

If he found the hallway familiar—as he had found Mazarin's room upstairs disturbingly familiar on his first clandestine visit—that was because he had been brought here and taken care of when he was suffering from amnesia six months ago.

Yeah, taken care of good, Bolan thought. They'd sure been quick to spot the possibilities offered by a patient who had been trained to kill, but couldn't remember which side he was supposed to fight on! For some reason he recalled the shootout in the Maginot lobby and the dying watchman, Gerhard. *As if you didn't know!* the boy had cried bitterly when the Executioner had posed some question concerning the terrorist plot.

Well, he hadn't known, not consciously. But now he was damned well going to find out!

Noiselessly turning the handle, he eased himself into the study and closed the door behind him.

Friedekinde, seated at the desk writing, had his back to the door. "What is it, Mazarin?" he asked testily without raising his head. "Who rang the front doorbell? Did you knock something over? I thought I heard a noise."

Bolan made no reply. For ease of movement he was armed only with the Beretta in its shoulder rig—fully equipped with suppressor. He drew the autoloader from leather and held it loosely in his right hand.

"I asked you a question, man," the doctor said angrily. "I expect an answer when I—" The sentence died on his lips as he swiveled his chair to face the doorway.

"Mazarin is temporarily—shall we say—indisposed," Bolan said softly.

"Baraka!" Friedekinde exclaimed. "How did you—?"

"I rang the front doorbell. You heard me."

"But, my dear fellow, how good of you to come by. We're always happy to see an old patient." The clinic boss was effusive. "Although how you happened to...never mind. Now put that thing away and let me fix you a drink."

"What are you offering?" Bolan said. "Psilocybin? LSD? Soma? If it's telepathine, I prefer it on the rocks, with a twist of lemon."

Beneath the thatch of white hair, Friedekinde's florid face blanched. His mouth opened, but no words came out.

"The name—" the Executioner's voice was no more than a whisper "—is Bolan. You see, I know about Baraka and how you and your thugs treat him. What I don't know—" now the voice cracked out like a whip "—is what you are programming him to do. And you're going to tell me that right now. Or die."

The blood drained from Friedekinde's face. "I d-don't know the d-details," he stammered. "I swear it. It s-started as an...well, as an experiment. It was Schloesser and Hansen who... All I did was provide the laboratory space. It wasn't my idea, the imprinting. They swore it w-would be—"

"Okay, I'll accept that for now," Bolan said. "You may or may not be in on the details. But I want to know about the whole plot. The bombs, the killings, the hijacks—there has to be an overall reason."

"I know nothing, n-nothing at all," Friedekinde babbled. "I was asked to provide a certain service...a professional service...to allow members of my staff—"

"Nonsense," Bolan interrupted roughly. "You're in it up to your neck, even if you have nothing to do with the actual planning of the hits."

"I c-can't tell you."

"Okay, it's your life," Bolan growled, taking a threatening step forward.

"All right. What do you want to know?"

"I told you." Bolan stepped back, keeping the gun trained on the doctor's forehead. "The object of the terror campaign."

Friedekinde breathed heavily. Finally he spoke. "It's a c-consortium, a group of the world's most powerful men. They're connected with extreme right-wing or neofascist political groups or paramilitary organizations. They fund them secretly and support—"

"Their names?"

"It's more than my life's worth to tell you."

"You said it, not me." The gun barrel came up fractionally.

"Al-Jaafari," the Swiss said hastily. "Sayed Mahdi al-Jaafari, the playboy oil billionaire. Farid Gamal Mokhaddem. He's in oil, too, but he has an enormous religious following in the Arab world. There's an American senator—"

"Shell Pettifer. A big wheel, perhaps the biggest, in electronics. I just saw him leave. One of your board of directors—and you say you're just an innocent bystander? Don't make me laugh."

"There's a man called Nasruddin, who organizes—"

"I know about Nasruddin. What about the other directors? Caversham, the Brit? The French admiral? Giotto?"

"They don't take an active part. But they have...well, connections. They could swing a lot of support our...that is to say, their way, when it became necessary."

"Okay. So who calls the tune?"

Friedekinde stared at him pathetically. "I don't follow."

"The boss man. The brains behind the terror campaign. There has to be an overall planner, an organizer. Who is he?"

"I never heard his name," the Swiss cried abjectly. "He has nothing to do with the foundation. He's only been here once or twice. He's American. The others call him Al."

"That's a great lead," Bolan said. "If you're telling the truth..."

"I swear it," Friedekinde said.

"What's the aim of the operation? These scum are paying Nasruddin and his hit men to eliminate prominent figures and stir up a climate of terror. Why?"

"They're hoping, planning to create a situation where the Communists—local parties, not the Soviets—will attempt to move in. There'll be opposition—people will think it's a Moscow takeover. Things will get even worse, almost up to the civil war level. And at that point, there'll be such an outcry, such a demand for a peaceful, lawful existence, that our right-wingers can move."

"You're deliberately provoking a total breakdown of law and order with the hope that the Communists will move, right? And at that point your neofascists will take over—by popular demand—and claim after all the heads have fallen that they're in power legally. Is that it?"

"Yes."

Bolan remained silent. He didn't like it at all. It was exactly the way Hitler had put it. And once in control, with oil and electronics in their power and a terrorized work force to kick around, there was nothing they couldn't achieve.

He looked at the Swiss again. "There's one more thing you're going to tell me. It seems that Baraka, my other self, is being prepared to make a hit that will be the high point of the campaign against law and order. What is it? And when?"

There was a look of resignation in Friedekinde's eyes. Bolan thought he saw something there. Regret, perhaps? He couldn't be sure. In any case, it appeared as if the man had consigned his fate to the Universe. And Bolan had a pretty good idea what that fate would be when the others came to collect.

Friedekinde broke. "Very well," he croaked. "It won't do you any good and it will kill me, but it's the *Nimitz* . . . at Monte Carlo."

"The *Nimitz*? The U.S. Sixth Fleet flag carrier?"

Friedekinde barely stopped himself from nodding. "A g-g-goodwill visit," he choked. "There's a reception at the Sporting Club . . . heads of state, movie stars, the world's richest people. It's . . . a big event. There may be informal talks on America's . . . on help to deal with the law-and-order threat. Secret agreements perhaps."

"And I'm scheduled . . . you mean Baraka is scheduled to make his first hit there? Is that what you're telling me? What's on the shopping list? A bomb aboard the *Nimitz*? A U.S. Marines liberty party machine-gunned? An elder statesman eliminated?"

"I warned you, it won't do you any good," Friedekinde whimpered. "Even when you know, you won't be able to do anything about it. You're already programmed. All the details. Once they catch you again—and they will—all they have to do is pump the right dose into you, point you in the right direction and you'll carry out the program as efficiently and mechanically as a clockwork toy."

"The program being...?"

Something that was almost a hysterical laugh escaped the Swiss's foam-flecked lips. "You're going to assassinate the President of the United States," he said.

29

For the second time on this mission, Mack Bolan was numb with shock.

The monstrousness of the plan astonished him. The fact that he had been scheduled to engineer the biggest atrocity of all horrified him. And still more disturbing was the idea that he had already been programmed to do this.

Inside his head, utterly concealed from his conscious recollection, a group of cells among the billions in his brain held the secret blueprint of the evil operation. Like a cancer festering unseen in an otherwise healthy body, he carried within him the seed of an evil flower that, when it bloomed, would shake the world.

Worst of all, the knowledge he tried desperately to hide from himself, was the conviction that, given the right backup and briefing, he had the skill and the power to get away with it.

It was this that really scared him.

But before he could free his mind to examine the implications—and estimate his chances of foiling the plot—other problems, more urgent, more immediate, claimed his attention.

He heard the crunch of tires on gravel followed by the slamming of a car door. Then there were footsteps rising to the porch, a key grating in a lock, and finally confused shouting, presumably when Mazarin was discovered.

Bolan dropped the lamp and leaped back behind the door. He was ready with the silenced Beretta when it burst open, but Klaus, the chauffeur, was standing outside the window with a submachine gun, and behind him, half obscured by a stone urn filled with geraniums, stood the Marksman with his twin-barreled rifle.

"If you don't want us to come in shooting," Max Nasruddin's voice drawled from outside the door, "throw your gun on the floor where we can see it."

Bolan's lightning glance took in the whole scene. There was no other exit from the study. Behind him, a hatchway that probably connected with a butler's pantry had slid open. On the far side a man held something with a long barrel that glinted in the light from the study window.

Covered from the front and rear, Bolan had no choice. "Say nothing about Baraka and save your own skin," he whispered to Friedekinde. "Keep quiet and I won't let on that I know." He threw the Beretta onto the carpeted floor in front of the open door and raised his hands to shoulder height.

Nasruddin strutted into the room. He was unarmed, but the tow-haired youth behind him with flinty eyes beneath a jutting forehead was carrying a Detonics Combat Master. He looked eager to use the .45 automatic whose stopping power was as lethal as Bolan's own AutoMag.

Looking at the pathetic figure of Friedekinde, still slumped abjectly in his swivel chair, Nasruddin said with scarcely disguised contempt, "All right. So Mister Big here put the bite on you. What did you spill?"

"I couldn't help it. I...he was threatening to shoot me!" The voice, quavering at first, rose to a defiant yelp.

"What did you tell him?"

"About...the plan. Just the general layout. He wanted to know what the hits...what he called the t-terrorist acts...were in aid of," Friedekinde said wretchedly.

"And you told him?"

"There was nothing else I could do, Max."

"All right, that's enough. He didn't ask you anything else?"

"He was g-going to, but then you arrived."

"I wanted to know when and where the next hits were planned," Bolan said with a meaningful glance at Friedekinde.

"You do know. It's all in your mind!" Nasruddin said. He laughed. "You're familiar with the whole damn thing—only you can't remember any of it."

Okay, they did know he knew he was Baraka. In the meantime, it looked as if they must also be wise to Julie's betrayal.

"Yeah, your little friend was also a little indiscreet," Nasruddin said as though reading Bolan's thoughts. "You were getting too close for comfort, too often. So we ran a check. The Belgian hit was organized specifically to bring you back within range. You fell for it all right. But just to make sure our suspicions were correct, we fed the Marco girl a different story from everyone else when we set it up. The real target was always the Kennedy tower block—but she was told, when she activated the dossier, that it was the

Culture Center. And that's where you went when you hit town, the Culture Center. Who needs more proof than that?''

Well, as far as Julie was concerned, time was running out, Bolan thought. And right now there was nothing he could do about it. He posed his own second question.

"Tell me one thing," he said. "You're safe enough, after all, if I'm not going to remember a thing about it. What is this big hit I'm supposed to be training for? What's the target? Where?"

Nasruddin turned to pin him with a level stare that was equal parts dislike and suspicion. "You'll know soon enough," he said gruffly.

Strikeout.

Klaus and the Marksman had come into the room. The chauffeur still held his SMG at the ready. They were followed by Mazarin, clasping both hands to his gut and glaring at the Executioner. The tow-haired youth's Combat Master was pointed at Bolan's abdomen, and he supposed the fifth member of the assault squad remained on the far side of the hatchway at his back.

"The timing's a mess," Nasruddin said, plucking his lower lip with a forefinger and thumb. "And it means the original schedule is shot to hell. Plus we'll have to keep him sedated damn near a week. But since the bastard's here...well, it'll save us the trouble of bringing him in the normal way. And I don't like to let him loose after his talk with Uncle Wilhelm here." He glared at Friedekinde. "Klaus, what time do you have to pick up Schloesser and Hansen again?"

"They're waiting in Berne with Senator Pettifer until his plane takes off," the bullet-headed hardman said. "I'll be leaving again in half an hour."

"Great. They can decide the appropriate medication when they arrive. Meanwhile, I figure our friend Baraka has earned a rest."

He turned to Mazarin. "Perhaps I could persuade you to help Mr. Bolan sleep until the medics show?"

Mazarin flexed his fingers. The backs were covered in black hair. He licked his lips. "It'll be a pleasure," he said, looking at his right hand. Slowly he curled the fingers into a fist, then drew back his arm.

Bolan prepared himself for the blow. It didn't come. Instead the bald giant used Bolan's own technique: his knee jerked up with paralyzing force into the Executioner's crotch.

Bolan doubled up as agony flamed through his loins and belly. It was then that the huge left uppercut rocketed up with enough force to lift him off the floor.

Before he could fall, the tow-haired kid seized one of his arms and Klaus the other. They held him upright as his knees buckled and involuntarily jackknifed toward his brutalized groin, then Mazarin hit him with the second murderous blow.

And the third.

Pain seared through every nerve end in the Executioner's body as the merciless beating continued hammering at his defenseless torso. The room went dark and began to spin. Through a red mist of agony he heard Nasruddin's faraway voice ordering, "Don't hit him in the face. I don't want the features marked."

His lungs were on fire. He felt himself vomit uncontrollably. He was hallucinating: he imagined he heard women screaming; the sound of Mazarin's fists smacking into his flesh accelerated, grew faster and faster until they sounded like the rotors of a helicopter; a freezing wind roared through the archway and smashed into his chest.

Then consciousness dwindled to a single point of blazing red light....

30

The helicopter was a French army-type Lynx, and it was real.

Bolan saw wisps of cloud stream past the rain-spotted ports when he opened his eyes. He groaned and turned his head. Apart from his feet, it was the only part of his body that didn't throb and ache.

He was half sitting, half lying on one of the folded-back canvas seats in the belly of the chopper. The man in the seat beside him was tall and snub-nosed, with pale blue eyes and red hair. His left arm was in a sling, and blood had seeped through the bandages swathing his wrist.

"Aaron Davis!" Bolan exclaimed thickly, struggling to push himself upright. "What the hell are you doing here...wherever here is?"

He looked around the cabin. Behind him half a dozen tough-looking characters in camouflage fatigues sat cradling Uzi submachine guns. One had a blood-stained strip of cloth tied around his head. "Where am I?" Bolan demanded.

"There were some problems down at the clinic," the Mossad man explained. "We thought it better to lift you out."

"Thanks," the Executioner said. "But I don't understand. How do you know about the clinic? How did you know I was there today? What gave you the idea I was in trouble? What are you guys *doing* here anyway?" His head was beginning to ache now, too.

Davis grinned. "We know about the clinic because we followed you there from North Africa. We knew you were there today because we've been staking the place out ever since. We figured you were in trouble when we saw the posse forming up outside the window with guns. As to what we're doing here and why, I told you in Tel Aviv—a watching brief on these new-style terrorists. We have to satisfy ourselves first of all that their campaign isn't directed uniquely at Israel."

"It isn't," Bolan said. "I can tell you that. It's against Europe as a whole. What do you mean—you followed me from North Africa?"

"When they took you away from Boardman's place. You were brought to the clinic a couple of days before they dumped you in Paris, right? Well, we tagged along to see what the score was."

"I don't get it." Bolan was more mystified than ever.

"When I say 'we,' I mean our agent in Algiers—she followed you."

"She?" Bolan sat bolt upright—and winced. "You don't mean . . . ? Your agent wasn't—?"

"Fawzi Harari." The Israeli nodded. "One of the best field operatives we had. She was a great loss."

"She was a great person," Bolan said. "Her killers have already been eliminated, but the account won't be closed until I've finished with Nasruddin." He sighed. "So that's why she handed me that phony story about the scooter, the overnight drive to Paris in an off-roader, and all that jazz?"

"Yeah. Actually, she tracked their plane in one of ours equipped with all the latest high-tech directional gear, radioed ahead for ground support and then reported back to us once the team had located where you were held. We sent her back to Paris when you were transferred there."

Bolan nodded. "So it was no accident she was ready and waiting to snatch me from the arms of the law. I can understand why she lied about the scooter, but what was all that nonsense about avenging her brother?"

"No nonsense. The boy was her brother, all right," Davis said soberly. "I guess she used his death as a reason—her instructions were to hook you and to talk you onto the team without letting you know who she really was."

Bolan eased his position on the canvas seat. The bruises were beginning to hurt. "How did you get me out of that place?"

"Standard antihijack activity and hostage release routine," the Mossad man told him. "Winched a couple of my men down to the roof. They didn't know they'd have several nut cases and a ward full of scared nurses to pacify, but it worked out okay. The rest of us jumped. We chuted into the grounds, rendezvoused at the stables and then took the place front and back. Son of a bitch in the butler's pantry pulled a knife on me and slashed my wrist." He lifted his wounded arm. "And some straw-haired psycho carved his initials on Shimon's skull with a .45. Luckily he was only creased. After that, broken windows and a brace of Slepoy stun grenades did the trick. You were out anyway, so you missed the party."

"What did you do with the prisoners?" Bolan asked.

"Got the hell out and left them there, once we had you. What else could we do? We were over Swiss territory without official clearance. By local standards that clinic's properly run. Nothing illegal goes on there, and it's not against the law to carry out psychiatric research. There's nothing to link the place with any terror campaign. All the links are buried in the Maginot bunker."

"We couldn't get the place closed down? Provide evidence that would send Nasruddin, the doctors and the gorillas to jail?"

"What evidence? You and I know what goes on. But there's no proof a court would accept. They may have employees with jail records, but right now they're officially clean." Davis paused. "But you, old buddy," he said, "are not! You made an illegal entry into their property, assaulted their butler and forced your way into the house. You held up the owner at gunpoint. Armed robbery with violence is the least they could throw at you. Same thing with us. Except we're breaking *inter*national law. An armed band crossing the frontier—that's practically an act of war! So far as the Swiss are concerned, if it ever came to trial, *we* would be the terrorists."

"Guess you're right at that," Bolan said. "Working alone I forget that two guys with guns make a paramilitary organization and three's an army. If they're on the wrong side."

The chopper flew on. In the distance, Bolan saw a wooded crest slide past through a gap in the low cloud. "Which way are we headed, Aaron?" he asked.

"We have a safehouse with a helipad in Luxembourg," Davis said. "From there, we can fix you up with transport to Paris or wherever."

"Could you drop me off someplace near Strasbourg?" the Executioner asked. "It's on your route, and I have to get there fast to tip somebody off. It's important...I mean life and death."

"Tell me about it," Davis said.

Bolan told him about Julie Marco.

"I'll come with you," the Mossad man offered. "There's a small private field near Molsheim. I'll radio ahead and have our Strasbourg resident meet us with a fast car." He pushed himself upright and walked forward to the Plexiglas bubble enclosing the flight deck.

JULIE'S APARTMENT was in the cathedral quarter of the old town. It was in a narrow cobblestoned street— a six-floor walk-up in a converted medieval house.

Bolan rang the bell set in the doorpost and then knocked. There was no reply.

Together they shouldered open the flimsy door.

The apartment was surprisingly spacious, with goatskin rugs on a polished pine floor, big-screen television, stereo system and filled bookshelves among items of furniture that had obviously been picked up individually at secondhand stores but chosen and arranged with some taste. Three steps, with a wooden railing on each side, led to the sleeping alcove.

The rope that had strangled Julie Marco had been passed over an exposed beam and tied to the frame of a heavy iron bed in back of the alcove. During her death struggles, the rope had jerked the bed a foot away from the wall, but her lifeless toes were still six inches off the floor. Deep scratches on her neck showed where she had vainly tried to claw the noose away from her throat.

Aaron Davis had never seen an expression as forbidding as the one on Bolan's face; it masked the fury seething within him. "It's not your fault, Mack," the Israeli said, averting his gaze from the murdered girl's bulging eyes and protruding tongue. "You didn't know they were wise to her until a couple of hours ago, and this was done yesterday. I've seen it enough times to know. There's nothing you could have done."

Bolan's eyes were chips of ice. "She was counting on me," he choked. "I failed her. But not one of the people responsible is going to live, I promise you. Not a single damned one."

31

"I want a last look at the Maginot dossiers," Mack Bolan told Hal Brognola. "There may be more intel there that could give us a line on their planning, not just on the Baraka hit."

"Don't you risk another . . . well, another Baraka programming yourself?" Brognola asked. "They know you've penetrated the place at least once before, and they must have strong suspicions that it was you who wiped out those guards in the farmyard. Won't the place be double-guarded now?"

"Could be. But if there are no cars, no bikes in the yard, it stands to reason the place is unoccupied inside at least for the moment. It's too far out in the sticks for people to arrive on foot, and no buses pass within miles."

"And if the guards are outside, like last time?"

"I'll ignore them. I tunneled my way out at the far end of an unused passageway before. No reason why I couldn't get back in the same way. And a stronger version of that magnetic lock pick should see me past the steel door."

"Yeah, but—"

"Look, Hal, the guards will never know I was there. It's unlikely they found my exit tunnel. Nobody goes along that passage beyond the steel door . . . and the two guys who did know how I escaped, well, they won't be talking.''

Brognola shrugged. ''It's your psyche,'' he said.

''Hal, in the summer of '86 a man called Alexandre de Marenches, a former chief of the French intelligence services, was questioned about terrorism in a TV interview. Do you know what he said? 'It's only just starting.' That night there was the bloodbath in the hijacked Pan Am Boeing in Karachi. Soon after Muslim extremists were responsible for the massacre at the Istanbul synagogue, and a bomb was found on the Paris subway. These bastards have to be *stopped*, Hal. And among them are two from the Middle East, one of them with a big religious following.''

Bolan stopped. Brognola knew that his friend wasn't usually a man of many words. But this time Bolan's determination was almost palpable in his fervid outburst. He was breathing heavily. ''Any single thing we can find out about them,'' he said, ''anything at all, will help to stop them.''

''Okay,'' Brognola said. ''Okay, Striker. Don't think I'm not with you. But don't say I didn't warn you either.''

The big Fed was right; the Executioner underestimated the opposition.

He was glancing at the biochemical lab reports and was less than twenty minutes into the office papers when he was surprised by a four-man team—two at the top of the spiral staircase, two blocking the exit to the walkway overlooking the computer room.

He recognized the two-haired little killer from the clinic. The other three were unknown to him.

The two Arabs by the door the walkway, one tall, one short, both with swarthy faces and hooked noses, seemed to be on some drug. They exchanged glances of complicity frequently and were having difficulty suppressing fits of giggles. Bolan didn't know it, but these two were the crazed terrorists who had carried out the supermarket slaughter near Brive-la-Gaillard on the road to Limoges.

The man standing beside the tow-haired kid was tall also—a thin character with a crew cut and pale, expressionless eyes. Nobody could have recognized him because all the passengers and crew of the jetliner he had sent hurtling to its doom over the Alps were dead.

Bolan, blacksuited, the 93-R and the AutoMag both firmly leathered, noticed that none of them carried guns. But they were all armed with weighted lengths of rubber hose, and the crew-cut man held a small bamboo blowpipe. The warrior didn't need to be told what that would be used for.

For an instant he considered making a run for it. He had beaten odds worse than four to one in his life as a fighter. But they had appeared too silently, and they were now too close to leave him room to maneuver.

Those lead-filled hoses would paralyze his arms before he could draw. The soldier knew that even if he drew on all his unarmed combat expertise, he couldn't take them all. In any case, a single well-aimed puff from the blowpipe would signal the end of the contest.

A savvy warrior doesn't waste energy when the situation is already hopeless. He conserves it for future use.

Bolan knew they wouldn't kill or even injure him badly—they needed Baraka, the "stolen" half of Bolan, with all his faculties intact. They would simply make use of this unscheduled capture to take the program one step farther.

Well, he could make use of it, too.

He'd asked Beth McMann to provide him with doses of the vitamins and drugs they hoped would neutralize or at least minimize the effects of the stuff Schloesser and Hansen pumped into him.

They were contained in four separate gelatine capsules, two of them with double, extrahard layers that would dissolve slowly in the stomach and release the contents in measured amounts only after some hours.

Rather than waste the seconds remaining in a useless display of courage, he would swallow these and see what happened. It would be a helpful trial run; the knowledge he gained could be vital when the time came for the big hit.

The four hoods were moving in on him.

They were only a few feet away. Bolan's right hand dived into a pouch clipped to his belt and then flew to his mouth.

A blackjack thudded with savage force against his forearm, sending pain flaming to his shoulder. But the capsules were in his mouth. He swallowed as the towhaired punk came in.

"This is for my pleasure," the kid said. His right arm swung back and then forward. The lead-weighted rubber hose thwacked with terrible force across the lower part of Bolan's belly. As he doubled up with a grunt of agony, the return blow on the backhand caught him a second time on the hip.

Bolan twisted as his legs buckled. And it was then that the tiny blowpipe dart stung the back of his neck.

After that there was chaos.

It wasn't a total blank as it had been each time they'd taken him before. But then Beth's antidotes weren't specifically designed to combat the knockout stuff. It was only when he was back at the Friedekinde clinic and the whirling darkness pricked out with occasional dazzling lights had faded that Bolan regained a blurred awareness of reality. But even then straight lines curved and curious waves of color washed between solid objects each time the doctors, sometimes dwarflike and sometimes giant, approached him with a drink or a syringe.

He knew he was taken south in an ambulance. He knew that in a house high above the harbor he sat for a whole day in a chair talking and being talked to. There was a map and an architect's model of the principality.

He knew that, but Baraka knew much more. Baraka was digesting information, evaluating it, making and rejecting decisions. And it was only from time to time that Bolan and Baraka connected, became a single entity.

Certainly it must have been Baraka who asked to be taken for a walk around the port and the casino quarter. Parts of that filtered through to Bolan: sunlight warm on his farm, a group of nuns against tropical shrubbery, a boatman with a bright green face and torso rowing across the chocolate sea.

Another time, in another life, there were stairs, flights and flights of stairs ... and companions eager to stop him making too much noise.

At some point Baraka made a decision. He made up ... *his* mind? Or was it Mack Bolan's mind, only Bolan didn't know?

Then, quite normally, there he was in the late-afternoon sunshine, talking to his friends Max Nasruddin and the Marksman.

"That time in Paris," he said with a smile at the Marksman, "when I was trying to get across the vacant lot and you were firing at me, were you missing deliberately, or was I just lucky—or too difficult a target?"

"Difficult!" The Marksman's saturnine, cadaverous face creased into an expression of disbelief. "What do you think? You think I could have missed, in that light, at that range, with that gun, if I'd really wanted to take you? Don't make me laugh. My job was to make you run...and convince that punk Graziano that I was really trying."

"And convince me that Graziano was really trying so I'd get mad at him?"

"That and the bikers. We never expected them to make it," Nasruddin said genially. He put an arm around Bolan/Baraka's shoulders. "Hell, those kids were expendable. The point was to get you to the Las Vegas."

Later Bolan remembered the whole exchange—and recalled with incredulity his own bland acceptance of the parameters involved. But of the twenty-four hours between the conversation with the Marksman and Nasruddin and his awakening in a hotel room in Dijon, central France, he retained only the haziest, unreal recollection.

"WHAT I CAN'T UNDERSTAND," Aaron Davis said, "is why you don't just alert the President. Change the date and the venue. Call off the gala altogether. Or simply keep Bolan under lock and key until the presidential visit is over.''

"You don't understand, Aaron.'' Hal Brognola had decided—as he often did in moments of extreme stress—to quit smoking. He was sucking noisily at an unlit cigar. "Bolan is imprinted . . . he's programmed to kill the President . . . and the exact mechanics of the hit are left to him. That's why they need a guy with his skills. If he didn't make it this time, he'd try again, as soon as the plotters briefed him—or his pseudoself that they call Baraka—with details of another time, another place.

"Naturally we have to warn the President,'' the Fed continued. "Whether or not he goes through with his own program as scheduled is up to him. But like I say, even if this particular hit is averted, even if we jailed Striker for the duration, the guy would still be at risk.''

"Which guy?''

"Both of them.'' With a grimace of distaste, Brognola laid the soggy cigar down in an empty ashtray. They were in a private suite overlooking the ocean in the Hotel de Paris in Monte Carlo. "What you have here is a situation in which one of the world's most talented infiltration specialists is in a position where, unknown to himself, he can be used as a tool by a group of the world's most unscrupulous men.''

He reached automatically for a fresh cigar, but checked his hand just in time. He said, "Anytime in the future that they can slug him or get close enough to dope his drink or shoot a sleep dart into his neck—and, hell, we can't keep him under wraps forever—they can use his military know-how any evil way they want. That's what I mean—he'd remain at risk as a potential assassin. So would the President.''

"Until?"

"Until this goddamn imprintation has been neutralized."

The Mossad man nodded. "And so?"

"So before he's safe—before anyone's safe—this whole setup has to be smashed. Bolan's exposed most of the ringleaders, but we still have no name for the top man."

"What do you know about him?"

"That he's apparently American, and the others call him Al," Brognola said disgustedly.

"That's all?"

"That's all. If there's anything else, nobody told me. In any case, exposing the bastards isn't having proof. We don't have anything hard against a single one of them, except possibly Nasruddin, and that's only Bolan's word against his. So, if The Man agrees, we figured the best thing is to let Striker keep on playing along, to hide the fact that he's wise to the target, to allow himself to be shot full of dope once more...but to take the pharmaceutical precautions worked out by Toledo and Beth McMann, and hope to hell he comes out on top."

Aaron Davis shook his head. "Good luck!" he said.

At that moment, unknown to Brognola and Davis, the Executioner was less than two hundred yards away from them, talking to Nasruddin and the Marksman.

"IT WAS A KALEIDOSCOPE, a nightmare fantasy," Bolan told Brognola. "It was like a time-exposed still of Sunset Boulevard at night, but with all those long streaks of automobile headlights and rear lights weaving like snakes among the red, blue and green neon."

They were back in Paris. The Fed figured that if they were seen together in Monte Carlo—even if Bolan as himself were to go there—it could be a tip-off that he had tumbled to the hit for which Baraka had been programmed.

"But there's one thing I don't get, Hal," Bolan said. "I left that Dijon hotel at three o'clock in the morning. I took an all-night coach to Paris. Like one of our Greyhounds. I was the only passenger until the coach stopped at Chaumont, and then only a priest got on, with an old peasant couple on their way to the Paris fruit market. No car and no bike followed that coach, and I'd stake my reputation nobody saw me drop off at the terminus. It was still dark and the place was deserted. I took a cab to a small hotel in the northwest. That wasn't followed either. And yet look..."

He moved to the window of the embassy interview room and drew a net curtain one inch aside. Brognola looked over his shoulder. A tow-haired youth with a jutting brow was leaning against the wall beside a drugstore across the street, pretending to read a newspaper. "One of them?" the Fed asked.

Bolan nodded. "And there's a Peugeot parked ninety yards away on this side, with another one behind the wheel. A lanky guy with a crew cut. How the hell could they know I was here?"

"The priest?"

"He got out at Troyes. Okay, they knew about the Dijon hotel because they dumped me there. But even if they watched it all night, they couldn't have tailed that coach to Paris, and then followed me to my hotel, without my noticing. Hell, I was on the lookout for tails. I swear nobody followed me."

"Then you must have been followed at a distance," Brognola said.

"You mean a bug they could home on? But we played that scene, Hal. We found the bug. And anyway I checked everything before I left the hotel—shoes, seams, belts, everything."

"We'll run another check on you," the Fed decided.

They took the elevator down to the specialists in the basement.

There was a bug.

It took time to locate it, but the experts finally hit pay dirt . . . in Bolan's silenced Beretta.

One of the tiny screws securing the butt plates had been removed and shortened half a millimeter. Then it had been replaced with the transmitter, no bigger than the head of a match, between it and the end of the screw hole.

"Very smart," Bolan said. "They used two bugs. One, in a fairly obvious place, that we were meant to find. And this one. They knew I'm never without this gun . . . and they relied on the fact that I'd have to unharness before a body search or an examination of my clothes. Once we'd found the first one, it was a fair guess that we wouldn't look any further."

"Look, Striker," Brognola said when they were back in the interview room, "does it really matter? The fact that they know where you've been doesn't tell them you know about the presidential hit. That's the important secret we still hold. And in any case, if you're going to go through with it, you *want* them to find you, don't you?"

"I'm going through with it all right," Bolan said. He walked to the window and looked out. The tow-haired punk was still there. So was the Peugeot. "There are a couple of other secrets they don't know that I know," he said. "I got a look at a new videotape before I was jumped last time. And I don't think the four guys who tailed me knew that I'd seen it."

"What did you see?" Brognola asked.

"A rehearsal. Baraka's next target is the French president. The hit can be made from an old bunker that's actually part of the Maginot fort. It looks over a valley, and there'll be a presidential motorcade crossing a bridge at the far end of the valley when he visits Alsace next month."

Brognola whistled. "And secret number two?"

"The camera operator was a little careless. The guys organizing the plot—Pettifer and the Arabs and the rest—were watching Baraka's programming. And for an instant they came into view. So now I know who Al is."

"Who?" Brognola demanded.

Bolan told him.

The Fed dropped into a chair and mopped his brow. "My God," he said. "This is dynamite!"

"For me," Bolan said, "it's this guy Baraka that's dynamite. A guy wearing my face and my body, and I don't know him from Adam. Until *I* can get inside *his* skin, this operation remains a gamble. And that scares me some."

"Trust Beth and Toledo," Brognola said with a confidence he was far from feeling. "The dose you swallowed on your trial run was a pilot. They didn't know how or when it would be needed or used. The Man's timetable is fixed. They'll know exactly, to the minute, when the antidote drugs have to be at their strongest."

"Yeah," Bolan said. "That's right."

He didn't tell the Fed what scared him most. He remembered it very well. Sometime during his walk with Nasruddin and the Marksman, they had passed a store with a mirrored door. Bolan had glanced aside and seen his own reflection—a tall, husky man with rugged features, blue eyes, and the cold, blank stare of a killer.

32

From the air, the principality of Monaco looked as if a giant hand had snatched a part of Manhattan and scattered it along a three-mile strip of hillside plunging into the Mediterranean. It was divided into three neighborhoods, of which Monte Carlo was the best known and most important, since it included the luxury hotels, the affluent apartment blocks, the famous casino and the banks.

Most of all the banks. For this nineteenth-century pleasure dome still hosted the world's highest concentration of oil sheikhs, billionaires, property developers and industrial tycoons.

Foreigners living there paid no tax.

"Maybe less money changes hands here than in Vegas," Hal Brognola said to Bolan, "but a lot more of it stays right here in town. You know why? Because it's safe. Because this is the most cop-riddled place on earth. They have three hundred guys in uniform, another coupla hundred in plainclothes, two hundred casino heavies and a palace guard of fifty—to look after a population of no more than twenty-seven thousand. There aren't many burglaries in Monaco."

"How many of them are genuine Monegasques?" Bolan asked.

"Fewer than six thousand. And you know something else? There are secret police, too, and they hold dossiers on every damned one of those twenty-thousand-plus foreigners. Every single telephone line in the principality is patched in to a listening post, which can be switched to record at the drop of a peaked cap. And they have more video cameras than you ever saw in your Maginot dump—one at each main intersection in town, twenty-six in all. And those babies can zoom in and read a newspaper headline from two hundred yards if the guys on the police monitors want to read the latest score in major league baseball or check out tomorrow's weather."

"Okay," Bolan said. "So the place is secure. They have it all sewn up. The rich dames can wear the real jewels when they go to the casino. I get the picture."

"Only the really loaded are welcome," Brognola told him. "A lot of folks try to get permission, but only about thirty a year are allowed to become what they call 'privileged residents'—best-selling authors, tennis stars, racing car drivers, wealthy actors. You know."

"Sure. Why are you telling me—?"

"One of the banks won't even let you open a charge account with less than a hundred grand. And you have to keep your balance above that. If you want to write a check for ten bucks, you have to have one hundred thousand and ten in the kitty. I'm telling you this," the Fed continued as he saw Bolan's expression, "because it may not be all that easy to get past all this security. Plus the President's own bodyguard."

"Hal," Bolan said gently, "it's already decided, the plan's already made. I don't know what it is, but my Baraka self does. He doped it all out on that visit with

Nasruddin and the Marksman." He shook his head. "It's a hell of a thing, knowing you worked out a complicated plan of attack—maybe a brilliant one, complete with fail-safe options—yet having no memory of it at all."

"Are there no clues you can give me? None at all?" Brognola demanded. "Nothing on the site, the range, the location you chose for the hit? Nothing on how you aim to break through security?"

Again Bolan shook his head. "I remember a stairway, sun on my face, a view of the harbor. I remember a party of nuns among tropical trees. I remember thinking that from there the casino looked like a wedding cake with two peppermills on top."

"From where?" Brognola shot at him.

"From the roof—looking over the trees sheltering the nuns." Bolan's jaw dropped. "You surprised that out of me. I didn't know I knew it," he said blankly.

"Try again. Anything at all," the Fed persisted. But the compartment of the Executioner's mind that had surrendered one secret had closed again; he couldn't dredge up any more flash memories of his stay in Monte Carlo or the plan he had made there.

Brognola sighed. "Okay," he said at last. "We'll cover the waterfront. It seems a likely enough place, where the shore party delivers him to the motorcade. The rooftops, too. We'll check which buildings overlook the casino across a belt of tropical trees. Not more than a hundred, I guess."

"That may not be the place chosen for the hit," Bolan pointed out.

"I know, Striker. But we have to cover every angle, don't we? In case Toledo is talking through his ass and the stuff they're gonna feed you is bad medicine."

"With what I can tell them about the trial run, they should be able to modify the formula so that it works."

"I sure hope so. Because from here on down it seems this is strictly a play-it-by-ear situation—for both of us."

"That's right, Hal."

"Well, I hope they're playing our tune, that's all. I hope you can somehow use the situation to flush these bastards into the open and wrap it all up."

"That's what I hope," Bolan said. "But you'd better keep your fingers crossed."

The man from Washington put an arm around the warrior's shoulders. For a split second again, Bolan saw Nasruddin next to him on the roof, but the image faded. "Listen, guy," he said. "You know my first responsibility, my first loyalty is to The Man, don't you? His safety comes before anything else...."

"That's understood, Hal."

"So I have to tell you that from now on the danger sits squarely on your shoulders. Because presidential security will have to be alerted to the possibility of a hit. The local law, too. The whole shooting match, no pun intended, will be on the lookout—and if there's any doubt, they'll shoot to kill."

Brognola fished a cigar from the pocket of his rumpled suit and stuck it between his lips. He made no attempt to light it. "I hope you understand the implications," he said awkwardly, "if Toledo's antidotes don't allow you to overcome the effects of the drugs and your Baraka self looks likely to succeed."

Brognola paused as the soldier turned to look him in the eyes. The man from Justice wished with all his heart that he didn't have to utter the next words.

Bolan's diamond-hard gaze never faltered as he looked at his best friend.

Very softly Brognola said, "We'll have to kill you."

ONCE MORE THE SUN was warm on Mack Bolan's face. He sat nursing a beer at a sidewalk café on Paris's Champs-Elysées.

It was crazy, he thought.

He had been programmed to kill the most important public figure on earth as part of an evil campaign to stimulate a left-wing uprising that would be crushed by the extreme right. Although he knew about the conspiracy, he was continuing to allow himself to be used, in the hope that his antidrug treatment would permit his conscious self to block the plans made by his secret self.

But he wouldn't know what those plans were, whether he could block them and eliminate the ringleaders of the conspiracy, until and unless the antidotes worked well enough to unite the disparate halves of his mind.

Or until they didn't—in which case, as Max Nasruddin had said, he would "read about it in the papers."

If they allowed papers in the cell for condemned inmates.

There was a copy of an English language newspaper on the table beside Bolan's beer, folded back to an inside page. Right now he could read about the man whose life was supposed to be in his hands.

The *Nimitz* was due to anchor off Monaco, along with a cruiser and a squadron of antimissile frigates, that evening. The next day, chase planes from the great carrier would give aerobatic displays above the principality, and there would be a presidential reception on board to which the Monegasque royal family, local dignitaries and various European heads of state were invited.

It was on the day after that that the festivity was scheduled.

Apart from the goodwill character of the visit, the paper said, it was thought that unofficial—but highly important—talks would be held between the U.S. President and European leaders on the subject of a firmer stand against Russian expansionism, the terrorist menace and the dictatorship of the oil producers. It was for this reason, the article stated, that the presidential advisers included the secretary of state, three Pentagon generals, two of them "hawks" and one a "dove," and Dr. Alwen Proctor, State's roving troubleshooter, who was also a notorious hawk in addition to heading the government's think tank on long-term strategic planning.

And among all these headliners, Bolan knew, Hal Brognola would be flitting from group to security group, from contacts in the CIA to NSA aides to incognito members of the FBI to Monte Carlo antiterrorist chiefs, doing his best to figure out a contingency plan for a potential assassin to be wasted in certain circumstances—when he knew no better than Bolan himself from which direction the attack might come!

In any case, Bolan thought, the attack on his own person would come soon. The reception was the day after tomorrow. To avoid alerting the terrorists, he had replaced the bug in his Beretta. The tow-headed kid was drinking coffee at a café on the far side of the street. The Peugeot was circling the block.

Soon, Bolan thought again, they or their bosses would make their play.

Bolan reached out a hand for his beer. The table tilted, and the glass grew immensely large and then dwindled to nothing. The tow-headed kid was running across the street, dodging the traffic. The Peugeot angled in to the curb, and the sidewalk swung slowly up to caress the side of Bolan's head. The last thing he heard was a voice saying, "I'm afraid our friend has been taken ill...."

"YOU REMEMBER WHO YOU ARE. Baraka. That's who you are," the man with the blue chin and wraparound shades insisted. "We have to take a trip because you have things to do, don't you, Baraka?"

"The enemy," Mack Bolan said thickly. "Get rid of him."

"That's right," the second doctor said. "If he is threatening you, you know what to do?" He removed his pince-nez and gazed enquiringly at the big American.

"Kill," Bolan said.

"And if he threatens the whole world?"

"Kill, to keep it safe." And astonishingly he seemed to be both inside and outside of himself. He was floating alongside his body, seeing his own blank stare and hearing the voice issue from his expressionless face, saying, "Kill while there is still time."

"Very good," the younger doctor said. "Excellent."

The Bolan who was talking knew exactly what had to be done—he glanced with hatred at a life-size photo of the President of the United States—and remembered now in precise detail the plan he himself had worked out: the approach, the climb, the firing point. And the comforting presence of the gun they were kindly lending him.

The Bolan standing outside recalled his last conversation with Beth McMann, the attractive Langley redhead, and the warning she had given him.

"The dosage," she had said earnestly, "is calculated on the assumption that you regain consciousness, that you know who you are, even if it's for a short time only, when the effects of whatever knock-out technique they use have worn off—but before they inject you with the psychotomimetics. We think there must be a period between the two comatose states—they'll need you conscious and organically normal to check out the cumulative initial effects of the drugs *they* use."

"I don't remember waking up the other times," he had said.

"You wouldn't because of the memory block they lay on you afterward. But that's when you have to swallow those first capsules. If you wait until after they treat you, you may already have taken off and be too... well, too stoned to remember."

The capsules were lodged in special miniature clips behind the front teeth of his upper jaw. He worked two of the three loose with his tongue and swallowed them. The older doctor was swabbing the arm of his other self with alcohol-soaked cotton wool. The man with shades held a syringe.

After that there was the dark man with the limp. But for a while back there things were confused. There was a journey by air. He remembered a lift-off—it must have been a chopper—and a view of the snowcapped tops of mountains. Then there was a blank, a lot of talk in a room with wide windows overlooking high-rise apartments, the blue sea below. Finally he was on his own, in control of his balance again, free to do what he wanted, what it was his duty to do, the way he had planned it.

Wearing the white pith helmet, white belt and dark blue uniform of the palace guard, he walked briskly past the beach at the inner end of the harbor, around the corner where security police supervised the erection of barriers and a striped awning above the jetty where the presidential launch would land the official party later, and on up the slope that led to the Hotel de Paris and the casino.

There was a leather-covered steel document case chained to his left wrist and a revolver in a white holster at his hip.

The cop on traffic duty at the intersection didn't give the palace guard a second look as he hurried toward the banks. He raised a gloved hand in a casual salute. Bolan returned it punctiliously, his face impassive.

The streets were crowded. Stars and stripes alternating with the French and Monegasque flags hung from the buildings in the business quarter fronting the port. Smaller pennants mixed with colored lights had been strung between the palms outside the Café de Paris and among the trees in the gardens that stretched between the Avenue de la Costa and the casino.

Traffic was crawling as motorists paused frequently to stare at the huge clifflike bulk of the *Nimitz* and its dressed escorts beyond the rocky headland on which the royal palace stood.

Up beyond the casino, Bolan-Baraka walked into the main post office. Urgent business for the palace perhaps, a passerby might have thought, perhaps some official telegrams in the prince's name, or maybe even royalty needed to use stamps for their letters.

The post office wasn't a separate building: it occupied part of the street level beneath a large business block. A long, wide marble hallway separated it from the entrance to the block. At one point, iron-railed stairs curled upward to office suites on the floors above; at another there was a bank of elevators. Between the two was a small door marked Private.

Checking that the hallway was temporarily empty, the big man in the palace uniform opened the door and slipped through.

He found himself in a corridor with offices on either side. He could hear a hum of voices and the clacking of typewriters. In one of the rooms some piece of electronic hardware was bleeping. He opened the door closing off the far end of the passage and passed through a sorting office with labeled wire trays racked along benches.

Sacks of mail had been dumped ready for collection on the platform of a loading bay. Two yellow delivery trucks were backed up to the platform, but the long room was empty.

Now, he knew, came the difficult part.

It was believable that a royal guard might have legitimate business as far as the post office, maybe even inside the sorting center.

But from now on, no way.

He raised the chin strap, removed the helmet and unlocked the chain from his wrist. Then he stripped off the uniform, belt and holster and stuffed them beneath the wooden platform. Wearing only his blacksuit, he turned the crank that raised the shutter blanking off the loading bay. It was well greased and moved silently. When the shutter was eighteen inches off the pavement, he let go of the crank and ducked beneath into the open air.

He was in an alley that led from the loading bay to the street... and the alley ended at a wall that enclosed a yard in back of the building next to the Sporting Club. Bolan seized the briefcase, leaped for the top of the wall and hauled himself over.

He dropped on the far side between a stack of empty crates and a row of trash cans. The air was pungent with the odor of overripe fruit, but it was more agreeable than the yard behind Las Vegas Nights. There was a restaurant in the block.

He drew a bunch of skeleton keys from the pouch clipped to his belt, unlocked a door and went into the building. From here on in it was enemy territory.

It was necessary to keep that in the forefront of his mind. *The enemy... the enemy... the enemy*. He had to be destroyed.

On the inner side of the door there was a storeroom, with stairs that led down to a basement housing the laundry and a heating unit. Both were unoccupied.

Bolan set down the document case, thumbed out six digits on the roller-type combination lock and opened the lid.

Inside was his Beretta, the shoulder rig and a Japanese Arisaka Type 99 rifle that was split into three sections, together with his favorite Bausch & Lomb Balvar sniperscope.

He shrugged into the harness, checked and holstered the Beretta and then started to assemble the rifle. He screwed the barrel into the breech mechanism, snapped the small of the butt onto the hinged portion of the stock and locked them together, then clipped the optical sight in place above the breech.

The gun was equipped with a webbing sling, and the five-shot magazine was loaded with old-type .303 caliber rounds. The slugs in front of the brass cartridge cases were nickel-jacketed.

Bolan slung the rifle across his back. He opened a door on the far side of the storeroom and edged cautiously into the lobby beyond.

Marble floor; multiple glass doors opening onto the wide private parking lot in front of the Sporting Club and a view of the tropical gardens; an antique elevator with a paneled mahogany car and an open shaft fenced in with a close-mesh grille.

The door of a glassed-in concierge's lodge by the entrance opened. An old man in a gray uniform came out. "Who are you?" he demanded. "What are you doing here? How did you get into that storeroom? You can't bring a gun—"

The words were choked off by a yelp of pain. Bolan hit the old janitor with the edge of a stiffened palm behind the neck. He crumpled, but the warrior caught him before he fell and carried him back into the lodge.

He found cleaning materials in a closet. He ripped cloth into strips, bound and gagged the old man, pulled a shutter down over the window and left the small office, locking the door behind him. He tossed the key through the accordion-type gate at the foot of the elevator shaft and pressed the button to call the car.

After it rocked to a halt behind the gate, he shoved the grille aside, pushed through the double doors and fingered the top button on the control panel.

The doors swung shut behind him, and the grille clanged across to close off the shaft. Bolan turned away from the doors.

There were mirrors on all three of the car's paneled walls. It was then, as the elevator jerked into movement and whined upward, that the struggle inside Bolan's head began.

He had to open the inspection hatch of the car. That was part of the plan. It was too high for him to reach on tiptoe. That had been allowed for. He unslung the rifle, reversed and jabbed the butt upward against the small trapdoor. The door sprang open and flipped over, leaving an opening wide enough for a man to climb through.

Or rather four openings wide enough for four men.

Lowering and reslinging the gun, the man in the elevator was aware of four identical black figures performing the same movements.

But not thinking the same thoughts.

It was the first time since he'd passed the door of the jewelry boutique that Mack Bolan the Executioner had invaded the implanted consciousness of Baraka the killer. But now, with the proliferation of image and the duality of personality, there came the added trauma of identity—which of those mentalities belonged to which image?

Crazy! Mack Bolan thought.

Yeah, crazy. There was only one real body, only one Bolan, only one brain that was being artificially split. But the images multiplied. His vision blurred; now he saw eight. The floor of the car had begun to rotate. Panic seized him. He had to get out.

That was part of Baraka's plan—getting out. Leaping up to grasp the edge of the inspection hatch, he dragged himself through the opening and up onto the roof. He closed the hatch. So far, so good. Now all he had to do was wait until the car stopped on the top floor.

The car stopped at the sixth.

A gate slid back, doors opened and shut, the gate closed. The car trembled as extra weight depressed the floor. The elevator began to sink.

The man crouched behind the cables rising from the roof cursed. Someone on the sixth floor must have called it an instant before he'd stabbed the button; the mechanism was overriding his own command.

On greased hawsers, the huge counterweight slid past him and up into the darkness. The car stopped at street level.

He heard footsteps receding on the marble floor. A man's voice said, "That damned concierge is out again! How many times do I . . . ?"

Now once more he must open the hatch and drop down inside to redirect the elevator to the top story.

As he raised the trap, the car shuddered into motion. For the second time he swore silently. Hunched there on the roof, he would be visible to anyone, on any floor, who happened to glance through the mesh surrounding the shaft as the elevator rose.

This time it stopped on the eighth floor. And there was someone standing back from the gate, staring at the roof—a dark-skinned man with a mustache, wearing an elegant Savile Row suit. He was holding a yellow rosebud in one hand.

The man on the roof of the car recognized him.

Farid Gamal Mokhaddem, director of the Friedekinde Foundation, a cynical manipulator of his Muslim coreligionists, with enormous interests in oil and armaments. "What the hell are you doing here?" Bolan said.

"You know what I am doing here, Baraka," Mokhaddem said. "My office suite is on this floor. You were here last week. How else do you imagine you got to know the geography of this block?"

"What do you want?"

"At the moment nothing." Mokhaddem wore an Old Etonian necktie, but his English was heavily overlaid with the gutturals of the Middle East. "Just checking that so far your plan works out." He opened gate and doors, leaning into the car to press a button. "You have two more floors to go. But don't forget— if you fail or try to cross us, we shall be waiting for you on the way down."

As Bolan was carried out of sight, he saw that the Arab was threading the stem of the rose through his buttonhole.

When the car reached the top of the shaft, he stepped onto a short, steel-runged ladder attached to the side of the shaft. Above this was a door, and on the other side of the door the roof of the building.

Bolan stepped out into the sunshine.

The roof was flat, asphalted, studded with television antennae, vents from the heating unit, occasional chimneys. Across treetops stirring in a warm breeze he could see the casino.

He unbuckled his shoulder rig and left it, together with the Beretta, behind a trumpet-shaped ventilator from the mouth of which drifted a wisp of steam and the smell of cooking. Where he was going, the extra gun would be an encumbrance.

His target was on the far side of the roof, where an air duct connected to the air-conditioning installation crossed the asphalt and then snaked up over the wall of the adjoining building, which was two stories higher.

The duct was rectangular, made of sheet metal and riveted every few feet to brackets set in the roof. Near the housing from which it emerged, a fine-mesh steel grating that was thirty inches wide and eighteen high covered an opening in the side of the duct. The frame of this grille, too, was riveted to the metal; there was no way of removing it short of using a blowtorch.

But the wires of the mesh, each one-eighth of an inch thick, were set at half-inch intervals around the frame.

Bolan intended to get inside that duct. He produced a pair of wire cutters. To open the mesh grille, so that he could bend the whole thing inward, he would need to sever a hundred and thirty-two separate wire strands.

He started to clip. It took a long time, and before he was halfway through, the muscles of his right hand were on fire.

It was during this period that the two sets of drugs within him started warring for ascendancy. He had no idea if it had happened before when he'd been playing Baraka, but he began to hallucinate.

The sky hardened into a glittering constellation of crystals; buildings wavered, soft as caramels, and started to melt; a sensation of extreme warmth washed over him as if he were deep within a coral sea. Through air as thick as molasses, his arms, hands, fingers continued their task.

The last wire parted. Lying prone, he pushed with all his strength. The grille bent at the top, slanted inward and folded toward the top of the duct.

With the .303 Arisaka slung across his back, he crawled through the hole into the ventilation conduit.

Its rectangular section was the same size as the grille: thirty inches wide by eighteen high. This gave him width but not too much height, especially with the gun barrel between his shoulders—there was a hollow boom that seemed to him to echo forever each time the muzzle knocked against the top of the duct. When he had progressed ten painful yards, he rolled to one side and managed to withdraw his arm from the sling.

After that, he held the weapon in his left hand, advancing slowly with his weight supported by both forearms and one drawn-up knee. The passage was too shallow for a proper elbow-and-knee crawl.

He had a long way to go. Dimly lit every fifty feet by a grating similar to the one he had forced, the conduit stretched interminably ahead. The really difficult part, he knew, would come when he hit the slope, where the duct climbed up to and over the parapet of the neighboring building, angling across the Sporting Club roof to feed or—he was not sure which—extract air from the auditorium.

For the moment it was a question of stifling the waves of nausea, of fighting to ignore the bands of livid color spiraling toward him and twisting underneath his eyelids when he forced his way grimly onward with his eyes squeezed shut.

From time to time the phantasmagoric quality of his journey was emphasized by a far-off roar of machinery and a hot wind that roared past him, sucking in air through the gratings, blowing his hair across his eyes and drying the sweat-soaked material of his blacksuit where it clung to his back and thighs.

He was tunneling his way out of a prison camp—the roof props ahead were breaking up and he would be buried alive. He was robbing a bank a mile beneath the ocean. He was huddling beneath the covers, plunging headfirst to the foot of the bed because he was scared of tigers and it was hours before he could get up and go to school.

And all the time, incessantly in harmony with each forward shuffle, the refrain hammered on with the pumping of his heart—a great voice shouting, *The enemy... kill the enemy... kill the enemy... kill...*

He could see the face of the enemy very clearly.

It was in front of him all the years it took him to coax his body up the slope, free hand scrabbling, the weight dragging him back down the smooth slant of metal and only the ridged rubber soles of his combat boots, digging in, to stop him sliding back. It was only because the rifle, more than forty inches long, was considerably wider than the conduit that he was finally able, by wedging it slantwise across, to drag himself foot by foot up the last section of the grade.

After that, apart from the risk of making a telltale noise, it was an easy ride until he reached the grating, above the proscenium arch, that looked out over the auditorium.

That one had to be removed altogether—one hundred and ninety-two separate snaps of the cutters and the hand burning again.

When it was done, he lifted the grille carefully out of the frame and set it down on the floor of the duct where it curved away around the auditorium. He climbed out through the opening.

A catwalk ran along behind the proscenium arch. He stepped down onto it.

Above his head rose the loft, that tall, hidden part of the theater where backdrops were stored until they had to be flown as decor for opera or ballet on the stage far below.

At the far end of the narrow gangway, a tiny red pilot light glowed among the controls on the lighting technicians' gantry. They wouldn't be used tonight: the reception would be a lights-up occasion. Bolan nevertheless stole to the other extremity of the catwalk and made himself comfortable between the wall and a huge spotlight.

Apart from a dim blue illumination filtering through from the wings on each side, both stage and auditorium were in darkness: the technicians, the maintenance men, and the security personnel wouldn't materialize until it was time for the festivities at the end of the afternoon.

Bolan leaned the Arisaka against the wall and squatted with his arms wrapped around his knees. Somewhere in the blackness of the grid above him, a piece of scenery creaked on its ropes. All he had to do now was wait.

HAL BROGNOLA WAS ANGRY. "What the hell do you mean, you lost touch with him?" he raged. "When you replaced that bug in his gun, you positioned another, didn't you, under the screw on the other side?"

"Yes, sir, Mr. Brognola," the electronics expert replied. "On a different frequency, like you said. With a three-mile pickup."

"And Bolan knew nothing about it?"

The man shook his head. "No way, sir."

Brognola ran his hands through his hair. It was his job to cover every angle: outside of his loyalty to the

Executioner there was his loyalty to his country and the man chosen to direct it. It had been a hell of a thing anyway, the President and his advisers allowing this thing to go through. And now one of the Fed's lines of communication appeared to be blocked.

He stared at the twenty-six monitors that had been put at his disposal in the Monaco secret police HQ. "You're certain it was him the camera picked up on the Quai Albert Premier this afternoon, near the jetty where the President will land?"

"No doubt about it, sir," the expert confirmed. "He was disguised as a member of the palace guard, but there was the height, and the eyes . . . and anyway the bug gave us a fix."

"And then?"

"The trackers monitoring the bug had him pass the beach and continue up the hill—where he was picked up again by the camera above the Avenue d'Ostende underpass, and once more at the Beaux Arts-Princesse Alice intersection. He was carrying a black document case chained to his wrist."

"And your bugmen then tracked him across the Beaumarchais Square to the post office, right?"

"Yes, sir."

"But now you're telling me he never came out of there?"

"He's appeared on no screen since. I'll swear to that, Mr. Brognola. And the bug is still transmitting—but from a fixed location. We lost movement on it twenty minutes after he went into the building. The operatives monitoring the frequency—they're parked on the far side of the square—report a steady bleep that neither swells nor fades. No more than one hundred yards from where they are."

Brognola frowned. "And that block's pretty close to the back of the Sporting Club. He must still be in there someplace."

He stared at the street scenes on the monitors. There was a festive air in the streets. Traffic was still heavy. A crowd had gathered around the barriers railing off the awning above the presidential landing stage.

"I'd give a lot to know what's in that damned document case," Brognola said savagely. "How do you read this no-movement bleep from the bug?"

"There was a lot of movement within a small area, sir, just after he went in, but our guys had been told to hold off if there was any risk of them being seen. After that, the bug was static. The way I read it, sir, he dumped the Beretta and the harness and went on without it."

"What would he do that for? He's never without that gun," Brognola growled. "The sharpshooters are all ready to take up their posts inside the auditorium?"

"Two hours before the festivities start, sir."

"Okay." Brognola sighed. "You better alert the local authorities. Check with the police captain and tell him we'll have to go in there, track down that bug and keep a watching brief."

FOR MACK BOLAN there was no longer any time, any place, not even any identity: there was only flow—the dancing kaleidoscopes of color that buoyed him up above the glowing coils and endless vibrating circles in his mind.

Wading through the tide, he tried desperately to reach the shore. But the flow slowed, solidifying, turning to jelly that clung to his arms and legs. Fernlike arabesques of brightness proliferated behind his eyes. The designs were as neat and geometric as the wiring patterns on a computer.

A computer? Now his mind was diamond-sharp, crystal clear. The mind *was* a computer, billions of neurons programmed only to make a limited number of connections. The drugs—he knew very well that drugs were affecting him, helping him to see more clearly—were consciousness-expanding. They opened his computer mind to newer, more varied and exciting programs.

The world around him was infinitely more complex than he had imagined. The jelly before his eyes separated and, to prove the point, the spotlight, the catwalk, the auditorium, the whole universe cracked apart into vivid globules that carried him away to the brilliance beyond the frozen waves. He was at one with the atoms that were the essential constituent of matter; he was an electron, an electric charge, the nucleus at the center of it all.

He went with the tide.

Yet something else clamored for attention...a task, a duty, an obligation that must be attended to before he could explore this wonderful new world.

Concentrate. Glaring lights below, with music and many voices. The auditorium was full. Now each line was hard and sharp—strange that he hadn't heard them all come in.

There was something he had to do.

Of course. He tongued the third capsule from the clip behind his teeth and swallowed it. *Apomorphine normalizes the metabolism and regulates the blood serum.* Who said that?

In a flash of clarity he heard the voice of Greg Toledo. "Dr. Charles Savage, of the Mental Research Institute of Palo Alto, says that the psychotomimetics have a less profound effect when the subject has physiological tests to perform or manual skills to show off."

More flashes now. A constant, aching flicker that transformed the auditorium below into a visual chaos that resembled the shattered electronic image on a badly adjusted TV screen.

The tasks, though. Yes, there were the tasks.

They were manual skills, weren't they?

He rose upright and took the gun away from the wall.

At once the picture cleared. The shift in position regulated the distortion, clarified the image. Waves of applause crashed around him like the raging of an angry sea. He peered over the rail of the catwalk.

The enemy was below.

The jet-set socialites lolling in their five-hundred-dollar seats didn't know it, but he was among the nine men seated behind a long oak table on the flag-draped, flower-bordered stage.

Prince Rainier of Monaco in the chair. The secretary of state, burly and solemn. Three uniformed generals with clipped mustaches, their chests bright with medal ribbons, as alike as tin soldiers stamped from a mold. Troubleshooter Alwen Proctor, tall, pink-faced, with white hair crimped close to his skull. A couple of broad-shouldered aides who were probably security. And The Man.

Bolan steadied an elbow on the rail. Organ music that had been thundering inside his head faded. He felt quite cold. The enemy was standing in front of the table, adjusting a microphone attached to a lectern. He was speaking. The echoes of his voice were lost in the loft.

The cross hairs of the Balvar sight centered on the speaker's back. There was a fresh wave of applause.

Kill the enemy.

Bolan pressed the trigger.

There were three shots in all.

33

Bolan was off the catwalk and into the duct before the shouts, screams and exclamations of outrage in the auditorium had reached their crescendo. In the shock and confusion over the killing of the man whose body still dripped blood from the lectern over which it was sprawled, it was not noticed at first that two others, sitting side by side in the tenth row, had also been shot.

Bolan scuttled crabwise through the conduit. So far there were no sounds of pursuit. Gradually the echoes of the hubbub behind faded into silence. It wasn't until he rounded the corner at the top of the slope, where the duct led down to the roof of the adjoining building, that trouble loomed ahead.

It loomed large. In the light from a grating he could see the huge bulk of Mazarin prone at the foot of the slope. Immediately behind him was the tough little chauffeur, Klaus. Mazarin's weight was on his elbows, and there was a .38 Police Special grasped firmly in his two hands.

Clearly he had heard Bolan coming and was waiting for him to appear around the curve at the top of the slope before he fired. He was quick off the mark, too. Almost too quick. The blast of the shot in the confined space of the metal tube was deafening.

Bolan ducked back his head as quickly as a tortoise retreating into its shell. In front of him a thin pencil of sunlight shone through the hole drilled in the duct by the heavy caliber slug.

Breathing hard, he collected his thoughts.

Mack Bolan, the Executioner, was at last imposing his will on Baraka, the programmed killer. Whether it was the positive action, the last capsule, or a delayed effect of all Beth McMann's magic potions, he didn't know. But now he was whole, he was one within himself, the programming was a remembered dream.

He was Bolan.

Colors and lights still flickered from time to time behind his eyes, the walls of the conduit tended to advance and recede, the metal beneath him risked softening, but mentally he was in control.

And as Bolan he was faced with a problem.

His escape from the Sporting Club auditorium had been programmed, too, worked out to the last detail—but worked out for Baraka, the assassin of the President. The plan was to get him away from the police, the security guards, the secret-service men, who wouldn't discover the killer's firing point initially, but who would take up the chase like crazy men once they found the hole in the rooftop air duct.

By which time Baraka would be away over the roofs and down the elevator shaft to safety and a getaway car.

But the first shot from the Arisaka Type 99 didn't kill the President. Instead it blew away Dr. Alwen Proctor, the White House hawk, who was about to introduce him to the audience.

Dr. Alwen Proctor, whose money and political clout were widely supposed to subsidize LAFF—the Loyalists of America Freedom Fighters, whose antisemitic, racist, neofascist activities were threatening the stability of the West and South.

Dr. Alwen Proctor—plain Al to his friends and fellow plotters—whose twisted brain had fashioned the evil and ingenious plan to goad the European Left into protest action that could be stamped on ruthlessly by the Extreme Right. A ruthlessness that the public would accept because the protest could be presented as yet another example of the terrorist violence of which everyone was so sick.

Mastermind Proctor, a contender in the coming presidential election, whose scenario, financed by Mideastern money, would permit him, along with the oil barons and multinational tycoons who supported him, to clean up once the panic was over.

The second and third shots had disposed of Schloesser and Hansen, the infamous medics whose perverted skills had allowed Proctor to make his domination dream a reality.

Or would have done if it hadn't been for the Executioner.

Bolan himself hated killing as such, but here he had no compunction. His targets, directly or indirectly, were responsible for the slaughter of hundreds of innocent men, women and children. They deserved to die. Alive they would somehow have continued their deadly work. Publicly exposed, they would have risked only prison sentences—commuted or quashed if smart lawyers plugged the no-hard-facts line of defense.

So Bolan had overcome the drugs. But crossing up Nasruddin and the others had left him with one hell of a problem.

Because the escape route *was* known to them. As Baraka, he had planned it with their cooperation to the smallest detail.

And, yeah, they'd sure be gunning for him now—as Bolan.

They had acted fast. But Mazarin would only be the first line of attack.

Bolan had to get out of the air duct.

There was only one thing he could do. The Police Special was already trained on the curve at the upper end of the slope. By the time he could raise and sight the unwieldy Japanese rifle, he would be dead meat.

He unhooked a lightweight Misar MU-50 plastic grenade from his belt, pulled the pin and lobbed the egg-shaped seven-ounce antipersonnel destroyer against the wall of the duct on the far side of the curve. It hit the metal, bounced and rolled down the slope.

Bolan heard a single hoarse cry from Mazarin...and then the deadening, thumping, concussive roar of the explosion.

He waited until the acrid brown smoke forced up the conduit had been sucked away behind him, then he slid feet first down the slope to the twenty-foot hole blown in its lower section.

The legs and lower half of Klaus's torso lay in a puddle of blood and viscera several yards behind the breach. The remainder of his flesh and bones, together with all that was left of Mazarin, was spread in a gory fan over the roof outside the jagged edges of the shattered pipe.

Bolan ran across the stained asphalt to recover his Beretta and its shoulder rig. He was fastening the clasp when the door at the top of the elevator shaft opened and Mokhaddem walked out onto the roof. ''You infidel pig!'' he cried, his voice shaking with rage. ''Worthless betrayer. I warned you!''

There was a Makarov automatic in his hand, and it was aimed straight at the Executioner's heart.

Bolan had no time to draw the sleek Beretta. And once more he was looking death in the eye. Incongruously he almost burst out laughing at his plight, after all he'd been through. Almost. Instead he fired the Arisaka from the hip.

The yellow rose that adorned the Arab's immaculate lapel disintegrated. In its place a larger, scarlet decoration blossomed, frothing and bubbling as Mokhaddem went down. Bolan fired again, the last round in the rifle magazine, before the Arab hit the roof. The high-velocity .303 nickel jacket cored through the top of his head and pulverized his brain.

As he twitched once and then lay still, yellow rose petals were still drifting down to settle on his contorted face.

Bolan dropped the rifle, hurried to the door and opened it, lowering a foot toward the first rung of the ladder.

He gasped, fighting back an unexpected twinge of vertigo. He was staring down into a ten-floor void, a perspective of parallels that converged on the elevator car's roof at the bottom of the shaft. Someone had called it back down.

Behind him now, over the bray of police sirens and ambulance bells, he could hear distant shouts. Looking back over his shoulder, he could see figures on the Sporting Club roof. He had to get out of there fast. In the eyes of the law, murder was murder, whatever the justification, however evil the victim.

Drawing a deep breath, he leaned in and seized one of the oiled wire elevator cables just below the pulleys at the top of the shaft and slid down into the yawning space until his feet rested on the great rectangular iron slab that formed the counterweight.

Way down at street level someone shouted. The wires jerked. Bolan saw the roof of the car advancing toward him.

The counterweight sank.

It was suspended on two hawsers, one at each side, with just enough space for a man between them. Grabbing hold of one cable, Bolan unleathered the Beretta with his free hand.

The car rose rapidly.

He was sure that at least one member of Nasruddin's gang, if not more, would be inside. But the three mirrored walls of the car were solid wood on the outside, and the inner doors, although they had glass panels, couldn't be opened while the car was moving. So although they were going to pass, halfway up the shaft, almost within inches of each other, the Executioner would be unable to see who was inside. And the occupants, if they had been tipped off by the man below that Bolan was there, wouldn't be able to spot the Executioner, particularly as the counterweight slid up and down the shaft behind the car.

This, of course, assumed that the warrior could flatten himself sufficiently on his perch above the weight not to be scraped off, mangled and then dropped sixty or seventy feet to his death in the inspection pit at the foot of the shaft when the two passed.

He angled his feet outward so that the toes wouldn't project, squared his wide shoulders, pulled in stomach and chest and held his breath, one arm at full stretch to hold the cable, the one with the gun held straight down by his side.

The elevator car approached, slid past and continued on up. Bolan expelled his breath in a sigh of relief. The paneled back had been so close to the waist buckle of his shoulder rig that he felt the displaced air beneath his chin.

The car reached the tenth floor, stopped and at once started to drop back down the shaft. Nobody had entered or left.

That could only mean one thing: whoever was inside was looking for him.

The point was proved on the return journey.

Silenced shots were fired from the interior as the car passed the fifth floor level; panels splintered and cracked as slugs cored through the wood to penetrate the mesh surrounding the shaft. Inside the car glass shattered. Fortunately the killers had miscalculated. Because of the space difference between the elevator floor and the inspection pit when it was at street level, and the top of the shaft and its roof when it was at the tenth floor, the travel of car and counterweight were unequal: they didn't pass each other *exactly* halfway up the shaft.

So the first volley passed above Bolan's head. And the second, when the car rose next time, splatted against the counterweight beneath his feet.

In between the counterweight itself with Bolan on it had dropped to the bottom of the shaft.

Standing outside the gate was the guy who had shouted—the tall crew-cut murderer with pale eyes. He was holding a large-bore automatic—it looked like a .45 caliber Detonics Combat Master—fitted with a silencer. The long cylinder of the suppressor tube was trained on Bolan as he descended.

Like many professionals in close combat, he aimed for the head. There was no comeback if you scored, while a body hit could leave an opponent free to fire back. But it was this very professionalism that saved Bolan's life. He ducked suddenly, dropping faster than the weight. The gun moved faster to cover him, but not quite fast enough, and the slug slammed into the gate, flattening itself on the junction between two of the crisscross steel braces.

Before the guy could correct his aim, the weight reached the limit of its travel. In the instant of inertia before it began to move up again, Bolan sighted the silenced Beretta through one of the diamond-shaped spaces in the grille and punched out a single upward-angled round that took away the hardman's crew cut and most of the cranium beneath it. The 9 mm slug continued on its way to star the top of the entrance lobby's mirrored wall.

The dead terrorist was slammed against the glass, leaving a semiopaque patch of brain tissue pricked out with bone splinters to cloud the reflection of the elevator gate before he and his image slid to the marble floor.

Like Baraka, there had been two of him; like Baraka, he was through.

But there were two real guys in the elevator car; Bolan could hear their voices.

As the insane seesaw continued up and down the shaft, he realized that he had a temporary advantage. From outside, he could judge the height of a man standing inside the car, whereas the occupants could only guess at the counterweight's position by counting the floors as they passed. And they no longer had a lookout below.

On the third pass, holding the Beretta tight in above his hip, the Executioner opened fire on the rear panel of the car, which was now peppered with holes and scarred where wood splinters had been gouged out. But unlike his enemies, Bolan scored. He heard a cry of pain, a stumbling fall. The car shook on its cables.

One down.

A second grenade was clipped to his belt. Should he drop it onto the car? He decided not to. The roof was metal; it might not kill. But the blast could cripple the car, jam it in the shaft, fracture a cable and send him to the bottom of the shaft with it. Apart from which, unless he wanted to brave the security men hunting the rooftops, the only way he was going to get out of this damned shaft was *through* the car. There was no other way that the exit gates on any floor could be opened.

The next time the car rose, it was halted at the seventh floor. Bolan guessed the remaining man was doing what he himself would have done: he had opened the hatch and was climbing onto the roof.

Lying flat there, with a gun trained over the edge, he would have the whole of Bolan's body to fire at as it rose toward him, while almost all of his own would be shielded by the car.

The cables tremored. The elevator was coming down.

Surprise was the warrior's only hope, and there was only one surprise he could pull.

Instead of standing centered on the weight with a cable on either side of him, he moved outside the right-hand cable, bracing one foot against the edge of the weight, holding the cable with his left hand and allowing his body to swing out over space with the Beretta in his free hand.

This way he would be displaced more than a yard to one side of his expected position.

It wasn't much, but he would give it a try.

The floor of the car sank past his head. Over the lip around the approaching roof, he saw a hand holding a Walther PPK automatic. The trigger finger tightened. The gun spat fire. The guy was firing blind, aiming between the two cables, hoping Bolan would rise automatically into the deathstream.

Three and a half feet off to one side, the splintered panels of the car brushing him as they slid past, Bolan held the Beretta across his body and let loose a single shot, coring the gunman's wrist at almost point-blank range.

He heard a yell of pain and rage as the hand was snatched back, the Walther spun away and dropped to the roof of the car and blood spurted into the shaft. Bolan's head rose above the level of the roof, and he stared into the hate-crazed face of Max Nasruddin.

As the counterweight carried him farther up and the car sank beneath him, he jumped onto the roof.

Nasruddin rolled away to pick up the gun in his left hand. He moved quickly, and flame jetted from the muzzle before the Executioner could reach him.

Bolan felt a searing pain in his right shoulder, temporarily paralyzing the arm. The Beretta dropped through the open trapdoor into the elevator car.

The terror boss was on his knees, lining up the Walther for a second left-hand shot, but this time Bolan was too near. He kicked the gun out of Nasruddin's grasp, and it hit the mesh sidewall of the shaft and fell from sight.

"Fucking doctors," Nasruddin snarled. "I knew I should never have trusted them to—"

The sentence was never completed. Bolan's round-house left caught him on the mouth, and he crashed over backward, bounced off the counterweight cables and slipped down into the gap between the wire mesh and the back wall of the car.

For an instant he clawed desperately for a hold with his good hand, his burly body rubbed between the moving car and the wire like cheese against a grater, then he lost his grip and plunged with a wild cry down the counterweight channel into the chasm below.

Bolan dropped through the hatch. The casualty was Willi, the Maginot doorman and would-be bomber of Liège. His left lung was punctured near the heart, and pink froth bubbled from his slack lips where he lay slumped in a corner. The Executioner picked up the Beretta and finished him with a mercy round in the back of the neck.

The elevator car jolted to a halt at street level.

Bolan jerked open the glass-paneled doors. The concertina outer gate was slammed back by someone else. Two men stood in the lobby facing the shaft. One held a small box with an open lid from which a steady, strong beep was audible. The other stepped forward with his hand outstretched.

"Well, Striker, we found you at last!" Hal Brognola said.

EPILOGUE

It was a clean wound, and the bone wasn't touched. Bolan sat with his arm in a sling and tried to forget that it hurt like hell.

"He never heard of you, he didn't know you were here, and neither did I," Brognola said, "but The Man sends his congratulations. At least that's one more danger out of the way."

"A lot of the bad guys got away, Hal," Bolan said. "We won a battle, but we haven't won the war."

"Don't worry," Aaron Davis said. "Our sights are trained on them now."

"That's good to hear," Bolan said, "but there are plenty more where they came from." He sighed. There were always more.

Greg Toledo turned away from the window and the view of the harbor. They were in Brognola's suite in the Hotel de Paris. "There won't be any more Hansens and Schloessers," he said. He sounded almost regretful. "That was a fascinating line of inquiry they started. What the hell. I guess I'll have to be satisfied—" this to Bolan "—with the labor of deimprinting all the stuff they planted on your subconscious, and then trying to reimprint you with your original conceptual standards."

"Be my guest," the Executioner said. "Start when you like, because they tell me Baraka could still be recalled, given the correct drug dosage, any time until you do!''

The door opened, and Beth McMann came into the room. The owl glasses were gone. Curvaceous in a low-backed pleated white dress and white high-heel pumps, she looked very desirable.

Bolan looked from her to Toledo to Aaron Davis. He grinned. ''This is too much,'' he said. ''Three freckle faces in the same room. I want out!''

Beth walked across and laid a hand on his undamaged arm. ''You had a real rough trip,'' she said. ''That cocktail I mixed you was powerful medicine. Is there anything I can do to help?''

''Sure is,'' Bolan said. ''According to those lab reports I copied out of the clinic files, one of the goodies they were shooting me with was called TMA. Can you tell me what the hell that is?''

She smiled. ''Sure can,'' she mimicked. ''It's an abbreviation for Trimethoxyphenyl-Beta-Aminopropane 3,4 and 5. That's the one responsible for those strobo phenomena.''

''I'm sorry I asked,'' the Executioner said. ''It's going to take a hell of a long time to explain that to me. Why don't we go to that little Italian bistro on the other side of the port and start in over dinner?''

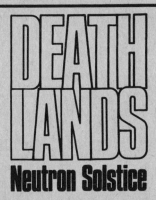

TAKE 'EM NOW

FOLDING SUNGLASSES
FROM GOLD EAGLE

Mean up your act with these tough, street-smart shades. Practical, too, because they fold 3 times into a handy, zip-up polyurethane pouch that fits neatly into your pocket. Rugged metal frame. Scratch-resistant acrylic lenses. Best of all, they can be yours for only $6.99. MAIL ORDER TODAY.

Send your name, address, and zip code, along with a check or money order for just $6.99 + .75¢ for postage and handling (for a total of $7.74) payable to Gold Eagle Reader Service, a division of Worldwide Library. New York and Arizona residents please add applicable sales tax.

Remove from pouch...

unfold once...

unfold twice...

and they're ready to wear.

GOLD EAGLE

Gold Eagle Reader Service
901 Fuhrmann Blvd.
P.O. Box 1325
Buffalo, N.Y. 14240-1325

Offer not available in Canada.